2023 RARE AUSTRALIA ANTHOLOGY

VARIOUS AUTHORS

SIGNING CHECKLIST

- [ ] Rebecca Zanetti
- [ ] Boone Brux
- [ ] Becca Jameson
- [ ] Sienna Snow
- [ ] Pepper North
- [ ] Jayne Paton
- [ ] K.L. Shandwick
- [ ] Elizabeth Safleur
- [ ] Nyssa Kathryn
- [ ] M.F. Adele
- [ ] Elise Faber

TABLE OF CONTENTS

ZERO HOUR & PROTECTED BY REBECCA ZANETTI

Dear Readers:

Here's a quick Scorpius Syndrome short story (how it all began), AND a short story from my Dark Protector series...

CHAPTER 1

A coyote mourned in the distance, the sound weaving through the southern Nevada desert. No wind, no breath, no sense of movement filtered in the rapidly cooling air. The moon rose high and full, cutting yellowish light through waiting blackness.

Dr. Sharon Haung sidled around scrub brush, scattering dust with each footstep. Hopefully the worn boots would protect her feet from scorpions and snakes. The metal detector weighed heavily in her gloves, and she flipped on the device.

A shadow fell across the moonlight in front of her. "If this isn't illegal, why are we here at night?" whispered Tim Norton, an assistant professor who taught with her at the small local college.

She shrugged and swept the detector in a wide pattern. "It's perfectly legal for a person to collect one meteorite a year so long as the material doesn't weigh more than ten pounds." Of course, that wasn't why they were hunting the elusive rocks at night. "From public lands, anyway."

Tim groaned. The light glinted off his spiked dark hair. "We're not on public lands, are we?"

Kind of. "We're on the boundary line of BLM lands and land

owned by a cantankerous old bastard who won't let us search on his property." But she'd viewed several larger meteorites hitting the earth the previous month through her telescope, and she'd made note of the locations. "We just want one or two."

Hunting meteorites in the Nevada desert was a sport for many, and tour guides earned decent money leading tourists to abandoned lake beds to find the hard rocks.

But these meteorites were new, and she needed to get her hands on one. NASA had watched and chronicled the Scorpius Comet two months ago. As it had veered away from the earth, a meteor shower had occurred.

Nothing new or out of the ordinary there.

But the comet? Yeah. Scientists believed the comet came from somewhere around the Antaras star in the Scorpius Constellation, hence the name.

Tim sighed and flipped on his metal detector. "Meteorites are all about the same—why do we need yet another one?"

Sharon jabbed the hat off her forehead. It was decorated with little Kangaroos for luck. "Seriously? We're looking for a rock from outer space, buddy. How can you say they're all the same? If we find one, it might have traversed galaxies we can't even *see* right now." Man. Talk about no imagination.

Tim sniffed. "You'll write me an excellent evaluation for committing a felony with you, right?"

"Yes, and trespass is just a misdemeanor. Especially if we accidentally cross over from public to private land." She smiled.

"We jumped over a fence. How was that an accident?" Tim groused.

Well, when he put it like that.

The wind flushed out of nowhere, skittering chills down her back. A ding nearly stopped her heart, and she dropped the metal detector to the side and fell to her knees. "Here we go," she murmured, her heart kicking into gear. A ten pounder, at least.

Clouds covered the moon, and she squinted to see better.

Tim aimed a flashlight beam at the rock. "Great sample, and it's a little bigger than the one I found."

Yeah, but his still weighed about five pounds, which pleased her. She nodded and carefully dug around to extricate the rock. "This has traveled from places we can't even imagine," she whispered.

He held out the sack. "Okay."

Truck lights rose over a sand dune.

"Crap." Sharon jumped to her feet and extended the sack toward Tim. "Run, and I'll get the equipment."

"I can't leave you."

"Trust me. Get those rocks back to the lab, and if you cut into yours tomorrow in the Intro class, leave mine alone." She tapped his arm. "Go, now."

The guy turned on his heel and burst into motion, much faster than she would've managed. She scrambled to retrieve her backpack and secure the tattered material over one shoulder.

The cloud cover thickened, and she couldn't see.

She patted the dusty ground for the metal rod. If she used a flashlight, the truck driver would see her.

The vehicle drew closer, careening over rocky terrain, the bright lights slicing through darkness like danger on the hunt. Anybody out this late at night wasn't seeking a friend. Stories of serial killers and images from every scary movie ever made shot through her brain.

She swallowed and tried to keep from being noticed. Hopefully the moon would remain in hiding.

Her fingers touched metal. Ah ha. She grabbed the detector and bunched to run.

The truck turned her way. More lights flashed awake into a blue and red pattern, and a siren trilled.

Shit, shit, shit.

A split second found her in the grip of a decision on whether to flee or not. If caught trespassing, she might lose her job. Both her jobs. Could she outrun the vehicle?

The police truck swerved to avoid a grouping of cacti, propelling her to make a break for it. Blood rushed through her veins and filled her head while her lungs compressed.

The moon managed to peek through clouds to help her, and she swiveled away from careening into a luminous rock and around a cactus to head north. Probably. Maybe east.

Right now, she just had to get away from the truck on her butt.

The moon plunged behind darkness again, throwing off her eyesight. Her foot caught on something, hopefully not a snake, and she flew through the air, yelping and trying to regain her footing.

She hit solid earth, her hands slapping the ground before her knees impacted. Pain cut into her palms, and sharp agony ripped up her legs.

The truck pulled to a stop, spitting dust in every direction.

She tried to shove to her feet, stumbled, and went back down.

A presence warmed over her. "Freeze, and show me your hands," a male voice ordered.

She froze. Head to toe. It couldn't be. It *really* couldn't be. She turned around, blinking into the harsh light of an industrial sized flashlight.

"Well, hell," he breathed.

Yep. She knew that voice. Her stomach dropped through her tail bone against the chilled earth, and she sighed, blinking dust from her eyes to see him. He stood silhouetted in the truck lights, big and broad, and definitely the most dangerous thing in the entire desert. "Brett?" she breathed, her nerves firing with instant heat.

Silence ticked for precious seconds. Long enough for her to realize she lay on the ground probably surrounded by creatures that wanted to sting or bite. "Brett?" she repeated.

"Fuck me." He reached down and hauled her up with one

strong arm. "When you divorced my ass, I figured I wouldn't have to deal with your craziness."

She regained her footing and shrugged off his hold. Awareness rose the hair on the back of her neck, and her body flared awake, even as a familiar hurt pummeled her chest. "You don't."

His chuckled swept along her skin as if he licked each inch. "Oh baby. I don't think you understand."

She tried to settle her stance, anger slowly boiling. Of course she'd known he worked as the sheriff in the small county, and she figured she'd run into him at some point. Not in the middle of the desert bathed in moonlight, however. All she needed was to tangle with Brett Pierce again.

His Stetson shaded his face, but even so, his bourbon-colored eyes lasered through her, easily overcoming the simple darkness. Dark hair brushed his collar, and more than a shadow covered his hard jaw. So much for the straight military cut and clean shave.

She fought to ignore her curiosity as well as her suddenly clamoring body. "I have to go, but it's been lovely." The bite in her voice matched her ram-rod posture.

He chuckled again, smoothly pivoted, and somehow slid handcuffs over her wrists. "Nice try."

The cold metal shackled her skin, and her mouth dropped open. "No."

He tugged the bracelets, and they held tight. "I'm takin' you in for trespass and for resisting arrest." His good old boy twang was smoother than silk. "You have the right to remain silent, the right—"

"Fuck you," she exploded, struggling against him. "You have got to be kidding me."

He turned her toward his truck. "Nope. Look at the bright side." All smooth muscle, he lifted her over an outcropping of rocks without breaking stride. "Now we can get closure."

* * *

5

BRETT SAT BACK in his chair and plopped his boots onto his battered metal desk, his gaze on his ex-wife. She sat in the cell, arms crossed, shooting pure hell at him through stunning eyes.

Brown eyes, black hair, fiery temper. God, he'd missed her.

For now, he had her exactly where he wanted her, and he intended to make good use of his time. "Why were you trespassing on Phillip MacKay's land?" he asked.

She somehow glared harder.

He bit back a smile. "Your face could stick like that, you know."

"Screw you," she said quietly but with impressive authority.

He let the grin loose. "Still as feisty as ever, I see." They hadn't seen each other in ten years, which made her what? Twenty-seven? Yeah, they'd married young when they thought they had to, and when she'd lost the baby, she'd escaped the small town. He'd never blamed her for that. "Are you enjoying your time in Nevada?" he asked.

She lifted an eyebrow. "Guest lecturing at Nevada Desert for a semester and taking a sabbatical from the National Geological Foundation has been a lot of fun, actually." Slim fingers wrapped around the bars.

He shoved down at groan, remembering full well how those fingers had felt wrapped around him, even so many years later. "I'm surprised you're the sabbatical type."

"No, but my boss forced me into a vacation."

"Good." Brett smiled.

She blinked, and a cute frown wrinkled between her brows. "Let me out of the cell, Brett."

"You want out?" he asked.

Her stubborn chin lifted again. "Yes." Then she waited, daring him. Definitely daring him.

This was the most fun he'd had in years. "Fine. I'll make you a deal."

Her lip curled. "No deal."

He shrugged. "If I tell MacKay that I caught the trespassers he called 911 about, then he'll press charges. If I don't tell him, he won't know about you."

She lowered her chin. "You're going to blackmail me?"

He wouldn't, but interest lingered in her eyes. "Sure. Why not? Agree to one date with me. You do that, and I'll forget all about the trespass."

She huffed out air. "Wait a minute. I'm thinking it's not much of a coincidence you and I are facing each other in Nevada again."

He kept his face stoic. "No."

Her nostrils flared. "What did you do?"

He shrugged. "When Samuel mentioned you were going on a sabbatical—"

She lifted her head. "Samuel? As in Samuel Kelso, my boss at the NGF?" Her gaze narrowed.

Man, she was pretty when riled. "Yes. You know Samuel served in the marines, right?"

"You're kidding me. You know Samuel."

"Yes." Brett smiled. "We served together."

Steam might soon come out of her head. "I've worked with Samuel for five years, and not once has he mentioned you. You've been keeping tabs on me."

He wouldn't lie to her now. "Yes."

Her mouth dropped open. "For how long?"

This time, he paused. "Ah."

"How long, Brett?" Her pitch rose this time.

He leaned toward her. Always." Yeah, they'd both needed time to grow up, but that didn't mean he'd forgotten her. "I care about you. Always have."

Her eyes softened. "You just put me in jail."

"You're cute in jail." True words.

She shook her head. "So you heard about my sabbatical."

"Yes. Samuel said you'd fulfilled your most recent grant requirements and had planned a sabbatical until grant cycle came around again. I have friends at the college, thought you'd jump at the chance to study meteorites, and they created the special courses for you."

"Why?"

He lifted an eyebrow. "I figured at some point we'd give it another shot, and the opportunity arose. What do you think?"

"I sure didn't expect to be arrested by you."

"That was fortuitous, now wasn't it?" He leaned back and pinned her with a gaze. "How about we give us another shot?"

Intrigue filled her eyes. "Let's start with blackmail and one date tomorrow night. But we are not going to have fun."

That's what she thought. He bit back a smile as he stood to release her.

For now.

CHAPTER 2

After a sleepless night and a busy day, Sharon finished putting away her lecture notes as the advanced class filed out, much quicker than usual. Ah. Spring Break. She smiled and shut down her power point presentation. Her mind had been filled with Brett Pierce all day, and she needed to get a grip.

Brett had been her boyfriend from third grade until graduation. Their first time together had been beneath a full sky of stars, and sometimes even now she wondered if it had been as good as she'd thought. Of course, then she'd gotten pregnant.

They'd gotten married, as was the way in their small southern town so many miles away from where they'd both ended up. Then when she'd lost the baby, she'd been devastated. It was a miscarriage at three months, which wasn't uncommon.

So she'd run. To a different life and an education. But sometimes…she wondered. What if she'd stayed?

A throat clearing tore her from daydreams, and she glanced toward the door at the back. "Tim. How was the intro class earlier?" Tim taught three of the Intro classes and seemed to enjoy the job, although she had almost gotten him arrested again.

"Fine. Did you get arrested?" Tim loped down the center of the lines of desks and dropped into a seat. His T-shirt stretched across a wide chest, although with his height he seemed more slim than built.

She grinned and shook her head. "Nope. You and I are record free, my friend. Now, about your class?"

Tim nodded. "It went well. We cut into the smaller meteorite, and I gave everyone a piece after we studied the rock."

"Was it made of Iron or Stony Iron?" she asked, tucking her files under her arm.

"Iron." He smiled a row of even white teeth. "With a mineral that seemed like salt. I had everyone take a quick taste—using your directive of all five senses, of course."

She laughed. "I usually don't go that far." Something to think about, however.

Tim grinned. "I managed to get enough pieces out of it for the whole class. Gave an extra-large one to Louise Patterson, since she brought donuts again."

Sharon chuckled. "Smart girl. You know she's interested in you, right?"

Tim smoothed down his dark T-shirt. "I don't know." He rubbed his eye. "Man, I'm fighting a raging headache. I hope nothing is going around."

"Why don't you go get some rest? I'll finish up here," Sharon said, noting his pallor.

"Thanks." He planted his hand against his stomach and strode toward the door. At the doorway, he glanced back. "When are you cutting into your rock?"

"After Spring Break," Sharon murmured. The guy looked like he might throw up. "Are you traveling?"

"Nope," he said. "I'm staying here. Talk to you later."

She nodded and waited until he'd cleared the doorway. Hopefully the flu wasn't going around. She didn't have time to get sick.

With a shrug, she shook her head and trumped through the empty classroom. Now she had to steel herself to meet with Brett again. In the years since she left, she hadn't loved anyone like she'd loved him

They could not go back. Yet...what about forward?

* * *

BRETT LEANED back in his chair and eyed the two battered men in the cell. Broad as barns and twice as thick-headed, the brothers had once again gotten in a brawl at Red's Tavern. "I should call your mama this time."

Bud Blare jumped for the bars, wrapping sausage-sized fingers around the steel. "Oh, Sheriff. You wouldn't do that to a friend, would you?"

His brother, Buck, sidled up to his side. "We didn't mean nothin' by the fight."

Brett shook his head. "You're both forty years old, for Christ's sake."

"Thirty-nine," the men said in unison.

"Then act like it." Brett tried to sum up anger, but truth be told, if the Blare brothers didn't get in a brawl once in a while, he'd be bored out of his mind. Between an occasional bar fight or car wreck, his keeping of the peace was a soothing job. One he'd worked hard to deserve.

Buck fingered a rapidly swelling cheekbone. "Ya didn't have to punch me, Brett."

The fool had been swinging a broken bottle at Brett's head at the time. "You're lucky I didn't break your damn neck." He could've, easily, and the thought rose bile to his throat. He wasn't that guy. Not anymore. His time in the service had ended, and he was ready to settle down for good.

Bud shoulder-checked his brother. "You sure can fight, can't you?"

Shit, yeah. He'd learned to fight as a kid from a dad who liked to hit, and then the military had honed his skills. "Yes, but next

11

time, I'm definitely calling Mother Blare. It isn't even suppertime."
He dropped his boots to the floor and crossed to unlock the cell,
making the same threat he'd made for the last two years.

The brothers trumped out, and Bud slapped him on the back.
"How about we hit the diner? Supper is on us."

"No thanks." He glanced at the clock. One of his two deputies
should be on the way soon to relieve him, and then he needed to
get ready for dinner.

Buck snorted. "Why not? You got a hot date?"

Brett flashed him a smile. "Yeah." A date that might be the
beginning of a new life...one he wanted with a family and nice
home. He'd never forgotten Sharon, and now she was in his town
again. Maybe she'd stay with him this time.

His cell phone rang just as he exited the small station. He
glanced at the face to see that Sharon was calling. He'd had her
number for years, just in case. Oh, she better not be thinking of
canceling on him. "Hello, Sharon."

"Brett? Something is going on." Tension rode her voice.
"Within the last hour, ten students from the Intro to Meteorology
class were all admitted to the hospital with some weird sickness.
I'm headed that way now."

A chill skittered down Brett's back. "All ten? At the same
time?"

"Yes. Can you meet me there?"

He broke into a run for his truck. "I'm on my way."

* * *

SHARON JUMPED out of her rented SUV, her mind spinning. If it
was just the morning class, they'd eaten donuts. Something had to
be wrong with the donuts. She hustled inside the bright lights,
stopping at a quaint welcoming desk and recognizing the receptionist, who moonlighted as a waitress at Sharon's favorite diner
in town. "Hi Helen. What the heck?"

Helen Ramridge pushed wild gray hair away from a classic face marred by mascara smudges. "Hell if I know. Group of students all from the same class. Doc is trying to track down Doris from the grocery about a bunch of donuts."

"That's what I figured." Sharon stiffened as Brett stalked inside, instantly bringing the scent of male.

Helen arched an eyebrow, looked at Brett, glanced back at Sharon, and then smiled perfectly set dentures. "Mornin', sheriff."

"Helen," Brett said. "What's the story?"

"You tell me, hot stuff," the ten times over grandma said, wiggling her eyebrows.

Sharon's face heated, and she tried to look innocent.

Just then, Doc Daniels stomped around the corridor to the room. Lines of fatigue cut into his weathered face, making the darker spots stand out. His faded blue eyes narrowed behind heavy spectacles, and he lifted dark gray eyebrows. "Sharon? You sick?"

She shook her head. "No. May of my students are, though."

"Were you in the classroom with these kids?" Doc asked.

"No." She rubbed her chin. "I didn't eat a donut, either." Her knees wobbled.

Brett grasped her arm and tugged her closer. "What's the story, Doc?"

Doc scrubbed his head. "Dunno. The infection is localized, so I'm thinking it's bacterial."

"Like Salmonella or E-coli?" Sharon asked.

"Yeah, except *not* Salmonella or E-coli," Doc said, sighing. "The locality is in the head. A migraine to the nth degree with a frighteningly increased fever."

Sharon's stomach clenched. The doctor had been the one to call her with the news that he and the students were all in the hospital and in pain. "Meningitis?"

Doc rubbed scruffy whiskers. "That bacterium does attack the central nervous system, but this ain't meningitis. I've seen that, and this is different."

Brett rubbed her arm. "How bad are the kids?"

Doc scratched his elbow. "Right now, the fevers concern me the most. One kid went into convulsions, but we got her hydrated." An alarm blared, and he blanched. "Shit. Gotta go." He pivoted on scratched cowboy boots and rushed back down the corridor.

"Can I see the kids?" Sharon asked.

"No." Helen nodded toward the four chairs in the empty waiting room. "Not until we have an idea of what this is."

Brett gently drew her toward a chair. "I need to call the school. We should be notifying parents." He waited for her nod, and then he headed back into the chilly air.

Sharon bit her lip. If it was just a bacterial infection from the donuts, antibiotics would be able to help. But unease still caught in her throat. What kind of bacterial infection mimicked a migraine? Not even meningitis presented that way. Slowly, she drew her phone from her pocket. It wasn't too late on the east coast. She started a video call and waited until a familiar face came onto the screen.

"Why are you calling so late?" Lynne Harmony asked, frowning into the phone.

Sharon grinned at one of her friends from graduate school. "It's not that late. I'm calling you first and Nora next." The two women were brilliant at their jobs and both had specialties she didn't study. "Are you at work?"

"Of course." Lynne's green eyes sparkled. "Don't tell me. You finally gathered enough courage to seek out Brett Pierce and give in to the true reason you're taking your sabbatical in the middle of nowhere."

Sharon's face heated again. "Yes, and we'll talk about that later. For now, is there a bacterial infection that presents in the head?"

Lynne pursed her lips. "Meningitis presents in the central

nervous system," she said, her smile disappearing. "There are others. Why?"

Sharon cleared her throat. Calling Lynne at work was probably premature. "We have ten kids suddenly down with a fever, and we think they all ate from the same batch of donuts earlier today. Incredible head pain and high fevers."

Lynne nodded. "That sounds like some type of food poisoning. How bad are the stomach cramps?"

"There aren't any," Sharon mused.

Lynne stilled. "None?"

"No."

"No nausea, throwing up, aches or pains in the digestive system?" Lynne asked.

"No." Sharon shook her head. "Just pain in the skull and fever."

Lynne bit her lip. "That is odd." She glanced at something off screen. "Tell you what. Keep an eye on it, and send some samples my way. We'll take a look." She leaned closer to the phone camera. "How is it being with your ex? I swear, between you and Nora both still mooning about men you'd left eons ago, I have to just wonder."

Sharon blew out air. She and Nora had bonded over the fact that they'd both married and divorced way too young. "It's weird seeing him as an adult. He's tough and pretty hot." Her face heated.

"Nice." Lynne smiled and then frowned. "I *so* want details, but I have to run to a late meeting with drinks. Get the good facts together and we'll dish later this week. Bye." She clicked off.

Sharon put her phone in her purse. She'd jumped the gun in contacting the CDC, but sometimes, instinct ruled. Those kids had to be all right.

Soon, Brett came back inside and sat next to her, taking her hand in his. "Investigators from Vegas are heading to the grocery store and bakery to see what could've happened with the donuts," he said. "I've had the college notify parents."

Soon several parents and other students filled the waiting room. The doctor poked his head out around ten in the morning to say that none of the antibiotics seemed to be working, but three of the patients seemed to be getting better anyway. A collective hope filled the room.

* * *

BRETT FINISHED CORRALLING people in the hospital waiting room, forcing everyone but immediate family to head home. He'd been in contact with the larger hospital in Vegas, which was sending an emergency team, but for now, they waited for the tests to come back. Within the last hour, three of the students were rapidly recovering while the others were not. The doctor was looking for how and why.

Why the infection or poison was hitting each student different, Brett didn't know. His expertise had never lay in science. But the possibility existed that the poisoning, if that's what it was, had been deliberate. So he'd been questioning people as he'd taken over the situation.

Finally, when he'd gotten everyone settled, he stepped through people to where Sharon sat in a chair by the window. Her hair curled wildly around her shoulders, and smudges darkened the skin under her eyes. Sitting with a cup in her hands, she looked lost. So he crouched down until they were eye-to-eye. "How are you?"

Her sigh moved her entire torso. "I'm all right. Confused and wish we had answers."

Brett brushed a curl off her cheek, reassuring himself that she was all right. "You're sure you didn't come into contact with any of the donuts?" If it was the donuts. Teams were testing the bakery, and the empty donut box from the school had been sent to the lab. So far, no news.

"I didn't eat anything at school," she replied. Her lips trembled into a near grin. "I've been watching you get everyone organized. When you get all sheriffy and in control, your drawl deepens."

The smile on her face, however slight, eased the tension inside him. "Sheriffy?"

She shrugged, her voice softening. "Yeah."

He couldn't help it. As if drawn, he leaned in and kissed her, going deep. It was like coming home.

She kissed him back, moving into him with a soft sigh. All woman. Still his.

He broke the kiss. What was going through her head? He rested his palms just above her knees, enjoying the warmth through her jeans and trying to give her comfort. "I just heard that three of the patients had their fever break and are being let loose."

Relief filled her pretty face. "That's fantastic. So whatever it was—"

Brett shrugged. "Appears to be running its course for those three, so we're hopeful for the rest. But I do want those lab results to make sure it was an accident." He turned as two of the patients, one male and one female, checked themselves out of the small hospital. "Looks like Doc gave them the go-ahead."

The male turned, his gaze immediately seeking out Sharon. Something unfolded in Brett, something he hadn't felt in a while. Alertness. Okay. Possessiveness.

The man, and there was no doubt he was older than the other student, loped their way. Dark spiky hair, blue eyes, handsome even in the pallor after a fever. "Sharon?" Pleasure gilded color in the man's cheeks.

Brett shifted to the side, just enough that the guy had to stop his advance.

Sharon blinked and stood. "Brett Pierce, this is Tim Norton, an associate professor at the school. Tim, this is the sheriff."

The sheriff. Brett jerked his head in a nod. Hell, he didn't expect her to introduce him as her ex-husband, or even as the man who'd just kissed her senseless. But something other than his job description would've been nice. "Tim. How are you feeling?" Yeah. His drawl came out dark that time.

"Better. Felt like my head was going to explode." Tim kept his gaze on Sharon, intent along his cut features.

The female student sidled up next to him. She'd pulled long blond hair back from a classic face, and with the ensuing pallor from the infection, appeared fragile. Breakable.

Sharon smiled at the girl, her shoulders relaxing. "Hi Louise. How are you feeling?"

The girl shrugged, and her lips trembled. "Like I could sleep for a year, but at least my fever broke. The doc says I'll recuperate if I take it easy." She eyed Tim, so much longing in her expression that Brett flashed back to his years as a teenager. The girl had to be about eighteen and obviously in the throes of a serious crush.

Tim ignored her and kept his gaze on Sharon. "I'm heading home. You want a ride?"

"I've got 'er," Brett said smoothly. "You should take it easy until you feel better."

Tim turned toward him. "I'm young enough I bounce back quickly but old enough to know what's best for me." His voice stayed low and pleasant, but a glimmer darkened his eyes in the way of beast challenging beast. "And I believe I was asking Sharon, not you."

Brett showed his teeth.

Sharon frowned, her body stiffening. She placed her hand against his arm in a not-so-subtle warning. "I'm fine, Tim. But definitely give me a call later to let me know how you're doing."

Tim didn't turn his focus from Brett. "Sounds good. I'll call you later. Nice to meet you, *Sheriff.*" He turned on his heel and headed for the doorway, his gait natural and easy.

Louise hustled to catch up with him.

"That was seriously odd." Sharon stared at the closed door.

Brett looked down at her. "I don't like him."

"He's not usually like that, and you're kind of overreacting." She shook her head, her hair flying. "You haven't changed a bit."

Brett lifted an eyebrow and waited a beat to make sure he had her full attention. "Sure I have. Ten years ago, I would've had that moron's head on the carpet until he begged for mercy." True statement, that.

Sharon paused, thoughts flying across her face. "I guess that's true."

Of course, if Sharon hadn't been there with a restraining hand on his arm, he might've still taken a bite out of the young professor. There was a glint in the kid's eyes Brett didn't like...he'd seen it before, too many times in the eyes of predators. He didn't like it at all.

Doc came into the room. "Four of the students just dropped into comas."

CHAPTER 3

*B*rett finished reading the lab reports in Doc's office at the hospital and tossed the files on the desk, frustration crawling through him. "Doc has no clue of the infection still." If there had been deliberate poisoning, Brett hadn't figured out a motive.

Sharon glanced up from typing at the computer. "I have another call into the CDC."

He opened his mouth to argue that point just as Doc shuffled in and dropped into the other guest chair. "Lab called. There wasn't anything on the donuts, and they haven't yet identified the bacteria. Tests show it is a bacteria, however. A deadly one."

Brett nodded. "Bacteria can normally be killed by antibiotics, right?"

"Yep, but this bastard kills fast." Doc scrubbed gnarled hands down his face.

"So if it wasn't the donuts?" Brett asked.

Doc shrugged. "We're tracing history, but the only time those kids were together all at once was in that classroom."

The computer dinged, and Sharon clicked a button near the screen. "Hi, Lynne."

"Howdy. Why aren't you making out with your hottie ex?" came a chipper voice.

Sharon flushed red.

Brett stood to cross around the desk to view the woman in the screen. Light green eyes, brown hair, impish smile. "You must be Lynne." Sharon had told him about her friend earlier.

"I must be." Lynne's fine eyebrows arched. "Aren't you a handsome southern boy."

He kept the smile, not sure what to say. "We seem to have a problem." A quick recitation of the events made Lynne lose her smile.

She squinted. "If it wasn't the donuts, what else could it be?"

He shrugged. "Dunno."

She glanced around. "Well, let's trace. What was going on in the classroom?"

Sharon leaned toward the camera. "Nothing unusual. We'd found a meteorite in the desert and the kids cut into it, each taking a piece. We've done that several times."

Lynne's gaze sharpened. "They all took a piece?"

"Well, yeah." Sharon glanced at Brett and then back at the screen. "But we do that all the time."

Lynne's eyebrows drew down. "Didn't I read somewhere that NASA is worried we're sending bacteria into space with each space shuttle?"

Sharon bit her lip. "Yes, and we've put bacteria in space on purpose to see how it survives." She sat back in the chair, her gaze sharpening. "You don't think—"

"Maybe. Bacteria can survive in space, and isn't it possible it could remain dormant in spores for a long time?" Lynne looked to the side and seemed to rifle through a bunch of files before turning back. "I mean, isn't it possible?"

Sharon frowned. "I don't know. I mean, well, yes. It is possible. Highly improbable, but I guess, possible."

Lynne nodded. "Good enough. We need to bring everything

here to my lab. I'll be in touch with directions for transport." She paused in pushing a button. "And don't go near the meteorite without proper protection." She clicked off.

Brett scratched his chin. A meteorite? "Is that really possible?" he asked Sharon.

She turned to the side, her face set in thoughtful lines. Finally, she nodded. "Yeah. It actually is."

He scrubbed both hands down his face. How the hell was he going to keep the town safe?

The outside door opened, and Tim Norton walked in. "Sharon, I really need to talk to you." His eyes were wide and his pupils enlarged. His skin was so pale as to be nearly translucent. "Now."

Warning ticked through Brett. He slowly stood. "Are you all right?" he asked.

"No." Tim yanked a gun from the back of his waist. "The voices have to go. They won't' stop. Stop them."

* * *

Sharon jumped to her feet. "Tim. What is going on?" she breathed, adrenaline flooding her system.

He looked at her, his eyes wild. "I don't know. It hurts. My head hurts. All the voices in it want out." His hand shook around the gun.

Brett moved toward her, partially blocking her with his big body. "Tell me about the voices. If you can explain what's happening, then I can help you." He inched closer to Tim, his body visibly on alert, the muscles in his arms vibrating.

Tim shook his head. "I don't know. Ever since the headache started, it won't stop. God, make it *stop*."

"Okay." Brett kicked the gun out of Tim's hand and took him down to the ground. Easily flipping him over, he almost gently handcuffed the guy.

Tim keened.

Sharon rushed forward and pushed back his hair. "It's okay. You're going to be okay."

"I want to hurt somebody," Tim moaned. "I don't know why, but it's all I can think about."

The nurse ran in and plunged a sedative into Tim's arm.

Brett relaxed. "Get him into a bed and secure him."

Two orderlies hustled around the corner and complied.

Sharon looked at Brett. What the hell had just happened? "I don't understand."

He grasped her forearms and helped her to stand. "Is it possible a bacterium can change a brain? I mean, strip it or anything? Cause insanity?"

Her mouth opened and closed. Her mind spun. "I really don't know. We'll have to get some tests going and fast." That wasn't her field of expertise. "We're going to have to hand this over to the CDC, you know."

He nodded and stepped into her. "I have a feeling, sweetheart. Something bad is coming, and this is just the beginning." His kiss against her forehead felt like a promise.

"Me too," she whispered.

He lifted her chin, and his gaze swept hers. "I need to know. Before this all gets started and we have to launch into reaction mode, are you with me?"

She breathed in. Next to him, warmed by him, felt like home. "Yes."

He brushed her mouth with a kiss. "I mean *with me*. No matter what happens? All in?"

She smiled against his lips. "Yeah. I'm all in."

He exhaled. "This is just the beginning. That bacteria is going to spread across the world, and we might need to head to the mountains and safety for a while. I promise I'll keep you safe."

She nodded, fully understanding what they now faced. "I agree, but let's wait for Lynne and find out everything we can while we still can." Gut instinct told her life was about to change, but they'd save everyone they could, and then they'd hunker down. For now, she was going to help the students still in the hospital get better and leave. It was all she could do.

He kissed her nose. "You with me?"

"No matter what, it's you and me." She could almost see the difficulties in front of them, in front of the world, and she knew they'd win. Their time for growing up and exploring on their own was over. For the rest of this life, she wanted to be home with him. "I've always loved you, Brett."

He kissed her, going deep. Finally, he let her breathe. "I've always loved you, too. Forever this time, Sharon."

* * *

PROTECTED BY REBECCA ZANETTI

A DARK PROTECTORS SHORT STORY

This short story was included in the Nightingale charity anthology, which is now out of print. I get asked about it a lot, so I thought I'd include it here for you. :) This one features Janie and Zane when their daughter Hope was around five years old.

CHAPTER 1

*J*anie Kayrs-Kyllwood sat straight up in the bed, her heart hammering against her rib cage. She gasped and sucked in air, trying to breathe. Her mate stretched his arm across her and flipped on the bedside lamp.

"Nightmare, Janie Belle?" Zane asked lazily, his unreal green eyes sleepy.

"Vision." She shoved her light brown hair away from her face. "Two-pronged. Somebody is making a move against Garrett and Hope at the same time. We're being attacked." Garrett was her younger brother and Hope her daughter, and fear nearly froze her in place.

When Zane wanted to move fast, he did. In a second he was out of the bed, tossing her jeans over his shoulder to land near her, his phone already to his ear as he barked orders. The male sounded like the head of the demon nation, which he was, going from sleep to battle-ready in less than a human heartbeat.

Which his was not. He was half-demon and half-vampire, with the demon lineage pulling dominance.

Janie was human. Well, immortal human since she'd mated Zane. She scrambled to pull on her jeans and a blue sweater, bumping her hip on the closet in the small room. They'd rented the cabin for a weekend getaway up in the mountains for some snowy fun, and she was too far from the center of the camp. Too far from her five-year-old daughter, and way too far from her adult brother, who was somewhere in Oregon. Or Washington State. She didn't know.

She yanked on socks and her tennis shoes before running into the quaint living room, where Zane was pulling on boots. "What's happening?"

Zane turned, his dark hair falling over his forehead. "Phone just went dead."

Janie paused. "Dead? Our phones can't go dead." There wasn't even a storm going on outside right now. They were in a protected camp with the rest of the family coming the next night. Right now, it was just the two of them and her parents with her daughter across the camp—way too far away. "What do you know?"

Zane stood outlined from the dawn light peeking through the blinds, his body strong and solid muscle. At six and a half feet, he should look gangly, but he was all brutal strength. Even the harsh angles of his face looked dangerous, and right now, he appeared deadly. "I don't know. When did you start having visions again?"

She lifted a shoulder. After having given birth five years ago, her visions had waned. "I don't know. Lately they've been coming back a little. Nothing strong but glimpses into the future that I can't decipher yet." She'd never been able to control the visions, and they often led to contradictory options, so it was a little terrifying to know they were returning. If only she could somehow force the images of the future into her brain that she needed to know about. "Please tell me you found Hope before the phone died?"

"No. But she's having a sleepover at the other end of camp with your parents, and I'm sure she's still there. It's too early to go anywhere." Zane's voice remained level and calm, but tension rolled off him faster than an oncoming storm. "I'm so pissed I can't teleport any longer." The ability for all demons to do so had ended with an abnormality that had something to do with string theory and the p-brane, and hopefully would return someday.

"We still have the snowmobile." Janie took in a deep breath and hustled to grab her coat off the hook by the door. If anybody could keep her baby safe, it was her parents. Her adoptive father, Talen Kayrs, was arguably the most dangerous vampire on the planet, and Cara had spent decades learning to fight, although she was also an immortal human with mere human strength. "I wouldn't have the vision if there wasn't danger coming." She couldn't point to a factual basis for that claim, but she knew it with her very being. "We have to get to her and somehow warn Garrett." Why weren't they running out the door? "Zane?"

He dug into a pack and tossed her a green gun. "I don't know. I sense something. Someone. Shoot anybody who comes through that door."

"Absolutely not. I'm coming with you." She moved for the door just as the front window exploded.

* * *

ZANE KYLLWOOD LEAPT for his mate, taking her down to the ground and protecting her from the flying glass. Was that a grenade? In one smooth move, he had her up and covered by his body as he carried her into the bedroom and kicked the door shut with his boot. The entire camp was under attack? "Stay down." He placed her between the closet and bed so she could shoot toward the door or the window, if either were breached.

Then he went out the window, his senses settling into the intensity of battle. All questions of who was attacking or why, not to mention how, went right out of existence.

There was only right here and right now and destroying

28

whoever had just threatened his mate and might be going after his child.

His boots hit the snow and sunk a foot, but he was already moving around the side of the cabin to the front, his gaze searching the tree line. He couldn't see them, but he could sense them. Maybe smell them. Burnt hamburger and whiskey. Seriously? He scanned the heavily snow covered pine trees, zeroing in on the scent.

Two men. Human. What the hell?

He scratched the shadow of his whiskers, noting the sun rising over the mountains and sparkling on the snow. He could go straight at them, even though there was wide open land between them. If humans were attacking him, it was just a mistake. A deadly one, but not one leading to war. They probably had no clue who he was or that he was the leader of the demon nation.

One thing he'd learned from watching the humans was that when a leader of a superpower was weak, the world burned. When the leader of the *most* powerful nation blinked, enemies struck with no conscious across the globe.

Zane Kyllwood never blinked.

He'd keep his family and his people protected regardless of the cost. So he ducked his head and barreled across the snowy landscape straight at the trees. Gunfire erupted and bullets slammed into his shoulder. Human bullets? He shoved the irritating metal out with his mind and reached the duo, tackling them both into a massive pine tree. Guns dropped and the first guy grunted in pain while the other passed out cold.

Zane stood and brushed snow off his shirt, staring down at them.

The unconscious man was around thirty with a thin wool coat over jeans, and his nose bled through the snow. The other guy was a little older with deep lines extending from his eyes. He just wore a flannel and it looked like Zane's assault had broken both his right arm and his clavicle.

Zane frowned. Killing humans wasn't his thing, and they couldn't hurt him. But they had attacked his cabin with Janie inside. A grenade wouldn't kill her, but she could've been injured. "Talk."

"Ug." The guy spit blood and then wiped off his mouth, leaving a trail down his ice-crusted beard.

"Try again." Zane cocked his head.

The guy's eyes were bloodshot and his body shook. "We needed the money. Were hired to throw a grenade through the window."

Was he tweaking? Zane leaned forward. "What are you on?"

"Everything." The guy smiled and blood slid along his teeth.

This wasn't making sense. Unless...Zane turned in time to barely miss a sword slicing toward his neck. The blade glanced off his shoulder and pain burst through his arm. He ducked his head and charged the attacker, catching him mid-center and plowing them both into another ancient tree. But with two immortal bodies hitting it, the tree cracked in the middle, shooting a schism up to the highest boughs. With a furious roar, the tree split in two and fell, destroying other trees on the way down. It hit the ground with a resounding boom.

Zane backflipped to his feet just as three enemy immortal soldiers bounded out of the trees. They'd learned to mask their scents?

Damn.

CHAPTER 2

*J*anie jumped as the ground shook from what sounded like a forest blowing apart. Grasping the gun, she moved for the window and eased herself into the chilly morning. Her breath fogged the air as she shoved through thick snow to the snowmobile and jumped on. She could hear fighting in the trees, and she could sense the enemy close.

While born human, she'd inherited some of Zane's gifts when mating him, and she knew when the Kurjans were near. Her mate was one of the most powerful fighters in the immortal world, but their child was in danger, and she didn't have time to wait behind and just shoot people infiltrating the cabin.

She didn't have the patience for it.

If somebody came after her family, she just couldn't wait for rescue. For years she'd trained to fight—her entire life actually. As a human, even a mated one, she'd never have immortal strength or speed.

But she had a snowmobile.

She ignited the machine and swiftly turned it toward the trees, following a very clear path across the snowy ground left by Zane. Zipping between two spruce trees, she quickly took in the scene.

Zane grappled with two Kurjan soldiers as a third stayed to the side, weapon pointed at the melee. It was a green gun, like hers, that shot lasers that turned into bullets that harmed immortals. Terror coated down her throat. For centuries the Kurjans had been unable to venture into the sunlight with their pale translucent skin. Their scientists had been hard at work to create an antibody to the sun for them and had recently succeeded.

Their skin was pale and their hair either black tipped-with-red or red tipped-with-black. These all had black hair with blood red tips.

She turned the Polaris again and shot forward, straight at the soldier with the gun. He pivoted and tried to fire, but she plowed into him, tossing him up into a tree like he was a beach ball. He fell back down to the ground hard, still firing, and landed on his face. She flipped around and ran him over, the snowmobile making a nice jump as she did so.

"Damn it, Belle," Zane bellowed, throwing one of the Kurjans so far he almost hit the damaged front porch of the cabin.

Janie slid off the machine, gun out and firing at the prone Kurjan on the ground. The immortal's body jerked with each bullet and his blood ran the icy ground red. Finally, he lapsed into unconsciousness.

The guy wouldn't die, but he'd be out for a while. She paused and sank to her knees in the snow.

Zane cracked the neck of the other soldier and then stood, facing her as the body dropped.

Her heart caught and seized. Sometimes she forgot. He was her mate and she loved him with everything she'd ever be, but even so, sometimes she forgot the raw beauty of the sheer deadliness in every line of his immortal body. He stood in the snow after having battled immortals and humans, a thin line of blood sliding down the side of his angled his face. His eyes blazed an unreal green fire, and power cascaded along his steel-cut form.

"I told you to stay inside the cabin," he ground out, his voice low and garbled. Blood dotted his shoulder but he'd probably already healed the wound.

"We have to get to Hope." She shook herself out of the stupor and kicked through snow to the machine, not surprised when Zane beat her there.

He plucked her in front of him as he sat. "We'll talk about disobedience and danger after."

"Humph," she said, grabbing the handlebars as he opened the throttle. She felt better after having run over the enemy a couple of times, but she needed to see her daughter. Yet she knew, deep in her soul, that her father would never let anything happen to Hope. Even so, she couldn't help but breathe in relief as they drove up to Talen's cabin to see him standing over three prone Kurjan soldiers, all unconscious and bleeding in the snow.

"We were attacked," Talen said, sounding bemused. He was as tall and broad as Zane with thick dark hair and a jaw made of pure stone. He kicked one of the Kurjans with his boot, watching the body flop. Then his golden eyes rose to check out Zane and Janie. "You two okay?"

"Yes." Janie jumped off the sled and rushed for her father, hugging him. "Is Hope all right?"

"Of course." Talen tilted his head to study the bodies on the ground. One stirred, and he kicked him in the jaw, ending the stirring. He looked at Zane. "Attacked." He sounded more bewildered than angry. "They're not very good. It wasn't even a good fight." Now he sounded regretful.

Zane nodded. "Let's take them away from the cabin and have a little discussion. Our phones were knocked out, and that's problematic. The Kurjans apparently have a new electronic weapon." He pushed off the snowmobile. "Belle? Stay inside this time." His voice was mild but a thread of pure menace flowed through it.

Considering the discussion with the attackers would probably include torture, maybe, she didn't argue. Instead, she rushed inside the cabin where her mother was sitting with Hope at the table, both eating cereal that looked like it had extra marshmallows in it. "Hi." She reached her daughter and gathered her in a hug. "I missed you."

Hope absently patted her arm, chewing happily on the sweets. Her light brown hair was already tied in braids and her blue eyes danced with the happiness found in too much sugar. "Hi, mama. Talen gots in a fight." She sighed and wiped milk off her lips. "It was too short for him, though." She sadly shook her head.

Janie sank into a chair at the table and looked at her mom, who still appeared to be around twenty-five or so. They had the same hair color and blue eyes, so most people upon meeting them figured they were sisters at this point. Being immortal definitely had its advantages. "Any word from my brother?"

"No. Why?" Cara asked, concern for her son bright in her eyes. "Is Garrett in trouble again?"

"I don't know. I had a vision of danger coming for him as well as Hope." But there wasn't any time limit to the vision, was there? "It might not be immediate?"

Cara poured another mug of coffee from the pot on the table. "I'll try to get ahold of him when the comms come back on."

Janie gratefully took the warm drink. "It's so weird seeing Kurjans in the sun."

Cara winced and reached for her coffee mug. "Right?

Hope kicked her little feet beneath the table, wearing her favorite Kangaroo T-shirt and jeans. "The ones outside didn't come to hurt us. I donna know why they came." She smiled, showing yellow marshmallow in her teeth. "They don't want us to know they want more war yet."

Janie's stomach went cold as Cara stiffened. "How do you know that, baby?"

Hope shrugged.

Janie reached for her daughter's small hand. Hope was the only female in the world with vampire blood in her, considering vampires genetically had only made males until Hope had been born. She was a miracle—perhaps made by science or perhaps by fate. Either way, she had gifts Janie very much feared she hid. "Did you have a vision?"

"Maybe." Hope chewed thoughtfully, her eyes looking much older than a five-year-old's ever should. "Visions or dreams are the same, right, mama? I dunno. I want the Kurjans to wanna be friends. Don't you?" She returned to her cereal bowl.

Friends? Could one become friends with their mortal enemy? It'd be nice, but not all people wanted the same things in life. Janie would love peace. The Kurjans didn't see peace as an interest, and without the same goals, how could they reach a peaceful existence, especially when the Kurjans just wanted more power? It was a mistake to assume that everyone would fight for the same things.

The sound of a helicopter split the silence outside.

Cara sighed. "Guess we're done camping and snowmobiling here."

CHAPTER 3

*B*ack at demon headquarters in northern Idaho, just down the lake from the vampire headquarters, Zane waited until Janie had finished talking to her brother via a video conference. When she vacated her chair, he sat down and waited until she'd left the room to start speaking with his brother-in-law. "If your sister thinks you're in danger, you probably are," he murmured.

Garrett was a solid form of strength, even through the camera. His sizzling gray eyes remained somber. "I can handle any danger. Just take care of my sister."

Zane lifted one dark eyebrow. "It's time for you to come home, G. Whatever secret mission you're on has to end. Now."

"No." Garrett grinned, for a second looking like that smartass kid Zane had once known. "Now get busy and get me a nephew, would you?" He clicked off without another word.

Zane rolled his eyes and wandered through the secure home to the bedroom, where he found Janie unpacking from their interrupted weekend. "Your brother wants a nephew." Was it possible they'd ever have another girl? Hope was a miracle and those probably came along only once in a lifetime, if ever.

Janie partially turned, her pretty face still looking stressed. "Hope is only five. He knows immortals take forever to procreate. It's shocking we have so many little ones running around right now. I think there's something to that old adage that any population grows after a war." She rubbed at a bruise on her wrist that must've happened when she'd driven a snowmobile into a Kurjan.

Yeah, that had been hot. Zane wanted to be irritated that she had plowed right into danger, but her ferocious heart was one of the reasons he loved her. Besides, the danger level had been rather low, and he'd known that the second he'd stepped into the wind. "So. Visions again?"

She bit her lip. "Maybe. I was hoping that since I had a vision, Hope would stop having them, but I doubt that's how it works." She removed her earrings. "Not that I'm positive she's having visions. Could be just dreams or that she knows things. Is psychic."

Zane wrapped an arm around Janie's waist, pivoted, and tossed her on the bed. "Something to worry about another day."

His mate's eyes sparkled as she landed softly and bounced. "Same with Garrett?"

"Your visions rarely have a time line. That kid could be in danger in a century." Not that Garrett was still a kid, but to Zane, maybe he always would be. Who knew? "The Kurjans did knock out our comms, which I think was the real reason for the attack. It was a test run." Which was why he'd dropped the captured soldiers outside of a Kurjan encampment all tied up and in the sun. Their new defense against the sun didn't last for too long, so they probably would've had a blistered sunburn by the time they were picked up. He couldn't bring himself to kill an inexperienced scouting team. Plus, he'd implanted trackers in their heels and recorders in their earlobes while they'd been out.

Janie slowly unbuttoned her shirt. "I'm surprised you let them all live."

He kept his face calm. "I let them live so I could gather information." She didn't need to know about the show of force his nation would take the next day to deter any future attacks by small Kurjan bands. He learned a long time ago that the enemy stood down when faced with a viable threat, and he'd also learned to always strike back with more force than the enemy had shown. It was the only way to keep his people and allies safe. "Now. About that son?"

"You immortals are so odd to have kids through centuries. Most of you, anyway. Can you imagine having a sibling hundreds of years younger than you?"

"It'll probably happen," he agreed, standing tall by the bed. "If my mother would take a break from robbing banks, I'm sure she'd like another few sons." He yanked his shirt over his head to toss onto the floor. "Are you worried about new visions?" He was.

"No. I've had them most of my life. But it'd be nice to be able to control them."

He sighed. While he wasn't angry with her, if she was having visions and if the Kurjans were doing test runs with new technology, danger was coming for them. Again. "We do need to talk about obeying orders in the field."

Her eye roll did nothing to ease his mind.

* * *

JANIE LOVED PUSHING HIM. Zane wanted so badly to be modern and kind, while every instinct in his immortal body roared for him to control and protect. The war between his mind and his heart, in so many different areas, was what made Zane Kyllwood an excellent leader for the demon nation. It also made him the perfect mate for her. "I don't know how to obey."

"I'm aware." His jeans hit the floor as he moved forward, all male animal and muscle. "Take off your shirt."

All the fear, all the emotion of the morning pooled into one hot flare of desire. No matter how long she lived, she'd feel this for him. She narrowed her eyes even as flutters danced through her abdomen. "You want it off, you take it off."

He smiled like a panther finding prey in the brush. "My pleasure." Faster than she could track, he reached and yanked her shirt over her head. One snap and her bra flicked open. She removed it, scooting further up the bed, her gaze on the warrior still smiling at her. A killer smile, full of lust and something else. Something that would always be just for her.

His briefs hit the floor and fully aroused, he put one knee on the bed, reaching for the button of her jeans. With one hand he unzipped and slid them down her legs, pushing her onto her back. His head dropped and sharp teeth teased sensitive skin as he tugged her cotton panties down to her ankles where she kicked them off.

She groaned as he nipped at an ankle before moving back up. Desire whispered along her skin and love filled her heart. She'd loved him since the first time she'd looked into the heated eyes now above hers.

"Ah, my Janie Belle. When are you going to learn?" A rough shadow ran along his jaw. His full lips quirked as he settled his bulk against her skin, the shadows ever present in his eyes lightening for this moment.

She reached up and ran her hands through the thick black hair he'd allowed to grow to his collar. "Never."

His lips twitched and one hand grabbed her ass to tug into his hardness. "I could handle anything in this life but losing either you or Hope. That matters." His eyes lost all amusement. "You gave yourself to me. Your mine to love and protect, no matter what." He shook his head, slowly entering her, inch by swollen inch. About half way in, he paused, dropping his forehead to hers. "You're perfect."

She lifted her head, brushing his lips with hers. Need, hot and full, pulsed where they met and she wrapped her legs around his hips. "Safety is an illusion, Zane. You know that as well as I."

39

Although she believed in her very soul that he'd protect their little family to the death. Maybe beyond.

"True." His green eyes flared with a light nowhere near describable with the human language. "I would greatly appreciate it if you kept yourself out of danger, although you're a true menace on a snowmobile." He thrust hard, fully embedding himself in her.

Janie cried out, feeling him through her body, through her heart, possibly to her soul. Her tumultuous soul with its power and future destiny, whatever that might be. Immorality drew out fate, didn't it? Was it possible to have many destinies or fates to fulfill? She often thought so, and so long as Zane was by her side, she could handle them all.

Zane gripped her hips with both hands, one with a mating mark on his palm. "Do we understand each other?"

She grinned, even as desire warred with caution throughout her. "I seriously doubt that."

"You will," Zane said in an agreeable tone that gave her pause. He pulled back and slid slowly back again. Several times.

Love and heat consumed her from the inside out. "Zane," she breathed, tracing his ribs one at a time down to the hollow of his back. Her thighs clutched him harder, urging him to go faster. "Go faster."

He chuckled against her collarbone, nipping a path to the soft spot where her neck met shoulder. He bit down, his mouth enclosing the space in heat while desire quickly replaced the sharp flash of pain. Nibbling up her jaw, moving too slowly inside her, he brushed her lips with a kiss. Then he descended and went deeper.

His tongue took hers, his mouth engulfed hers, his body heated hers.

"I love you." The words escaped from somewhere deep she couldn't fathom, from somewhere reality couldn't reach. There was only the two of them there. Forever.

2023 RARE AUSTRALIA ANTHOLOGY

He stilled, a warm flush cascading through his body as it covered her. His head lifted and the heat in his expression warmed that place so far from reality. "I have no doubt your love has saved us both through the years and will continue to do so. You're all mine, Belle."

A soldier with the heart of a poet. Janie smiled. Hers. Forever. "I'll protect you."

Almost all the way out of her, he slammed home with a grunt. "That's my job, baby." He increased his speed and the strength of his thrusts, and she urged him on, digging her feet into his butt. Sharp light filled her head and behind her eyelids as the orgasm rippled through her. She cried out his name.

He followed her into bliss, his fangs slicing into her shoulder in a mark as old as time.

She mumbled and was asleep before he moved. His chuckle followed her into a deep sleep where dreams left her alone until the morning and another vision struck.

This time, she turned over in the bed to see Zane on his side, watching her.

His gaze was alert in his rugged face. "I felt it. You had a vision."

She didn't question how intune they were to each other. "Yeah."

"Do I need to get up?" He stretched lazily but the intensity didn't abate.

"No." She pressed her hand over his heart. "The vision is cloudy, but I saw both of our brothers in danger from their mates. Or in danger from the *threat* around their mates." She couldn't get it straight. "Sam and Garrett are together, riding motorcycles, with women riding behind them."

Zane played idly with her hair. "When?"

"I don't know. There's fire chasing Sam and something invisible and sinister chasing Garrett." Why couldn't she see more?

Zane sighed. "Sounds about right." He rolled her onto her back and covered her. "Since there's no timeline, we'll call them later. For now, let's get busy on giving them both a nephew."

"Or niece," Janie said, tunneling her fingers through his thick hair.

Anything was possible.

* * *

I HOPE you liked this glimpse into the Dark Protector and Scorpius Syndrome worlds! I write thrillers, romantic suspense novels, paranormal romances, and some small town humorous women's fiction. If you're interested in my books, drop by my website for more information and reading order for each of the series: www.RebeccaZanetti.com

NEW YORK TIMES, USA Today, Publisher's Weekly and Wall Street Journal bestselling author Rebecca Zanetti has published more than seventy novels, which have been translated into several languages, with millions of copies sold world-wide. She has ridden in a locked Chevy trunk, has asked the unfortunate delivery guy to release her from a set of handcuffs, and has discovered the best silver mine shafts in which to bury a body…all in the name of research. Honest.

SOUL SURVIVOR BY BOONE BRUX

A DARK REAPER SHORT STORY

Welcome to the new world of Dark Reapers. Bad deeds done for a good reason might just get you a second chance at life.

CHAPTER 1

*E*ven in the dimly lit alley, Thomas recognized her. This was the woman who'd made him smile. The woman who'd been the ray of sunshine in his empty existence. The woman he'd died for.

Why was she here? More importantly, why was she crouched over a body? "August?"

Her head snapped up, that familiar brown gaze ghosting across his partner Cain to settle on him. Now void of the warmth he remembered, the cold stare of a Shadow Demon peered back at him. "August doesn't live here anymore."

"Fuck." He flinched as her answer rasped from her throat. Goddamn demons. How had they managed to possess her? Usually, they set up shop in drug addicts or a willing host. There wasn't a chance in Hell August would have allowed herself to be possessed. "Where is she?"

She pursed her full lips in a mocking pout. Lips he'd once fantasized about kissing. "She's been indefinitely evicted." Her pupils constricted. "Thomas."

"I take it you know her?" Cain growled from beside him.

Thomas nodded. "I used to, anyway."

"Shit. Try and stay focused." The solid weight of Cain's hand came down on Thomas's shoulder. "The only way to help her is to free her."

"Don't worry about me." Big words spoken with a conviction he didn't feel. "I've got this."

At least he had until the second demon rounded the corner. "Mutha fucker!"

"Let me guess," Cain said, "you know him too."

"That asshole's name is Throttle." August had been why he died, and this asshole had been how. "He's one of those dicks from the Scavengers."

"That motorcycle gang is really starting to chap my ass."

"I'm way past that." Thomas pulled his scythe blades from their holsters. "I could have sworn I killed that bastard…right before his boss put a couple dozen slugs in me."

Taking the info in stride, Cain nodded. "That sucks."

"Tommy, my man." Throttle opened his massive arms in greeting, the tattoo-covered muscles bulging. "What a surprise. Let's see, the last time I saw you, you'd just shoved a knife into my host's chest." A jagged grin stretched his thin lips. "Thanks for that, by the way. I managed to slip in a second before Throttle kicked off the mortal coil." Locking his fingers together, he cracked his knuckles. "This body is way better than the last."

"Sorry you won't be keeping it." Thomas's gaze slid to August as she slowly rose to her feet. "What about her?"

"Weak." In a display of ownership, the biker draped a meaty arm around her shoulder and hauled her against him. She went willingly, her sneering smile sending a shiver of dread up Thomas's spine. "After you died, all she did was cry every goddamn day. So annoying. She was easy to possess." As if the reason for Thomas standing in front of him finally dawned, he cocked his head. "Don't tell me they made you one of them Dark Reapers."

"Okay, I won't tell you," Thomas said.

"Aww, damn, now I've gotta kill you all over again." He released August and dragged a serrated blade from his waistband. "That's okay." He spun the knife around his index finger. "I don't mind."

"First off, you didn't kill me. Your jackass of a boss did. Secondly, you're not Throttle. You're just some underworld piece of shit squatting in his body."

A have smirk quirked the corner of the demon's upper lip. "Why do you gotta be like that, Tommy?"

"I don't know." He shook his head. "It's like...everything about you makes me want to stab you—repeatedly."

Throttle shrugged. "That's fair."

"What's your name, demon?" Cain asked as he threaded his fingers into the brass knuckles of his double blades.

"How rude of me." Executing a half-bow, the demon grinned. "Ma'dik, loyal servant to the Shadow Empire."

"Seriously? That's your name?" Thomas asked.

"Yes, Ma'dik, the mighty." The demon threw open his arms. "Ma' dik, defender of the true god."

"Dude, don't you hear it?" At Throttle's confused expression, Thomas grinned. "My dick. Your name is my dick?"

The demon's confusion morphed to anger. "Funny." Spinning the knife again, Throttle gifted Thomas with a humorless smile. "I'm going to enjoy killing you."

"Uhh, no you're not." Gripping his blades tigher, he raised the weapons. "But I'm sure going to enjoy vanquishing your ass. This time I'll make sure it sticks."

His gaze drifted to August and leveled on her. Everything about her was nearly the same. Same big brown eyes, coppery curls that hung past her shoulders, and the tight body that had gotten him hard more than a few times. What wasn't the same was the malevolent look in those gorgeous eyes that used to gaze lovingly at him, and the pulsating black of the Shadow Demon's aura surrounding her.

"You want the big one?" Cain asked.

"No." Thomas shook his head. "I want her."

"Good, the little ones are usually meaner." Cain lifted his blades and whispered his Latin chant against the metal, igniting the power of his scythes. Blue flames raced along the edges, and then faded back to black. "This will be a good test for you."

Thomas harumphed. "Yeah, this should be super fun." He raised his daggers to his lips and whispered, "Producat in lucem." Bring the light. Like Cain's scythes, the blue fire sped along the honed blades and then dimmed. Now the weapons would exorcise the demons but leave the humans alive. Though…it was always a tossup how bad off the host would be afterward. "Let's do this."

As August stalked toward him, she dragged a long dagger from the inside pocket of her coat. Determination burned in her eyes, her approach steady and purposeful. He wouldn't make the mistake of thinking he could reason with this demon. No, there was only one solution, and he prayed he could make a clean strike.

When she was about five feet away, she launched herself forward with a flying leap. Endowed with the demon's strength and speed, she lifted above him, slamming her knife straight down. Thomas dropped to one knee. Clasping his blades together overhead, he formed a shield. Her attack bounced off, and as she landed on the ground behind him, Thomas spun and swept his leg in an arc. The hit caught her at the calf and knocked her off balance, causing her to stumble. Trying to remain upright, her arms windmilled.

If this had been any other possessed person, Thomas would have taken advantage of the split-second gain, but this was August, the woman who had fed his fantasy of a happy life. The idea of sinking his blades into her twisted his gut in a knot. His attack faltered, the hesitation costing him.

August took a step back, catching herself. Seeing his mistake, Thomas charged forward., but she bent backward and propelled herself into a backward flip. Her foot landed a solid kick to his chin as it followed her body.

The force of the hit slammed into him. Pain ricocheted through his jaw, and stars danced behind his eyes. Stumbling, he went down on one knee, but the tip of his right blade dug into the asphalt, stopping his fall.

August rocketed toward him, her knife poised for the strike. Triumph glinted in her unwavering stare, and a sneer pulled at her mouth. For a split second, her body hung in the air, blades raised overhead.

All hesitancy melted away, his mission crystalizing. He struck. Lunging forward, he buried his blade in her chest. The sickening sensation of the metal sinking into her soft flesh shook him to his core. Delivering the second blow, he rammed his right hand forward. The blade flared to life, the blue flames licking along the incision and burrowing into August's chest.

She dropped to the asphalt, but he held her upright. Her body convulsed, her eyes wide, and her mouth rounding. The dagger in her hand clattered to the ground and skidded out of reach. Slowly, she grabbed his fingers. Even with two eight-inch Shadow Blades buried to their hilt in her chest, the demon's grip tightened to a painful level. Her nails dug at his fingers, scraping off a few layers of skin. Still, he held fast. Never letting up on the tension, Thomas pressed to his feet.

"You can't have her," the demon hissed.

He leaned in until they were nose to nose. "Fuck. You."

With that, he shoved the blade upward, slicing a wide gash in her chest. A scream tore from her throat, her fingers clawing at his face as he released one of the scythes and plunged his hand into her chest.

A viscous liquid surrounded his hand, slowing his forward motion. The sensation of a million biting ants tore at his fingers and wrist, but he thrust deeper into the thick oily substance until he felt the hard nugget of the demon's soul. It recoiled from his touch, but he snatched at the putrid lump and yanked it free. The black liquid turned to vapor and seeped from the wound in August's chest, trying to reach the demon soul.

Tossing the fetid mass in the air, he hauled a blade free from her body, spun, and slashed at the clump. Blue flames raced along the razor-sharp edge of the scythe and engulfed the soul, burning it to ash. As if caught by an updraft, the vapor expanded outward, and then exploded in a sudden burst, and then evaporated.

As he watched the black mist disperse, his shoulders sagged in relief, but his reprieve was short lived. August's body pitched forward.

"Shit." He spun toward her just in time to catch her from falling to the ground. Holding her with one arm, he pulled the second blade free and shoved it into its holster at his back. "August." He lowered her to the ground and laid her flat. "Can you hear me?"

No response. Her chalky pallor sent a pang of alarm through him. After stowing his second blade, he bent to examine the gash. Though the skin was scorched and puckered, the incision was healing. By tomorrow, hopefully there would be no sign of his reaping—if there was a tomorrow.

"August." He slid his arm under her shoulders and lifted her. "Come on, baby, wake up."

Still nothing.

The thud of light footsteps jogging toward him sounded to Thomas's right, and a second later, Cain appeared. Sometime during the fight, Cain and Throttle had disappeared down the alley. From the scowl on his partner's face, things hadn't ended well.

Cain crouched next to them. "She alive?"

"Yeah, but unconscious. Throttle?"

His glower deepened. "Escaped."

Thomas harrumphed but didn't comment. Cain was the oldest Dark Reaper living. If he'd lost the demon, there had been a good reason. Shifting August higher, he said, "Help me get her back to my place."

Cain's dark gaze leveled on him. "Do you think that's wise?"

Probably not, but nothing on Earth would make him abandon her now. Not when he'd just found her again. "Wise or not, I'm taking her home?"

Cain didn't argue. He liked that about the guy. Just let things be. He helped Thomas to his feet and then went to check on the unconscious guy still laying next to the trash bin. After a minute of examination, he prowled back to Thomas. "Drunk. He'll be fine."

Thomas nodded, hefted August into his arms, and strode to the street. It looked like becoming a Dark Reaper wasn't the only second chance he was getting.

CHAPTER 2

*S*unlight danced just beyond August's eyelids, but exhaustion made it impossible to open them. Silence blanketed her. No motorcycles revving. No yelling or laughing. None of the pandemonium that was the constant din at the Scavenger's clubhouse. Even the smells of gas and oil were missing. Where was she, and why couldn't she remember anything?

Her mind sifted through the shattered fragments of her memories, trying to piece together something coherent, but just as she latched onto an image, it evaporated. She let it go, seeking the next clue as to how she got here, wherever here was. Without warning, the image of Thomas flared to life in her mind, bringing with it the raw grief she'd been living with since his death a few months ago.

A whimper slipped from her lips as the sadness swamped her. He'd been the only happiness in her miserable life, but before anything beyond friendship could develop between them, he'd been killed. The vice around her heart tightened. He'd tried to protect her from Throttle's drunken rampage and paid the price. Because of her. Now that she remembered, she wished she could go back into the haze she'd been living in.

As she rolled to her side, her body curling in on itself, a sharp ache spread across her chest. She gasped against the pain, her eyes popping open. It took a second for the sight before her to register. Then, all pain vanished.

Not a foot away sat Thomas, elbows resting on his knees, his stare intent. "Hey, Sunshine."

"Whoa!" She bolted upright, her body pressing against the back of the couch. "What the hell?" Her gaze skated around the dingy apartment, but she didn't recognize it. "If you're here...then I must be...dead?"

The same crooked smile she remembered kicked up the right side of his mouth. "No, you're very much alive."

"But...you're dead, right?"

"Uhhh, well." He grimaced. "Not exactly."

"What do you mean, not exactly?" Surely, she was having some kind of drug induced delusion. "You're dead."

Leaning forward, he covered her hand with his. Warm and heavy. So unlike the last time she'd touched him. "I'm not."

"Yes, you are." She yanked her hand away and scooted to the end of the couch. "I saw you get shot. I checked your pulse. You didn't have one. You were dead."

"True." He slid back into the chair, again resting his elbows on his knees. "But, I'm not dead now."

"I don't think it works like that." She should be happy that Thomas was sitting in front of her, apparently healthy and breathing, but he'd been dead. That was the one thing she'd been certain of. "Slayer shot you. You bled out on the floor of the clubhouse." Her head shook involuntarily, her mind unable to reconcile the living Thomas sitting in the chair. "Dead. Dead. Dead."

His brow pinched together as his gaze dropped to his hands. "It's...complicated."

"Well." Waving wildly in his direction, she grasped for understanding. "Uncomplicate it for me."

His blue gaze lifted again, settling on her face with the same intensity he used to watch her with. He looked exactly the same as she remembered. Except for the being dead part. Same short clean-cut hairstyle that had made him stand out in the crowd of longhaired or bald Scavengers. He hadn't fit in, and that's why he'd been special. More than anything in her entire life, she regretted the day he'd been shot. The guilt had become unbearable. Maybe that was it. Maybe she was having a psychotic break. That's the only thing that made sense.

His stare never wavered from her face, but his jaw flexed as if struggling for an explanation. Finally, he exhaled a heavy breath. "I did die but was brought back to life."

"How? Who brought you back? Doctors?"

"That's where it gets complicated." He pushed to his feet and paced a few steps before turning back to her. "I need you to bear with me."

She scowled, wondering where this was going. "Okay."

"What is your last clear memory?"

"What do you mean?"

"Obviously, you remember me getting shot. After that." He moved back to the chair and perched on the edge, his eyes locking on hers. "What's your most recent memory."

"Waking up here."

"And before that?"

She opened her mouth to reply but stopped. Again, the murky recesses of her mind refused to cough up a clear memory. "I guess it was of Throttle coming to check on me in my room. I'd been really depressed, and he was oddly nice to me that day."

"When was that?"

"I don't know. What day is it?"

His gaze narrowed on her. "Thursday."

"Then, a couple of days ago."

"It's Thursday," he repeated. "September third."

"No, it's not. It's October."

"No, August. It's September third. Your memory is from a year ago."

How could she have lost eleven months and not realized it? Drugs? Had Throttle kept her doped up so she couldn't leave? Bile rose in her throat, her head shaking in denial. "That's not possible."

"It is." Thomas stood and renewed his pacing. "This is where it gets complicated. Do you remember when I stabbed Throttle, and then Slayer plugged me with a dozen rounds?"

"All too well." A thousand questions tumbled through her mind, but she didn't ask them, wondering where he was going with his explanation. "You were dead, and Throttle was bleeding all over the club house."

"Right. So, when I killed Throttle, and his soul left his body, a demon named Ma'dik slipped in."

Whatever she'd been expecting, this explanation hadn't been it. Slowly blinking, she tried to process what he'd just said. "Ma'dik?"

"Yeah, he's a nasty fucker. Real sadistic."

"You're telling me Throttle is possessed by a demon named Ma'dik?"

"Yeah."

Disappointment stole through her. For a minute, she thought she was actually going to get answers. Now, it was clear that Thomas was mentally ill, having delusions of demons. Whatever he'd gone through had broken his mind. She nodded, unsure what to say. "Okay."

"You don't believe me." It wasn't a question. He sat again, leaning forward in his usual pose. "But here's the kicker. So were you."

"Me?" Shifting on the couch, she sat straighter. "Thomas, I'm not possessed."

"Not now. I exorcised the demon from you."

Yikes, he'd really gone around the bend. "Okaaaay. Thanks."

His crooked smile pulled at his mouth again. "When I died, I was given a second chance to atone for my sin. I'd killed a man, but I did it to protect you. A bad deed done for a good reason. I'm a Dark Reaper now. We hunt Shadow Demons. That's what's possessing Throttle, and that's what possessed you for eleven months. You don't remember because the demon controlled your body and mind." From behind his back, he withdrew two razor-sharp weapons. A jolt of panic hurtled through her, but she remained rooted on the couch. "These are my scythes." Bringing the blades to his lips, he whispered something she couldn't understand.

Blue flames shot along the edges, flaring to life before extinguishing. Her eyes rounded, her mouth dropping open. "How did you do that?"

"Each Dark Reaper chooses a Latin phrase that embodies his journey. It ignites the blades so that they exorcise the demon but leave the person alive." He motioned to her chest. "You may still have the marks."

With trembling fingers, she undid the buttons of her shirt. Red raw welts slashed across her chest, one of them running from her sternum to the base of her throat. A dull sting burned along the scar as she ran her finger up the raised ridge. "Impossible."

"Improbable." After setting his weapons on the table, he moved to the couch and sat beside her. "But not impossible."

Like wiping away the steaming mist from a mirror, the magnitude of her situation gelled, understanding pushing its way to the front. "Then, you're really alive."

His gaze locked with hers. "Yeah, I really am."

With her heart racing, she edged toward him. At the clubhouse it had been impossible to be together. Early on, Throttle had claimed her, and there had been no way out, but her heart had always belonged to Thomas. She cupped his face. "I can't believe this."

The warm weight of his hand pressed against her waist, but he didn't pull her to him. "You're happy then?"

55

The darkness and desolation that had threatened to shatter her soul melted away. "So happy," she whispered.

"Good." He hauled her to him and slid his fingers into her hair. "Because it would really suck if the woman you died for didn't give a shit."

"You never have to worry about that." Thomas had given his life for her, and she knew she'd do the same for him a thousand times over. Leaning closer, she rubbed her lips against his. "I've waited so long for this." They'd escaped the Scavengers, and hopefully this would be a new beginning for them.

CHAPTER 3

Despite the need to crush her against him, he remained still, letting her take the lead. Clad in his oversized T-shirt with a kangaroo smoking a joint on the front and her panties, she lifted her leg and straddled him. When she settled, a moan of pleasure hummed from him, her heat penetrating his jeans.

Gripping her ass, he pushed his erection against her. "So sweet." She smiled and ran her tongue along his bottom lip. Fuck waiting. He was ready to explode and needed to be inside her. His finger hooked the string of her panties. "Take these off."

"You're wearing too many clothes too," she said, gliding off him to stand. "Condom?"

"Reapers don't get sick or pregnant."

Her hand stilled, taking in that information. Had she wanted kids? Would she regret her decision to become a Reaper? Finally, she nodded. "Understood."

As she skimmed the scrap of material down her legs, he kicked off his boots, his jeans and boxers quickly following suit. As her shirt and bra fell to the floor, he snaked his arm around her waist and dragged her into the straddle position again, her hot core pressing against him. With slow circles, she gyrated, whimpers of pleasure escaping her lips.

His cock tightened, needing to be inside her. Pulling her mouth to his, he positioned himself at her entrance. Slow progression had been his plan, but she gripped the back of the couch, arched and seated him deep inside. He groaned, the feel of her tight channel pure heaven. "August, shit."

She took control, thrusting and circling, searching for what she needed. Her pink-tipped nipples stiffened, begging for attention. Cupping the mounds, he sucked, nibbled and tongued the tight buds, drawing a keening moan from August.

Her hips drove faster, her breath huffing from her with each thrust. Tingles of pleasure sparked at the base of his cock, building. He mentally cursed at his lack of restraint, but the way she moved drove him over the brink. "I'm gonna come."

"Do it," she panted

He'd get there, but not without her. Reaching between them, he thumbed her clit and thrust. Her slick canal constricted around him, pushing him over the edge. Locking her body against his, he plunged into her one final time and shattered.

A cry ripped from August as her body stiffened. Her nails dug into his shoulders, adding pleasurable pain as he released inside her. His muscles seized, and all conscious thought bled from his head. Pure fucking magic.

Tremors rippled through both of them as they floated back from their climax. Taking her with him, he stretched out on the couch. Locked in each other's arms, they lay staring at each other, breathing heavily, lost in euphoric happiness.

At some point, August's stomach growled, breaking the mood. "Hungry?" he asked.

"A little."

Though reluctant to move, they dressed and called for pizza. There was a lot to do now that she knew about him and his reincarnation. Meet with the reapers. Get her sorted out. Plan a whole new life—together. After cleaning up, their discussion turned to the nuances of being a Dark Reaper. She appeared to take everything in stride, accepting her destiny as his mate. It almost felt too easy.

Lifting one of the scythes, she examined it. "This thing is pretty wicked."

"Careful. Don't reap yourself."

Her eyes rounded. "Could that happen?" When he chuckled, she rolled her eyes. "Jerk." A loud knock sounded at the door. "Finally, food." She held up the scythe as she made her way across the room. "Ya know, this thing would make a great pizza cutter."

He scowled at her. "Don't disrespect my weapon."

Laughter tittered from her as she looked over her shoulder. "Never."

Her eyes glinted with mischief as her hand came to rest on the door handle. Everything about her filled the emptiness he'd lived with his entire life. He loved her, and nothing would stop them from being together now that they'd been reunited.

As she pulled open the door, Thomas's gaze cut to the man standing in the hall. Not the pizza guy. Throttle. "Hello, beautiful."

Thomas's breath slammed to a stop in his throat, and August's head snapped toward the door. She gasped and stumbled backward. "No!"

The jagged scar on his lip curled upward. "Miss me?"

Thomas launched from the couch and dove for the second blade still on the table. He slid across the surface, shouting the chant. Fire not only raced along the blade he was holding, but August's as well. As the demon produced his knife, Thomas's brain raged against the inevitable. He was too far away to prevent the strike.

Instead of fleeing from Throttle, August drove into him, burying the blade deep in his chest. The shock of her attack took a couple of seconds to register—just enough time to drive his knife downward through her heart, and then jerked it free. Her body crumpled to the floor, tearing a cry from Thomas.

He hurled himself at Throttle and slammed the tip of the blade into the demon's throat. The metal sunk deep, and with a downward pull, he tore open the massive chest, plunging his hand inside. The gnawing agony was no match for the fury pulsing through Thomas. For him, the man and the demon were one. Both sadistic and rotten. There was nowhere for the abomination to run, no punishment too great, no torture too painful.

Thomas yanked the rotten soul from Throttle and pulled his other blade free. The black vapor blasted from the gash, trying to merge with the soul as his body dropped to the ground. Before they could unite, Thomas slammed the blade's edge into the putrid lump.

The scythe carved deep into his palm, burning his skin, but he held fast. Blue flames licked along the gash and surrounded the demon's soul, engulfing the toxic clump. Thomas gritted his teeth against the pain until the soul finally crumbled to ash and the mist vaporized.

The surging adrenaline bled from him as he shook the ash from his hand and kicked the door shut. Somebody would have to deal with the body, but right now, August was his only thought. He tossed his blades aside and dropped next to August. "No." Brilliant red spread across the front of her shirt, a stark contrast to her white tinged lips and ashen complexion. "Please." Nestling her body against his, he began to rock. "Don't take her from me." Tears clogged his throat, his grip tightening. "I'll serve a million lifetimes for one with her."

How long he sat holding her, he didn't know. It felt like a lifetime and yet, not long enough. Despair crashed through him, stealing all the joy the last couple of hours had brought. As the minutes ticked past, reality reared its ugly head. She wasn't coming back. Fate was such a cruel bitch.

Tucking his mouth next to her ear, he whispered, "I love you, August. Please, don't leave me."

She gasped and coughed, her body shaking. Inhaling deeply, she said, "You're not getting rid of me that easily."

Thomas reared back to see her bright brown eyes staring at him. "August. Oh God, August." Struggling to his feet, he lifted her and strode to the couch. "You were dead." Cupping her face, he peered into her eyes. "How?"

"They heard you." With a gentle brush of her fingertips, she caressed his cheek. "A million lifetimes for one."

For the past two years, he'd reaped with no message or connection to the Divine, but this was proof that somebody up there was keeping score. "They granted it?"

"Oh yeah, they granted it." Her eyebrows lifted. "On one condition."

Unease snaked through him. "What condition?"

"That you take on a new partner."

His brow pinched in confusion.

She stared pointedly.

His gaze narrowed on her.

Her smile stretched.

He blinked, understanding dawning. "You?"

"Meet the newest Dark Reaper."

"You chose to be a Dark Reaper?" He shook his head. "But...why?"

"It was that or die. I thought this was the better choice." Her smile faltered. "Also, as much as you wanted one lifetime with me, I wanted it too." As she shifted to straddle him, she clutched the front of his shirt. "Is that okay?"

The sacrifice she'd just made rendered him speechless. She had no idea what this life entailed, but she hadn't wavered in her decision to be with him. He threaded his fingers into her hair and pulled her mouth to his. Everything he had, everything he felt he poured into that kiss. They would be together forever.

When they finally broke the kiss, she exhaled an exaggerated breath. "I guess that means you're okay with it."

"More than okay. This life can be lonely, August, but I promise I'll never stop trying to make you happy."

"I like the sound of that." She ran her hands over his shoulders and around his neck. "Can we get matching reaper outfits?"

"No."

Her lips pursed into a pout. "I thought you said you'll spend eternity trying to make me happy."

"No matching outfits. The second we start to dress alike, then we start to look alike, then the other reapers will make fun of us."

"Well, I'm incredibly disappointed, and I think you should find another way to make it up to me."

"That's one wish I can grant." Flipping her onto her back, he covered her body with his. "I plan on spending the next millennia demonstrating how much I love you."

"I love you, too, Thomas. I always have."

August's smile shown like the brightest sun as he pressed into her. No doubt their future would hold many hot and scorching moments. Still, thousand lifetimes wouldn't be enough with her.

* * *

BOONE BRUX IS a USA Today Bestselling Author. Her books range from high fantasy to romantic comedy. She lives with her daughters and a myriad of animals in the icy region of Alaska. Always looking for the next adventure, it's not unusual to find her traversing the remotest parts of the Alaskan bush. No person or escapade is off limits when it comes to weaving real life experiences into her books. Read more at: boonebrux.com

SHENANIGANS BY BECCA JAMESON

Dear Readers,

The following short story is from the viewpoint of one of my most beloved characters, Lucy, from my Surrender series and my Blossom Ridge series. Lucy and her friends live in Dom/sub relationships with their Daddy Doms. They can be quite naughty at times, and their shenanigans will make you giggle!

CHAPTER 1

Lucy

"PLEASE, PLEASE, PLEASE, PLEASE, PLEASE!" I'm giddy as I jump up and down, trying to get Daddy's attention.

Roman is at his desk. He's working, but I've taken this week off from my job, so I'm in a week-long Little space. Usually, I'm only Little in the evenings after work. When I'm on vacation though, I have more time and slide into a deeper space that helps me fully relax.

It also brings out a bit of my naughty side. I don't usually have time to get into much trouble on work days. Plus, I'm too tired to waste my evenings standing in a corner with a sore butt, but on vacation weeks all bets are off.

Roman smirks. "Day one of your vacation and already you're plotting something mischievous." He pauses what he's working on and turns his desk chair to face me, reaching out with a hand.

I go to him, letting him pull me between his legs. He chooses all my clothes when I'm at home. And he's a huge fan of dresses that would be suitable for a toddler. Ones that barely cover my panties. He's also a fan of very youthful panties.

Today I have on pink cotton panties and a lavender dress. It's got a Peter Pan style collar, puffy short sleeves, and smocking across my chest. Daddy loves torturing me with smocking. He has forbidden me from ever wearing a bra when I'm in Little space, and he knows how much I squirm when my nipples rub against the smocking.

Roman's number one rule for dresses though is that they barely cover my bottom. Every one of my dresses is just long enough that if I lift my hands, people will see my panties. Everyone who lives in the house has seen them, but everyone who works for Daddy is extremely familiar with our lifestyle and they all indulge my Little to the fullest. No one cares if they see my panties.

I'm pretty sure the reason Daddy likes these dresses has more to do with what he does next. He slides his hand under my dress to pat my bottom while he holds me between his legs.

His eyes are dancing. "Tell me what has you so excited, Lucy."

I roll my eyes in exasperation because he already knows what I'm going to say. He's already spoken to Craig and Foster. I heard him on the phone. That's why I ran into his office from my playroom.

Of course, he hung up the phone and pretended to be engrossed in something on his computer the moment I entered, but he knows.

His expression turns serious, and he narrows his eyes at me in that way that tells me he's about to reprimand me. "Did you roll your eyes at me, naughty girl?"

I sigh. He always notices that. "Maybe?"

"Were you listening in on my phone conversation too, sneaky pants?"

"Daddy…" I groan. "You weren't quiet. I was just in the other room. So can we?"

"Can we what?" he teases, rubbing my bottom, teasing the edge of my panties because he knows it drives me wild.

I can't stand the suspense, so I blurt out my request. "Can we go to the zoo with the other Little girls and see the baby kangaroos?"

"Who said anything about the zoo?" he teases. He slides his other hand up the front of my dress but stops short of actually touching one of my breasts. He's distracting me. Tormenting me. He even tugs the smocking a bit so that it abrades against my titties, making me squirm.

I shove at his hand to no avail. I won't be distracted. "All the girls are going. I know about it. Please say we can go too. Please?"

"How did you hear about a trip to the zoo?" he asks as his hand slides under the smocking to directly play with my nipple.

I gasp as he tweaks my tender bud. My panties are wet, and I know he's going to reach between my legs in a moment. I'm wearing frilly white socks folded over and lavender mary janes because Daddy is indulgent and often makes my shoes match my dress. I keep my feet planted wide because that's a hard rule and I don't want to end up with a spanking.

Trying to focus and stick to the subject, I squirm in his hold as I inform him, "Leah told Amelia who told Brea who told Stella who told Juliet who told Giana who sent me a text."

Daddy chuckles. "That was a long line of telephone. Are you sure the original message wasn't something more like 'we're going to the pool to see the roosters'?"

I giggle. "That's silly, Daddy. They don't have roosters at the pool."

"Still, that's a lot of naughty Little girls. *Nosy* Little girls," he amends.

"Daddy…" I whine in exasperation. I shove at his hand again, but he ignores my efforts and shifts his fingers over to my other nipple. He pinches it hard enough to make my breath hitch.

He pulls me closer and sets his lips on my ear. "You're so wiggly this morning. Did Evelyn feed you jumping beans for breakfast?"

I shake my head. "No, Daddy. It's your fault. You're distracting me." I rise onto my toes, trying to escape the hand on my bottom that's slowly trailing down between my legs.

I hold my breath and wait for the inevitable. It's part of our dynamic. He's not going to be deterred. His fingers will be in contact with my pussy any second now. The question is will he drive me to the edge of orgasm and leave me hanging? Or will he tug my panties aside, thrust his fingers into me, and let me come? It's always a tossup.

I moan the moment his fingers rub along my slit, pressing my wet cotton panties between my lower lips.

"You're soaked, cherry blossom," he whispers.

I whimper and lean into him, giving up the fight. At this point, I need the release. Will he give it to me?

He keeps speaking against my ear. "Should I take you over my knees, pull these wet panties down to your thighs, and spank your naughty bottom for rolling your eyes and eavesdropping?"

I shake my head as I grab his shoulder to steady myself before I turn into goo and slink to the floor. "No, Sir. I'll be good all day. I promise."

He slowly eases the soaked cotton to the side and touches me with his finger, finding my clit and then easing his finger deep into my pussy.

I moan as my head rolls forward onto his shoulder. "Daddy…"

"That's my girl." He releases my swollen nipple and shifts his hand back to the other one, tweaking it just as hard. "Come on Daddy's fingers and then we'll talk about possibly going to see the roosters at the pool."

I can't even laugh or correct his bad joke because I'm lost to him. I'm always lost to him. He's my Daddy. He's my Dominant. He's my husband. I'm putty in his hands every day of the week.

When he adds his thumb to my clit and a second finger to my tight pussy, I stiffen and come, the pulses of my release making it hard to focus. Good thing he holds me up. He always holds me up. Nothing bad will ever happen to me as long as I'm with him.

Nothing. It's inconceivable.

CHAPTER 2

"*A*re you sure about this?" I ask Roman as he parks the SUV near the entrance to the Kangaroo Ranch. Daddy had informed me that playing telephone with my friends had indeed caused the story about the kangaroos to change slightly. We aren't at the pool seeing roosters. It wasn't that bad. But we aren't at the zoo either. We're at a ranch that's more like a petting zoo. They happen to have kangaroos.

"Sure about what, blossom?"

"No one is going to see me? I mean like, vanilla people?" I twist my neck to look all around me. Several other cars are pulling in, but they belong to my friends.

Daddy reaches across the console and takes my hand. "Do you trust me, blossom?"

I nod. "Of course, but…" *I don't trust other people.* I'm very comfortable in my skin. I'm Little. I've been Daddy's Little girl for many years. But I prefer not to explain myself to vanilla folks. I'm always Little in our home where I trust the staff. I'm also Little when we're at Blossom Ridge, the mansion-turned-bed-and-breakfast we own where all the guests practice age play. I'm Little when I'm at Daddy's club, Surrender, where all the members respect each other's preferred kinks.

I do not take my kink out in public.

Daddy holds my chin. "Look at me, blossom."

I take a deep breath and face him, ignoring the activity outside our car.

"I know the owners of this ranch. Besides the fact that the owner and his wife are also in a D/s age-play relationship, their staff is aware and accepting the same as my staff at home. I booked this private party. Only my guests will be here today. That's you, your friends, and their Daddies. No one else can get through the gate."

"Yes, Sir," I murmur. I should know better than to doubt him.

"I want you to have fun. I want you to have time outside with your friends in your preferred skin without worrying about anyone judging you. Can you do that?"

I nod, which doesn't dislodge his grip on my chin.

"Good girl." He releases me, opens his door, and gets out to come around to my side.

As soon as he lifts me out of the SUV to set me on the ground, I tug the hem of my dress down.

"Stop fiddling with your dress, Lucy," he admonishes.

I glance down. "Is it long enough? Are my panties showing?" It's a warm day, which can be a curse for someone who practices age play. On cold days, Daddy will dress me in leggings and long sleeves. I'm even more protected when I get to wear a jacket.

Not today. Today, I'm wearing a sleeveless navy tank dress. The bodice is fitted around my chest, which means my nipples are obvious. The skirt has loose flowy layers that keep catching in the breeze and lifting up around me.

As usual, the length is incredibly short, and to embarrass me further, Daddy put white panties on me, which means every glimpse of them will be obvious. I also have on white tennis shoes and frilly folded socks. My hair is in high pigtails with navy bows.

I look like I'm going to a toddler's birthday party, except we're here with other adult Littles to see the kangaroos.

Daddy lifts my chin and meets my gaze. "What if your dress *isn't* long enough and people *do* see your panties?"

I swallow. He's right. I don't care about my friends and their Daddies, but I get self-conscious when we're with strangers, even if Daddy did vet them and determine they were kink friendly.

"Would you like to start the day with me leaning you over the seat of the car, pulling those panties down to your ankles, and spanking your naughty bottom?"

My face heats as I shake my head. "No, Sir."

"I didn't think so. What are the rules?"

"Stay where you can see me. Be polite to the owners. Be kind to my friends."

"Good girl." He shuts the car door, cups my face, and bends down to kiss me. It's a panty-melting kiss that scrambles my brain and reminds me why I love him so much.

As he slowly releases my lips, he slides his hands down to my breasts and tweaks my nipples through the cotton dress.

I whimper. "Daddy…"

He chuckles. He knows I like this game. I love the embarrassment. I love how he can tease me and keep me on edge even in a crowd so I'm wet and needy no matter where we are or what we're doing.

"Lucy!"

I spin around at the sound of my name and see Leah skipping toward me. She and her husband, Craig, are the managers of Blossom Ridge. Amy is skipping alongside Leah.

"This is going to be so much fun," Leah declares as she gives me a big hug. "I've never seen a kangaroo up close."

"I heard there are two babies right now. We might get to see them peek their heads out of their pouches," Amy adds.

"Amelia. What did I say about running across the gravel?" The stern voice comes from her Daddy, Foster. He's the groundskeeper at Blossom Ridge. Amy is the chef. They are both employed by my Daddy, Roman. Well, technically, me too, of course. I'm just as much an owner of Blossom Ridge as Daddy I suppose.

"Sorry, Daddy," Amy responds. "I got excited."

"You're not going to have much fun today if you fall and skin your knees before we get started."

I'm pleased to see Amy and Leah are also dressed similar to me. Apparently their Daddies had the same idea of keeping us in toddler age range today.

The three of us Little girls lock hands and head for the entrance where we meet up with Brea, Stella, Juliet, and Giana. Brea's Daddy, Niko, sometimes does construction work at the Ridge. Stella's Daddy, Walker, is a lawyer in Seattle. Juliet's Daddy, Aldric, owns a ballet studio and teaches dance at the Ridge. And Giana's Daddy, Kendric, runs a philanthropy for underprivileged youth.

These are some of my best friends in the world, and I'm so glad we can all get together for something as fun as seeing baby kangaroos. I know Daddy had a lot to do with planning this and making it happen, and I twist my head around to smile at him.

He's looking right at me, also grinning indulgently. He loves pleasing me.

I'm truly blessed and lucky.

"Welcome, everyone."

I turn back around at the entrance to find a friendly-looking older man beckoning us forward with his arms.

"Come on in. Welcome to the Kangaroo Ranch."

The seven of us Littles follow the kind man to a pavilion where we take seats on benches in front of a small stage. Our Daddies sit behind us.

I'm giddy as the man introduces himself as Mr. Barlow. His wife soon joins him and waves at us, telling us her name is Priscilla. Two other men arrive. They make me nervous at first, and I glance at Daddy to make sure he still thinks this is a safe environment.

He's smiling and nods at me, so I twist back around to pay attention. The two new additions are Braxton and Harwin. They show no evidence in their expressions that we are even slightly out of the ordinary. That makes me relax.

After all, seven grown women are sitting on the front row anxiously awaiting this presentation. We all have on short, childish dresses, youthful shoes, and hair bows. There is no mistaking we are Littles. A vanilla person would do a serious doubletake and stare, eyes wide.

Seven men are behind us with serious Dom faces that no one could possibly overlook.

"Before we take you girls out to see the kangaroos, we'd like to tell you about our marsupials and how they came to live with us on the ranch…"

I swing my legs while I listen intently. The ranch is an amazing place that rescues animals but also breeds them and educates people. By the time Mr. Barlow is done telling us all about the kangaroos, I'm so excited to get to see them up close and pet them that I almost can't contain myself.

The beauty of being Little is I don't have to. Who wouldn't be excited to see kangaroos? Even grownups love animals, especially ones we don't see often in our country. But Littles… We get to clap and squeal and jump around because that's the skin we live in.

Leah takes my hand as we leave the seating area. "I can't wait to see the babies," she exclaims.

"Me too."

We follow Mr. Barlow, Braxton, Harwin, and Priscilla out to a fenced area where we get our first look at the kangaroos as they wander toward us.

"They're domesticated," Harwin explains. "You never want to walk up to wild animals in their natural habitats. Even so, kangaroos are still wild animals. Be calm around them and don't do anything to frighten them."

"Say cheese," Daddy says behind me as I reach out to pet one of the kangaroos. He's holding up his phone, and I bend down to let him get the picture.

We have the best afternoon I've had in a long time, filled with laughter and fun, friends and memories. My face hurts from smiling. The babies with their tiny little heads sticking out of their mommies pouches were the cutest things I've ever seen. We each kept saying we wanted to bring one home.

"I need to use the restroom," Leah says as we're leaving the kangaroo habitat.

I take her hand. "I think I saw the sign over by the pavilion." I give a tug and the two of us take off in that direction. Sure enough, we easily locate the restrooms.

It's not until we come back outside that I realize my mistake. Both Daddy and Craig are standing outside, arms crossed over their chests, eyes narrowed.

"Oops. I'm sorry, Daddy."

"What's the first rule when we're out?"

"Stay where you can see me at all times," I murmur.

Craig clears his throat. "Leah? You know the same rule applies to you."

"Yes, Sir."

Craig wraps his hand around the back of her neck and leads her away.

I clasp my hands behind my back and rock on my feet, waiting to find out how mad Daddy is.

"There are several more fun things planned for today. Would you like me to spank you now or wait until later?"

"Later please, Sir." I stare at the ground, using my toe to push the dirt around.

"Shall we rejoin your friends?"

I nod. "Yes, Sir." I'm contrite because it's expected of me. But getting into trouble and getting spanked is also expected of me. It's been a while since Daddy has spanked me. I'll probably do a few more things today to ensure my perfect day ends with an amazing round of impact play.

Daddy takes my hand and leads me toward the parking lot.

When we get there, I notice Leah's eyes are red and she's adjusting her panties under her dress. I guess her Daddy chose to spank her now. He wipes away her tears and kisses her sweetly.

I feel bad for dragging her to the bathroom without telling anyone, but she knew the rules too, and she likes to get her bottom spanked as much as I do.

After we all gather in the parking lot, Daddy speaks to the entire group. "Did everyone have fun seeing the kangaroos?"

A unanimous "yes" is shouted by all of us.

"Well, guess what? We Daddies have a surprise for you. The fun is not over. Guess where we're going next?"

"Where?" we all yell excitedly.

"Who wants to move this party of fourteen to Blossom Ridge for a fun afternoon and evening of movies, games, and snacks?"

I jump up and down, not caring that everyone can see my panties every time I bounce. We all do. We Littles rush toward each other for a giant group hug as we all talk on top of each other, plotting the rest of the day's upcoming antics.

I'm certain by the end of the day, we'll all end up with sore bottoms from poor choices, but that's half the fun.

CHAPTER 3

"*H*ave you ever seen anything that cute in your entire life?" Giana asked as she dipped her shoulders under the water in the hot tub where we are all huddled after a fun afternoon of games and pizza. "I wanted to take those baby kangaroos home with me."

"Right?" Juliet responds. "They were so tiny and their little eyes…" She sighs.

Stella nods. "This is one of the best days ever. I haven't had a day off from the café in weeks." She owns a café in Seattle. Even though she's got amazing employees, it's still hard for her to take time off.

"I feel like all I ever do is study," Brea adds. She's going to college.

Amy giggles. "I can't complain about my job. I love cooking. It feels weird not to cook for all of you while you're here, but Daddy insisted I'm having a girls' day. I'm not permitted to lift a finger."

"You deserve it. You work every day," Leah points out.

"At least you both get to be Little nearly all the time," I say, envious of Leah and Amy who live and work here at Blossom Ridge. "I only get nights and weekends. I've been looking forward to this vacation week for a while. It seems like most evenings I'm just getting into my Little space emotionally when it's time to go to bed."

Giana nods. "That part is hard. Separating. Kendric and I have been working more hours than usual at the afterschool program. Even though I defer to him and subtly submit to him all the time, it's not the same. I have to be in my adult headspace when I'm working with the kids."

Juliet, the quietest one of all of us, speaks, "I get that. I've been helping Aldric with several ballet classes lately. It's weird for me because I'm nearly always dressed in a leotard, whether or not I'm in Little space. I have to catch myself when I'm talking to the kids."

"That would be hard," Stella agrees. "Plus, I know days like today are stressful for you."

We all know Juliet was nearly agoraphobic when we met her. She's been working hard to leave her house more, especially alone. Coming to Blossom Ridge isn't difficult for her, but I suspect the morning at the Kangaroo Ranch was challenging. More for her than any of us.

Leah stands up in the hot tub and peers over all our heads toward the men who are sitting on the other side of the pool at two glass tables, talking and keeping an eye on us.

She looks back at us with a grin. "Who's in favor of getting into trouble?"

We all giggle.

I'm already going to get my bottom spanked for wandering away from Daddy to go to the bathroom earlier, but I knew this would eventually happen. Either organically or by design. We're Littles. We get into trouble.

"What do you have in mind," Amy asks.

Leah looks devious as she dips back into the water until it rises above her shoulders. "I say we start a splashing war. Screaming out of control, soaking the deck and the windows and the pile of towels. When the Daddies come over to find out what's gotten into us, we don't stop. We get them wet too."

I smile. It's so naughty. So devious. We will all get our bottoms spanked. But I'm totally in. I'm usually pretty well behaved. It's been a long time since I pulled intentional antics like this. "Let's do it," I say.

"Yes," Amy adds.

I glance around at each Little to make sure no one is opposed. I don't want to get other Littles in trouble if they aren't up for it. Not every Little I know likes to misbehave and end up with a sore bottom. I'm aware everyone in this group is usually game for joining the shenanigans though.

Juliet is the most timid. She's biting her bottom lip, but her eyes are dancing. She glances toward the men and then back. "I never misbehave," she admits. "Daddy will think I've gone mad."

"But?" Leah asks her.

"Oh, I'm in." She shudders. "My ass is going to hurt for a week." She giggles and rubs her bottom. "Longer if he finds out I used a naughty word."

"Everyone's okay with this?" Leah clarifies.

We all nod.

"Ready? Set? Go!" Leah starts splashing, and we all join in.

The only actual misbehavior so far is that the Daddies told us not to get our hair wet. We are soaked in seconds. So is the deck and the windows along the kitchen, and the pile of towels.

I'm laughing so hard I can't breathe, and it's difficult to draw in a breath anyway with six other Littles splashing so hard we're practically drowning each other.

I keep turning my head away to suck in oxygen. The water level is lowering in the hot tub. With seven of us in it, the water had risen to the very top. We're splashing it out as fast as we can.

"Girls!" someone shouts. I have no idea which Daddy. We're so loud, I can't identify the voice. It could even be Roman.

"What the heck has gotten into you all?" This booming voice is definitely Foster.

"Are they fighting?" one of the men shouts.

"No. I think it's a water fight. They're all laughing," someone else responds.

"Girls!" Another attempt to get our attention. Useless. We're ignoring the Daddies.

I can hear them talking, but their voices are lower now, so I can't make out the words anymore.

We keep splashing until we're exhausted. By the time we stop, we're all panting. Our hair is dripping wet. The deck is soaked. The water is much lower in the hot tub. It's also not on anymore. Someone turned it off. Probably a good thing.

The giggles continue, but when I tip my head back, I find seven stern men with their hands on their hips. They're all soaked to a varying degree. Even their shoes. Oops.

I purse my lips, trying to look chagrinned, but it's impossible.

Glancing from one face to the next, I find the same expression on every Daddy. They've already spoken. They are a unit. They have a plan. It's enough to make any Little shudder.

The most important thing to note is that no one is seriously angry. That's the beauty of our lifestyle. It's an agreed upon power exchange. It's expected that we will occasionally misbehave. We mostly do it on purpose.

The men have their brows furrowed in mock horror and condemnation, but they can't keep the slight lift from the corners of their mouths. They're enjoying every moment of this.

We fall under the fetish umbrella. Lots of people in the BDSM community enjoy impact play. Lots of Doms enjoy providing it. Lots of subs enjoy receiving it. In our case, we like to turn it into an age-play lifestyle, one where we get the spanking we crave even though it's often a product of mock misbehavior.

"Are you naughty Little girls done?" Roman asks in his sternest voice.

We are breathing heavily as we collectively nod.

"Are you ready to get out?" Craig asks.

We look at each other and shake our heads as planned.

Foster chuckles sardonically. "I know seven Little girls who are going to have to stand up to eat dinner because their bottoms are going to be too sore to sit down."

I'm chilled now. We're all standing, and with the water level lower, half of our bodies are no longer under the heated water. We're shivering.

Walker shakes one of his legs. Water drips off the end of his jeans. "Even my feet are soaked." He makes a big deal of stretching out his fingers as if warming up for the spankings.

Aldric has his arms crossed. "Mostly I'm in shock. Juliet never misbehaves."

Kendric nods. "Peer pressure."

Aldric takes a step closer. "Yep, and it's not a good enough excuse to keep her little bottom from turning red."

It's my Daddy who finally turns the tide of our shenanigans. "You girls have ten seconds to get out of the hot tub and join your Daddies. If you apologize sweetly and accept your punishments without fussing, we'll consider the slate wiped clean and head inside for snacks and movie night. If you're not standing in front of us apologizing by the time I count to ten, your fun night will not happen."

We all gasp. He doesn't even need to start counting. We fly out of the water so fast he wouldn't have been able to get to the number three anyway.

I step up to Daddy, shivering cold. "Sorry, Sir."

He tips my chin back and meets my gaze. He's got that partial grin going. The one that tells me he's not even remotely angry. "You really needed a spanking today, didn't you, blossom?"

I nod. "Can I have a towel?"

"Nope." He takes my hand and leads me toward the tables and chairs on the other side of the pool.

I glance around to find all the rest of my friends being led in the same fashion. We did splash the towels, soaking the pile, but there are others on the shelves we didn't hit. Apparently, the men bumped heads on this issue because their movements are collective.

Daddy sits on one of the chairs and pulls me between his legs. When he reaches for the top straps of my one-piece and starts pulling it down my arms, I gasp.

"Daddy," I whisper. I'm not alone though. Most of the other girls are being stripped too. A few are too modest, and their Daddies would never subject them to that kind of exposure. They've been pulled over their Daddies' knees wet bathing suit and all.

Roman tugs the wet material down my legs and off my feet, leaving me naked.

I'm shivering worse now. Freezing. The air is chilly now that the sun is going down.

He brings me to one side of his lap and lowers me over his thighs. "Arms at the small of your back, naughty girl."

I reach back to clasp my hands behind me.

Daddy wraps his fingers around both my wrists, holding me firmly against his lap. I can't count the number of times we've been in this position in all the years I've known Roman, but I'm not usually naked, wet, and cold. Not often outside. I've rarely been spanked in a group where I wasn't the only one being naughty and we're all getting disciplined together.

"Spread your legs, Lucy," he commands.

I whimper as I part them. The position I'm in has already made me needy. My pussy is pulsing, and I know I'm not going to get to come. Not right now. Possibly not tonight at all.

Daddy palms my bottom before he starts to swat my skin. The cold air keeps me from relaxing, so every spank hurts worse than usual. He builds up the speed and pressure quickly. He can do that because I know what to expect from him. This isn't my first rodeo.

He spanks me harder and longer than usual. He knows I need it. I need the release. I need the deep submission. I needed this very Little day badly. It's been too long. We all did. Getting our bottoms spanked is icing on the cake after a day of fun.

Eventually it starts to hurt. My butt is on fire. Each swat of his palm makes me wince. That's when I really let go and start crying. The tears fall down my cheeks and drip onto the wet concrete. Tears of release. Cleansing tears that wipe away not only my invented transgressions but the stress of a long workweek and anything else weighing on my mind.

I'm sobbing when he's finally done. He doesn't let me up just yet. He rubs my bottom for a few minutes, still holding me against his thighs.

When Daddy releases my wrists, he eases me to my feet between his legs. I'm trembling too hard to stand on my own, but he has a hold of my waist with one hand.

"Keep your legs parted, blossom," he says softly as he reaches for a towel on the table. He doesn't use it to dry my body or wrap me up. He uses a corner of it to wipe my face, my tears.

I'm sniffling, struggling to get back under control. My shoulders heave every few seconds. I shudder from the exposure. My nipples are hard points. I don't dare touch them or cover them. Daddy wouldn't hesitate to take off his belt and swat them next if I "play with my titties."

"Better, Little cherry blossom?" he asks as he kisses my forehead.

I nod, chattering. "Yes, Sir."

"What happens to naughty Little girls who get their bottoms spanked while they're at Blossom Ridge?"

I swallow hard and glance at the wall of windows that lead into the kitchen. I notice all my friends are in a similar situation, getting comforted by their Daddies.

I know what he's referring to. This huge kitchen has a worn spot in the corner on the hardwood floor. It's a spot where decades of Littles in Roman's family have stood in timeout.

"What if someone else wants to use the naughty corner?" I mutter on a hiccup. I mean, my Daddy owns the Ridge. He should definitely reserve the timeout corner for someone who is more of a guest.

He chuckles. "Oh, blossom. Don't you worry. All of you are going to stand in the corner."

"All of us?" I want to lift my hands and rub my arms, but I don't dare.

"Yep." He stands and takes my hand, leading me toward the glass doors with everyone else. They seemed to have timed this well.

"I'm cold, Daddy," I tell him, my teeth really chattering now.

"Is that why your nipples are so hard?" he asks as he guides me into the house.

"Probably," I lie.

He laughs and points toward the corner. "You take the center. Nose to the wall. Hands at the small of your back. No moving. No complaining."

"For how long?" I ask, my voice squeaking. I'm naked. Most of us are. I see I'm not the only one with wet hair still dripping down my back.

"Quite a bit longer than before you asked," he informs me, brows raised.

My breath hitches, and I purse my lips as I head toward the naughty corner. I take up my spot, legs spread wide, hands clasped behind my back. I quickly realize I'm not really cold. It's warm in the house. I wonder if someone came in and turned up the heat in the kitchen knowing about this naked, wet, timeout event.

I am, however, exposed. My nipples are so hard they ache. I'll be in ten times more trouble if I let them touch the wall, so I'm careful to keep them from grazing the corner.

Low voices fill the room as all my friends join me, shoulder to shoulder, along the walls. There's sniffling, which isn't surprising since everyone just got their bottoms spanked. But we are well behaved and know when to stop pushing buttons. We stand perfectly still and wait. We have to be good now or we'll lose the privilege of movie and snack night in the basement theater. No one wants to risk that.

CHAPTER 4

"Thank you, Daddy," I say several hours later when we're finally in our room upstairs for the night.

He smirks as he turns on the bath water and sits on the edge of the tub to remove my clothes. "What are you thanking me for, blossom?"

"The most perfect day." As soon as I'm naked, I throw myself at him and hug him tight. "I had so much fun."

He chuckles as he tucks an arm around me and pats my bottom, making me wince. "Even with the shenanigans that led to a hard spanking."

"Uh huh." I set my lips on his ear. "Especially the spanking. I needed it."

He gives my sore bottom a pinch. "I thought so. That's why I spanked you a bit longer and harder than usual. It's been a while since you've needed my palm on your sweet bottom."

"That's because I'm well behaved," I announce, standing tall as if he could take me seriously in my naked state.

He laughs. "Were you well behaved when you were stashing sexy bras and panties in your work drawer and changing into them after you got to work for months?"

I cringe. I fessed up to that and got punished for it months ago. Actually, I'm still being punished for that incident. Well, it was more than one incident I guess. I was changing in the bathroom before work for a while before Daddy found out.

I'll be paying for a while too. I now wear the plainest white and nude bras on the planet to work. No lace. Nothing sexy. Nothing revealing. They cover more skin than a sports bra. And I shudder every time I think about the babyish panties Daddy puts on me every morning under my professional skirts. He says they help remind me who's Little girl I am while I'm at work, and he's right.

He's still chuckling as he pulls me closer. "Did you know I have eyes in the back of my head, Little one?"

I nod slowly, wondering where he's going with this. "Yes, Sir."

"I've kept a tally of all the naughty things you've done in the past few weeks. We haven't had time to deal with your behavior."

I hold my breath. Sometimes I do naughty things he doesn't know about. Which ones is he aware of?

"Now that we're alone and we don't have to get up early tomorrow and we have plenty of time, I think we should address some issues, don't you?"

No. Goodness no. We shouldn't address any issues.

He lifts a serious brow, but he's also almost smiling. He has that expression nailed down. "Would you like to confess a few things, or would you like me to list them for you?"

I open my mouth, but he holds up a finger to stop me. "Let me warn you, if you confess, I'll go easier on your punishment. If I have to remind you what naughty behavior you've engaged in, I won't be as easy on you."

Shit. Oh, that reminds me... "I cussed when I stubbed my toe really hard in the play room the other day. Did you hear me?"

"Nope."

I sigh. *Well, shit.*

"Anything else you'd like to mention, Little one?"

I know my transgressions. After all, I know the rules, and I know when I break them. I didn't meet Daddy yesterday. I lean against him. "Daddy…" I whine. I don't like this game he plays. It's not the first time we've done this either. He likes to keep a running tally of my naughty behavior and then see if I will fess up. He also likes to wait until I'm naked and vulnerable to do so.

"How about if you think about what you're going to say while I give you a bath?" He lifts me up and swings me into the tub before turning off the water.

I reach for a bath toy, but he plucks it out of the tub and sets it on the side. "You need to think, not play." He pours water over my head and grabs the shampoo while I squirm. I don't like this at all.

"Can we do this at home instead?" I suggest.

"Nope. We can do it now."

I wince as I shift my weight, reminding myself how sore my bottom is. "Are you going to spank me again tonight, Daddy? My bottom is very stingy."

"I haven't decided yet. Depends on what's on your list and how contrite you are and whether or not you can convince me you'll do better in the future."

I close my eyes and focus on his hands on my scalp. I love when he washes my hair. I love when he washes the rest of me too. I suspect he's not going to linger anywhere important tonight.

"Start talking, blossom." He rinses my hair.

I might as well list some of my sins. I'm sure he knows most of them anyway. He really does have eyes in the back of his head, but he also has a lot of cameras in the house. Usually, I assume he can't possibly take the time to watch all the footage in every room to keep up with my shenanigans, but sometimes I get caught.

I drag my fingers through the water while I confess, "A few nights ago while you were asleep on the other side of the bed, I woke up restless and played with my titties and my pussy." I lift my gaze. "I swear I stopped myself before I reached orgasm. I knew it was wrong."

He tweaks one of my nipples. "It was entertaining to watch though."

I gasp. "You were awake?"

"Yes. You were wiggling around so much I couldn't help but wake up. When I heard you panting, I decided to watch the show. Made my cock hard. I'm proud of you for stopping, but are you permitted to touch yourself in the first place?"

"No, Sir." Darn, he knew that one. Or maybe I should be glad.

"Go on." He pours soap on a washcloth and starts to lather my arm.

"Twice last week I poured some of my breakfast milk down the drain when Evelyn left the room," I confess. Daddy is a stickler about me drinking my milk in the morning.

"Mmm. I didn't know that."

Shoot. Now I won't get away with that again. He'll have eyes on me.

"You can start drinking your milk from a sippy cup before you get out of bed in the mornings, while I'm still in the room and can keep an eye on you."

I gasp, my eyes going wide. "Daddy, I'm not that young."

"Is that so?"

"Yes."

"Your behavior suggests otherwise."

I sigh.

"Anything else you'd like to list?"

Darn it. I really, really dislike these confessionals. They put me on edge. I take a deep breath. "I spilled a tiny bit of nail polish on the hardwood floor in my playroom last week. I cleaned it up really fast with a tissue though."

"So that's why the rug was moved."

I sigh loudly. Now I'm thinking he doesn't really know much of anything. He's playing me.

"No nail polish for two weeks then. Not because you spilled it.

Accidents happen, but because you tried to hide it when you should have just told Daddy."

"Yes, Sir…"

"What else?"

"That's all, Daddy," I say with confidence.

"You sure?" He's working his way up my leg with the washcloth.

I nod, trying hard to look trustworthy. Hopefully I'm calling his bluff.

"Positive?"

"Yes, Daddy."

"So, you didn't run through the entire downstairs with scissors in your hand because you forgot to get them before you started making paper dolls?"

Shit. "Oh, that."

"Yes, that. The scissors are in timeout too. They're hanging out with the nail polish."

Gah. Darn.

"Were you not the Little girl who changed her panties for another pair and hid the first pair in the hamper while I was in a virtual meeting on Saturday?"

I gasp. How did he know that?

"Did you have an accident?" he asks.

My eyes widen. "No, Sir." I may be Little, but I don't wet my panties.

He lifts both brows in question. He's like some kind of all-knowing deity.

I might as well tell the truth. He might be able to read my mind. "I was playing on the floor in my play room while you were on the phone, and your voice was so sexy, and I kept picturing you touching me, and…" I draw in a breath. "My panties were soaked, Daddy. I didn't touch myself, but I didn't want you to know."

"Mmm. Should I put all your panties in timeout with the nail polish and the scissors?" he teases.

I shake my head. "No, Daddy."

He slides the washcloth between my legs and rubs my pussy. His voice is low and sexy when he speaks. "If you were wearing panties right now, would they be wet?"

I nod. My pussy is swollen and needy. It's been all day. I grip the sides of the tub and enjoy his touch.

He slides one finger into me, pushing the washcloth up inside me.

I whimper. Even after all these years, I still get so hot when Daddy touches me. I need his cock inside me. I hope he's not going to deny me.

He leans closer, his lips on my ear. "My voice makes you horny, huh, blossom?"

"Yes, Sir," I breathe out.

"I can't really punish you for that, can I?"

"No, Sir."

"Do you think I would approve of you sneaking off to change your panties without permission, Little one?"

I shake my head. I'm struggling to listen. He's still fingering my pussy.

I'm panting and I might actually cry when he removes his finger and pulls the stopper to let the water out. I don't dare ask him to let me come.

"Your punishment for playing with your titties and pussy in the night will be one week sleeping all night with your hands restrained to the headboard."

I sigh. It could have been worse. I don't like to sleep in that position, but I keep my mouth shut.

"As for the panty incident… I'll be moving all your panties to a locked drawer from now on. You don't have to specifically come and tell me when your panties are soaking wet, but you won't be able to sneak around and change them without permission."

"Yes, Sir."

He lifts me out of the tub and stands me on the rug to dry me off. When he's done, he sits on the edge of the tub again so we're eye to eye. He reaches between my legs and strokes his fingers through my folds. His voice is husky. "I love that my Little girl gets wet at the sound of my voice. I love that she still gets wet often. I love that nearly every time I reach between your legs to touch your pussy, your cotton panties are soaked."

I whimper and grab his shoulders. My legs are wobbly.

"I bet sometimes it's not comfortable to sit around in wet panties though, is it?"

I shake my head.

"How about you just tell Daddy when you need to be changed?"

My face heats. "That's embarrassing, Daddy."

"I bet your embarrassment is half the fun." He pushes a finger up into me. "This wet Little pussy is mine and I would be happy to help you change your panties in the middle of the day if you need me to."

My face is a hundred degrees, but I mutter, "Okay, Daddy."

Holding my hip with one hand, he adds a second finger to my pussy and thrusts them deep and hard. "I'm pretty sure we still own the same bottle of lube I bought once years ago thinking we might need it someday." He pulls his fingers out and brings them up between us. "We haven't needed it yet." He touches my lips with my own arousal and then sucks his fingers clean.

As he reaches between my legs again, he kisses me with all the passion we've had between us from the very beginning. Even before I knew I was his Little girl, I was already his. I was already wet and squirming and needed him.

I need him just as much today.

"We should take a day off to do fun things more often, blossom," he whispers against my lips.

I'm not going to argue that point. A moment later, I gasp as his thumb finds my clit, and I detonate. I come so fast I nearly fall on my butt. But Daddy has me. He slides his hand from my hip to my bottom and grips me firmly. The burn from his earlier spanking makes itself known, adding to my orgasm, intensifying it.

"That's my good girl. I love it when you come so easily on my fingers."

I do too, but I can't voice my thoughts right now. Before I can recover, he swoops me off my feet, turns toward the masculine Daddy bedroom in our suite, and eases me onto the big bed.

It takes him moments to strip naked, and then he climbs over me. His mouth comes to my breast, and he suckles my nipple hard. I swear I have the most sensitive titties on the Earth.

When he releases me with a pop, he lines his cock up and thrusts into me hard and fast, just like he had with his fingers.

I grab his biceps and press my knees wider so he can get deeper. There's nothing in the world I love more than a day of shenanigans followed by a good hard spanking and a night of sex. This is my perfect day.

Daddy loves these days too. It's obvious because he's breathing heavily in moments and can't hold back. His fingers ease between us to find my clit, and he rubs it as he meets my gaze. "I love you, Lucy."

"I love you too, Roman. So much."

"Come for me, Little one."

I do. I can't deny him anything. I come so hard my vision swims. I'm only marginally aware of him reaching his own climax seconds after me, but I'm very aware of him holding me tight, kissing all over my face, whispering words of love.

He's the best Daddy in the world. The best husband. The best man. The best life partner.

I'm the luckiest woman, Little, and wife too.

Yeah, today was the perfect day.

I can't wait for the next time me and my friends cap our day off with wild shenanigans that land me over Daddy's knees and then in his bed.

I'm grinning from ear to ear as he holds me close, not pulling out yet because he knows I like the pressure of him on top of me and inside me for a while.

Not surprising. After all, he knows everything.

* * *

THANK YOU FOR READING SHENANIGANS!

Becca Jameson is a USA Today bestselling author of over 100 books, most well-known for her Wolf Masters, Fight Club series, and Surrender series. She ives in Houston, Texas, with her husband and Goldendoodle. Two grown kids pop in every once in a while too! She has dabbled in a variety of genres, including paranormal, sports romance, military, and BDSM.

RUTHLESS MISCHIEF BY SIENNA SNOW

Read Devani and Sam's love story from the beginning in Ruthless Heir at -> https://geni.us/ruthlessheir.

CHAPTER 1

✑

Devani

"Is everyone in position? This is going to be down to the wire," I asked my team as I navigated into the passageways leading toward the elevator shafts of the twenty-story Melbourne highrise owned by the King Brothers of New York City.

The Kings were the epitome of danger wrapped in a façade of civility. Well, maybe not all of them, but one, in particular, had it down to a science.

Tonight, I'd play a little game of cat and mouse with him.

"You realize this will get our asses in trouble if we're caught? I have no idea how I'm going to explain this," an annoyed, British-accented voice commented through my earpiece, and I couldn't help but smirk.

My sister-in-law, close friend, and mentee from years past, Lilly Lennox-King, loved to break the rules as much as I did. Her being the voice of reason made no sense whatsoever.

"Just say you had no choice since your director told you to do it."

"Don't you mean former director?" Danika, my best friend, an internationally wanted hacker, and one of my other sisters-in-law chimed in.

"My title remains, even if I retired from everyday operations. Now, let me concentrate. These crawl spaces are tight as fuck."

Technically, one could retire from the spy game, but the game never left the system, especially if said spy entered the life at the young age of fourteen.

I slid into a barely two-foot-wide area and leveraged my way to a second-story ledge.

"I'm breaking the no secrets rule with Rey, and it's all your fault. I swear you're still as manipulative as ever." Lilly's annoyance made me want to needle her a little more.

Ever since Lilly and Rey King, my brother-in-law, reconnected, they shared every damn thing. Much to the dismay of everyone around them. Yes, I understood that it all stemmed from Lilly keeping her status as an agent in Solon, the underground spy agency I formerly led, from Rey. But Rey wasn't all squeaky clean either since, at the time, he was running an operation for the CIA.

"Hasn't Rey heard of the saying that a woman had to have some secrets?"

"We started our relationship on lies and half-truths. We don't do that anymore."

I sighed and asked, "Then I suppose he knows about the bean you're carrying in your uterus that you haven't told us about?"

"He knows. What is it with the brothers and figuring out before we do? I literally had no clue."

I sighed, making my way up a service ladder. "According to Sam, he knew he knocked me up because of my boobs."

"Bullshit," Jayna, the last of my sisters-in-law, mock coughed through the transmitter. "Or maybe the Queen of Diamonds dared to show emotions when everyone believed ice ran through her veins."

"Whatever," I muttered. "Aren't you on kid duty? Why are you even on this feed?"

"Because I'm the lookout. Or did you forget a certain King brother calls the penthouse for his nightly bedtime chat with his offspring and spouse? I could tell him you aren't in North America and are back to your old, wicked ways."

"Okay, point taken," I grumbled for a second and then smiled, thinking of my nine-month-old daughter. "How's my girl?"

Never would I have believed me, Devani Maya Patel-King, would one day be a mother, much less married.

Since the age of fourteen, all I'd ever known was violence and manipulation. My parents and brother were murdered, and I'd inherited a billion-dollar diamond empire. As with most stories that started this way, there were always greedy relatives waiting in the wings, and I was no different. My uncles, who were left to raise me, shipped me off to boarding school and took over my family business.

However, at the age of fourteen, a teacher at the school took an interest in me and recruited me into an underground organization. Something my beloved husband believed was reprehensible at best, especially since my recruiter had turned me into a human weapon by the time I hit sixteen.

"Veda is in dreamland next to her cousin. They had such a fun time with their toys that they fell asleep in the playroom."

"You are the only person I know who can get him to sleep without trying, and Nik and I are practically begging the beast to calm down enough for us to take a nap." This was Danika's daily complaint about her son, Arin.

Arin had more energy in his pinky than ten people held in their whole bodies. The fact that Jayna seemed to have this ability to calm him down enough to pass out for a few hours made us all wonder what kind of magic she used on the kid.

"It's the fact I put a kid-size punching bag in the playroom and let him have at it. Once he expels all his energy, he's out for a few hours."

"Of course, the MMA fighter of our quartet would put a punching bag in a playroom with a nine-month-old and a fourteen-month-old." I couldn't help but laugh.

"Are you or are you not the one who bought your infant child custom-made handguns as a six-month birthday gift?" Jayna asked with a defensive tone. "At least what I'm doing won't require someone taking my gifts and locking them in a safe until my child can understand what a deadly weapon is."

"In her defense, she isn't normal. Child assassin and all," Danika said.

I could always count on my bestie to come to my rescue.

"Putting my gift-giving to the side and circling back to Lilly." I stepped onto the platform that would take me toward my final destination in the King building. "When are you making your announcement to the family?"

"You just made it for me."

"I did, didn't I," I responded in the same deadpan tone and then said, "I mean to the world."

"After we tell Papa. We must tell him first, so act surprised."

"Understood," Jayna, Danika, and I said in unison.

Lilly's father was none other than the notorious German syndicate boss Joseph Lennox. The man held a reach well beyond Europe, and Lilly was the apple of his eye. Without giving two shits that he was stepping on the territory of other bosses, the man single-handedly coordinated a war with the Kings and Solon North America to protect his daughter.

Respect went a long way in the world of organized crime, and since the Kings and Solon lived on the periphery of it, we followed the rules. Allowing Joseph to believe he'd learned of his newest grandchild first was among them.

"What's the ETA on your arrival for the drop off?" Danika

asked. "I traced Nik's phone, and based on the information, the gents are thirty minutes away."

"I'll be long gone before any of them step foot in the building. I've done this a time or two. Lennox can vouch for me."

"You mean Lennox-King," Lilly corrected.

"Yes, let's not forget the King part," I muttered.

"You're one to talk. Devani Patel-King. Sam is your King, after all."

I rolled my eyes. "Shut it, Jayna. That was a private conversation you are taking out of context."

"Oh, tell us more about what you walked in on." Danika's amusement made me want to reach through the earpiece and shake her.

"Let's say big brother had his assassin wife in a very compromising position and refused to set her free."

Only one man on this earth could make me want to bend, submit, to lose control—*Samir Krishan King.*

He knew all my secrets, saw all that I was, including the good, the bad, the ugly, and would still burn down the world to protect me.

"Oh, I need more details. Was she on her knees or something?" Lilly chimed in this time.

My cheeks heated. "Are you assholes here to watch my back or gossip?"

"Did we touch a nerve, Director Patel?" Lilly asked. "Oops, I meant Director Patel-King. Wouldn't want to upset your King by using the incorrect name."

"I really hate you three sometimes." I pulled my ski cap from over my head, shook my hair as I walked to the elevator shaft, and stepped onto the top of the cab.

"Well, the feeling is mutual. I don't understand how you rope us into your escapades." The clicking of keys told me Lilly readied to unlock the hatch for the elevator. "I was just this innocent girl at a boarding school in Switzerland, and this bossy woman barely older than me comes into my dorm room and tells me I have to come with her, and now she's fucking with my life as an in-law."

"It's because I'm a world-class manipulative bitch who saved you from a boring existence of popping out syndicate babies."

"Isn't that the truth? Could you see me as a syndicate boss' wife? I'd shoot him before we reached the altar."

"Umm, Lilly. Rey isn't a gun-toting mailman," I reminded her. "And for the record, you did shoot him."

"I'm going to ignore you now." The sound of a spring releasing indicated that the lock disengaged.

Now to wait for Danika to turn off the security system.

God, I loved having badass criminals like myself for sisters-in-law.

"The network for your area is down for the next twenty minutes. I'll monitor the parameter to ensure everything else is working as usual."

"This will take less than ten."

"Remember to get my list of goodies before you board the flight home."

"I went shopping the minute I landed. If I wasn't sure you were already preggo, your list would have given it away, Lilly."

"It wasn't that bad."

"Not that bad. I nearly cleaned out the whole shop. Tim Tams in every flavor possible. Do you know the number of flavors out there? Caramello Koalas, Twisties, Anzac biscuits, Minties, Violet Crumble, and Lamingtons."

"Please tell me you didn't forget the Vegemite."

I wanted to gag at the thought of putting that on toast, but to each their own. "No, I did not forget that."

"Did you get at least five packs of each thing on the list?"

"Lilly, you know we can order the same items and have them shipped to the States so Devani wouldn't have had to bring it back with her?" Danika seemed as exasperated by the list as I was.

"This is the least she can do for getting me into a situation where I'm forced to lie to my husband."

"Oh, for the love of God. I'm going silent now before I say something to make preggers cry. Let me know if anything changes on your end."

I lowered the volume on my earpiece to keep the chatter from distracting me, opened the ceiling door to the elevator, dropped down into the cab with a soundless crouch I'd mastered over the last nearly twenty years, and then stood.

Using the security code for the penthouse, I directed the elevator to the designated floor and waited for the doors to open.

I rubbed my hands together, loving that I'd finally got one over on my dear husband.

The second I arrived at my destination, I went directly to Sam's suite. As I crossed the threshold, I closed my eyes, inhaling his scent filling the room: crisp, clean, intoxicating.

Over two weeks.

This was the first time since we married that we'd been apart so long.

I truly missed the asshole and his bossy ways.

Damn.

When the fuck had I become such a sap? I was cold, calculating, and manipulative. The woman with a heart as hard as the diamonds in the many mines she owned.

A throat cleared in my earpiece. More than likely, it was Lilly reminding me to get moving before my time ran out.

Reaching behind me, I unzipped the pocket of my utility pack and pulled out a stuffed kangaroo. I positioned the creature so he'd see it when he neared the side of the bed he preferred.

I patted the front pouch of my gift and hummed to myself.

Mr. "I know everything about you" would get a wicked surprise tonight.

If only I could be a fly on the wall to see his reaction when he discovered the note and picture inside the pulse animal.

Turning in a smooth pirouette, it tiptoed through the dark penthouse back to the elevator.

I re-entered the code for the metal doors and waited for them to open, but nothing happened. Glancing at my watch, I saw I still had fifteen minutes.

I touched my earpiece and whispered, "Ladies, what the fuck. Open the elevator."

"It's not us," Devani responded. "Let me see what's going on."

That was when I heard Lilly say, "Oh shit, we are so fucked. Well, I'm fucked. Rey is halfway back to New York. I swear to God, if Neil ratted us out, I will slit his throat. I don't care if he is Sam's biological brother. He's Solon and, therefore, was ours first."

I tuned out Lilly's tirade about my replacement at Solon as the electric sting of one man's presence washed over me, and goosebumps prickled my skin.

And then, a light clicked on.

"Hello, love. You're a bit far from home."

CHAPTER 2

$\mathcal{S}$am

I TOOK a sip of my scotch and waited for Devani to face me.

My lovely wife wanted to play games. I'd oblige her.

She might have, on paper, put the world of spying and illegal maneuvering behind her. But the thrill, the sneaking, the risk would never leave her blood. She'd find some way to purge her needs.

I understood it. Hell, I lived it. I'd used my fists and smarts to survive the streets of a shit neighborhood in New York City and then used the same knowledge to undermine the elite of Wall Street.

However, she placed something precious on the line by being here. I couldn't allow that.

I almost cringed inside just thinking those thoughts. She'd probably castrate me the second she heard the word allowed. No one permitted Devani Maya Patel-King to do anything.

My Highness did whatever the fuck she wanted.

Well. With me, there were exceptions.

No matter how shocked or surprised she might have felt at my appearance, the moment she turned, I saw a mask of cool disinterest.

My queen never gave an inch.

I took another sip of my drink and said, "I'm sure your co-conspirators can hear me."

Devani stood, not saying a word.

"Ladies, thank you for watching her back. We will no longer need your services. Lilly, I'm sure you've figured it out by now. Rey will arrive in a few hours. He wants to revisit that no secrets rule of yours."

As Devani lifted her hand to her ear, I added, "Oh, and, Jayna, give my princess a kiss from me."

Devani cringed as if the sisters-in-law were in an all-out argument in her ear.

"How did you find out?" she asked, throwing the transmitter to the floor and smashing it with her heel to ensure no one could hear what came next. "Was it Neil?"

No, the new director of Solon North America hadn't betrayed his sister by choice to his brother by blood. I'd learned of my wife's plans when a little boy who was just over one told his father, "D go on pane." And the only other D in the family was his mother, whom he called Ma.

I bet the last person she believed would rat her out was her nephew. Then again, we King men stuck together.

Instead of answering her question, I said, "I have one word for you."

"That is?" Heat entered her eyes, and her lips parted just a fraction.

"Strip."

"Sam."

I held her molten gaze. "Highness."

Her breath grew unsteady, and I fucking loved how she reacted to me.

Only I could pull this out of her. Anyone else, she'd eat alive and use their bones as toothpicks.

"I gave you an order." I shifted forward, adjusting the legs of my pants to give my hard-as-hell cock some relief.

Her brown eyes shifted to my crotch, and at the same time, she swept her wet tongue over her plump lips, giving me visions of what her mouth could expertly do.

With the grace of a dancer, she slid her backpack to the floor and slowly undressed. When she stood before me completely naked, her breathtaking body entirely on display, I couldn't help but admire every inch of her.

She'd grown curvier since having our daughter, something I loved more than she would ever know. And yet she was no less muscular than before, maybe even more so now, since she trained harder with her former agents.

Then there were the faintest traces of stretch marks on her toned abdomen, a perfect reminder of how our little girl had forced her mother's hand into no longer taking death-defying risks. That alone made me want to keep Devani pregnant for the rest of her life.

Which was another thing Devani would punch me in the face for, if she ever got wind that I'd even had the whim.

Her nipples pebbled into hard, stiff peaks as I perused her gorgeous body, and a light flush touched her soft golden skin.

I crooked a finger, telling her to come toward me, but when she took a step, I shook my head and pointed to the ground.

"Crawl."

She narrowed her eyes for the briefest of moments, and without a word, she lowered to her hands and knees and moved in my direction.

It took all my strength not to groan, seeing the goddess before me. She was perfection incarnate. Her heavy breasts bounced, and her full hips swayed in a seductive dance, making me want to forget my original plans for her and fuck her right there on the floor.

But my queen needed to know she left the protection of New York City with something very precious in tow. Sometimes the best punishments came with a bit of pleasure added in.

I'd learned long ago to make a point with Devani. I couldn't give her any signs of weakness.

She was a queen, and she only submitted to her king.

When she reached me, she sat back on her heels. A slight trail of arousal coated her swollen pussy lips, and she inhaled in and out with short, ragged pants.

"Sam," she whispered, unable to hide the depth of her need. "It's been over two weeks."

"Is that why you flew halfway around the world? You wanted me to service you?"'

"I had other reasons."

"Why don't you share them with me."

"Later." She squirmed, pressing her thighs together and clutching her fists against her legs. "Right now, I need you to make this ache go away."

"How would you like your situation remedied? My mouth, my fingers, my cock?"

Her palms settled on my thighs, and she leveraged up, staring at me. "Yes."

"Yes, what, Highness?"

"I want all of it."

"Do you deserve it?"

A calculating smile touched her beautiful lips. "Abso-fucking-lutely. Your mouth, fingers, and cock belong to me."

I couldn't help but chuckle at her surety. "Is that right?"

She crawled up my fully clothed body, straddling my hips, and brought her face a hairsbreadth from mine. "Did I stutter?"

I grabbed her throat, cutting off her airflow for the briefest of seconds before easing my grip.

Her pupils dilated, and she whimpered, "More."

"You'll get what I give you."

"You're an asshole."

"And you're a manipulative bitch. We established this long ago. And yet, we're together. What does that say about us?"

"It's true love." She wrapped her arms around my shoulders.

I brushed my mouth against hers. "Yes, it is."

I deepened the kiss, letting her taste engulf my senses, a mixture of elderberry candy and her natural sweet essence. She drew me to her like no other woman ever had. She made me crave, want, and need.

I'd grown up on the streets, lost all that I'd ever cared for in life at a young age, and then I found solace in the arms of a socialite known as the Queen of Diamonds. However, the role she played for the world wasn't the woman I knew, the queen I'd protect with my last dying breath.

She'd build the icy facade to protect herself from the vultures of society. She'd become a weapon as a means to survive a childhood where she'd had no control. Then we'd found each other, all because of a dare at a poker table.

And thank God I'd taken up her challenge instead of going with my initial instinct and telling the Director of Solon she was too much trouble.

Sliding the palm of my other hand up her spine, I arched her back, breaking our kiss, but keeping my fingers wrapped around the column of her neck.

"I'm not going to make it so easy for you. You're on the wrong continent."

"I do what I want. I don't answer to you, Mr. King."

"Liar, liar, Director. I'd say pants on fire, but you aren't wearing any."

"You promised to take care of my needs. If not, then why did I marry you?"

"I must have missed that part in our vows."

She pressed her nails into the skin at the nape of my neck. "I mean it, Sam. Fuck me, or I'll break our deal and take care of it myself."

Oh yes, our deal where I owned her pleasure. Without me, there was none.

I pulled her arms down and pinned them to the hallow of her back.

Then I took the tie I had waiting for this exact moment from the side table and wound it around her wrist, securing it in a knot.

"You aren't going anywhere."

"Didn't we establish years ago that nothing can hold me if I don't want it to? I can break this with ease and then your wrist as you try to subdue me."

"But would you?" I leaned forward and bit the juncture where her shoulder met her neck, causing a whimper to escape her lips. "We know you enjoy giving up control too much to risk damaging the hands that leave the marks you love so much."

"I know you plan to punish me for being here. So I say, get on with it."

I gripped her hips and rubbed my thumb over her swollen clit, poking out from her slick sex. "The punishment is the wait."

Before she could respond, I slid two fingers inside her weeping pussy, curling them to rub against the sensitive spot that drove her desperation higher.

"Oh, God." She gasped and bucked, flooding my hand with her arousal.

I fucking craved her cries, and my cock hated me, hard as it was, wanting nothing more than to bury itself deep in her cunt.

However, until she begged, neither of us would get our desires fulfilled.

I understood her need to be near me and the games we played. I felt it too, but her safety would remain a priority.

Her existence made her a target. Not just because she was an heiress of a billion dollars, or her assassin status, or the fact she was one of the most notorious directors of an underground vigilante spy agency. But as my wife, people would use her to get to me.

My role as a broker between civil society and the underworld made me a person who knew everyone's secrets and, therefore, the one to focus on when things went south.

She rode up and down, grinding herself against me. At the same time, my thumb circled the pearl at the apex of her pussy lips. Just as her muscles contracted, pushing her into a freefall of release, I gripped her shoulder, holding her down and stopping my ministration.

"Bastard," she ground out through clenched teeth.

"True enough."

I brought her to the cusp two more times. She writhed, needing relief, glistening with sweat and flushed with unquenched desire.

A fucking goddess before me.

I pulled my soaked fingers from her body and brought them to her lips. Immediately, she parted them, taking them deep into her mouth and sucking them clean.

"Please," she begged. "I need to come."

"I know you do. But first, we need to clear up something."

She narrowed her gaze. "No, you need to make me come. Then we can have any discussion you want."

She rolled her hips, sliding her drenched bare pussy against the steel rod that had become my cock. Her heat soaked through my slacks and pulled at the urge to drive into her and force her submission.

However, I reined in my raging need, not giving her the

concession she expected, and asked, "Do you really want to prolong your pleasure?"

A calculating gleam entered her dark brown eye, and in the next second, she grabbed hold of the collar with one hand, and with the other, she fisted my cock through my pants. Just as fast, I pinned her wrists to her thighs.

My woman's skills were lethal, but I had pure body mass on my side.

"You put yourself in danger." I leaned forward. "You didn't even bring a small team with you."

"I can protect myself."

"Tonight's situation says otherwise."

"That's because you had insider information. Who's the traitor?"

"No changing the topic, Highness."

"Sam, I wasn't in danger. I got off the plane, stopped at a shop for Lilly, then came here. Once I left the building, I planned to go straight back to the jet."

"Why did you come here?"

She lifted a brow. "No, changing the topic, King."

If that was how she wanted to play it. I'd oblige.

I stood, holding her ass and hands, and walked toward the primary bedroom.

Once inside, I noticed the kangaroo on the pillow. She came halfway across the world to put a stuffed animal on my bed.

Pushing the thought back, I unceremoniously dropped her on top of the covers. Immediately, she jumped to a crouching position as if ready to attack me.

CHAPTER 3

*D*evani

I CLENCHED my jaw and glared at Sam, ready to take his eyes out. First, he sexually tortured me, leaving me hanging, and then tossed me on the bed as if I were a sack of potatoes.

"I'm not a damn rag doll to throw around."

He smirked, his hazel eyes full of mischief.

He unbuttoned his shirt, discarding it behind him, and then his fingers went to the waistband of his pants.

"I didn't throw you. I placed you on my bed."

"Placed? I'll show you pla—" All my outrage evaporated as his slacks hit the floor, and my attention shifted to the tent his dick formed in his boxers.

Damn the man. He definitely had an incredible cock.

"Cat got your tongue?"

"Are you planning to use that or waste my time?"

"You'll just have to wait and see." He pushed his boxers down and slowly stalked in my direction.

My core clenched, seeing the predator coming toward me.

His thick, heavy veined cock wept with precum, making me wish for just a taste of his salty-sweet essence. His honed, sculpted muscles bunched and flexed, readied. As if he expected me to pounce.

If we were in a different situation, I might have obliged.

I loved it rough, untamed, raw; everything a cultured, refined, civilized socialite should ever crave. This man gave me everything I desired and more.

The more was what always scared me the most. He softened me and showed me a vulnerable side of myself I never knew existed.

Now here I was, caught in the spell of a cobra. Correction, considering our location, he was channeling the Australian western taipan, the most venomous snake in the world.

"Is that a look of surrender in your eyes, Highness?"

"I haven't conceded, King."

"Then why haven't you attacked? Don't you want my marks on you? You usually beg for them. I'm the one who has to say no."

"Maybe, I want something a little different for a change."

He paused, stopping at the foot of the bed and studying me. "And that is?"

"How about…" I crawled toward him and set a hand on his tattooed chest. "Something a little gentler, maybe without the gymnastics?"

He slid his hands around my waist, drawing me to him. "And the edge you love so much?"

"I didn't say I wanted it tame." I glided my fingertips over his forearms and shoulders. "I have a question for you."

"Go ahead."

"Can we stop talking and start fucking?"

In a flash, he grabbed my throat, my heartbeat jumping in reaction. "You have a one-track mind, Highness."

"I have needs you have to satisfy." I wanted to feel him deep inside me, quaking, shivering, lost in me as I was in him.

This man rarely let go, except with me.

Pressing the heel of his palm to my chest, he tumbled me back and came over me. His giant body caged me, cocooned me, making it so all I saw was him.

I gripped his cock, pumping up and down, letting the bead of moisture at the tip drip onto my bare mound.

"Please, I'm desperate for you."

"I know." He pushed my hands aside, notching the brad head of his erection into my waiting, aching slit.

He pushed in a fraction, retreated, and repeated the motion.

"What are you doing?"

"Before I give you what you want. I must make something clear."

"You will not use this moment to make anything clear." I shoved his shoulder, ready to toss him to the side.

As if suspecting my plans, he used his knees to push mine too far apart to use, all the while keeping his cock firmly posed in my opening.

"Now, where were we." He leaned down, bit my lower lip hard enough to sting, and continued, "You aren't alone in this anymore. When you take risks, it affects other people."

I cupped his face. "This isn't that serious. This trip was just for a little amusement at your expense."

"You're mine. I won't risk another woman I love. I'd burn the world down if anything happened to you."

I sighed. There it was. The reason for this whole setup. His fear he'd lose me just like his mother.

Sam had attempted to build an impenetrable wall around his heart, and then we'd crossed paths, and neither of us had been the same afterward.

How could I have forgotten that sometimes my risky antics,

which he enjoyed, for the most part, could scare the shit out of him if he wasn't in the loop about them?

"Understood, Mr. King. I'll try not to relieve my solo mission days without adequate backup or keeping you informed."

"It's not exactly what I wanted to hear, but I suppose that is as good as I'll get."

"I'll take my wins as they come. Marriage is all about compromise."

"That it is." Sam hooked an arm under my knee, shifted his hips, and thrust his engorged cock to the hilt, making me cry out.

He rolled his hips, tunneling his penis deep as if claiming every tiny bit of space inside me. The muscles of my pussy flexed around him, quivering and contracting, loving the feel of him.

"Fuck me hard, Sam. I need it hard."

"You asked for it." He reared back and then plunged in again, starting a relentless pounding.

My nails clawed the skin of his back and neck. I had no doubt I'd drawn blood, but neither of us cared. This was how we were together—desperate for the other's marks, craving them. The bruises, the scratches, the bites.

Powerful spasms rocked through my core, making me clench around his pistoning cock. I heard his gusts of hot and fast breath in my ears, and sweat dampened both of our skins.

The second he grazed my clit, I detonated. A cascade of violent shudders washed over me, engulfing my senses and filling me with a pleasurable pain I wanted to live in forever. I basked in ecstasy, enjoying the ride, barely registering Sam gripping my face and kissing me as he called my name, fucking me through his climax.

CHAPTER 4

$\mathcal{S}$ am

I ROLLED Devani to the side, keeping her in my arms as our breaths calmed.

"Want to tell me why you flew across the world to sneak a stuffed animal into the penthouse?"

She lifted her head, a smile touching her full lips, and reached for the plush kangaroo dislodged from its previous place against the pillow during our carnal activities.

"There is a secret inside. I wanted you to discover it."

"Let's see the reason for causing all of this mischief." I plucked the animal from her grasp and studied it.

After a few seconds, I noticed the kangaroo's pouch held something. I tugged a little tab, and out came a little joey with a tiny image attached.

This woman was something else. She'd fought me every step of the way before agreeing to be mine, and now she played her crazy game to give me the one thing I never had before her.

A family of my own.

She rubbed a hand down my chest. "This time, I get to say I knew first."

"Nope. I figured it out before I left New York."

"No fucking way." She sat up, a scowl on her beautiful face, and I wasn't sure whether I should smirk or keep a straight face at her outrage. "How the hell did you do that?"

I reached up and cupped her full breast. "These. Just like last time. They gave it away."

"You're obsessed with my boobs."

I shrugged. "They're great boobs. Besides, I'm positive the only ones you'll allow me to be obsessed with are yours."

Fire lit her dark eyes, and she narrowed them as if readying to attack. "If you know what's good for your longevity."

"I rest my case."

In a quick flash of movement, she straddled my waist and pinned my shoulders back with her body looming over me.

No matter our size difference, the strength in her body never ceased to amaze me.

"One day, I will get one over you."

"That's like when you said you don't submit. And we know that statement is a lie."

"I'm a queen. A queen doesn't submit to any man."

I slid my hands into her hair and rubbed my thumb over her lips.

"I'm not just any man. I'm a King."

She leaned down. "That's right. Mine."

* * *

Sienna Snow is a USA Today bestselling author who loves to serve up dark and super sexy romances about anti-heroes and the strong and unapologetic women who bring them to their knees. Her books will take you into a world of indulgence, suspense, and most definitely steam.

You can find out more about Sienna at www.siennasnow.com

FINDING SANCTUM BY PEPPER NORTH

SANCTUM welcomes those looking for a very special relationship and needing the protection that only a Daddydom can provide.

CHAPTER 1

Dear Shelby,

Is there any way I can come visit you? I really need to get out of town. I'm afraid of Nate. If only I could find someone to love me as much as your Daddies adore you.

Gia

Before she could reconsider for the eighteenth time, Gia sealed the letter and dropped it, with double postage to make sure it got there, through the mail slot at the post office. She crossed her fingers, hoping Shelby would get her letter soon.

Jumping as the jarring song Nate had selected for his ringtone blared, Gia fumbled for her phone and answered. She'd learned it was never a good idea to ignore a call from him.

"Hello?" she whispered quietly as she walked out of the post office.

"Where are you?" he demanded.

"I had some errands to run," she hedged.

"Tell me where to meet you."

"Oh, I won't waste your time as I flit out of one store into another. How about if I meet you in a couple of hours at the park?" she suggested. There should be plenty of people there now.

"No freaking way. Last time, you just wanted to swing. I'll be at O'Grady's. Be here in an hour," he warned and disconnected the call.

Gia could tell he'd already been at the pub for a while. His words didn't quite slur together like he was truly drunk, but he was close. She shook her head. How did she ever fall for his good looks and charm? She'd totally missed the clues in front of her face and ignored the warning from his last girlfriend. Brenda's face popped into her mind as she'd tried to get Gia to listen.

Wow! Do I owe her an apology? Brenda wasn't around anymore to correct that error. She'd fled across the country immediately after making a stop to talk to Gia.

A light jingle vibrated her phone. Gia looked at the screen before quickly answering. "Shelby?"

"Hi, Gia! Jeremy and Beau came to pick up some parts they needed at SANCTUM. Can we take you to lunch?" Shelby's sweet voice suggested.

"Oh, Shelby. I need help. I just sent you a letter."

"Where are you?"

"In front of the post office." Gia heard rapid whispers being exchanged in the truck as Shelby updated the two men.

"Beau says go back inside and wait. He'll come inside to get you. It will take us five minutes to get there," Shelby told her.

Three minutes later, the door to the post office rattled open and everyone looked to see who entered with a clatter. Gia immediately rushed to the handsome man's side. "Hi, Beau. I'm sorry to bother you."

"No bother. Shelby's in the car. Let's go," he suggested, placing a hand at the small of her back to usher her outside.

The truck was parked illegally at the curb. Gia rushed forward at the sight of her friend waving at the window. Shelby pushed the door open to scramble out to greet her. The two girls hugged briefly before climbing in the back together. Beau closed their door securely before jumping back inside.

"Let me pull into a parking lot and you can tell us what's going on, Gia," Jeremy suggested.

"Could you drive to the park? No one will notice us there," Gia requested.

Without asking any questions, Jeremy turned off Main Street and followed the directions Gia gave. When they reached the park, he pulled into a space and turned around.

"Is it safe to get out and talk?" he asked.

"It should be. I'm having trouble with a guy I've been dating. He's at his favorite bar. I have," Gia paused to look at her watch, "forty-five minutes left—really seventy-five. He'll get mad if I'm late but won't come after me until I'm thirty minutes late."

"I don't like him already," Beau muttered with a dark expression.

"Me, neither. How can we help?" Shelby asked.

"Can I come stay in SANCTUM for a while? If you have a tent, I could just set it up somewhere," Gia offered.

"You're not staying in a tent," Jeremy laid down the law.

Before he could continue, Gia's phone rang. Quickly, she answered, "Hi, Nate." At Jeremy's signal, she clicked on the speaker so they could all hear.

"… your phone is at the park. Didn't I tell you to come here when you were done with your errands?" Nate's voice was harsh and slurred.

"I finished and wanted to swing. You know me—airhead who loves the park. I'll be there before my hour is finished. Promise," Gia spoke quickly.

"Fine. Swing now because you're not going back there again this month." The call disconnected.

Gia looked down at the phone and slowly shook her head. "He's tracking my phone."

"Text him that your battery is dying," Jeremy instructed. "Then hand me your phone."

Gia did as instructed, then watched Jeremy fly through several screens on her phone, tapping buttons before powering it off.

"I've disconnected the share location feature on your phone. Unless he's loaded a tracking app on your phone I don't recognize, he shouldn't be able to tell where you are. Just in case, keep it turned off," he suggested.

"O-Okay." Gia stumbled over the word. Nate was going to be so mad.

"Of course, you're coming to SANCTUM. Are you living with him?" Shelby asked.

"No, thank goodness, but he knows where I live and the code to get in the apartment building."

"Let's go pick up anything you'll need for a while. Are you okay to miss work?" Beau asked.

"Nate came in last week and caused a scene. He made me quit. I just paid the rent and bills, so I'm okay for a while," Gia assured them. She didn't want them to think she was trying to mooch off them.

"Did you walk to the post office?" Shelby asked.

"Yes. I'm… I don't have a car anymore," she admitted.

"Get back in the car, everyone. Let's head to Gia's apartment and grab some clothes and supplies," Beau ordered.

When they reached her complex, Jeremy stayed with the truck to keep an eye out while Beau emptied the refrigerator. Gia quickly threw most of her clothes and most precious possessions into a couple of bags. Into a large tote bag, she tucked her stuffie, Roopert. She couldn't leave him.

"Your apartment came furnished, right?" Shelby asked.

"Yes. I've got pretty much all my stuff with me now. If worse comes to worst with Nate, I can give notice that I'm leaving my apartment and move to another town and start again," Gia suggested sadly. She hated that she'd made such a mistake in choosing the wrong man to get involved with and now had to flee. *Stupid mistake!*

"You couldn't have known," Shelby comforted her.

"Time to go, ladies. Do you have everything?" Beau asked, picking up the two bags.

"Sorry I've got so much. I promise I'm not moving in to stay," Gia rushed to assure him.

"That's not what I meant, Gia. We've got a truck to fill if there's anything else you need to take," Beau said gently.

"Could I take that?" she asked, pointing to an ugly lamp. "It was my grandma's."

"Find a blanket and wrap it up. Then come to the truck," he directed.

The two women scampered to follow his directions. Shelby asked, "This may be your last chance. What else?"

"Really, that's it. I hate this lamp, but it was my grandma's. It's all I have of hers."

"It isn't the prettiest thing I've ever seen," Shelby agreed, making them both giggle.

It felt good to laugh. Gia didn't know how long it had been since she'd had fun with a friend. Jeremy drove out of the parking lot and Gia didn't look back. She was too busy catching up with her friend.

CHAPTER 2

❧

"*B*oth of them?" Gia mouthed and waggled a finger behind the front seats.

"Both of us," Beau confirmed without turning around.

Embarrassed to have him know what they were talking about, Gia felt her cheeks flame. Shelby's, "Oh, Daddy!" comment made her even more curious. Obviously, there would be no secrets in the car. Gia suspected Shelby didn't hide anything from the two men in her life—ever.

"They're your Daddies? Like in the books?" Gia asked in amazement.

"Even better than in the books," Shelby assured her.

"How do you feel about Daddies and Littles, Gia?" Jeremy asked.

His tone sounded like an everyday question, but Gia sensed there was more to it. Taking a deep breath and releasing it to calm her beating heart, she admitted, "I've devoured every book I can find. I should have known that Daddies existed in real life, but I haven't ever met one. I thought Nate might be a Daddy because from the beginning, he always told me what to do and not do."

"Daddies exist," Beau confirmed. "I haven't met Nate, but I'd bet my left arm that he isn't a Daddy."

"Me, too," piped Shelby. "Daddies love you and make you feel good. They don't make you stuff all your things in a bag and flee town. Well, unless you're scared. Littles are allowed to make mistakes. Daddies help with those."

"I don't think leaving Nate was a mistake. Dating Nate was my worst choice ever," Gia shared.

"Well, that's over and you're on your way to SANCTUM. How much has Shelby told you about the place she lives?" Jeremy asked.

"Just that she's happy and has a cat and a dog," Gia answered.

"Want to tell her, Shelby, or shall we? Gia should know where she's going," Beau suggested.

"Is it something bad?" Gia asked. She could feel her forehead wrinkle and tried not to feel anxious.

"Not bad at all," Shelby rushed to assure her. "SANCTUM is a protected community of Daddies and Littles. It's a place where Littles can be themselves and Daddies can be, well... Daddies."

"That doesn't sound like a bad place. I mean, I'll be the only one there not in a relationship. Will that bother the other Littles?" Gia asked, watching her friend's face to capture her genuine reaction.

"Of course, it won't bother anyone! And there are more Daddies there. A bunch have built homes in SANCTUM while they keep looking for their Littles."

As if on cue, Beau's phone rang. "Hey, Lincoln. You headed out to get the last of your things?" There was a short pause. "Here, let me put you on speaker so you can ask her that question yourself," Beau suggested with a laugh before turning on that feature. "Go ahead."

"Hi, Shelby. How's the prettiest Little in SANCTUM?" a deep voice asked.

"You tell everyone they're the prettiest Little in SANCTUM,"

Shelby answered with an eye roll and a laugh. "I'm good."

"Repeat your question," Beau reminded him.

"I asked your Daddy when you're going to bring one of your Little friends to visit?" Lincoln asked jovially. "I need some help to find my perfect Little."

The two men in the front seat exchanged meaningful glances as did the women in the back.

Shelby recovered and answered, "Gia is in the car with us, Lincoln. I can't tell you if she's Little or not. That would be up to you to find out yourself, but she knows what SANCTUM is. She's coming to stay with me for a while."

This time, the brief pause was on the other end of the line. "Well, I walked right into that, didn't I. Hi, Gia. I'll look forward to meeting you. Don't worry, no pressure. You come have fun with Shelby. Beau, you owe me a bonfire tonight," Lincoln declared.

"You got it. Spread the word," Beau suggested.

"Will do. Drive carefully. You have precious cargo," Lincoln instructed.

"Don't we know it," Jeremy answered. "See you tonight."

After Beau disconnected, Gia asked, "How do I know if I'm Little?"

"You don't worry about it. Let a Daddy help you figure it out while you recharge your batteries and relax at SANCTUM. Lincoln will never pressure you—nor will the other Daddies there," Jeremy promised.

"There are other Daddies without Littles?" Gia asked.

"In SANCTUM? There are several. A few might be at the bonfire tonight."

"I'm not really looking for a new boyfriend. I haven't even officially broken up with Nate yet," Gia pointed out.

"No pressure, Gia. You move at your own pace. You might find a special relationship here. You might not. It doesn't hurt to give them a chance if someone makes you feel special," Shelby pointed out.

"That makes sense. I wonder if Nate knows I'm gone yet?" Gia asked, looking at her phone.

"He'll know where you are if you turn on your phone. Borrow Shelby's and make any calls you want to," Beau warned.

"I don't really have anyone to call. No boss. I have casual friends, but they won't worry if they don't see me for a while— maybe forever," Gia confided.

"Family?" Jeremy suggested.

"My folks retired to Florida. I'll call them next week to update them," Gia answered.

"Then just sit back and enjoy the ride. Let's play Shelby's favorite game," Jeremy suggested. "I'm going to SANCTUM and I'm bringing an anteater."

"Woo hoo! It can suck up all the ants. Me, next," Shelby cheered. "I'm going to SANCTUM and I'm bringing an anteater and a bajillion pieces of bubble gum!"

"Your teeth are going to rot out, Little girl. We'll need a dentist at SANCTUM," Jeremy pointed out. "Your turn next, Gia. Just say…"

Gia jumped in. "I know! I'm going to SANCTUM and I'm going to take an anteater, a bajillion pieces of bubble gum, and a cow!"

"We've got plenty of those," Beau assured her. "Hmm. It's my turn…"

"You've got D, Daddy!" Shelby reminded him, leaning forward eagerly.

Distracted by trying to remember the list, Gia forgot about her phone and her troubles she'd left behind. Already, she felt her shoulders settle down into place as her stress level ebbed down. She patted Shelby's leg as a thank you and received a hug in return.

"I'm glad you're here. We'll have so much fun," Shelby told her.

"I'm ready for some amusement."

CHAPTER 3

Gia was exhausted by the time they arrived at SANCTUM. She took one look at the massive gate in front of her and felt safe for the first time in forever. Nate had never hurt her physically. He had gotten so aggressively angry when she didn't do exactly what he wanted that Gia had worried about being hurt. Here, he couldn't find her. She didn't have to talk to him ever again.

"Let me show you the guest room," Shelby said, linking her arm with Gia's when they'd tumbled out of the truck. "My Daddies will bring your things in soon."

"I can't forget Roo," Gia said, grabbing her tote from the truck.

"Does Roo ever come out to say hello or meet new people?" Shelby asked, peering into the bag.

"Of course. He's very friendly."

Gia pulled a kangaroo stuffie out of the bag and carefully unwrapped the scrap of blanket from around his well-loved body. "This is Shelby, Roo. She has stuffies as well."

"Hi, Roo." That deep voice from the phone made Gia jump. Quickly, she hugged Roo to her chest to hide him.

"It's okay, Gia. That's Lincoln. I bet he came to unload the truck and get the bonfire going."

"That's exactly right, Shelby. I'm sorry I scared you and Roo, Gia," he said from a polite distance.

"That's okay. He didn't expect you. I'm going to go see where I'm sleeping. I'll see you at the bonfire," Gia said, excusing herself quickly and linking arms with Shelby to escape.

"Are you okay?" her friend asked as they got far enough away that Lincoln couldn't hear.

"You didn't warn me he's a twenty on a scale of one to ten!" Gia accused in a shaky voice.

"He is handsome. I like that gray streak over his temple," Shelby agreed. "Sorry, I don't think of him that way."

"There's no way he'd be interested in me," Gia answered, waving a hand at herself. "I'm not wearing makeup and I'm in slouchy clothes."

"Daddies don't care about that. My Daddies let me put makeup on for special occasions, but not every day. I'd much rather be me than someone else," Shelby said with a shrug.

"Do you think Lincoln is the same way?" Gia asked.

"Daddies always are."

* * *

SHELBY HELPED Gia unpack all her clothes into the drawers. She even tucked her nightshirt under the pillow so Gia would be ready to go to sleep whenever she wanted. Shelby even found a toothbrush for her when Gia discovered she'd forgotten hers.

"Are you hungry?" Shelby asked.

"Starving," Gia admitted.

"Let's go get something to eat," Shelby suggested, leading her friend to the backyard where a bunch of people had gathered.

Shelby waved her arms and announced, "Hi, Everyone! This is my friend, Gia!"

"Hi, Gia!" came at her from all sides.

Overwhelmed, Gia waved and tried to look friendly.

"Come get something to eat," that deep voice announced Lincoln's presence.

"What are we having, Lincoln?" Shelby asked, towing Gia over to the food table.

"Chicken tacos! How many can you eat?" Lincoln asked with a grin.

"Forty-two!" Shelby announced.

"Four, it is. Go get your tacos all fixed up," he said, pointing to the table of yummy additions before looking at Gia.

"How many can you eat, Little girl?"

"I'm not sure I'm Little," she whispered, not wanting to mislead anyone.

"You just be yourself and I bet you'll figure it out," he answered with a smile. "Did I hear you say four tacos? Coming up!"

Lincoln handed her a plate of four tacos and nodded his head to where Shelby piled lettuce, cheese, and salsa on her plate.

"Thank you!" Gia said, leaning over her plate to inhale the delicious aroma as she listened to the next person ask for one hundred tacos and Lincoln announce her four tacos.

"Does everyone get four tacos?" Gia asked as she dropped sour cream on her plate.

"Always from Lincoln. He says four fit perfectly on a plate. No matter how many you ask for, he gives you four. It's fun to tease him," Shelby explained.

"That's fun. Are all Daddies nice?" Gia asked.

"There are all sorts of Daddies. Some Littles like dark Daddies. And I'm sure some Daddies are jerks, but I haven't met any like that. Everyone here at SANCTUM would climb mountains and crawl through quicksand to save their Little. They're amazing men as well as Daddies."

"Sounds almost too good to be true," Gia commented, sprinkling cheese over her food as the final finishing touch. "Where do we sit?"

"Let's go join that group over there. I'll introduce you to Hannah and Lindy. Lindy moved in with her Daddy right after me and Hannah has been here for about a year," Shelby shared before leading the way over to a couple of empty chairs.

"Hi, Gia! Welcome to SANCTUM," a slender brunette greeted her. "I'm Lindy."

"Hi! I'm Hannah. Come join us."

"Hi, Lindy. Hi, Hannah. Thanks," Gia said as she sat down.

"Do you have a Daddy?" Hannah asked.

"I don't," Gia said uncomfortably. She didn't like feeling like she was in the spotlight.

"That doesn't matter. We're glad you're here. Hannah and I were chatting about sweet talking Lincoln into teaching us how to make bread," Lindy confessed.

"That would be fun. I love making bread," Gia said before taking a bite of her first taco.

"Yum!" she mumbled.

Someone settled into the seat next to her and she turned to see Lincoln settling in with a plate as well. She smiled to see that he had exactly four tacos.

"I didn't see you pick up anything to drink," Lincoln commented, cradling three cans of root beer in one arm. He opened and handed one to both Shelby and Gia before popping the tab on his own.

"Thanks, Lincoln," Shelby said.

"Yes. Thank you," Gia echoed.

"Lincoln, can you teach us to make bread?" Hannah asked, leaning forward eagerly.

"Just regular old white bread?" he asked.

When the three Littles nodded, he agreed. "Come to my house tomorrow at ten. We'll make bread. While it's rising, I'll put you to work helping me get a swing tested out."

Gia sat quietly as the others cheered and chattered about their plans. She took another bite of her tacos. They were so good.

"I have enough room in my kitchen for five people to work together. You'll come too, won't you?" Lincoln said quietly to her alone.

"I know how to make bread. My grandmother taught me," Gia confessed.

"Perfect. You can be my assistant. When everyone has their hands covered with gooey bread dough, you can help me dole out more flour," the handsome man suggested.

When she hesitated, he added quietly, "I'd like to get to know you better, Gia."

"I just left a boyfriend," she confessed, not wanting to mislead him.

"Beau gave me an overview. You should be very proud that you asked for help. Come tomorrow and make bread. You deserve to have fun with the other Littles," he suggested.

"I don't know if I'm Little," she hedged.

"Then it's time to figure that out, isn't it?" Lincoln tapped his soda can against hers.

She couldn't help liking him. "Okay, I'll help with the bread making."

"Thank you, Gia. My day tomorrow just got a lot more interesting."

CHAPTER 4

*A*fter going to sleep early that night to allow both herself and Roo to recover from the long trip, Gia ate breakfast with Shelby and her Daddies after waking up refreshed. Shelby was not a morning person. Watching her struggle to wake up as she sat on one Daddy's lap and then the other amused Gia. The two men took wonderful care of her as they tempted her to stay awake with choice nibbles of food on their plates.

"She's eaten all my bacon again," Jeremy complained. His indulgent smile clued Gia in that he didn't mind at all.

"Sorry, Daddy."

He kissed her temple and stole a piece of toast with butter and jam from Beau's plate, disregarding her other Daddy's protest to hand it to her. "Eat this. Tomorrow, we'll eat bread you make," Jeremy suggested.

That perked Shelby up. "What time is it?"

"You've got time to finish breakfast. Then we'll brush your teeth and get you dressed."

Shelby accepted the toast and took a big bite. "Yum! Thank you, Daddy Beau."

"You're welcome, sweetheart. I can't wait to try your loaf later. You'll have fun at Lincoln's."

A half hour later, Shelby and Gia set off for Lincoln's house. "We could let my Daddies drive us, but I like to walk. I can't wait to swing on Lincoln's swing set. A bunch of the Daddies worked on it."

"I like to walk, too. It's so pretty here," Gia complimented.

"I love living here. Have you turned your phone on?" Shelby asked.

"I hadn't even thought of it," Gia said with a shrug. "I definitely don't miss mean phone calls. Last night, no one was on their phone."

"Daddies like to focus on their Littles. They use phones for business and emergencies, of course, but they'd rather talk to us in person. We have a lot of gatherings like last night."

"Does Lincoln always cook?" Gia asked.

"No, but we love when he does. Everyone takes turns and has their specialties. Do you like him?" Shelby asked, looking sideways at her friend.

"He seems unlike anyone I've ever met," Gia confessed.

"Daddies are," Shelby answered with a smile.

"I can tell you love your Daddies, and they love you."

"With all our hearts. It took a bit to get everything settled between my Daddies. It was hard for them in the beginning, but they knew I needed them both, so they worked it out. Look! There's Hannah and Lindy. Let's go have fun!"

* * *

"THANK GOODNESS YOU WERE HERE," Lincoln said as he wiped up flour that somehow had gotten tracked away from the kitchen.

"It was fun. You're a brilliant teacher. I learned a few things, too," Gia told him.

"Thanks for staying to help me clean up. Your loaf looks pretty good," he complimented, gesturing to the last loaf of bread left on the cooling rack after the other women had all scurried home to show off their prize creations.

"I was glad to search high and low for scattered remnants of hurricanes Lindy, Hannah, and Shelby. But you didn't make any bread for yourself."

"What would you say about joining me for dinner and sharing yours?" Lincoln proposed.

It took her one whole second to say, "Yes."

"Perfect. If you like lasagna, I can pop it in the oven."

"I love it. The bread will go wonderfully with it."

"Let's cut off a couple of pieces while the bread's hot and go for a walk as the lasagna bakes."

When she nodded eagerly, Lincoln put the casserole dish in the oven before cutting two thick pieces of bread and slathering them with butter. Handing her one on a napkin, he grabbed a bottle of water and ushered her out of the house.

"This is so good," Gia said, taking another big bite.

"Don't eat too fast, Little girl."

"What is a Little girl?" Gia blurted.

"The men that founded SANCTUM met years ago," Lincoln shared as they walked down a well-worn path. "We were all drawn together because we all identified as Daddies. Each of us recognized our need to care for the one we love on a different level. We are all dominant and were searching for our submissives—a special kind of submissive."

"What makes them special?"

"I can only tell you what I've searched for. For others, it might be different. My perfect match is a Little girl who needs someone to look out for her, protect her from the negative side of life, reward her when she's good, and correct her when she's not," Lincoln answered.

"Like spankings?"

"Or standing in the corner, writing sentences, missing playtime with your friends—there are a lot of ways a Daddy might choose to address bad behavior."

"Like a Little girl?" she questioned.

"But with a woman's mind and desires. Littles often enjoy simpler things in life: a treasured stuffie, having someone to kiss a booboo and make it better, sometimes even very little things like bottles and diapers."

Gia squeezed her thighs together. Lincoln's explanation was like he saw her fantasies and understood them completely. She rushed to say, "No diapers."

"That depends on what the Little and her Daddy need," Lincoln stated firmly.

"Do you think I'm Little?" she asked, studying his face.

"I think there's a good possibility, but that's something only you can decide. If I had a checklist for Littles, it would be something like this:

Would you like to be someone's cherished center of attention?

Could you love someone so much that you trust them with your heart, mind, and body?

Could you let someone take care of the daily chores we all have? For example, would you be happy if someone takes care of all your living expenses, schedule, clothing, etc.?

Could you allow your significant other to make rules for your relationship?

Could you let yourself be rewarded when you're good and punished when you break a guideline?"

"I don't know. I'd say yes to everything, but number four scares me. Nate, my former boyfriend, always told me what to do. Then he did whatever he wanted. Life wasn't very fun," she admitted.

"He wasn't a Daddy. They have rules, too," Lincoln shared.

"Like what?" she asked, popping the last piece of her bread in her mouth and wiping her hands and lips on the napkin.

"A Daddy loves his Little. Her needs and happiness are most important."

"You don't think he loved me?" Gia asked.

"No."

She looked at him closely after that curt response. They walked together for a couple of minutes in silence. The birds flew overhead, and the sun shone on the path in front of them. Gia hadn't just existed and hung out for so long. This felt wonderful.

"I don't think he loved me, either. I was convenient and biddable. He was nice in the beginning, but that disappeared fast."

"Sounds like you weren't listening to that voice in your head that was sounding the alert. Do you hear it now?" he asked.

"I do."

Gia didn't want him to know what that voice was saying. It urged her to make the first move. When Lincoln's fingers brushed hers, she daringly slid her hand into his. Instantly, he squeezed her fingers gently.

"I want you to stay here, Gia. We need to see if this attraction we have to each other is something we both crave. It has to be right for both of us," Lincoln told her.

"Does it feel right to you?" she asked, peeking up at him.

"You know when you put a jigsaw puzzle together and you get to the last two pieces? You're so excited because you're almost done, but you can't find those last pieces. So, you hunt everywhere: under the table, in the toy chest, under the box. They aren't anywhere to be found."

"I hate that," she confirmed.

"So you pick up the box to throw all the pieces back inside and something rattles," Lincoln added.

"And when you open the box, there are the two pieces even though you've looked in there a hundred times!" Gia said triumphantly.

"You fit them together first and then press them into the hole to enjoy the entire unmarred picture before you. It's more beautiful in real life than you ever expected."

"I love that. I never want to tear them apart and put the pieces back in the box," Gia said with a sigh.

"What if SANCTUM was our puzzle box, and we never had to destroy the awe-inspiring picture we make together?"

Lincoln stopped and turned Gia to face him. He set Gia's hand on his shoulder and he wrapped one hand around the back of her head to pull her closer. "I'm going to kiss you, Little girl."

She nodded eagerly and lifted her lips to meet his. Soft and sweet, his kisses promised everything she'd ever wanted. Wrapping her arms around his neck, Gia pressed herself against his hard chest as she rose to her tiptoes to demand more kisses as passion flared between them. His powerful arms wrapped around her to lift her to his chest as he deepened their exchange.

When he raised his head, they both were breathless. She looked into his brown eyes and thought, "This is what home feels like."

* * *

JOIN ALL the happy couples in SANCTUM! May you find your own SANCTUM. Please visit my website to find all my series and a list of all my books: www.4peppernorth.club

Ever just gone for it? That's what USA Today Bestselling Author Pepper North did in 2017 when she posted a book for sale on Amazon without telling anyone. Thanks to her amazing fans, the support of the writing community, Mr. North, and a killer schedule, she has now written more than 70 books!

RECKLESS RIDERS BY JAYNE PATON

DADDY HARVEY'S REVELATION

Two people from different worlds find something special in the walls of a BDSM club. Will Harvey's need to take it out of the club with Reckless Riders president, Rivka, bring joy or heartbreak?

This is part one of Rivka's and Harvey's story and is only the beginning.

CHAPTER 1

$\mathcal{R}$ivka

AN AIR of electric excitement always followed after the new prospects became patched members. Tonight was no different. Only, I wasn't feeling it. I itched inside my skin in a way that suggested it had been too long since I'd played. I could use all the mental techniques to shift my thought patterns, but when I got into one of these moods, only one thing worked. Playing at one of my favorite BDSM clubs in Jacksonville with Daddy Harvey. The man could make me submit to him in ways that those in the club would see as weakness. I kept that part of myself tucked away from prying eyes.

Being a female and president of Reckless Riders brought with it a need to prove too many that I had balls bigger than anyone else's. That was easy with a mom who'd trained others and me in martial arts, both unarmed and armed combat. I could take a full-sized man down by the time I was five. She'd also taught me the difference between being a pushover and willingly submitting to someone. Only some folks couldn't figure that shit out, and I got fed up with kicking ass while trying to explain I wasn't anyone's pushover. Heading over to Jacksonville was my way to combat that. What I had with Harvey was… complicated. I'd met him three years ago, and from the moment I'd laid eyes on him, I'd wanted him. He, like me, wasn't after a long-term commitment.

Isn't three years a long-term thing?

"Rivka, you need another drink?" came a voice from my left, loud enough to compete with the chatter and music, distracting me from my uneasy thoughts.

I glanced sideways at the newest club member, Vale. She was pretty in a wholesome way that fooled many. Underneath the sexy curves, blonde curls, and blue eyes was a woman who'd learned to fight dirty, use her cunning, and rip out folk's eyes before they blinked and realized what was happening. She was loyal and protective as a dog, making her a simple decision to patch this time around. Patching a prospect only happened once a year, and the inner circle was fussy about those who joined.

I glanced at my near-full beer bottle and shook my head. "This'll do me."

And it would. If I headed to Jacksonville tonight, I needed to keep my wits about me.

With a quick nod, Vale moved on, going from member to member, getting requests before heading back to the bar she staffed with several other members.

My old colonial home had become the clubhouse around the time of Mom's death. The old building's roof was a mess after a tropical storm. I'd offered my house as a temporary solution, but it somehow went from temporary to permanent without me noticing.

I had the ground floor adapted. The sunroom was now a bar that opened into the living area. I'd gotten the kitchen extended and modernized out back to cater to the meals Donavan cooked for everyone. The rarely used dining room was now the church.

My gaze narrowed as one of the older members got handsy with Savannah, then I laughed when she gave them a hard enough whack that I could hear over the music. Laughter erupted around the room as I rested back in my seat. There wasn't a person in the room that couldn't handle themselves, which made it interesting when things occasionally got physical.

"You're quiet tonight. Something up?" My sergeant-at-arms, Blaze, slipped into the vacant seat beside me. His scowl, when aimed with cruel intention, could make a two-hundred-fifty-pound man piss his pants matched the air of authority. A jagged scar ran down his neck and disappeared into his black T-shirt, ending just below his sternum. It added to the menacing look he'd mastered. I'd dealt with the owner of the knife, but not before he'd tried to gut Blaze in a bar fight in Orlando two years back when we'd gone on a ride-out.

"I'm not feeling it, so I'm gonna head out for a ride."

One brow arched. "You're leaving? The party just got started." The surprise wasn't concealed.

"And your point is?" I asked, my voice hard enough to snap metal. He knew I didn't tolerate being questioned... by anyone.

His gaze held mine for a moment before it dipped, and he glanced away. "No point."

Not one to make a big deal of something when there wasn't a need. I swung my leg from the chair arm and got up. No one paid attention, which was expected, given the amount of liquor being consumed.

I nodded to the newest members. "Make sure they keep out of trouble. Pistol hasn't quite learned to tame his ass down."

There was a flash of something in Blaze's eyes as he searched for Pistol. "Will do," he replied, sounding distracted.

I shook off the odd sense there was something I was missing and threaded through the crowd, nodding but not stopping to chat. Chatting was not what I wanted. At least not the kind being offered here tonight.

One glance at my black skinny jeans and fitted black shirt as I walked through the clubhouse, I detoured to grab my leather jacket and open-faced helmet. Outside, the night sky was clear, the stars creating a bold tapestry across the inky black.

I inhaled the scent of the night. The spring teased the air as I stopped and took a moment to appreciate the metal beast sitting at the bottom of the steps. The Harley Davidson 1962 Electra Glide classic had been my granddaddy's, and he'd passed his passion on to me along with his hog.

It was a passion I indulged in as often as I could. I'd learned the mechanics of a motorcycle engine so I could fix anything on my hog because I didn't trust anyone else with my baby. The paint job was a custom black and silver skull and antlers with Reckless Riders in calligraphy on the tank. The motorcycle was recognizable everywhere in these parts.

Seconds later, helmet in place and hair tucked into the collar of my leather jacket, I reached for the ignition, starting the engine. The vibration and sound of the low rumbling shifted my thoughts to the ride and the night's potential.

The club in Jacksonville had lockers where I stored clothes. I was prepared for occasions such as tonight. Not that anyone would question me taking a backpack. It would waste time, and since I'd decided, I was eager to be on my way.

How long had it been? A month? Two? Fuck, where had the time gone? It also explained the way I was feeling. The gap between visits had decreased for a while, but with prospects vying for the limited patches, it made things more hectic than normal.

At the end of the long drive that led away from the house, I indicated left and took off. The roads weren't a problem as I skipped past the slower-moving cars. Rock Springs disappeared behind me as the motorcycle ate up the miles to Jacksonville. The hundred miles distance took less than a couple of hours on average and allowed my brain to switch gears for what was coming.

Being in control came naturally. Relinquishing it to someone else did not, unless it was the right person I trusted fully.

The ride was uneventful, and it let the tension ease a little from under my skin. I checked vehicles in the parking lot at the back of CKJ. A small smile tugged at my lips when I spotted the red Chevrolet Silverado. Harvey wanted to show it off the last time I'd been at the club, and we'd christened the back seat.

A buzz of excitement shot straight to my core as I got off my motorcycle, recalling how he'd spanked then fucked me right there in the parking lot. Pocketing the keys, I removed my helmet, striding around the side of the building to the front entrance.

This was a members-only place, so there was no line. Inside the door, the receptionist staffing the large black counter smiled. The cute twink, Ruben, had been working at the club as long as I'd been a member. He was always polite and friendly.

"Hey, Rivka. It's been a few weeks."

"It has." I dropped my helmet on the counter and slipped off my leather jacket. He took both from me. The coat room was separate from the locker room because it wasn't big enough to hold anything more than kink wear.

"Anything special on tonight, Ruben?" The jacket slipped onto a hanger, then placed next to my helmet before he walked to the large key cabinet holding members' locker keys.

He returned to the counter. "It's alternative lifestyles tonight." His smile widened. "Daddy Harvey arrived an hour ago. *Alone.*"

"Is that so?" I answered, matching his playfulness. I didn't kick playful puppies, regardless of how they saw more than I liked.

He winked cheekily at me. "I think he's been missing you."

Ruben was the kind of person who wanted to see everyone happy. It was something about the kid that I liked. But Harvey and I would never be more than whatever this was we had in the club. If there was a strange sensation of disappointment at that, I'd learned to push it aside. I reminded myself there was no conversation about life outside this place, and there was a reason for that.

In these walls, he was Daddy, and I was his girl, Riv, who liked to be naughty and get punished.

Yet tonight, his comment piqued my curiosity, and against my better judgment, I asked, "Why do you say that?"

His brows knotted together. "He's not played with any of the other girls in forever. He waits for you, and if you don't show, he leaves alone." His gaze moved to the door behind me as it opened, and the smile was back.

"I'll see you later," I murmured, ignoring the two women behind me, running through Ruben's revelation. Was Harvey only interested in me? Some butterflies came with a dose of pleasure I wasn't sure how to cope with. Would the intensity between us be the same outside these walls?

Thoughts heading in a direction I didn't like, I walked to the door leading to the locker room. It allowed the members to change before entering the club, keeping things private. The space was clean and well-lit.

I opened my locker and checked out the several outfits inside, none of which were suitable to wear anywhere near Rock Springs. I reached for a pink pinafore dress with layers of frills that sat over my backside and rustled when I walked, offering a view of the matching panties. The little white top under the dress barely covered my ample breasts.

Stripped and dressed before the other women appeared, I slipped the key chain around my wrist. The little kangaroo charm I'd added to distinguish it as mine clinked against the key.

All members had identifiers on their key chains. I'd always been fascinated by kangaroos, especially after watching two males boxing. There was something captivating about watching two alpha males fight.

Donning cute white shoes with small kitten heels, I contemplated putting on the stockings, but the women entered the room and made my decision easy. Both women smiled, and the anticipation between them made me wonder if they were a couple. I nodded, walking to the door that led into the club.

I inhaled and exhaled slowly, letting the anticipation of what was to come run through me before opening the door and stepping inside.

CHAPTER 2

⚜

Rivka

THE SIGHTS, sounds, and smells of sex drew me like a magpie to a shiny object. My gaze swept the room, searching. My pulse leaped at the sight of others engaging in many acts that ensured I soaked my panties before I'd taken more than a few steps into the club.

The place was classy, with hardwood floors and silver-gray walls that complemented the pewter-colored leather furniture situated around the room. They placed seats strategically in areas for those who like to watch others take part in sexual acts. The music was a low sexy throb that teased the skin with its base, but wasn't loud enough to block out the sounds couples were making. There was a bar, but it only sold soft drinks. The club had a strict no-alcohol policy.

A sliver of disappointment came when I didn't notice Daddy Harvey at his usual spot over by the long bench I could fully lie on. The piece of equipment had the ability to morph. The lower part could split apart and allow a Daddy to do all sorts of wicked things to his baby girl while cuffed.

Was Ruben wrong? Had Harvey left early?

A familiar scent came before a solid, warm figure pressed against my back. I swallowed a moan as a hand appeared in front of my face, holding a lollipop.

"Hey, baby girl," came a dark sultry voice that sent shivers down my spine. His masculine fragrance surrounded me. The flex and movement of his body were familiar, as was the cock pressed against the middle of my back.

A whimper escaped my parted lips when the lollipop came closer to my mouth and the scent of cherries filled my nose. Lips brushed my ear, warm breath touching the shell. "Have you been a good girl for Daddy?"

The husky words whispered next to my ear released the last feelings of tension, knowing Daddy would take care of me. I melted against him, heat running through me as I let him take charge. "No, Daddy."

A sharp nip to my ear followed the tutting. The sting didn't last long as he sucked the flesh into his mouth and soothed it with his tongue. "What to do with a naughty girl?"

It wasn't a question I needed to answer. After we'd hooked up the first couple of times, we'd set boundaries, including safe words, if I needed them. There was no playing allowed without permission and parameters. The club owner had strict rules to protect their patrons.

I shifted my weight so he would know what I was doing as I parted my thighs in invitation.

His free hand slipped under the ruffles of my skirt, and his warm flesh brushed against the back of my bare upper thigh. The hand inched slowly toward my panties as I held my breath, waiting for his touch. When it came, it was barely the brushing of one finger caressing from back to front, lingering on my clit.

"Already so wet for Daddy. Such a naughty girl." His teeth

grazed my neck before he nipped at the delicate skin of my throat, marking me.

I shivered in delight.

"Daddy's perfect little girl." To make his point, he pressed the wet silk against my clit. The pressure was nowhere near what I wanted or needed and made me want to beg. It had been too long. The wild fluttering in my belly increased as he drew circles with the tip of his finger against the wet silk. It took very little time to have me drenching my panties. Excitement was something that I could never hide from Daddy Harvey.

The couple sitting in the seats right in front of me paid a little more attention when the hand holding the lollipop disappeared from my view. There was a slurping sound next to my ear and lips smacking together. It reappeared in front of my face, covered in spit.

The moan was low and needy as the lollipop disappeared once more but down the front of me. A gasp turned into a moan when he eased my panties to the side, exposing my bare pussy to the couple wearing hungry expressions. My heart thudded hard against my ribs. I loved to be watched, and Daddy Harvey liked to show me off.

The slick, sticky lollipop he dragged along the folds of my wet pussy. My thighs quivered along with my belly at the arousal Daddy Harvey never failed to ignite. My juices flowed and soaked the lollipop.

I groaned as he pushed the round head inside me and held still. Time slowed as he teased us before slowly rotating and coating it in my essence. The stickiness was no match against the arousal coating my inner thighs.

Whimpers poured out of my parted lips at the potential of what came next when his cock thickened and pressed more firmly against my back. It was thick and long. He liked to make me choke on it when the occasion suited.

"Daddy, please," I begged. For what? I didn't know, but he did. I squeezed my inner muscles to hold on to the lollipop, acting out.

"Begging so soon, baby girl." His teeth were back to nipping at my throat before he sucked hard on the skin. The bite of pain wasn't enough. "Daddy is in charge, and you made him wait." Another nip, sharper than the last, and I shivered. "You don't get to come, naughty girl, until Daddy says you can."

My chest rose and fell as he tugged the lollipop from my body, leaving my clit throbbing with the need to come. Fingers stroked my pussy lips, not touching my clit. Then he pulled the wet silk back into place, and I groaned in resignation because he was making me pay for not returning sooner. That, however, didn't mean I wouldn't push him to see if I could get what I wanted.

He eased back, making sure I was steady, before turning me to face him. His features were tight with control. A full-lipped mouth was set in a square jaw with a cleft. Jet-black hair framed his angular face, threaded with silver at the temples. His eyes were captivating. They had a navy ring around a pale-blue center. The navy was more prominent when he became aroused.

I watched him suck the lollipop, his heavy-lidded, desirous eyes meeting mine. My pulse leaped hard enough to make breathing difficult, but it wasn't the desire that caused it. No, it was an expression I'd never seen before. Longing?

A moment later, it was gone, and I could pretend I'd never witnessed it.

Fuck!

Was he gonna mess things up?

I was always honest with myself, and I worried for a second about what it meant for me.

He licked the lollipop like it was my clit, causing my thoughts to flee faster than rats on a sinking ship. The throbbing need between my thighs had me clasping them together. My imagination worked to remind me just how that tongue could make me beg.

A rumbling noise came from him. "Your pussy is sweeter than the lollipop." He offered it to me, a wicked light in his eyes. "Suck it."

I moved closer, my lips parting as I rose on my tiptoes to reach the lollipop. I held his gaze as I slid my tongue around the wet, sticky goodness, putting on a show. The cherry flavor was prominent, but I could still taste myself and Daddy Harvey. The combination added to the desire pulsing at my core. I fluttered my eyelashes and sucked the lollipop fully into my mouth, making obscene slurping noises.

His nostrils flared and a dark hue coated his tanned cheeks as he watched my mouth with an intensity that never failed to arouse me. No one had ever competed with him. I'd had a couple of hookups at the beginning of whatever this was, and they were totally dissatisfying. Nothing I'd discovered competed with the high of having Harvey focus his sole attention on me. I worked the lollipop around my mouth until he tugged and showed he wanted it back.

I held on to it until his brows rose and the light in his eyes became a warning. "You are in a naughty mood. Are you trying to get a spanking?"

Hell yes, I was. I licked my sticky lips and coyly lowered my gaze. "No, Daddy."

"Tut-tut, you know what happens to a baby girl who tells Daddy fibs." The dark quality of his voice was all part of the game and made it hard to focus. He took hold of my hand and guided me toward our favorite spanking bench, which was free. He dropped the lollipop without care into an empty glass sitting on a table as we passed.

All around us folks dressed up or undressed for the occasion. Tonight, I wasn't interested in anyone but Daddy Harvey. It had been too long since I'd felt the heat of his hand striking my bottom.

His commanding presence drew attention. It was what had

caught mine. There was no one else in the club who had his powerful confidence. It wasn't his clothes. It was the aura that surrounded him. Not that the black pants and button-down he favored didn't add to the dominant vibe. They did. They fit him as if handmade. The quality of his clothes suggested he had money to spend, as did the OMEGA watch on his wrist and the vehicle outside.

I wasn't interested in his money. I had more than enough of my own. His attention, all of it, was what I wanted.

The stickiness between my legs increased as he positioned me on the spanking bench face-down. His hands slid under my ruffled skirt, slipping my panties off. I was acutely aware of those around us as I rested my cheek against the soft, padded leather. The room was warm, yet shivers of anticipation caused the tiny hairs on my arm to rise. Handcuffed to the top of the bench, my breathing rate increased.

A large hand stroked over my arms. "Color?"

"Green," I answered without hesitation when his face appeared in front of mine.

He nodded, the lines around his eyes deepening as he came forward and kissed me softly, belying the desire in his eyes. It crackled in the air between us as his tongue licked over my lips, seeking entry. I could taste myself on his tongue as it touched mine. I swallowed our groans as his hand ran down the side of my body. A second later, a leather cuff circled my ankle.

Moments later, he stopped kissing me, and a wicked grin caused me to squeeze my thighs together. His laughter followed as he disappeared, and he cuffed my other ankle to the bench. Then the table beneath my lower body moved, and it spread my legs wide. Excitement thrummed through me at how defenseless I felt while utterly safe in Daddy's hands. Warm air bathed my wet pussy, and I wondered if anyone was looking at me.

A finger ran from the front of my pussy, dipping briefly inside before moving to my asshole. He ran the wet tip of his finger over my hole, making me squirm. I sucked on my lower lip as he repeated the move and teased my asshole. The sensitive nerves awakened as he tormented me, adding a little pressure with each pass of his fingertip. More heat flooded my core as two fingers plunged into my pussy, then didn't move. The thickness was nowhere near what I needed.

I wriggled, unable to get any pressure on my clit, and squeezed my inner muscles, unable to move my legs. The metal chains of the cuffs clinked, alerting him to my antics.

A husky chuckle tickled my skin as he lifted the ruffles of my skirt. "Always so impatient." Teeth sank into my bottom cheek, and then his tongue lapped at the stinging flesh.

I moaned in complaint when he stopped the torment. The seconds ticked by, each one feeling longer than the next as I wondered what he'd chosen to spank me with. Daddy Harvey liked to use his hand, but occasionally would use a wooden paddle. Lying as I was, I couldn't twist my neck far enough to see what he was doing behind me.

I felt the weight of gazes on me as the sounds of others didn't compete with the buzzing in my ears. Was he staring at my naked pussy?

I jerked, sucking in a breath at the unexpected stinging slap to my pussy. The wet, lewd sound alerted anyone interested in how aroused I was by the treatment. The next slap to my wet flesh was harder, the sting lasting longer as I exhaled noisily. I lifted my ass, begging shamelessly for more.

"Such a dirty little girl," he growled and slapped my pussy repeatedly until the burn in my clit and lips morphed into a wild pleasure like nothing I'd experienced.

Arching into each spank, I needed more, desperate for him to take me to that floaty place.

"More, Daddy," I cried out at the next set of fast-paced spanks. My clit felt triple the size, yet his wet fingers didn't touch it. His hand position showed he was standing facing my feet, his fingers pointing down toward my untouched clit.

The spanking stopped, and he pushed three fingers into my pussy, the squelching sound loud. He instantly stopped moving, and I moaned, milking his fingers with my inner muscles. I wasn't disappointed when he spanked my ass, leaving his fingers where they were.

He spanked the cheeks alternatively, in different spots as his fingers widened inside me until I lost my focus. The stretch sent delicious curls of pleasure to my throbbing clit. I lost count of the spanks, my ass and pussy burning. My cry was low and mournful as my inner muscles rippled at the hot, flowing rush of pleasure. Lewd wet sounds continued as the fingers thrust in shallow pumps. The roughness of his thumb stroking over my soaking wet clit stole my breath.

The pain and pleasure bloomed together, and I screamed, my body melting against the padded bench. My pussy spasmed repeatedly. My eyelids fluttered closed as I dragged in ragged breaths while his fingers prolonged the white-hot pleasure.

Hot breath touched my ear. "Did Daddy say you could come?" he whispered in a menacing tone that wreaked havoc on my pulse.

I met his gaze and shuddered. "No, Daddy."

I didn't apologize. What was the point? I wanted this as much as he did.

CHAPTER 3

✣

ℋarvey

DRESSED AS SHE WAS, it was easy to see she'd flipped back to the woman who would cut a man's balls off for so much as suggesting she get on her knees to suck his cock. One look at her, and I'd wanted her. Bluebell-colored pretty eyes were wide, set in a face that ended with full lips and a pointy chin. One she led with when spitting mad. Something I'd only witnessed once when a dude touched her motorcycle.

That was the defining moment when I realized my feelings were deep. I was about to step in and deal with the issue when Rivka dealt with the three-hundred-pound man like he was a two-year-old toddler. The guy didn't know what hit him, and it left me with an understanding of exactly what Rivka offered me when she came to the club.

The only issue was going about showing her I wanted more. She had control. She picked when we played and what we talked about. For a while, it had been enough, but now...

"You didn't need to see me out," she said in a smoky rasp that stroked my cock like her hand.

I'd never tire of hearing her speak. "What kind of southern gentleman and Daddy would I be to not escort my *baby girl* to her ride?"

One slim brow rose, but she didn't correct me. Was that a good sign?

At her motorcycle, she tucked long blonde-and-brown curls into the collar of her leather jacket before holding out her hand for her helmet. "Thanks."

I stepped to her, ignoring the outstretched hand, placed the helmet on, and fixed the strap under her chin to secure it. Never once taking my eyes off hers, I noticed the moment she relinquished control, and my heart wanted to burst from my chest. I lowered my lips to an inch of hers, keeping her gaze. "Daddy wants to see you on the weekend for a date."

Her breath hitched and hit his face. Her lips parted and, convinced it would be a no, I pressed my mouth to hers gently. Teasing us both, I brushed our lips together, doing no more until she moaned, and her lips parted in invitation. I deepened the kiss degree by degree. My tongue stroked against hers before I slowly sucked it into my mouth, mimicking what I'd done to her clit only an hour ago.

Her body pressed against mine, her legs parted, and one threaded through mine. The other went around my thigh, and she wrapped herself around me. Nowhere near as tall as me, her hands came around my waist and dropped onto my ass. Her fingers dug in as she ground against me, taking exactly what she wanted.

It was these two sides that made her irresistible. Breathless and fast losing control, I eased back. Being a temptress, she didn't relinquish her hold. Her hips rolled and the flush in her cheeks increased. "Are you gonna come on Daddy's leg?"

She moaned, her pelvis pushing harder against my thigh. Her

eyelids fluttered closed for a second as her lips parted, and she released a guttural moan. One that made my cock throb hard enough that I wasn't quite convinced I'd be able to control myself.

The security lights and cameras watching us in the lot were no deterrent. Why would they be when this was my club? Something the woman getting off on my thigh was clueless about. She sagged in my arms, more than a little breathless, as a slow, sexy grin appeared. "One for the road, Daddy."

I chuckled at her cheekiness. "You know I'm going to make you pay for leaving me hard." I lowered my voice into a menacing tone that never failed to make her wet. "Don't you?"

She shivered in my arms, her eyelids dipped, and a coy look appeared. "Yes, Daddy."

I spanked her bottom hard enough to make my hand smart. The groan and backward push didn't help me. Breathing in the scent of her sex, I stared at her, knowing we'd both played the distraction game. But I wanted an answer.

"Daddy wants a date with his baby girl. Are you free this weekend?" I persisted, hoping I wasn't pushing her away, but I needed more than what we had.

She licked her lips, her brows drawing together. The air got stuck somewhere between my lungs and throat. "I ain't the kind of girl," she nodded toward the club, "a guy wants to date outside of there." She said it with utter seriousness.

"Do you think I don't know who you are?" I glanced at her motorcycle and ran a hand over the helmet. "Rock Springs ain't that far away, darlin'. I knew who you were the second I got a look at your hog. There ain't nothing that's gonna put me off. We've been doing this for three years, Rivka. I want more. What we have is special, and I want to see what it can be like outside of the club."

The frown deepened, and my heart took flight when she shook her head. "My world... fuck, you have no idea. You might think you know who I am, but you don't. I run Restless Riders. I'm the president."

If she thought she was knocking the wind out of my sails, she was wrong. "I know." It was my turn to nod toward the club behind her. "This is my place. I scrutinize every application. I'm careful about who joins the club. It's why we have the six-month short-term membership option for new members."

She let go and took a step back, a barrier forming between us. It was there, regardless. I couldn't see it, but I damn well felt it. "Listen, don't decide now. Go home and think on it," I coaxed, using my Daddy voice.

Her sigh was heartfelt as she pinched the bridge of her nose. "This ain't a good idea."

Taking the lack of conviction in her tone as a good sign, I removed the distance she'd put between us. Brushing my lips against her soft ones, I murmured, "It is. Daddy wants you to take a chance." I deepened the kiss until she was breathless, her chest pressing against me. "And I will reward my baby girl for taking the risk for me."

She moaned at the meaning behind my words. "You ain't playin' fair."

Kissing her once more, I reluctantly let go and stepped back from temptation. "When has Daddy ever played fair when he knows what's best for his baby girl?"

The hesitation was long and lasted over ten seconds—I counted—before she nodded slowly. "I'll think about it."

I kept the grin to myself as she spun around and walked to her motorcycle. Her ass flexed in her tight jeans as she swung her leg over the seat. The engine's roar filled the night and gravel spat at my legs as she took off without a backward glance.

Watching her leave was hard, but this time, there was hope, or I fucking prayed there was. She was complex, with many layers that I wanted to unwrap. Would she see I could offer her what she wanted without making her less than she was?

I hadn't lied. I knew who she was, having vetted every applicant to prevent issues we'd had in the past with fake IDs and those

2023 RARE AUSTRALIA ANTHOLOGY

not genuinely interested in the lifestyle. Yet, when we'd played those first few times, I hadn't associated her application with the woman who wanted a Daddy. It surprised me when I escorted her to her motorcycle, and it finally registered who she was. Her reputation as a ball breaker was renowned in these parts. Rock Springs might be over a hundred miles away, but a motorcycle chapter like Reckless Riders had a far reach.

There wasn't much, it seemed, the club hadn't been associated with, and if I believed everything on the internet, it was up there with some of the most renowned clubs out there. Did I care? Nope, not one fuck. I wasn't lily white, and many would class me as a bad boy. I owned a fucking BDSM club where I got off on punishing women to orgasm.

The problem was that lately, there'd only been one woman I wanted that with. These last two months had been hell as I'd waited for her to show up every day. Second-guessing myself when she'd be a no-show. It was pathetic, is what it was. Tonight, when I'd seen her arrive, I'd known I'd broken my own rules about falling for a woman who should only be someone to play with. Things were going to have to change.

The dying sounds of the engine roaring away brought the reality that I was standing in the parking lot, staring into space. I sighed and walked around the front of the building, going back into the club, which was also my home.

"Hey, boss, you okay?"

Ruben was a sweet boy, and I resisted snapping at him when the unsettled feelings in my gut had fuck-all to do with him. "I'm fine." I was far from it. His worried look said the same.

I kept walking, not needing or wanting his concern. I keyed in the code for the door that led up to the second floor where I lived. The apartment covered the entire floor above the club and was open-plan. When I'd had the place renovated, I ensured there was a door leading up to my apartment in the lobby area and one accessible from the outside if I wanted to escape prying eyes.

Checking the time, I headed into the kitchen. The sleek gray countertops and kitchen cabinets matched the rest of the open space. I liked gray. There were splashes of red dotted about to add color. I'd gone with black for the rugs covering the wooden floor.

I opened the door of the large silver fridge and eyed the plated meals. The woman who took care of my home, Maisy, also cooked a batch of meals for me once a week. I took out a plate of chili and placed it in the microwave.

While I waited for it to heat, I grabbed a glass and filled it with Pepsi. Two minutes later, I sat at the counter and dug into the spicy food, contemplating the odds of me having to chase after Rivka. As I saw it, it was a fifty-fifty shot either way. What would tip the balance in my favor?

I stared unseeingly at the food, chewing without tasting it, my mind running through the few things I knew about Rivka.

My lips turned up in a smile, one that was full of mischief. What woman didn't like gifts? Pretty gifts that came with side benefits?

CHAPTER 4

$\mathscr{L}$

Rivka

"Rivka, there's a dude at the door. Says he's got somethin' you need to sign for," Pistol called from the hallway.

"What the fuck? Someone break your hands, Pistol?" I shouted back, annoyed that he'd broken my concentration while I was checking the income spreadsheet for the club.

There were seconds of silence before he hollered back, "Nah, the dude says he's got instructions you gotta sign for the package. It seems I ain't allowed."

I rolled my eyes, my pulse spiking for a moment at what or who would insist on me signing for a package. We'd had run-ins with rival chapters over the years, one of which had sent a dead opossum boxed up. Sick fucks.

Resigned, I placed my laptop on the small table beside the couch where I was doing the bookkeeping. Pistol stood by the front door, glaring at the guy holding a big box. The dude looked as if he were about to piss his pants.

"What do I need to sign?" When his eyes swept over me, I asked, ignoring the wide-eyed stare. I was used to that type of reaction. I was full-figured, with long blonde-and-brown-streaked curls that lay over ample breasts, and my face wasn't unattractive either, I supposed.

He held out an electronic pad with a plastic pen. "Sign here."

Doing as he requested, I eyed the brown packaged box. I had no memory of ordering anything, and definitely nothing that would require my signature.

A second later, Pistol shut the door on the guy without saying another word to him. He eyed the box I was holding. I looked to see if there was a label or anything indicating who sent it. The shipping label caught my eye. *Jacksonville!*

Would he send me a gift?

I ran my tongue over my teeth and swung around, heading for the stairs leading to the part of the house off-limits to the club members.

"What is it?" Pistol called out behind me.

Not stopping, I snapped back, "I look like I got x-ray vision to you? And what fucking business is it of yours?"

There was a mumbled, "Sorry," before boots clumped off in the opposite direction.

Up in my bedroom, I locked the door with trembling fingers. It had been two days since I'd left the club. Two days of doing anything to avoid thinking about Harvey's suggestion. Of how much I wanted to say yes. At the time, I'd put it down to the sex high I was riding. But the urge to say yes hadn't waned, and why I was doing my best not to think too hard on it. Only the fuck wasn't playing fair.

I eyed the box I held. It wasn't heavy, and with the shipping label, along with the request for my signature, there was no doubt in my mind Harvey had sent it.

Going to the unmade bed, I set the box on the covers and stared at it like it might bite me. I shook it, which didn't give me any information. "Fucking open it!" I muttered angrily at the edge of excitement I refused to fully acknowledge.

I'd never been given a gift just because. Searching for a gap in the tape, I blew out a breath. I ripped into the brown paper, letting it drop to the floor at the sight of the pretty box. Breath hitching, I flipped open the lid only to gasp at the dress laid in pink tissue paper.

It was a Macgraw silk and wool baby doll dress worth around nine hundred dollars. Something I'd never waste my money on. Oh, I'd looked at it online a time or two when I'd been looking to add to my collection for the club. The frivolous expense wasn't for me, but that didn't mean I didn't want one. I had to give Harvey kudos for knowing this would be something that would appeal to me.

With a shuddery breath, I lifted it out of the box. The scooped neck and puffed sleeves were gorgeous. The mix of wool and silk made the material flow under my fingers, and I couldn't resist stroking it. It was too much to resist the need to try it on.

I eyed the locked door before stripping off all my clothes, wanting to feel the silky material against my naked skin. Raised to wear practical jeans and T-shirts, they didn't take thought when getting dressed.

The side of me that got excited over dresses I kept for the BDSM club. It was more than obvious that everything I'd done to keep the two sides of my life separate collided as I put on the dress. Damn the man!

It fit perfectly. They cut the top to cup the wearer's breasts in a way that allowed me to go braless. The flick of the hem showed off my bottom when I twirled. I danced in front of the mirror inside my closet door. The pink complemented the golden tan on my long, lean legs. My gaze returned to the box. Wondering whether there was a card or something inside, I noticed what else they'd tucked into the tissue paper.

Back at the box, I groaned. My body heated, recalling the last pair of panties I'd worn like the ones in the box. Picking up the pale-pink ruffled panties, I released a shuddery breath, knowing I was going to break another rule. Don't date outside the club. *It was dangerous, but the fucker wasn't playing fair!*

At the bottom of the box was a white card with a bold script.

Daddy requests the pleasure of his Baby Girl's company at six p.m. this Saturday.

Please don't disappoint Daddy, and wear the dress.

Underneath was the club's address, but the first line was for the second floor. I presumed it was his... home?

There was no number, not that it wouldn't be hard to find one for the club to leave a message if I wasn't going to go. I caught my reflection in the mirror and didn't miss the smile I wore.

Damn! This was a mistake!

Then why was I excited?

* * *

IT WAS easy to slip out midafternoon when everyone was busy doing whatever they did during the weekend. It would be late evening before the club would become busy. During the weekends, the place was open to members and their partners. But they had to be affiliated with the club to get inside as a member or a prospect.

Prospects had six months to prove their loyalty and honor to the club and must complete the initiations without complaint. Not all made it through. The hazing by other members could be brutal.

Having a bar inside the clubhouse and prospects working for us had been Blaze's idea of keeping the townsfolk from complaining about members being drunk and starting fights. It also stopped cops from knocking on our door, looking for any excuse to arrest members. It had been too regular, and though we weren't too worried about keeping a low profile, it made sense not to invite trouble into our backyard. As most were fiends for liquor, it also made good sense because the profits flowed back into the club. The cash helped fund the ride-outs that went out of state for chapter get-togethers. There were four every year, so members could meet and catch up on what was happening with other club members.

The other chapters were all run by men, and I could imagine what they'd have to say about this side of my life. It was a hard world to live in as a female, with it being mainly male-dominated. Seeing where my thoughts were headed, I pushed them aside like I'd been doing since I'd booked the hotel and give myself this one night.

I pressed the electronic key card against the lock of the hotel door. I'd booked a place just two miles from the club, and it was fancy enough that folks were polite and didn't give me a second look. I dropped my helmet, leather jacket, and backpack on the bed. I reached to unzip my pack to check to see if the dress had survived the trip. I grinned when I unrolled it to see the hack I'd found online had worked to prevent creases. There was no way I'd have been able to transport it in a dress bag on my motorcycle and not draw unwanted attention.

Blaze had already given me odd stares after I'd explained about leaving for the weekend, so he needed to keep an eye on things for me. He hadn't asked where I was going, but I could see the questions in his eyes. It was unheard of for me to go anywhere overnight without other club members.

The uneasy feeling that I was standing on train tracks with my feet tied to the metal rails, about to get hit by the oncoming train, was there waiting to surface. I wasn't one to make mountains out of molehills. That wasn't me. I dealt with what came at me the only way I knew how: head-on. Was that going to be enough?

You're gonna find out when you step into that club tonight!

One more look at the dress, and I checked the time. I had an hour before the rideshare I'd scheduled would arrive. Going into the bathroom, I stripped off to shower. I hadn't bothered before leaving because it was warm enough to make me sticky while riding. Waiting for the shower to warm, I eyed my body critically.

I'd gone to the beauty parlor the day before to get waxed. My skin was smooth and silky. There was none of the redness that could sometimes happen when getting waxed so soon after the last one. I had long, lean legs and my bottom was full and firm. Round hips balanced my large breasts. I liked my curves, regardless of the unwanted attention they'd drawn when I'd filled out at fourteen.

I'd learned to use them to my advantage in my late teens, but I was in my twenties before I had my first encounter with a man who wanted a baby girl. The couple of times we'd hooked up, I'd discovered being that way wasn't a weakness. It was a powerful turn-on. Knowing those close to me wouldn't be accepting, I'd sought information and places to go where I could keep my needs private and get to fulfill my fantasies.

The first place I'd attended, fifty miles from Rock Springs, got too close for comfort when I spotted one of the prospects there. That lead to a search for a place far away in Jacksonville, ultimately leading to Harvey. I shook my head.

He owned the club and had known all along who I was, and it hadn't put him off. I had to give him credit for that. Men I'd encountered in the past couldn't escape fast enough when they found out who I rode with. It was why I'd made a rule only to date men affiliated with the club. There'd been no dates in nearly three years, and I didn't need to be a rocket scientist to figure out what and who was the reason for that.

Fucked up was what it was!

It didn't stop me, which was the actual issue.

Hot water cascaded down my body, and I tried to be annoyed at Harvey for moving the finish line, bringing me to this point. Reaching for the soap, I lathered up and rubbed soapy hands over my breasts, then down my body, following the path of the soapy water between my legs. I was in a semi-aroused state and had been since the dress had arrived. Anticipating what would happen tonight ensured I got a brief reprieve, especially when I was in a hotel planning my first actual date with Daddy Harvey.

A knot developed in the pit of my stomach, and I sucked in a scented, steamy breath. My thoughts were on Harvey as I stroked my slick skin. The man oozed confidence that pressed every button I had. He didn't question what I enjoyed. Didn't make me feel less about wanting him the way I did. It was refreshing when I was always on guard to protect myself and those I chose as family.

My granddaddy was the one who introduced me to Reckless Riders. The club members reciprocated his passion for motorcycles. He'd been a member for two decades when I joined. Mom had been spitting mad, and there'd been a knock-down fight between her and my granddaddy that I'd watched from the sidelines. They'd gone toe-to-toe and, after that, hadn't spoken again. Mom had focused on training me rather than loving me, which he'd pointed out was to her detriment.

His death, a year before hers, didn't mellow her any. She'd turn in her grave if she knew I was president, whereas I could imagine my granddaddy kicking up his heels, wanting to celebrate for me. Those in the club were my family now. Would Harvey understand that?

I finished washing my body, no closer to finding an answer. *This is only for one night, so what does it matter?*

Fuck!

I turned my attention to washing my hair, and half an hour later, with my hair dried and flowing over my scented shoulders, I spread the remaining jasmine oil I used on my body to my legs. Once applied, I washed off the excess oil, drying my hands before walking back into the bedroom.

Hesitating in the middle of the room, the seconds ticked down before I exhaled and slipped on the dress. Zipped up, I reached for the panties and slid them up my legs. The kitten-heeled pink shoes I'd found in a sale and never gotten around to taking to the club went perfectly with the dress.

My pulse picked up as I caught my reflection in the mirror opposite the end of the bed. I didn't wear makeup because I didn't like the feel on my skin. The evening sunlight coming through the window caught the rosy glow in my cheeks and the sparkle in my eyes.

Picking up my purse, I rolled my shoulders like a fighter in a boxing ring and walked out of the bedroom before I changed my mind.

I headed down the passageway and out of the hotel, hoping this wasn't the biggest mistake of my life.

The sun glinted off the metal frame of my motorcycle in the parking lot. The knot was back in my stomach, but this time, it came with a throbbing at my temples.

Our worlds were vastly different. Who the fuck was I kidding?

CHAPTER 5

*H*arvey

IF EVER THERE was a temptation to pace, tonight would make me do just that. Instead, I'd sat on the couch, channel hopping while listening for the door buzzing. It was two minutes after six, and I wasn't going to believe she wasn't coming. She'd not returned the dress, and I hadn't received a call to say she wasn't coming.

Rudeness was not something I'd expect from Rivka. She'd been nothing but direct and honest in all our interactions. The three days to think about our past had given me a lot to mull over. There'd been sixty-one nights that she'd come to the club. A couple of hours here and there, while other nights she'd stayed longer. Over the last year, I'd watched and waited for her every night. What I'd come to realize was that she never once approached anyone else. And as far as my memory served, I was the only one she'd ever shown any interest in. Did she realize that?

My gaze flew to the door at the sound of the buzzer, and I was off the seat fast enough to make my head spin. I flicked off the TV and threw the remote on the table, walking to the door. Inhaling and exhaling to calm my ass down, I pressed the intercom. "Hello."

"It's me," she snapped, making me grin.

I pressed the button to open the lower entrance, going to the door to wait for her. The hard knock of my heart against my ribs stunned me as much as the woman coming up the stairs. She wore a pissed-off expression that made my blood pump faster because I was a perverse fucker who loved that curl of her lips. Blonde-streaked hair cascaded over the delicate skin of her shoulders and the tops of her breasts. The pink of the dress made her tan glow. The skin below the hem of the dress at the top of her thighs gleamed like polished bronze.

"What a beautiful baby girl you are!" Her foot faltered on the top step, her uncertain gaze meeting mine. It was a first, and my heart flipped with the need to declare my feelings at the sign of vulnerability.

Patience, something I had in spades, held me in check. I smiled, oozing the confidence she loved, and went to kiss her plump pink lips.

"I hope you're hungry," I breathed against her mouth. I kissed her with deep emotion after her lips parted. Her taste was sweet and irresistible.

Her moan tugged at my arousal, and I took a step back, wanting to show her this wasn't all about sex. I took her free hand and guided her inside.

She looked around as I shut the door. "You've got a thing for gray."

It was a statement, but I answered anyway. "I do. It gives a sleek, sexy vibe and can also be calming."

I pointed to where the doors were. "Through there is the guest bathroom if you need it. My bedroom"—I indicated to the door to the left of the bathroom—"is in there, and the room on the other side is my playroom."

Slim brows arched up before her gaze narrowed on the closed door. "You have many folks up here to play?"

There was something in her tone that got me looking closer at her. Was she jealous? Stupidly pleased at the notion she could be, I set her straight. "No. *Up to now,* I've invited no one into my home."

There looked to be both shock and disbelief in her gaze. "I bought the club four years ago after a breakup with my long-term girlfriend. I needed a fresh start." When her head tilted to the side, she had a question in her eyes. "It wasn't an amicable breakup, shall we say."

She placed her purse on the arm of the couch as she passed it, walking deeper into the room, offering a view of her ass covered in silk ruffles.

"Were you unhappy with the breakup?"

It took a moment to register her question. "Yes, but not in the way you might be thinking. Letty liked to play with others too, which was fine when we were together in the club. It became a problem when she liked to do it in our home when I wasn't there."

"Oh." Rivka turned, and her expression was impossible to read. "What was the difference if you liked to share her in public?" Her tone had no inflection, making it impossible to read her.

I walked to her, enjoying the scent of jasmine on her warm skin. I took hold of her hands, pressing kisses to the knuckles of both before answering honestly while enjoying the furrow between her brows as she looked at her hands in mine. "She needed more than I could offer her. She invited men into our bed when I was working after we'd discussed it wouldn't happen in our home. I accepted she needed more than just me, and in the club, I agreed to that because of being included."

Her fingers tightened on mine. "But you didn't like it, did you?"

"No, I didn't. People watching my partner and me together I enjoy. I won't deny it. I don't particularly like it when others touch what I deem is mine," I said in utter seriousness. So there were no illusions between us because I was possessive and I wanted to make that clear. Rivka got off on being watched—there was no denying it—but to date, she hadn't seemed inclined to let anyone else join in. A part of me knew if she asked, I wouldn't be able to deny her. My feelings for her were stronger than those I'd had for Letty.

As if plucking the thought from my head, she fluttered her eyelashes at me, giving me a meek smile that did crazy things to my pulse. "Would you let someone touch me if I asked nicely?"

"Would you ask me?" I fired back in a firm tone that got her eyes glinting with desire.

"No. You know what I like." She glanced down at the dress and back at me. "Folks watching me is fine, but touching I reserve..." The pause was long, but I waited, needing to hear her say it aloud. To ease the fear that she was dating one member of Reckless Riders when she came to see me. "For one person at a time."

The breath I'd held hissed through my teeth, and before I could think twice, I tugged her close, kissing her upturned mouth. The heat between us was faster than someone switching on a gas burner. I imprisoned her hands against my chest as I devoured her lips, hungry to take what she offered. She melted against me, and once more, I had to take a moment and step back from the temptation to forget my evening plans of getting to know each other. We'd already been dating in reverse, not that I'd say that aloud. I wasn't sure she was ready to acknowledge that.

I kissed the end of her nose. "Come on. I didn't slave over a hot stove for nothing."

She had an adorably confused look on her face, something I also wasn't going to point out. "You did?"

"It's a date," I pointed out, wanting to make it clear it wasn't a club hookup. "I made pot roast. I'm just hoping you don't have any food intolerances or are vegetarian."

Her nose wrinkled, and she glanced from the stove to the table tucked into the corner of the room next to a large window that looked out toward the beach, giving the illusion we weren't in the heart of a big city. There were glasses and silverware on the table with pretty napkins I'd found in a drawer, probably something Mom had given me. "Nope, I'll eat anything. And I love a good pot roast."

"Great." I let go of one hand, keeping hold of the other while leading her to the counter. "Beer, wine, or something stronger? Or are you riding back tonight?"

I eyed the dress, considering where she might have changed before arriving. She always got changed in the club and used the option the club offered to launder clothes for members. The club didn't open until nine p.m., and I couldn't see her riding her hog dressed as she was.

"I booked into a hotel for the night."

The kick to my pulse came with all the possibilities. "You have the entire night free?"

The nod came, but slowly. "Just tonight. It's a first and a last. It won't be happening again." The warning was there in the seriousness of her tone.

This time, my heart kicked up a stink for a completely different reason. The stubborn line of her jaw had me reconsidering and biting back my initial denial at her words. If I wanted her, I needed to play smart.

Instead of demanding she acknowledge what was between us, I deepened my tone ruthlessly using my Daddy voice. "Then Daddy better make the most of the time he has with his baby girl. You will spend the night with me." It wasn't a question.

She shivered, and her fingers clasped mine tightly, as if she didn't want to let go. "Yes."

Changing tack, we went to the table, and I pulled out a seat for her. A furrow between her brows showed she was confused. I refrained from chuckling when she didn't sit, but stared at the chair I'd pulled out for her. The gentlemanly gesture was clearly alien to her.

I brushed back her hair to expose her neck and kissed the scented skin. "Daddy likes to treat his baby girl like a princess. Sit for Daddy." The pulse under my lips bounded before she lowered into the seat. "What would you like to drink? I have a bottle of Bryant cabernet, which is a treat for the palate."

Shapely brows rose. "I don't normally drink, but I'll try your fancy wine."

Going to the counter where I'd left the bottle I'd opened to let it breathe, I poured two glasses. Leaving one on the counter, I returned to Rivka. She took the glass, and I waited as she sniffed, then sipped. "It's... nice."

I chuckled at her comment. "I'm sure they were hoping for more than 'nice.'"

She shrugged, and silky strands of hair fell over the creamy flesh of the tops of her breasts. "I ain't no expert who's gonna prattle on about the undertones of this and that." She sniffed once more. "Smells like wine."

The deep belly laugh got her grinning at me, and a little of the tension that had reared up at her earlier comment dissipated with the relaxed way she reclined back on the chair, glass in hand.

"You got me there. Let's hope you like it as much in the pot roast." I returned to the kitchen, chatting as I took the plates from the warmer and pulled the large pot from the oven. The scent of roasting meat and vegetables received a groan from the woman watching me closely.

"Who taught you to cook?" she asked when I lapsed into silence while plating the food.

"My mom. She said it was the way into a woman's heart. Said the first time Dad made her dinner, she fell for him head over heels." I picked up the plates and walked back to the table, where the frown was back as she eyed the plates I held. My stomach dipped as I searched for something to say. "What about your parents? Did your mom teach you to cook?"

As I placed the plate in front of her, I didn't miss her flinch. "Mom taught me how to fight."

I hesitated at the seriousness of her response. "Fight?" I asked when she didn't quite meet my gaze.

"She taught martial arts, contact and non-contact. It was her thing. It was how she met my father. He was her teacher."

Each word felt like someone was attempting to extract a tooth from her mouth. I took my seat and watched her pick up her napkin and place it on her lap before picking up her cutlery. Her movements were stiff. "I'm sorry, baby girl. Have I touched on a hard subject?"

She stiffened fully as her eyes sparked with temper. "I don't enjoy talking about past shit. Who wants to talk about my deadbeat father who skipped out of town faster than a damn tornado, leaving behind a devastated young pregnant girl who couldn't see past the fact that he wasn't coming back, no matter what she did to train me to show him how good she was?"

Her chest was heaving, tightening the dress's fabric with every breath. I stood and came around the side of the table, kneeling next to her, needing to soothe her.

I took the cutlery out of her trembling hands and laid it down, seeing I caused her upset by wanting to get to know her. "I'm sorry. I didn't realize your past would upset you like this," I breathed.

The chair shot back as she stood, glaring down at me. She fisted her hands, and I resisted reaching out when stubbornness competed with anger. Both of which I was sorry I'd caused. "Why do folks need to do this?" A hand swept the table, and I rose as she continued to rant. "Sex works just fine without this. I knew this was a mistake. I ain't cut out for this, can't you see?"

Carefully, I lifted a hand and cupped her flushed cheek, monitoring her hands. "I want to get to know you beyond the sex. I don't think it's wrong. It's just different." I was pretty sure from her reactions that she hadn't dated much.

I stroked my thumb over her silky skin, desperate to soothe her. "As a Daddy, I want, *no need,* to get to know you so I can take care of my baby girl in the way she needs."

She growled low and mean, but didn't move back. "Who says I need you to do anything for me? I've been taking care of myself for decades. I could rip your damn balls from your body before you could figure out you'd fucking lost them."

Refraining from shuddering at the menace I knew wasn't pretense, I brushed a light kiss over her parted lips. "I know," I murmured, "it doesn't mean Daddy wouldn't want to be there for his baby girl when she needs him to be. It's not a weakness to allow someone to hold you once in a while and share any burdens." I deepened the kiss when she didn't pull away.

Her moan was low and needy, whereas her body remained tense and unyielding. The fear of her pulling away before I had a chance kept me kissing her. Could I sway her? Make her see what I had to offer before the night was over?

CHAPTER 6

Rivka

Every fiber in me fought against the need to give in. The kiss continued until I was breathless and aroused that one touch would have been all it would take to make me come.

"Please stay and give me the night," he begged, appearing uncaring that he was the one begging.

A shuddery breath escaped as he released me to bend and pick up the napkin that had fallen off my lap. My legs were shaky, and I used that as an excuse to sit back in the chair. His behavior, his home, was all so normal and not anything I was used to dealing with. I couldn't find my balance in what he perceived as normalcy. I should have expected he'd want to know more, but I was used to those around me not asking. I hadn't given it any thought. If I was honest, when he suggested a date, I'd expected it would be pretty much what happened in the club, only in his bedroom behind closed doors. When he'd initially mentioned he'd hoped I was hungry, I hadn't registered he meant for food.

On top of that, I was still reeling from the feelings of furious jealousy over him talking about an ex-girlfriend. The woman was a fool if she hadn't seen what a catch Harvey was. To cheat in their bed, what kind of woman did that? I wanted to hunt her down and...

And that was the fucking problem. Everything he was doing for me and the feelings that surfaced was... too much and scared me. I'd promised myself one night, yet sitting and watching him ready a meal for us, I envisioned more nights like this. But this wasn't my life. It was the stuff of dreams, and I didn't do dreaming. It was costly in a soul-crushing way.

He silently placed the napkin over my lap and then returned to the counter to retrieve his forgotten glass of wine. Back in his seat, glass on the table, he picked up his cutlery, aiming a smile at me that oozed sex appeal, yet around his eyes was the strain I'd put there at freaking out.

"Daddy's sorry for upsetting you. Shall we eat before the food gets cold?"

Once more, I picked up my cutlery, being led by him, unsure the knot that had formed at his questions would allow me to swallow the deliciously scented food.

"I was born in Florida. My parents still live here." He spoke after I'd started to eat and kept the conversation about him and his family, which I was grateful for.

Feeling safer, I asked, "Is your brother older?"

He swallowed the mouthful of food and then took a sip of the wine. "He's forty-one, two years younger than me. Something he never lets me forget." He chuckled. "We are both very competitive. But there's little I can do about my age."

"Does he still live in Florida?"

"Yep, near to where we grew up. He bought a house with his boyfriend five years ago, and his boyfriend refuses to move now that they've set down roots. They have three dogs, so Oswald doesn't travel far because of the dogs getting carsick."

"Don't your parents help?"

His rich laughter boomed out. "Mom's allergic to dogs, so that would be a big no. Dad won't stay over there without Mom, so until Oswald can find someone he trusts with his fur babies, he doesn't travel."

"Oh." There wasn't anything more to say about that. I'd never had a pet, so I didn't get what the fuss was about.

The conversation stayed light. He talked a little about the club and the one he'd owned in Orlando, which his parents were aware of. Something else we didn't have in common was his parents accepting him and his lifestyle.

The list was growing, and over the evening, I tried not to tally them as I drank his fancy wine and ate the meal he'd cooked for me.

With the meal finished and his refusal of my help, I watched him over the rim of my third glass of wine as he filled the dishwasher. The apartment was clean and tidy. "Do you have someone who keeps the place clean for you? Or do you do it yourself?"

He stopped what he was doing and grinned. "If I say I have Maisy, the woman that cleans daily in the club and comes up here too, would that lose me some points? And I have to confess she also makes my meals once a week, so I don't starve."

I frowned at the pot on the counter. "Didn't you say you can cook?"

"I can and do, but running the club takes a lot of time and energy, and cooking for one isn't as much fun as cooking for two."

"So, you made the meal tonight?"

The grin was infectious. "I did. I don't tell lies, and I'd do anything for my baby girl." The sincerity was hard to ignore.

Bringing the glass to my lips, I swallowed a big mouthful, letting it wash away the silly urge to ask what that would entail. One meltdown this evening was enough, and I was pleasantly relaxed now that he'd kept the conversation away from my personal life.

Once he returned to the table after refilling our glasses, he suggested I sit on the couch. There I continued to watch him, which was an easy habit when he was so attractive and moved confidently no matter what he was doing. Moments later, music, something bluesy and relaxing, filtered through speakers I couldn't see. He came and sat next to me on the couch, his arm going over the back of the cushion after he'd picked up his wine.

"How many members are there in the Rock Springs chapter?"

The sip of wine I'd taken went down the wrong way, and I coughed, feeling like we'd gone back a step to when he'd wanted to talk about my family. I placed the glass on the low table in front of the couch.

The sigh was soft, but I heard it. His mouth opened, but I answered before he could say more while I settled back and looked at him. "In our chapter, there are a hundred and twenty-six members."

"Do you have a clubhouse?"

There was no way I'd talk about club business, but since it was my home, there was no harm in mentioning that. "It's my home. The original place got damaged in a tropical storm."

"That's awfully generous of you. It must make things hard when you want some downtime."

I eyed him suspiciously.

A hand moved under my hair and gently stroked the skin at the base of my skull. It was gentle but firm enough to help with the tension I held there. "I'm used to it," I finally answered when he raised a brow.

"I love my club, and I spend a lot of time down there, but I still need a space to come and just breathe."

My eyelids fluttered as his fingers slid into my hairline, rubbing my skull. "I have the floors upstairs. That's off-limits." Was I slurring my words? The magic fingers continued to move between the base of my neck and the back of my skull.

"That's good to know." His voice sounded far away, but for

some reason, I wasn't bothered when he shifted, and I found myself tucked into his side. I rested my head on his shoulder and tilted it just enough to give him freer access to the top of my shoulders.

The music, the solid feel of his body pressing against me, and his scent, along with the touches, had me drifting into a dreamy state.

* * *

A SOLID WARMTH pressed against my back, and the weight of an arm laying over my stomach caused my brain to surface slowly. I licked my dry lips, a dull ache at the back of my eyes as I registered the aroused cock nestled against my lower back. Oh fuck! How had I gotten into bed?

It was obvious I was no longer in Harvey's living room. The scent in the room was easily identifiable. Light filtered through the edges of the blinds, announcing it was no longer night but morning.

I had no memory of getting undressed or how I'd gotten into the bedroom. Had he carried me? Undressed me?

I expected panic over the lack of control, at never having slept a night in with another person, but there was nothing but warmth circulating through my loose-limbed body. The man behind me shifted, and I held my breath as he rolled the other way. The loss I felt was immediate, and that was when the panic came.

Holding my breath, I slid out of bed carefully. With my pulse pounding hard enough to feel it pushing into my throat, I stood beside the bed, staring at the sleeping man. The dim light was enough to make out how peaceful he looked. Dark, long eyelashes lay over his cheekbone. His lips were slightly parted as he breathed deep and even. There was something so compelling about him, even in sleep. I wasn't going to deny that he wanted more from me than I was willing to give. That I would consider trying sent me over to the clothes laying on a chair next to the bed. I picked up my clothes and shoes, tiptoeing out of the room, glad he'd left the door open.

Dressing quickly, I didn't look back at the open bedroom door. Purse in hand, I dashed out of the apartment when the urge to go back and crawl into bed with Harvey became a sharp pain in the center of my chest. I ran down the stairs and out into the bright sunlight, blinded for a moment. I blinked to clear my blurry vision, which I blamed on the sun.

I sniffed, wiped the back of my hand over my eyes, then looked up at the second floor, giving myself a moment to consider what life could be like with Harvey if things were different. I rolled my shoulders, turned away, and walked down the block toward the direction of the hotel. Life wasn't different, so there was no point in wishing.

I didn't look back, knowing with certainty I would never return, regardless of how much that hurt my heart right then. *It would ease*, it would.

Reckless Riders was all I needed, was all I'd ever needed, and no man would change that.

* * *

THEIR STORY CONTINUES in Part 2 &3 of Reckless Riders coming soon!!!

Eccentric cake lover who has a passion for words of all kinds. I'm Jayne or JP, and my pen names are, J Paton (Crime), JP Sayle (MM paranormal, romance) and Jayne Paton (M/F romance). I live in the Isle of Man which is a tiny place in the Irish sea where all the magic happens. I'm a confessed bookaholic and if I'm not writing I love to snuggle with a book or two...if you catch my drift.

I've a wondering heart, a love of the sea and travelling to different places. Some of the places I've been, can be found in my world of books all you need to do is open the pages.

PIPE DREAMS BY K.L. SHANDWICK

RARE ANTHOLOGY

I hope you love the RARE experience in Melbourne and this short anthology piece of my work.

CHAPTER 1

"Stop!" I hissed in a whisper. "There's no way we're gonna get away with this." I blinked rapidly in the dark likethis was suddenly going to give me the superpower of seeing clearly, I eventually gave up and stared wide-eyed in the pitch-black corridor. Why I'd listened to my ride-or-die bestie Sasha, I'd never know.

I concluded Sasha Callan was a witch. That was the only explanation for her having the ability to talk me into sneaking backstage in the hopes of a five-minute meeting with her favorite rock idol. Sasha's determination to meet him had been fueled because she'd written a self-published book after being inspired by the lyrics of one of his songs.

"What the—" I muttered in a stage whisper when she'd acci-dently grabbed my boob in the dark.

"Shh. That was me. I tripped over my own foot."

"God, this is insane," I mumbled as she roughly tugged me along the drafty, windowless passage.

"Keep your voice down," she admonished.

"You know we'll most likely be arrested and thrown in jail for the night at the very least—" My breath hitched when a sudden shaft of light cut into the blackness at the end of the corridor and a door creaked open. In a nanosecond both Sasha and I simultaneously plastered our backs against the wall, hiding in the shadows like a pair of Japanese ninjas. I almost caved in and abandoned her when I heard her stifle a chuckle.

Low, growling voices quarreled somewhere in the distance. Unfortunately, we were too far away to hear what the argument was about, and I couldn't see anyone inside. Unexpectedly, the door slammed shut plunging the corridor back into darkness, and my heart stalled for a second. I forgot to breathe in that moment until my lungs almost burst and I remembered to breathe. The moment I took a breath, I heard the hollow echo of heavy footsteps as they came in our direction. That time, I made a conscious effort not to breathe as the footfall drew nearer.

"Fucking asshole," a raspy voice fumed so close to my face the air shifted. As adrenaline coursed through me, my lungs burned and my lips tingled from the lack of oxygen. A lightheaded feeling washed over me as I heard my heartbeat roar in my ears with the anticipation of being caught until the footsteps fell silent.

A rush of air left Sasha's mouth and swept over my face. "Sheesh, that was close," she muttered.

"Shh," I quickly warned. "I don't know why I let you talk me into this. It was a fucking crazy idea."

"Okay, so it wasn't one of my better ones, but we're here now," she countered.

"Here? Where exactly is here?" I snapped, tripped over her foot and fell on my ass.

Sasha began to chuckle which soon became muffled laughter. Unfortunately, she had one of those infectious laughs and mine wasn't exactly quiet. We both cracked up, laughing hysterically in the dark. In that instant, I was afraid of nothing and I no longer cared if we were found.

The next moment, the door that had opened before instantly flew wide and strip lighting above us flickered, transforming the corridor into a blinding, well-lit hallway. Squinting at the onslaught of light, we peered cautiously down the hallway. Standing in the doorway Mason Fox, aka Sasha's target, cut an imposing alpha male figure with his bare, muscular arms folded and his thighs so wide apart anyone would think his balls hung down to his knees.

"Where the hell did you two come from? And what the fuck are you doing down here?" Mason boomed. His tenor tone made my legs buckle as it bounced loudly off the painted concrete walls.

Holding her breath, Sasha stared toward him then to me, her eyes big and round. Instinct told me she was trying to pull herself together, but she lost it, snickered again and that one exhale sparked her second wave of giggles.

"Kenny, get the fuck down there and see what those two chicks are on. They're obviously stoned. Better bring them in here."

The fact that Mason thought we were tripping cracked me up and I laughed myself breathless. My sides ached so hard I had to clutch them for support. I'd never laughed so hard in my life.

A huge guy, who I guessed must be Kenny, came charging toward us. He looked dangerous with muscles so big his frame made his head look as if it had shrunk.

"Boss wants you." Kenny grabbed each of us by a forearm, and half walked, half dragged us toward Mason.

"How the hell did you get in here?" Mason barked in a frustrated tone.

"Ticket," was the best Sasha could offer before she became racked by another attack of the giggles.

"What the fuck did you take?" Mason probed. He cast his suspicious eyes over Sasha before he turned his attention to me.

As I turned my head from Sasha to Mason, I felt an instant connection. Seconds passed but I became enthralled by the deep, brooding stare in his serious, hazel eyes. The weight of his stare felt hypnotizing and took my breath away.

Onstage, Mason Fox oozed testosterone and sex appeal, but

the off-stage version was a whole other ball game yet to be invented.

At over six feet tall, Mason's muscular frame was ripped, tatted and pierced to perfection. The guy was a God-like creature of alpha male, book boyfriend status. Shamelessly, I paused long enough to take all of him in and I almost swallowed my tongue in the process. As if he also found it hard to break the connection, his eyes narrowed, dropped to my mouth, and he slowly licked his lips. Before I realized what I was doing, I was licking mine.

Remembering why we were there, I tried again to focus on the matter at hand and managed to look away.

"You better come inside." Mason nodded toward Sasha. "God's sake, get her some water and let's see if we can flush the hysterics out of this chick," he ordered his guard.

Taking his instruction, the security detail attempted to fill a little cone shaped, paper cup from the water cooler.

"Fuck, not that. Get a tumbler, on second thought, no she may bite it, fill that plastic bottle over there."

Kenny did this and attempted to hand Sasha the drink. Sasha was standing cross-legged and she'd been laughing so hard, I figured she might pee herself. Taking the bottle from Kenny, she lifted it to her lips, tried to drink, but lost it yet again. Water squirted out of her nose and mouth, and for a second I thought she might choke. I chuckled at how ridiculous she looked and figured if she'd hoped to make an impression when she met Mason Fox, she'd certainly achieved that. Although I doubt it was the impression she'd had in mind.

How I managed to bite back my laughter at the ungodly shambles she was right then, I'll never know. There was no doubt she'd grabbed her rock star's attention, but wasn't the alluring image she'd imagined that day when she'd dressed to the nines for him.

CHAPTER 2

"*You.*" Mason's probing eyes became locked in another protracted stare when they met mine.

"Yeah?" I asked breathily.

"What did y'all take? This trip she's on is insane. Your friend here is gonna bust a gut if she doesn't get her shit together and quit laughing."

An unintentional chuckle left my mouth and I immediately tried to suck up the humor and appear concerned. I was about to answer when Sasha took her humiliation to a whole new level when she suddenly broke wind. It sounded like a pop gun on repeat as she let herself go.

Mason was bearing down on me only inches from my face when he snickered himself, then burst out laughing, causing Kenny to join in as well. By then all bets were off as each of us stood creased up with laughter.

It was the rock star who tried to pull himself together first, wiping tears from his eyes and winding down his laugh as he turned to look at Kenny.

"Is this the most hilarious thing you've seen in a while, or what?"

he challenged. He grinned wide, showing a perfect set of straight, white teeth. Instantly it felt like the sun had come out in the room. "Grab her and sit her the fuck down on the couch," he said, pointing toward Sasha. "Let's see if we can get any sense out of them."

Mason slipped his huge hand into mine and slowly led me over to a second couch. He sat me down and landed heavily beside me. A bout of shyness hit me the moment I was back in control of myself. He caught my attention by squeezing my hand in his

and I turned to face him. I wasn't prepared for the slow, enigmatic smile he gave me. It was hard to know what he was thinking.

"Want to tell me what's going on here?" Mason asked in a surprisingly even tone.

I nodded, unsure if I'd lose it again if I started to speak as Sasha was still rolling around breathless, making cackling noises on the couch across from me. Kenny sat next to her, staring deadpan as he shook his head.

"Sasha wanted to meet you," I blurted by way of an explanation then flashed him an embarrassed smile.

"Well, she's sure made it a memorable meeting. I don't reckon I've ever had a chick that's made her way backstage, collapsed in hysterics and farted her way onto my couch in quite the same way as this one has before."

A giggle burst from my mouth.

"Don't you start again, or we'll be here all fucking night," he warned, then tried to scowl as he gave me another intense stare. I didn't miss the quirk of his lips as he fought another smile.

"Sorry," I ground out as I wiped tears of laughter from my eyes with my sleeve.

"All right, let's start again."

Inhaling deeply, I sighed, and realized Mason was still holding my hand. As I tried to pull it free, his fingers tightened firmly around it. "Let's start with a name," he probed as he gave it a squeeze.

"Mercy," I said, introducing myself.

"Are you shitting me?" He grinned as though what I'd said was ridiculous.

"What are you laughing at?" I asked.

"Never mind? What did you do?"

"We aimed to sneak back here... I knew it was a bad idea. I tried to tell her, but you don't know Sa—"

"No. I'm not asking how you got here. I meant what did you guys take?"

"Take? Drugs you mean?" I clarified, shaking my head. "Nothing, I mean we had coke— but the drinking kind. Nothing else. I've seen Sasha laugh, but never for this long. Perhaps, she's overly excited. She's been desperate to meet you."

"And you?"

"Hmm?" I queried, frowning.

"What about you?" he questioned.

"Excuse me?" I asked, confused.

"Were you desperate to meet me?" Mason's tone was playful, and he gave my hand another squeeze for good measure.

"Me? No. I could have cared less. It was all Sasha," I assured him, then cringed as I realized what I'd said.

"Pity. You're extremely pretty. I would have enjoyed getting to know you better."

"I don't think you would. I'm not a groupie, Mason, and I'm not a fan of rock music."

"Ouch. Enough already." Mason chuckled again. "Well, this is the weirdest stalking I've had to date, huh?" he asked, addressing Kenny again.

"No shit, boss."

Sasha quickly pulled herself together enough to look both mortified and hurt at the same time. "Oh, God," she muttered, covering her face in her hands and then started to cry.

Rising to his feet Mason wandered over to Sasha, pulled her up from the couch and wrapped her in a hug. "Oh, Fuck, I preferred her when she was laughing. It's okay, sweetheart. Not much sways me these days. What say you dry your eyes, and we can have a no-drama chat?"

Mason pushed her away from his body and looked down at her. Sasha stared up at him doe-eyed and slowly nodded. "I'd like that," she mumbled.

Digging into my purse I brought out a travel packet of tissues and passed them to my friend. "Here wipe your face and blow your nose," I instructed.

"Thanks," she mumbled. Her mascara wasn't the waterproof kind and had left rivulets of wet, black squiggly lines all the way down to her chin.

Turning her head, she eyed the huge water dispenser and leaned over. Holding a tissue under the faucet she wet it and swiped roughly at her face. When she was done, she discarded the tissue, plumped up her hair and turned to look at the rest of us as though nothing had happened.

"I'd say my behavior was embarrassing but I know you'd all tell me I was exaggerating," Sasha said it with such a straight face, the rest of us burst out laughing again.

"Babe, this is the funniest encounter I've had in my entire life," Mason disclosed. I felt his comment was supposed to make her feel better, but she cringed as soon as his words were out.

"Great way to make an impression, by snorting and hee-hawing like some deranged donkey that's fresh out the pen," she grumbled.

"And farting… don't forget the farting," Kenny piped up, causing Mason to chuckle again.

"Oh. My. God." Hiding her face in her hands, Sasha looked like she was beyond humiliated. I jumped to my feet, walked over toward her and hugged her again.

"Personally, I'm totally impressed you didn't pee yourself, girl.

That was some funny turn you had," I offered in a moment of solidarity.

"Shut up, Mercy, I'm trying to create an impression and you're not helping my case at all," she muttered. I could counter her comment on that but decided to hold my tongue.

CHAPTER 3

*M*ason continued smiling to himself as he wandered over to the small dressing table and picked up a bottle of Scottish malt whiskey.

"You girls want a drink?" he offered, as he upturned a fresh whisky tumbler and poured a very liberal measure.

"Thank you, but I don't drink," I replied, while Sasha nodded. She looked as though she was ready to inhale the rest of the bottle in an attempt to forget the previous fifteen minutes.

"Such an innocent, huh?" Mason probed, narrowing his eyes again as he searched my face for the truth. "Don't like rock music, don't drink, what about drugs?"

"Nope. I respect my body," I stated, firmly.

"Hmm, I can get behind that," he muttered in a seductive tone. I was sure there had been a double entendre in his comment, but not enough to call him out on it. Falling silent, his roaming eyes trailed from my head to my toes, and I swear the places his eyes had appeared to linger, became heated and wired. I instantly understood why Sasha was so smitten with Mason. He was a mixture of dangerous bad boy, dirty rock star and he was so fucking charismatic he made my ovaries ache.

Heat rose to my cheeks from his persistent gaze, and I was almost certain he could read my mind. I was oblivious I'd stared back until Sasha cleared her throat. Turning my attention to her I winced at the death glare she gave me.

"Anyway, the reason we're here is because Sasha wrote a book inspired by the lyrics of one of your songs. What is it called again, Sasha?" I asked prompting her to join the conversation.

"Pipe Dreams," she stated. She riffled in her purse and handed him the glossy paperback.

"I wanted you to have a copy… I've signed it," she said, handing it to him, suddenly focused on the task that had brought us here before our fiasco in the hallway.

"Racy cover," he mused as he smoothed his long masculine hand down the glossy spine and turned it over to read the synopsis. "Romance, huh? Is it riddled with hot sex scenes?" he inquired, staring Sasha straight in the eye.

"You'll have to read it to find out." She swept her hand carelessly through her hair.

"Ya think?" he asked, raising his brow. He glanced at me as if he were considering it.

"Tell you what. I'll not only read it but I'll review it as well, if Mercy here will agree to a date with me."

A growl tore from Sasha's throat. "The book has nothing to do with her."

"I know but I get shit sent to me every day by someone or other. If I'm endorsing something it should be mutually beneficial." Mason glanced from her to me and flashed me a wicked smile. "Don't look at me like that. I don't bite. Would it really be a hardship to spend one night with me?" The questioning look coupled with his low, sexy timbre suggested it would be a wild night with him.

"Are you two best friends?" he asked, changing tack. My eyes darted toward Sasha.

"Yeah, we are," Sasha mused in a tone that suggested we may not be if Mason got his way.

"Then wouldn't you want to do this for her?" he asked me.

Mason had put me in a dreadful position.

"Forget it, Sasha, come on, let's get out of here." No matter how hot I thought Mason was, I'd walk away to save our friendship.

"No. Do it. I want him to read it. I need the feedback. I want you to do it."

Mason's instant smile almost split his face. "Excellent. Tomorrow night? I only have one more day here. A thrill shot down my spine with how urgent his tone had sounded.

Sasha forced a smile. "Honestly, Mercy, it's cool," she coaxed.

"All right. I'll do it." My stomach flipped over the moment I agreed.

For twenty minutes after this Sasha had her brush with fame, snapping umpteen selfies in various poses and making the poor guy autograph just about everything in her purse. Eventually, Kenny called us a cab and saw us off on our way.

"That was fucking insane," I muttered still not understanding what I'd agreed to. Sasha looked conflicted about Mason's deal.

"Are you okay?"

"Yeah, but I'm annoyed with his attitude. It was plain he wasn't into me, but exposure from him will be worth the book's weight in gold. With his endorsement it could be a best-seller."

Personally, I didn't like the idea of bargaining with me. It felt like emotional blackmail. Even with that thought, butterflies fluttered inside at the thought of seeing him again.

CHAPTER 4

*"D*on't you go getting all dolled up. From everything I've read Mason can really turn on the charm. You're giving him your time. That's all you agreed to," Sasha advised.

"I'm a big girl," I countered.

"I know you, Mercy. You're a good girl. But sometimes you do stuff that scares the shit out of yourself as well as everyone else," she confessed.

"That won't happen tonight. I know why I'm doing this. I'm going there for you." Even as I said the words, a voice in my head said, liar.

"Not that one," Sasha instructed when I was about to pull on a baby blue dress that was one of my favorites. "That makes your tits too pert and your eyes pop too much. He'll want to take it off."

"Don't be absurd. He'll probably send me home an hour after feeding me."

"God, I hope so, because if he fucks you I'll be jealous.

Suddenly the seriousness of the situation hit me square in the chest. Her words weren't lost on me. We'd been here once before when a boy in high school liked her instead of me. I'd encouraged her to go out with him and they were still together after almost five years.

Eventually Sasha settled on my outfit of low-rise skinny jeans and a gray non-descript hoodie then insisted on tying my long dark hair into a severe-looking high ponytail. The look was grungier teen than sexy siren and I looked years younger than my true age of twenty-two.

"No makeup," she demanded. When I stared in the mirror at my reflection, the girl looking back at me wasn't someone about to embark on a hot date with a rock star. "Here," she said, throwing some beat-up old chucks from the back of my closet at me. "These will do nicely. It's not like he's taking you anywhere."

That part was true. Due to privacy, our date had been set to take place at his suite at The Four Seasons hotel in midtown for six o'clock that the evening. I prayed he wouldn't be expecting me to sleep with him in return to review Sasha's book.

"All right remember what I told you. Don't drink alcohol, you're a lightweight lush on booze. One drink and you're…" she sighed. "If he offers you anything other than soda tell him you're on antibiotics."

* * *

A CAR ARRIVED to take me to the hotel. On the way there I fought an urge to pick at the fresh nail polish I'd applied. I took out my cell phone to scroll social media and saw a text from Sasha.

Sasha: Remember no drinking and do NOT drop those panties.

This was such a bad idea.

I stared out of the window as a bus zoomed past in the next lane with a Visit Australia mural on the side. The vibrant browns and burnt orange colored background featured kangaroos jumping in the distance. I glanced down at my dowdy attire and convinced myself that Mason would be turned off the moment he clapped eyes on my outfit.

"Evening, Miss," the doorman greeted as he pulled the door open.

I'd never been in such a grand place before; the nearest I'd gotten to posh was a wedding dinner at a Double Tree by Hilton during a family wedding in Idaho.

The lobby of the hotel had intricate brown and cream marble flooring, pale beige stone wall decor and huge ornate light fixtures. My wonderous eyes feasted on the grandeur and from the frowning glances of the patrons, I saw they knew I didn't fit in. I cursed myself again for having agreed to do this, it was ridiculous.

The front desk receptionist was dressed in a crisp white shirt and black tie under her navy-blue suit jacket. Distain flashed in her eyes as she raked over my ensemble. I winced before standing taller and tried to look as if I was born to be there.

"Mason Fox," I requested determinedly.

"Excuse me?" she asked with a raised brow.

"Mason Fox... I'm here to see him."

"I'm afraid we have no one here by that name," she said, politely.

it occurred to me they'd probably deny Mason was a guest. Given my attire, I figured she assumed I was chancing my luck. I smirked at her assumption. Never judge a book by its cover, I wanted to say.

"Please contact Mr. Fox's suite and tell him Mercy Rivers is here."

"Sorry, there is no one here by—"

"I know he's here. His driver brought me here a few minutes ago. Mason is expecting me. Please call his suite and tell him I'm here," I stated more assertively.

Hesitantly, she did as I asked.

"Sorry for the intrusion, this is Destiny from the front desk. I have someone by the name of Mercy Rivers in the front lobby."

"Very good, thank you," she concluded and hung up. Glancing back at me I saw the moment her attitude toward me changed. Destiny flashed me a beaming smile like the previous conversation had never occurred.

"Somebody will be right down, Ms. Rivers."

CHAPTER 5

"This is some place, huh?" I asked Kenny nervously as the elevator shot skyward.

"Seen one hotel, you've seen 'em all."

For some reason I'd expected the elevator to open inside the suite like I'd seen in the movies, but the door opened into a hallway a short distance from the suite itself.

"Just a sec," Kenny stated, halting me with his huge shovel like hand after I'd stepped into the hallway. "I need your phone and I gotta take a look in your purse."

"Huh? Why? What for? Do you think I keep a Taser in here or something?" I asked.

"When the boss has private time, he doesn't want it being recorded and sold to the highest bidder," he muttered, pulling my purse off my shoulder. Before I could protest, he'd cradled it into his large meaty arm and had begun rummaging through it.

"He what? And what exactly does Mason think is going to happen in there that would be worth recording?" I questioned in an indignant tone.

"Not a thing, so you won't mind leaving this with me."

I felt naked without my cell phone. The device should have

been my security. What if I had to get help in a hurry or something happened behind those doors I wasn't prepared for?

Too late, I realized I was at the mercy of these people, no pun intended. They were strangers and I had forgotten all my usual precautions for the sake of Sasha's book.

"What about me? Who is to say I won't need protecting? How am I supposed to call for help if you take my cell phone away?" I protested.

"If that's what you think, then why did you come?" Kenny challenged. "This is about Mason's privacy, nothing else. No one's gonna jump you and tie you down or make you do anything you don't want to do. Mason won't relax if he thinks what he says will appear in the papers tomorrow."

My rising anger dissolved because I figured being a famous rock star, Mason had likely had something happen before. I nodded, accepting Kenny's point.

After Kenny tucked my purse under his right arm and strode toward the light-oak penthouse suite doors. I couldn't help but chuckle as the meathead swaggered along the hallway with my silver, oversized purse.

Opening the door with his keycard, he pushed it wide and gestured me inside.

I hadn't known what to expect when my eyes were drawn to Mason lying sprawled out in front of an open fire, with his right arm tucked behind his head. His left hand rested across his chest, and he had a set of earbuds in his ears. I turned to look at Kenny because Mason obviously hadn't heard us arrive.

"He doesn't know you're here yet. I screen his calls from my room," Kenny informed me. As I looked back toward Mason, I noted the twinkling city lights of New York City's skyline stretching far beyond us through the floor to ceiling windows.

Striding over to Mason, Kenny tapped his shoulder to get his attention. Mason's apparent lack of anticipation to my arrival made me feel insignificant. However, I took that thought back when he glanced over his shoulder and saw me.

He sprang to his feet so fast he did an extra couple of kangaroo bounces as he pulled his earbuds from his ears.

"Jesus, is that the time? I'm sorry I was listening to something my record company sent me." He flashed me his sunshine smile and the anxious feeling that had been crushing my chest instantly vanished.

"Glad you could make it. Come, Mercy, make yourself comfortable." He nodded toward the large twin couch opposite to where he stood. When I didn't move, too transfixed on his gorgeous face, he gestured to the couch again.

"Thanks, sorry for..." I indicated the way I was dressed, then noted he was in sweats, a tank and an open, soft cotton shirt.

"You look perfect," he offered, dismissing my outfit as he stared at my face. My heart raced as I felt myself blush from his compliment.

"Hardly, I've never dressed down this much for an outing before," I stated, honestly.

"This isn't an outing it's a date... and it's nice to know I'm worth it," he remarked and chuckled as he sat down directly opposite.

I gave him a grimace and shrugged. "The outfit was Sasha's idea."

"What else could I expect from a girl who farts in public?" We both laughed at his throw away comment. "If I remember correctly, you don't drink alcohol. But maybe you'd like a white wine spritzer or something?"

"Coke?" I asked.

"Ah, your drug of choice. Of course," he replied playfully before he stood and wandered over to the full cocktail bar near a pool table. When he pulled out two cokes and a couple of beers and placed them on the coffee table. "I'm saving my energy for more exciting activities instead of going back and forth."

Needless to say, my throat went dry and I swallowed roughly. "How long are you here for?" My attempt at conversation was bland.

Mason sat back down and eyed me curiously. "Another day, which means if this evening goes well, we could squeeze in a second date tomorrow before I leave in the evening," he offered.

I pulled the ring-pull and went to drink out of the can. "Stop," he barked. "Fuck, sorry," he said as he darted across to the wet bar and came back with a crystal glass. "Sometimes, I forget to be attentive. Living alone, will do that to a man." He smiled. "Okay, we're going to order dinner and then we'll take things from there."

CHAPTER 6

"*I* only came here for Sasha. You said if I came, you'd read her book and review it?"

"I did say that, didn't I? Do you mean if I asked you on a date and there was no book you would have refused?"

"If there wasn't a book, we would never have met."

"Then we have Sasha to thank, but I do think you're attracted to me," he challenged.

"Yeah, it would be hard not to be," I admitted. As his gaze locked with mine, I studied the green flecks in his hazel eyes that I hadn't seen before.

"Refreshing, a girl who says what she thinks." He broke the stare to pick up an 'I love Australia' novelty bottle opener, flipped the beer cap off and chugged down half the bottle's contents. With each swallow his Adam's apple bobbed seductively under his silk-looking skin which almost made me drool.

"You make me thirsty, Mercy."

I laughed. "Does that line work?" I challenged.

"Mostly, but I'm rarely serious when I say it."

His comment made me squirm in my seat. For a moment I was dumbstruck, and I sat silently blinking as Mason nonchalantly stood and made his way around the large coffee table from his couch and sat alongside me.

"You know what? I love this," he informed me as he gently tugged on my long, dark brown ponytail. He sifted his fingers through it while I sat like a cold fish, paralyzed by Mason's attention until I found the will to speak.

"Now I know you're playing games. I don't think I've ever looked less attractive in my life, wearing this." I pointed out my clothing. "You obviously get off on getting a rise out of girls."

"Hm," he muttered as his fingertips grazed the nape of my neck before he proceeded to wrap my ponytail around his fist and scrutinized it. The intent in his eyes almost appeared predatory, but when he glanced from my hair to my face my whole body vibrated with desire under the weight of the look of desire in his eyes.

"Is that what I'm doing?" he whispered. "I don't play games. I have no patience for them. Its wasted effort. I prefer frank conversations. This outfit you're wearing is far sexier than silk lingerie, satin babydoll pajamas or any other piece of clothing designed to turn someone on. It can be more thrilling to imagine what's hidden underneath."

My gaze dropped to his lap and took in the large bulge in his jeans and desire coursed through my body before I glanced back up to his eyes. The wicked grin on his face confirmed he'd noticed me fact checking his remark.

My eyes fell to his hand before they wandered up his powerful forearm before returning to stop at his wrist. There was something sexy about the weathered leather band and the thick steel bracelet he wore. His huge hand looked soft and strong. For a moment I spaced out and imagined how his palm would feel running over my body, until Mason drew me back into the conversation.

"You haven't answered my question," he prompted.

My eyes flitted from his hand to his beautiful face and

lingered. "Huh," I muttered almost trance-like. Mason smiled like he guessed how difficult I found the connection between us. "I have no idea what the hell I'm doing here and what you're trying to do," I disclosed and swallowed hard as a curved smile his lips.

"I wanted to see you again because I felt our instant connection last night. You intrigued me, and I want to get to know you better." Mason shrugged like inviting me there was nothing. I considered this and figured, to him, it most probably was nothing. I was a one-night encounter, when Mason would otherwise be at a loose end.

CHAPTER 7

"All right, I'll bite," I offered. "What is this connection you feel we have?"

He shrugged. "I'm struggling to make sense of myself."

"How do I know that's not just another line? I mean, you must have an encyclopedia of them by now."

"I don't use a line to pick up a girl when I believe they matter."

"Right," I muttered, unsure with what I was agreeing. Mason smelled faintly of a woodsy cologne and his unique manly scent, and everything about him drew me in. It was all too easy to let my mind wander into dangerous territory where my head could become filled with inappropriate thoughts, raw dirty thoughts, and a burning desire to explore the more intimate parts of his body hidden beneath his clothing. He was right, more is less instead of less is more, if you allow fantasies to burst to life.

My heart and mind began having emotions I had no business having for someone who had used me like a tool for the benefit of someone else.

Despite my resolve not to be swayed by Mason, my will had already crumbled. I was already falling for his charm due to the mesmerizing attraction that had pulled us together. That magnetism should have been a stern warning of how easily my boundaries would shift once we were alone.

"Tell me something about yourself," he encouraged.

"What do you want to know?"

"Do you have a guy?" he asked gruffly.

"Do you think I'd be here if I had?

"I don't know. The truth of the matter is that I'm not into drama or cultivating something where there's some kind of mess attached. The press brings enough of that shit to my door without my help. So, I'm asking again, is there someone waiting for you while you're here with me?"

"I thought I'd answered that," I stated.

"Not in so many words."

"No, there's no guy. But this isn't meant to be that kind of a date."

"I find that difficult to believe. I mean, look at you," he said, lifting the hand I'd been so absorbed with moments before and stroked my cheek with the back of his fingers. "There's something about you, Mercy," he whispered softly.

"This is ridiculous," I protested, swallowing hard but I couldn't deny the desire burning in his eyes. "What could you see in me? I mean you're a worldwide superstar with a following of millions. I've got fifty-four friends on my social media accounts." I chuckled at the irony.

"Maybe that's why I'm attracted to you," he suggested and smoothed my ponytail through his fist once again. He unintentionally licked his lips and I pressed mine together to prevent me from doing the same. Staring at Mason Fox in all his sexy-as-sin nearness was thirsty work. It felt both debilitating and thirsty work.

"Not sure what you mean," I confessed, feeling self-conscious.

"Last night in those crazy circumstances in the dressing room it struck me you didn't look at me in the same way most women did. Although I felt something shift in here when I looked at you,"

Mason said, tapping his chest. "I connected with you in a way that moved me, and that's RARE."

Despite his previous attempt to debunk that he spun women lines, I was convinced this was a highly polished line that had gotten him laid many times before.

"Is that right? You're very smooth, I'll give you that," I mused.

"That wasn't a line," he stated quickly, in a much more serious tone.

"I'm not the kind of girl that loses her mind and drops her panties because a guy pays me attention," I told him.

"I disagree. All girls will give themselves willingly if they're in the hands of the right guy," he answered flatly.

"So let me get this straight, you'd be the right guy in this situation?"

"Have I said this? Have I made a move on you since you've been here?"

"You've invaded my space, touching my hair, my skin and I'm supposed to believe you're not hitting on me?" My voice sounded an octave higher than usual.

"I'm a tactile person, but I haven't heard you object. Is it perverted that I needed to know how your skin felt, or to feel your hair running through my hand? You already told me you're attracted to me. Be honest why you're here, because I feel that attraction too. It's where we go from here that we have to figure out."

Standing quickly, I headed toward his suite door. "This body is not for sale. Sasha is my friend, and I came here for her, but no matter how attracted to you I am, I'm not going to be fucked by a rock star in order for you to read her book. This was a stupid idea. I'd like my purse back please, I want to go home."

CHAPTER 8

"*A*ll right I'll get you a car, but we both know you're running away because you're scared," Mason stated, his tone blunt and exasperated.

"You know what? Yeah, I am scared. I've never put myself in a position like this before. It isn't like I meet many rock stars in my day-to-day life. I not going to sell my soul for anyone. Sasha worships the ground you walk on, yet you've put our friendship at risk by placing the burden of her book's success on me."

"You do realize most of the people I meet want something from me?"

"Like you want something from me you mean?"

"How do you know what I want? All I wanted was a chance to spend some time with a beautiful girl who isn't here because of my music. Have you any idea how RARE it is to have a conversation that has nothing to do with my performance on stage? I can't even remember the last time someone said, 'Hi, Mason, how are you feeling today?'"

His comment gave me pause for thought and he was right. I wasn't giving him a chance. Sasha and I were the ones who had invaded his privacy.

Turning to face him again I bowed my head. "I'm sorry. I'm not used to any of this... to you. Men don't usually pursue me, especially someone like you."

"Come here," he said, holding one arm open but keeping the other close to his heart. My feet moved before my brain caught up, and in seconds I stood in front of him. Flinging an arm around my shoulder, he pulled me into his side. "I'm the one who is sorry. I guess this must feel weird to you. But meeting new people and cutting to the chase is normal in my world.

"Shall we start again?" I swallowed and nodded. "All right, name," he said prompting me like we'd only just met.

"Mercy Hall. Named after Mercy House, a mom and baby refuge center where my mom gave birth. My birth mom was encouraged to give me up for adoption and my adoptive parents, the Halls, kept my first name.

"Fuck and you said you weren't interesting," he muttered, wide eyed. "Did you ever get in touch with your birth mom?"

I shook my head as an ache formed in my chest. "No, after I was adopted, she left the center and just... vanished."

"Do you have any information about her?"

"Yeah, my mom helped me do some research, but every avenue so far has led to a dead end."

"Have you been looking for long?"

"Since I turned eighteen, so almost four years. We've all but given up now."

"No wonder you're guarded with people. That's a hard burden to carry."

"I'm luckier than most. My mom was forward thinking and took some pictures of her with me, so I'd at least I know what she looked like."

The conversation moved on from topic to topic and we found we had a lot in common. Mason had grown up in a tough neighborhood where he was surrounded by gangland culture.

For hours we reminisced about our childhoods, our families

and laughed about some colorful high school experiences. As we talked, I came to realize what a rounded, fun-loving guy he was.

"What time is it?" I asked, shocked when I saw a slither of light on the horizon.

"Damn, it's almost 5:00 a.m. Do you need to work today?"

"Yeah, I'm a copy editor and I have a rush edit on a short novella."

"I'll get my driver to take you home," he said, pulling out his cellphone.

After our lengthy conversation it felt like I'd known him for years, and I was reluctant to leave. I could tell from the frown on his brow and the intense way he looked at me Mason felt the same.

"I'll see you home." His tone matched the same sadness I felt. "Thanks for spending the night with me," he said with a mischievous smile on his face.

"Thanks for reading Sasha's book. She's a great person… and she loves you," I added, giving him a small smile.

"What about you? Do you love me now? Even just a little bit?" he teased, pouting.

"You're a dangerous man, Mason Fox. I reckon you could break a woman's heart," I replied honestly.

"I hope we can do this again." He flashed me a sensual smile with his beautiful lips, and I suddenly wanted to kiss him. I stared at his mouth a moment too long before I glanced back up to his eyes. A moment passed between us where we didn't move until Mason let out a breath, then looked past me toward the door. His lips twisted to form a wry smile.

With the connection lost he swiftly pulled me to his chest, held me a moment too long, then kissed the top of my head. Right, home." As we headed toward the elevator, I figured I'd be analyzing the night between us for days.

CHAPTER 9

*K*enny immediately appeared in the hallway. "Boss?"

"Go to bed, Kenny. I'm seeing Mercy home. Logan's waiting downstairs."

"But, boss…" Mason shot him a glare and Kenny reluctantly nodded. Turning, he took my purse from a small console table inside his door and handed it back to me.

"I'll be fine," I began, stepping into the elevator. Mason placed his long finger gently against my lips.

"No, I kept you out, I'm taking you home," he demanded, pulled his finger from my lips and smoothed it against his own lips in thought. A thrill of desire shot down my spine at his intimate act.

As the doors to the elevator car closed, he slipped his hand down by my side and took hold of mine. Wrapping his fingers tightly around my hand, he gave it a small squeeze that sent butterflies soaring through my stomach.

Mason snatched me quickly from the elevator car soon as the doors opened in the foyer and immediately led me to the open door of his waiting car. Climbing in, he quickly closed the door and slid back into the seat.

He smiled a little breathless. "That was smooth." He must have read my confusion and chuckled. "Sorry, life can get ugly flitting from one place to another. Fortunately, its only 5:15 a.m. There aren't many people around."

Not being able to move around freely without any harassment reminded me who I was with.

We sat in a comfortable silence during the journey to my apartment, and the nearer we got to my home, the heavier my heart grew. Mason was right, we really had connected and that reality suddenly felt like a burden, knowing that in one more day he'd be gone. Who knew how many people he'd connected with like this in the past?

"Thank you for a wonderful night. You really have been a gentleman," I said when the car drew up at my building.

"I feel as if I only began to know you when it was time for you to leave. I'll read Sasha's book and give her the review like I promised." When he leaned toward me, I thought for a second he was going to kiss me, and my heart raced in anticipation. Instead, he placed his large hand on the back of my head, drew me close and pressed a soft kiss on my forehead instead.

"Night, sweetheart. You're a very special girl, Mercy Hall." Mason clapped a hand on his driver's shoulder, who immediately got out and opened my door.

"Bye, Mason, thanks for…" I shrugged, at a loss for words. I turned and headed for my entrance when he called out.

"Mercy. I'll call you." I nodded and turned away as the lump in my throat threatened to choke me because I expected that the only place I'd ever see him again would be on the television.

As I fell into bed, part of me wished I'd never agreed to the date with Mason for a very different reason. I had no idea one night with Mason Fox would never feel like enough.

* * *

MY CELL PHONE danced around my nightstand, the vibration buzzing me annoyingly from my sleep. "Yeah?" I croaked sleepily as I cracked one bleary eye open.

"So?" Sasha demanded.

"He promised he'd do it," I mumbled sleepily. A sudden ache formed in my chest and I snuggled under the covers.

"Mercy. What happened?" she barked. Her sharp, bossy tone instantly jolted me wide awake.

"What time is it?" I muttered as I rolled over and sat up.

"9:40 a.m. Are you still in bed?"

"Yeah. I've only had four hours sleep. Can we do this later?" I asked, stifling a yawn.

"Four hours sleep?" she repeated in a high-pitched voice.

"Yeah, I only got home about 5.15 a.m."

"You were with him all night? Did you fu—"

"No, I did not fuck him," I snapped, cutting her off. "Mason was the perfect gentleman. We… talked is all."

"You talked? No one spends a night with Mason Fox and just talks," she argued.

"I did."

"Then the horrible outfit worked." I chuckled. "And he's going to do my book review?"

"Yep, he said so. We'll see," I replied. "Now, I need to go. I still have that novella to finish today."

While I showered, dressed, and had breakfast, Mason occupied most of my thoughts. Until reality set in and I had to concentrate on my work.

CHAPTER 10

"*I* love you, Mercy," Sasha gushed when I answered my cell that evening.

"You do?"

"Did you tell Mason the story?" Her question had me confused.

"What are you talking about?"

"Mason reviewed my book on Amazon, and he loved it. He plastered it all over his social media and the digital copy is a best seller. I mean, I'd rather he'd read it, but at least the review sounded as if he's read it."

"We didn't talk about your book."

"Then how come he's written a review already? You said you didn't get home until this morning."

"Then I guess he read the book. What did he say?"

"Let me read it for you. It isn't long but it's to the point. Pipe Dreams, A gut busting five-star read, by Sasha Callan. This is an honest review after Sasha stalked me with a paperback copy of this book. This romance book was inspired by my song lyrics with the same title as the book, Pipe Dreams. When I agreed to read this story, I had no idea what to expect. But I can confirm for everybody, this chick CAN write.

Although the story is a work of fiction, I related to the main dude in the story because he was an asshole at times when it comes to women. However, when he finally gets his sh*t together and realizes a few things, like working harder to be a good man for the woman he loves, the story flips the poor guy on his head.

During the story we see the characters grow closer, by breaking down their prejudices until the arrive on the same page. Let me tell you, I learned A LOT from this book. The storyline makes this read a must read for everyone. Go grab your copy. Mason Fox."

"Wow," I mumbled.

"Right?"

Mason's review felt like a hidden message to me. "It's fantastic. I'm excited for you, Sasha. He really did read it. I'm glad because I loved the story too. You deserve the best seller."

"I'd never have gotten him to if it hadn't been for you," she acknowledged. "And you really never slept with him to get it?"

"Of course not."

"Sorry I made you wear those horrible clothes to meet him."

"It's okay, he loved the outfit. He wasn't dressed any better."

"What did you think of him?"

"Honestly?"

"Yeah."

"I think I left this morning a little bit in love."

Sasha said nothing for a few minutes then sighed. "I'm sorry. I had a feeling that might happen. I saw he was into you and I felt jealous. Still do, but I can't make a man feel something that isn't there."

"He's your idol," I acknowledged because I didn't know what else to say.

"Yeah, but he didn't look at me how he looked at you. I'm not his type. I've never seen him date a tall blonde. They're always petite brunettes like you."

"Sasha, from what he said, I don't think any fan is his type. He said he wanted to spend time with me because I wasn't a fan of his music. We didn't talk about his work at all. Our conversation was about normal stuff like growing up, pets we had as kids, his high school baseball team and all the subjects he wouldn't get to reminisce about with anyone who follows him.

"Ah, well. I'm sorry if you've been left with a rock star hangover."

"I was dreading going there. But the evening turned out to be lovely." I heard how wistfulness my voice sounded.

"Did he kiss you?"

"Yeah, but not in the way you think. He kissed me twice actually. Once on the top of my head and once on my forehead."

"Wow. That sounds significant."

"Hardly. Anyway, he's moving on to better things today so there's no point in dwelling on it."

"There is nobody better than you, Mercy," she offered in a show of support for my feelings.

We concluded the call, and I went back to finishing the last few pages of the novella. Afterward, I skim read it again before I contacted the author with my notes and sent it back as I knew the author was on a tight schedule.

As my shoulders ached from sitting in one position I ran a bath, filled the tub with bubbles and climbed in. Stretching out, I placed my head on the tiny bath pillow Sasha had bought me the previous Christmas. I closed my eyes and sighed at the blissfully relaxing feeling that washed over me.

Settling comfortably, my mind flashed up Mason's gorgeous face and no matter how hard I tried, I couldn't think of a single person I'd met that had even come close to the effect he had on me. A wave of grief washed over me at the thought I may never have such an instant and deep connection with anyone else in my lifetime. Then I realized, I'd formed an instant attachment as well as the attraction I'd felt toward him during our time together.

I sighed to release the melancholic feeling that weighed on my chest, and I wished I'd ignored all my self-imposed moral boundaries and been careless with him for once in my life.

CHAPTER 11

The apartment door buzzer startled me awake, and for a moment I'd forgotten where I was. For a few more seconds I lay confused that I'd fallen asleep in the bath. I was still gathering my wits when the buzzer sounded again.

Once out of the bath, I wrapped myself in a huge bath sheet and answered my intercom.

"Hello?"

"Hey, Mercy. Can you let me in quickly before someone spots me?" My heart skipped a beat when I heard Mason's unmistakably low timbre. My hand shook as I hit the entrance button to buzz him up and my brain instantly went into melt down. For a few seconds I felt paralyzed as adrenaline flooded my body. Too freaked out by the fact he'd come back to see me. Being as I was only on the first floor I had barely had time to remember I wasn't dressed before my apartment doorbell rang.

I cracked the opened the door open and poked my head out.

"What are you doing here?"

"I needed to see you again. Is that okay?"

"Yes." *Fuck, think, Mercy.* My mind went completely blank as I stared out at his beautiful face.

"May I come in?" He glanced both ways down the corridor and I realized someone might see him.

"Sure, I was taking a bath," I explained as I opened the door wider to let him inside.

"Nice," he replied as he took in my towel and flashed me a lopsided smile.

Heat immediately rose to my cheeks and I clutched the tucked in the towel over my cleavage to make sure it didn't unravel like my mind appeared to have done.

"Grab a seat, I'll get changed," I said quickly when the initial shock had worn off.

"Don't get dressed on my account. I'm perfectly happy to talk to you as you are," he teased, smiling wider.

My body practically hummed in response to his flirty comment.

By the time I reached my bedroom I was breathing irregularly and my body shook so much from the hormones flowing through my veins that I could barely control my limbs when getting dressed.

Five minutes later, I reemerged in my sitting room wearing a pale pink tank top and some black yoga pants. I'd dragged a brush through my wet hair, was makeup free and imagined I'd managed to look even less attractively turned out than I had the night before.

"Damn," he remarked, as he cast hungry eyes over my body. "I thought you were beautiful the first time I saw you, and last night when you were totally dressed down, but this with your hair down and your curves on show like that... wow."

"What are you doing here?" I asked, as I tried to ignore his compliment.

"Yesterday you were forced to go on a date with me, I've come back to ask if you'd like to do it again, but with no strings attached this time."

My heart was shouting, YES! But my realistic head was having none of it. My heart was bruised after the little contact we'd had, and although my body yearned for the man, I felt my heart would get broken.

"What's the point? You're leaving tonight."

"I am. But I'll be back. The world isn't as big as you think. Not when you do what I do."

A frown creased my brow and Mason closed the space between us. "I was thinking after our lengthy conversation. You probably know more about me than anyone else I've met in years. That's because you took the time to get to know me."

I shrugged. "I'm not sleeping with you, Mason. You're wasting your time."

"Then I choose to waste my time on you. Do you think it's normal for me to ask for a date in exchange for something? I mean it's not the first time someone has brought me something one of my songs has inspired."

"Yeah, but it was due to the unique way Sasha presented hers," I reminded him.

"No. I agreed because of who she was with. Tell me you didn't feel that instant spark the moment our eyes met," he insisted.

I couldn't. "Yeah," I admitted.

"I didn't want last night to end. You made me feel restless after I'd dropped you off, and I've been unsettled all day."

"All right, say I go on this date with you. Where would you take me and what would we do? I mean you can hardly take me to Pizza Hut, can you?"

"Yuk. Come on, Mercy. Give yourself a break. Come out with me on a proper date."

"Okay, so what do I wear?" I asked, throwing caution and my bleeding heart under a bus.

"A dress and heels for a change. Let's switch it up, and make it the opposite of our first date. What do you say?"

Immediately I thought of the pale blue figure-hugging dress

Sasha had banned me from wearing and nodded. "Give me five minutes," I told him.

"That's my girl," he stated, sounding pleased with himself. When he called me his girl, even if it was just a figure of speech, my heart leapt, and as I got dressed, I couldn't believe I was risking another date night with a rock star.

CHAPTER 12

ou're not sleeping with him, Mercy, I reminded myself as I rummaged through a drawer for my sexiest matching underwear. I justified wearing it as a confidence boost rather than the possibility undressing in front of him.

I liberally applied moisturizer to my already bathed skin, quickly dressed and pulled on my sexiest stiletto heels... another boost to my ego.

By the time I opened my bedroom door, my heart was thundering at near capacity and my whole body was humming in anticipation of stepping out with Mason Fox in public.

"Wow, baby!" He cleared his throat. "How did you do all that in less than five minutes?"

All right, I lied. That was exactly the response I'd wanted.

Mason stepped close, placed his hands on my bare shoulders, smoothed his callused thumbs across my satiny skin, and swept his hands down my arms. By the time he grabbed my wrists I was a hot mess inside from the sparks of electricity firing off throughout my body.

He chuckled when he noticed my goosebumps, looked up and met my eyes.

Leaning forward, he pressed a small, soft kiss to my lips. When I didn't object, he kissed me again and I couldn't help kissing him back.

Mason's hands migrated; one to my waist, the other sifted into my hair. Grabbing a fistful, he wrapped it around his hand and slowly pushed my head closer to his. Our slick tongues tangled in a deep sensual kiss until he pulled away and took a step back.

"I just needed to do this to get it out of the way." He flashed me a small, wicked grin. "Let's get out of here before we do something you might regret."

Kenny stood with his back to the car when he saw Mason heading his way. He opened the door and we quickly climbed inside.

"I can't believe how lucky I've been not to be mobbed by the public. This is the first time I've been out in daylight for years without an incident happening."

I pitied that part of his life, that he felt excited because he hadn't been recognized.

"Where are we going?"

"Not far," he replied mysteriously. He gave me a slow smile that said he wasn't willing to divulge anything more.

He slipped his hand in mine as it rested between us on the seat, and gave me a small squeeze.

"I wasn't sure you'd agree to come out with me," he confessed as his thumb grazed back and forth over my skin.

"Neither was I."

He chuckled. "What are you worried about?"

"Maybe that I'll like you too much in the short time we have and that you'll probably hurt me."

"It's not my intention to hurt you," he replied quickly.

"But it could happen."

"I hope not, Mercy."

"Hope not?"

"Yeah, because I feel the same about you.

"It's difficult to explain, but I feel drawn to you. I've never wanted to know about any of the girls' lives. I was only interested in how they made me feel."

An unexpectedly strong pang of jealousy ran through me at the mention of other girls, and I scoffed at the arrogance of his statement.

"And how do I know you're not lying now?"

"Believe me, Mercy, this is no hook up," he said squeezing my fingers. "I don't know exactly what it is, but I missed you after I left you this morning, and I haven't stopped thinking about you since I met you."

My cheeks burned as I stared into his beautiful, bright hazel eyes.

"So, what happens after today?"

"After today?" he repeated. "I suppose I come back as often as I can for now until we know each other better... that's if my gut is right, and you feel the same way as I do."

Hearing his desire to build something made me ask myself whether I wanted to risk this, and I knew without hesitation, I wanted him all the more.

CHAPTER 13

"You're planning on coming back?"

"Of course. I've got to go down to Atlanta and Florida for a couple of gigs, but after that I've got a few weeks off. The rest is up to you."

I was nodding before my brain caught up with the words. "I won't tolerate being messed around, Mason. I'm not blinded by what you do for a living."

Letting go of my hand, he caught my chin instead. "Baby, that's part of the attraction for me. Meeting you has been the best thing that's happened to me in years."

"You poor soul, because I'm really dull."

"Can I kiss you?" he asked, like we hadn't already done this back at my apartment. His intense gaze fixed on my lips, and he licked his own. Personally, I thought I'd die if he didn't kiss me, right then. This time, my body hummed in heady anticipation of Mason's lips meeting mine.

Leaning in for a closed mouthed kiss he pressed his lips at the side of my mouth. "I've been wanting to kiss your pretty mouth since the moment I met you." His hand left my chin and tangled in the back of my hair as he pulled my head closer to his. This was where the tenderness ended. Passion is an understatement to describe the kiss that followed. In fact, there was no word in my vocabulary that adequately explained the torrent of emotions that ran through me. It was minutes later when we both pulled apart and struggled for breath as we got our feelings back in check.

"Wow," he muttered, unclipping my seat belt and his, then lifting me onto his lap before we got lost in another breathtaking kiss. Each of us gripped handfuls of hair from the other as our way of preventing our hands from wandering, until Kenny cleared his throat, and we realized the car had stopped.

Mason heaved for breath as his lips left mine before he let out a long, shuddery exhale through his nose. "Damn," he cussed. "You're so..." Lost for words, he growled. My confidence soared when I saw his reaction. He straightened my hair and moved me back onto my seat. Looking out of the window I noticed we were at a heliport and a helicopter waited about ten yards away.

"Where are you taking me?" I asked excitedly.

"We didn't get that dinner last night, so I figured I'd try to make up for it."

"In that?" I asked, pointing to the helicopter.

"It'll take us where we need to go."

"Which is where, exactly?"

"Ever seen Niagara Falls at night?"

I squealed like a child and bounced up and down in my seat. "I've always wanted to see them, but I've never been," I disclosed.

Kenny who got out of the car, let us out and Mason led me to the helicopter.

Once seated, I grabbed Mason's hand and gripped it tightly. Sensing I was worried he swapped hands, slid one over my shoulder and pulled me closer.

"You're not scared of this are you?"

"I've never flown before," I confessed. Kenny glanced around and I realized everyone could hear our conversation through the mic attached to the headset.

Leaning in, Mason bumped noses with me and kissed me again. Butterflies wouldn't begin to describe how he made me feel inside. I was in the arms of an attentive man, one so different from his public image and I loved how he made me feel.

Breathless, we kissed, then I turned and looked out of the window. It was dusk when we'd taken off but now the New York skyline was ablaze with lights against the dark shroud of the night sky.

"What're you thinking?" he asked.

"How perfect this is."

"Agreed." I turned to look into his eyes. "Best day of my life so far," he said.

I frowned in disbelief. "With all the amazing opportunities you've had?" I challenged.

"Yeah, because none of those were with someone I wanted to be with," he replied. I eyed him suspiciously, and he pulled me in for another kiss. This kiss was tender and sensual, less passionate than the one in the car. His hand wandered to my thigh but kept going and gently circled my neck. He applied a little pressure as his tongue probed deeper into my mouth. It was the kiss of an experienced seducer, and one I'd never forget.

A turbulent moment broke the kiss. I looked out the window again and saw beautiful pink and purple lights dancing over the water and illuminating the magnificent falls.

"Oh. My. God, this is spectacular," I gushed as I marveled at the natural wonder. Despite the noise from the rotors, I heard the roar of the white, foaming water raging down to the still water below.

"I aim to please," Mason joked like he'd designed the sight just for me. My gaze fell to the two large boats beneath us packed full of tourists. They were wearing bright colored ponchos. Some blue, some red. Suddenly the helicopter careered away from the falls and we landed a few minutes later.

CHAPTER 14

ot long after, Mason and I sat in a private dining area of a rotating restaurant overlooking Niagara Falls. I wondered how my life had gone from editing books to living a jet-setting high life, in just a matter of hours.

"Coke? Or can I persuade you to have a glass of champagne?" he asked.

"Champagne," I agreed, breathily.

"That's my girl," he praised. "As long as you don't go telling everyone I corrupted your innocent ways."

It felt strange that I'd trusted him.

When Mason spoke, I noticed how soft and full his lips were. My eyes fell to his hands, and I focused on him twirling the stem of his glass with his long, thick fingers as he spoke. More than once my mind to wandered to the kisses that we'd shared and how possessive his hands had felt when he'd held or touched me. All that from a kiss.

I'd had plenty of dates where my intuition had served me well. Ones where I'd recognized warning flags, but with Mason, despite his reputation, I felt none.

Our dinner of succulent chicken and fresh seasonal vegetables was simple yet perfect and strangely, we ordered the same. The champagne flowed freely and after three glasses I felt far less inhibited and our conversation had turned to sex.

"I'm not as innocent as you think," I suddenly confessed, making Mason almost choke on the mouthful of drink he was taking.

"Is that right?" he asked, playfully.

"Mm-hmm."

"How 'not innocent' are we talking here?" he asked, wide-eyed and using quotation marks with his fingers to quote me.

"Like a ménage kind of not innocent," I replied, giggling.

Mason banged on the table and threw his head back, laughing. "Damn." He raised a brow, surprised. "It's always the quiet ones." Straightening in his chair he narrowed his gaze and stared me straight in the eyes. "All right, I'll bite. What kind of ménage?"

"What do you mean?"

"Two men and you? Another girl with you and a guy?"

"Yeah," I said, feeling less confident about sharing this piece of previously untold information. I had no idea what had made me talk about it in the first place.

"Which?" he asked, his curious eyes darkened in interest as though my disclosure had turned him on.

"Take your pick," I offered quickly, and then covered my face, embarrassed.

"Fuck me," he mused, scrutinizing me further. He ran his forefinger over the seam of his lips in thought. "Are you shitting me?"

"I'm afraid not," I replied, cringing because I had no idea why I'd said it and it was too late to take it back.

"No, don't be. It's just… unexpected."

"It kind of was at the time as well," I replied, chuckling.

"Damn, baby. Just when I thought I knew you, you hit me with this snappy little curve ball."

"I've gone down in your estimation now, huh?"

"On the contrary, for the last couple of days I've been forming my opinion of you, kind of trying to see past the initial infatuation I felt for you. You appeared strait laced with your no alcohol thing and your 'I'm not sleeping with you, comment', yet I find you assertive, sassy and much more than I expected you to be. And now here you are telling me you're experimental in the sack?"

"Not all that experimental, I mean I've never done anal... you know the two dicks thing," I made a cross with my fingers.

Mason chuckled and shook his head. "Double penetration you mean?"

"Yeah, it was more like both guys liked me and I liked both of them, so we kind of got tangled once the alcohol flowed."

"Ah, so it's not so much you don't do alcohol, more like who you do when you drink?"

My cheeks felt as if they were on fire. "Erm, well on both occasions that's when it kind of happened," I confirmed, but not in so many words.

"And it was you and a chick and a guy the other time?" he probed, shaking his head at the waiter who gestured at the champagne bottle in the cooler when he approached the table.

"Coffee black?" he asked, I nodded. It was only after he'd ordered them that I wondered if he was avoiding me making another bad decision.

"Yeah... not Sasha though. It was when I was in college... and it was more of a dare than something I made a conscious decision to do.

From that point in our conversation we shared our sexual preferences, what we liked and what we weren't so keen on.

It was an honest conversation I never expected to have with any man. But when Mason told me he'd had three girls at once, I wasn't sure how I felt about that. When I voiced this, I was surprised when he suggested I thought he had taken advantage of them. Then, before I answered he asked, "There were three of them and one of me. Who's to say it was me that had taken advantage?"

Suddenly the illuminations went off over The Falls and my heart sank when I realized how late it had gotten. Time had flown and I really wasn't ready for my time with Mason to end. A long sigh left my body at the thought of setting off for home.

"Hmm."

"Sorry?" I asked in response not fully aware of what I'd done.

"I don't want this night to end yet. I'm not ready," he stated.

"Let's stay," I heard myself say. "Fuck it, I don't want this to end without knowing what this is and the only way I'm going to find out is by being with you."

"Being with me? You mean in my bed?" I nodded. "And what happens if you regret it tomorrow?"

"Will I? Right now, I'm thinking I'll regret it a whole lot more if I don't."

CHAPTER 15

"Can I just say this is a tiny bit weird?" I remarked as I followed awkwardly behind Mason and Kenny on the way to the suite his security guy had arranged.

"What is?" Mason frowned.

"Him," I whispered, pointing at Kenny who I felt was almost joined at the hip to Mason.

"Don't worry, he won't be in the suite with us," he murmured in my ear as we hung back while Kenny strode on.

"I should think not," I mumbled indignantly.

Mason smiled, swiped the keycard out of his bodyguard's hand and signaled for him to get back in the elevator with his eyes. "Go to your room for the night. I know we have a 9:00 a.m. start. Make sure to organize Mercy's transport home."

As Mason opened the hotel suite door, I questioned myself, *Am I really going through with this?*

With the door closed, Mason turned and smiled. His gorgeous eyes searched my face, and he swallowed roughly.

"You're sure about this?" he asked.

"Yeah," I replied, suddenly self-conscious and nervous again.

Slipping his brown leather jacket off his shoulders, he

shrugged it off and slung it over a chair. It gave me the time to take in his appearance and catch a breath before he wandered toward me.

Without trying, Mason Fox was stunningly attractive. Dressed in a silver-grey shirt and dark blue jeans, his plain looking attire did more to enhance how handsome he was, than if he'd worn an expensive suit. The way his jeans clung tight to his groin below his thick, worn belt drew my eyes to the bottom half of his body. There had always been something about that rugged cowboy look that instantly turned me on.

Stepping up toe-to-toe, his hot breath wafted close to my face and when he placed his hands on my hips, it triggered my own response. Wrapping my hands around his waist, he glanced down with a glint of lust in his eyes. I stared back, already submitting to his will.

"This, right here," Mason began. "This is the first of many nights. I promise you, baby." Strangely, I believed him.

Smoothing my hair past my shoulders, he slid my dress material off one shoulder and dropped his mouth to my skin. A shiver of delight ran down my spine and brought an involuntary smile to my lips.

"Mm, you taste good," he muttered, his tone low and thick. He traced a finger from my behind my ear to my shoulder that left a trail of goosebumps behind.

He smiled when he saw it and slid his other hand from my hip to my ass. "God, you have a fabulous ass in this dress," he mumbled as he buried his face in the crook of my neck. Then Mason leaned back to look at me, brought both hands up my back, over my shoulders and down across my breasts. Lingering there, his thumbs strummed and circled my hardened nipples beneath my dress.

"You're so fucking beautiful," he whispered before he moved his mouth close to my ear. "I know I should take this slow, but I don't think I can," he confessed as his hands skated around my waist again, then down past my ass and grabbed the hem of my dress. He swept the clingy material up over my thighs, hips and breasts and in another swift move pulled it over my head.

With my dress bunched in his hand, he cast his gaze over my body. "Fuck, baby, you look perfect." He cast my dress behind him and swallowed hard. Deftly he undid a few buttons on his shirt and pulled it over his head. My breath hitched when I took in his fit, muscular body, with hard pecs and toned abs.

Reaching out, my fingers nervously traced the lines of his abs before I flattened my palms and smoothed them up and across his pecs. Mason sucked in a breath, pulled me tight against him, and walked me to the bed. He shoved me playfully onto the huge bed and when I saw him prowling over me, my mouth went dry.

Dark, lustful intent shone in his eyes as Mason's hand flew to his belt buckle. The chink of metal and the whipping sound of soft leather being ripped through the loops of his jeans made my heart hammer in my chest in anticipation. My breathing was shallow and rapid, and my heart rate soared as every fiber in my body appeared to burst into life.

Not once did his narrowed hungry eyes break his powerful stare with me as he shoved his jeans to his ankles and stepped free. Mason didn't wear briefs under his jeans and his firm, thick cock sprang free. Climbing on the bed, his large frame surrounded me on all sides as he locked me in place with his limbs.

Flashing me a slow sexy smile full of intent, he dropped his forehead to mine. "I never thought this would happen," he whispered. The atmosphere between us felt heavy, suffocating, electric. Grabbing my wrists, Mason peppered tender kisses over each temple, each eye, and began a deliciously slow, torturous descent down my neck and stopped at my breasts. Moving back up he traced his tongue from my collar bone to my breasts, releasing my hands he used his to push my bra up, gave them a firm squeeze, then removed my bra.

The second he saw my nipple piercings his eyes darted to mine. "So fucking sexy," he whispered in a low gruff tone before taking one in his mouth and nipping it with his teeth.

"God," I muttered as my body vibrated under his touch.

Mason parted my thighs and settled his body between them. "I can feel how soaked you are through your panties," he muttered with a wicked grin.

"All this for me?" he asked as he slid his fingers down between us and slipped them under the elastic and grazed them over my folds. "Fuck you're bare," he mumbled before pulling his had out and coating his lips and sucking his fingertips. He leaned above me and kissed me again. "What I'm going to do to you," he promised. I spread my legs wider in response to his words. Exploring my sex again, Mason moved and circled my clit, before he pinched it tightly.

"Holy shit," I muttered, and he kissed me again.

When he broke the kiss, he dragged my panties down my legs and settled his cock at my entrance. We stilled as a wave of carnal desperation passed between us.

CHAPTER 16

"*D*o it," I demanded and tried to pull. His wet tip poked at my entrance, and I gasped.

"Please," I said as my heart almost beat out of my chest.

"Condom," he muttered.

"If you're clean, I'm on the pill," I muttered not stopping to think for a moment of the consequences of that. If this was only once then I wanted all of him, Mason Fox, skin to skin inside me.

Edging inside, we both said, "Fuck," in unison as he inched his way deep, stretching me tight, stealing my breath and making me the fullest I'd ever felt.

"Fuck," he said again when he bottomed out. His heavy, velvety ball sac brushed my ass as a deep groan left his throat.

He swallowed roughly. "God, you feel incredible. Are you okay?"

I nodded and he immediately began to move; first slow and tender, until he was sure I was ready for more and then he devoured my body, with his mouth, nipping at my skin and sucking my breasts.

A rush of euphoria took me by surprise and instantly I felt like

I was falling into an abyss. Through a convulsing haze, I screamed loudly, while I fisted the satin comforter, scored his back with my nails, and almost lost my mind completely until he covered my mouth with his. Our love making came to an abrupt end wen Mason suddenly quickened is pace, cussed under his breath and pulled out suddenly. I watched in fascination as long strands of cum pulsed from his slit until he couldn't bear it anymore.

Mason collapsed beside me and pulled me into his chest. His heartbeat strong and steady.

"I could have made that last a hell of a lot longer, but it would have been torture," Mason mumbled, glancing down at me. "Next time, I'll try to take my time." We lay there in the quiet for a few minutes before he rose from the bed and went into the bathroom.

I took my turn when he came back and smirked at the state of my smudged eye makeup and my bed hair in the mirror. After I'd peed and freshened up, I went back to the room, thankful Mason had turned the light off and I hadn't needed to face him.

"Everything okay? I didn't hurt you, did I?"

"Yeah. No, just freshening up," I replied softly as I climbed back into the bed. As soon as I laid down, he rolled toward me, spooned against my body and pressed a kiss to my shoulder. "Get some sleep, baby. This is the second night I've kept you up late. You must be exhausted."

I laid quietly and had began to fall asleep when Mason pressed another kiss on my shoulder. "I don't know how we're going do this. But I'm going to find a way."

I decided even if he couldn't, I wouldn't regret spending the night with him.

* * *

BEING DISORIENTED and shaken awake when you're used to living on your own is alarming. I sat bolt upright in shock and bumped heads with Mason. "Fuck," he cussed, nursing his head when I opened my eyes.

"Ow," I said, chuckling as I rubbed mine.

"Jesus," he said and pressed a kiss to my forehead.

"I've got to leave soon. I've arranged transport to take you home. A car will be waiting at 11:00 a.m., and a chopper will fly you back." Blinking, I stared at him, with an unsettling feeling. "Last night..." he said and shook his head. I held my breath and waited, expecting to be let down gently. "It was everything. I meant what I said. This is only the beginning... that is, if you'll have me."

For a few moments I became choked with emotion and couldn't talk, so I nodded.

"I'll get these two concerts out of the way and I'll be back." He leaned in and gave me a lingering kiss on my closed mouth. "I've got to run, but Kenny's left you the details for the transfer back to New York, order room service and I'll be in touch."

Mason pulled my head toward him again, kissed my hair, and left.

Once I was alone, I did as he said about room service. By the time it arrived, I'd showered, dressed and tidied my hair back in a high ponytail all the while trying to believe Mason hadn't deserted me.

The journey home was uneventful, but the moment I walked into my apartment and saw my answering machine flash with four messages, I instinctively knew they were all from Sasha.

CHAPTER 17

ℬ

*H*ow I dealt with my second round edits, I had no idea but somehow I got them done. Then it dawned on me, Mason hadn't asked for my cell number.

The arrangements for our first date had been made by his PA, who had contacted Sasha's author page on social media. Although he knew where I lived, Mason had no way of communicating with me.

As the days passed, I began scouring his social media for news, but I didn't learn anything new. After a week of no news, I became angry but resigned that I'd been used like hundreds of other stupid girls.

"Hey," Sasha said, when I finally felt strong enough to answer her calls. "I was about to call the police. Where have you been?"

"Sorry, just busy on my end… author deadlines," I lied.

"I've missed you. Should we grab a pizza, and watch *A Star is Born?*"

"No. No rock star movies," I snapped.

"Jesus. All right, already. Your pick," she appeased.

"Fine, give me an hour," I agreed, guilt-ridden.

I only realized how I much I'd let things slide in the previous week I'd been moping when I began tidying up. Sasha rang the buzzer in front of my building. As I let her up, I knew I needed to tell her what had happened between me and Mason.

When she knocked on the door, I swallowed hard, took a deep breath and opened the door wide. From the quizzical look on her face, I wondered what was wrong.

"Is there something you want to tell me?" she probed.

I dropped my head in shame. "Why?"

"As I stepped out of my car, this guy wandered up to the entrance and told me he was your boyfriend." She stepped aside and Mason's gorgeous face beamed a smile toward me.

"My boyfriend? I didn't even give this guy my number," I joked.

Mason strode forward and pulled me into his chest. "Hello, gorgeous, did you miss me?"

He lifted his head back and gave me a piercing look. "Well?"

"Guess I'm gonna leave you two to it," Sasha said with a shrug. "Thanks for the review by the way. Did you actually read the book?" she asked.

Mason nodded, cracking a genuine smile at Sasha. "Yeah, and like you said in the content, sweetheart, 'where some view the ambition of others as a pipe dream, those of us who believe, our dreams can become our destiny.'"

I'd never really listened to the words of Mason's song, but I had read Sasha's book. Mason was the kind of man book boyfriends were made of, and he was spot on when he'd said in his review that there were similarities between himself and the antagonist that Sasha had created.

Fortunately for me, I was the one woman he'd connected with who truly didn't get his fame. Wasn't impressed by it and wasn't intimidated by it.

After Sasha left, Mason flashed me his lopsided grin and my heart melted as he cupped his hand under my chin.

"You know how you said you work from home all the time?

How would you feel about working from my place? I want to spend time with you, and it is a little more private and secure than here. I'm not asking you to move permanently or anything, just to take a leap of faith while we get to know one another better."

I could have said no. Insisted on a long-distance thing. My gut told me to be spontaneous. That I could lose out on something wonderful if I didn't. "You've got a soundproof booth installed, right?"

Mason smiled widely and smoothed my hair in both hands. "If you come to California, I promise not to make you listen to my songs."

"Then it's a deal." I beamed.

Cradling my head in his hands he stared seriously into my eyes. "You know everyone's going to say we're insane," he muttered as he pressed a soft kiss to my lips. "But I've got a feeling we're going to prove them wrong because from the moment I set eyes on you, I knew I wanted you to be mine."

Who needs pipe dreams when fate has a hand to play? If a rock star had never written that song, and Sasha had never written her book based on the lyrics, little Mercy Hall from Queens would never have crossed paths with Mason Fox.

* * *

AT THE END : if you enjoyed this short story, you can find out more about my series and standalones at www.klshandwick.com

Writing came relatively later in life for K.L. Shandwick after a challenge by a friend led to The Everything Trilogy. She loves creating new characters and story lines. Her characters have flaws and she hopes this helps the connection between them and her readers. K.L. enjoys the journeys they take her on during the creation of her stories, and each character has his or her own voice. She doesn't use prepared outlines for her stories preferring the characters to take their own direction as the story progresses. These days K.L. lives in the Yorkshire countryside in the UK, and writes full-time.

GOOD GUYS BY ELIZABETH SAFLEUR

This short story is a good introduction to the Shakedown Series, a steamy contemporary, deep feels, second-chance-at-love series

CHAPTER 1

*A*spen slammed against the metal push bar of the exit door and stumbled into the street as Sol's curses rang out behind her. At least she didn't hit the pavement. She couldn't afford to fall.

Cold city air hit her in the face as she ran. Not fast enough, as the pounding of the man's footfalls grew closer. She picked up the pace.

If she could just get into a crowd, to a busier street, even if Sol caught up with her, she could scream and make a scene. Surely someone would help.

She glanced over her shoulder to see how close Sol had gotten to her. That was when she ran smack into a mountain of a man stepping out of a monstrous black limousine. His arms flew up and caught her.

"Help me." Her lungs screamed with pain. Were her words loud enough?

He twisted her so she ended up behind him just as Sol reached them.

"Step aside, man, and mind your damned business," Sol demanded.

"Mind your fucking manners," the guy returned.

She should say something like, oh, maybe, Sol's boss just tried to force her to give him *a blow job*. She'd only gone to his office to sign an employee contract, which was probably fraudulent, to ensure she got paid. Instead, she'd found him leaning back in a cracked leather office chair with his disgusting, fleshy dick in his hand. She'd have to bleach her brain to get rid of that image.

Sol pointed his finger at her. "She needs to be arrested for assault. We're pressing charges, bitch."

"He assaulted *me*." Aspen poked her head around the guy's shoulder. "Next time, I'll staple his entire dick."

"Get in the car, doll." The guy grasped her arm, but she wrenched it free. She never wanted to be touched again. Not by any man, ever, even if he was standing between her and an enraged bouncer who'd likely been told to haul her back to the strip club for punishment.

She only barely made it out. She'd slipped under Sol's beefy arms at the bottom of the stairs while his boss stood at the top, limp dick hanging out of his stained pants, hurling obscenities at them both.

Even if she had made $631 tonight, her career as a stripper was over.

That was when it hit her. She stared at her hands—her empty hands. God dammit, she'd dropped her bag in the slimeball's office. All her cash was gone. *Fuck. Fuck. Fuck.*

"Give me my money back," she spat at Sol.

He looked at her like she was the crazy one. Well, she was. Crazy with anger, disgust, and despair, and she'd had *enough*.

The guy she was using as a human shield pointed at the dancing girl embroidered on Sol's black shirt. "You're with Maxim's? Tell Jones to chill."

Sol's startled face made her feel a modicum better. "If you know Jones, you know he doesn't take orders from anyone."

"He'll take anything from Declan Philips." The guy's hand landed on Sol's chest. "*My* employer."

Sol's eyes narrowed. He cursed and turned away, stomping back toward the club.

The guy grabbed her arm and opened the limo door. "Doll, car."

"Stop calling me doll." She wrenched free again, her arm now sore as hell for being clutched at so often that night.

"I would, but you haven't told me your name." Was that an annoyed tone she heard? The nerve.

"Then we're even. You haven't told me yours, either."

"I'm Max. Work for Declan Philips. Just dropped him off for the night."

"Who?"

"Owner of Shakedown? Dance club? You should know it."

Another strip club? *Fantastic.* She stepped around him. Time to walk away. She was done with being groped, pushed, grabbed, cussed at, and, in general, being demeaned by anyone. That time, he didn't reach for her, which might have saved him from being punched even if he'd just saved her from God knew what.

The street was nearly deserted, with a few lone cars farther up the street, crossing the intersection of South Haven Street and O'Donnell and sending slices of light through the dark. What time was it? Had the buses stopped running? Her cell phone, along with her bus pass, was with her cash. *Whatever.* She could panhandle for five bucks at least.

She moved, each step a wince. The concrete was hell under her feet. By the time she'd gotten halfway up Haven, the blisters on her pinky toes were rubbed raw and stinging.

The rumble of a car engine got closer. "I'm not going to hurt you, for Christ's sake," a male voice called from the street.

She turned to face him. Max's arm hung out of the limo window, which crept alongside her, most definitely following her.

She stopped. "Thanks for the help, but you're off the hook. You can drop the knight-in-shining-armor bit."

"Left my armor at home. Look, I work for Declan Phillips—"

"So you said." She put her hands on her hips. "Hey, can you lend me twenty bucks? For a cab? Or let me order an Uber from your phone?" If he wanted to play savior, he could—with money.

"I've got your ride right here. You should know if Declan—"

"Jesus, who is this Declan guy?" Her arms fell to her sides with a slap. "You talk about him like he's the Pope."

"You work the clubs. I'd think—"

"No." She walked to the limo and slapped her hands down on the door frame. "I don't *work* the clubs. I'm an accountant." She straightened.

A shot of anger punched through her chest. Well, she used to be in accounting. So much for her Georgetown University degree. Fat lot that did for her.

He arched his eyebrows and let his gaze drop for a second to her clothes—a stupid Maxim's T-shirt they'd insisted she try on and her best jeans. "Look, Miss Accountant, just get in the back. I'll drop you off wherever you want, and we can both go home in peace. I gotta follow Declan's code." He scrubbed his five o'clock shadow.

She crossed her arms. "What code?"

"I'll tell you if you get in." He let his arm once more drop out the open window and bang against the car door. "Take a picture of me, my license place, and your location. Send it to a friend. Then you can sit in the back, and I'll keep the divider and a window down so you can jump out if I take my hands off the wheel."

Her feet would never make the eight-block walk to the nearest bus station, and she had no money anyway. So what if this Max guy turned out to be a kidnapper? Hell, maybe she could split the ransom with him. By the length of the limo, he knew people with money.

"Lost my cell phone."

He reached over to the seat and then handed her his phone. "Code is 1427. Take it with you in back."

She stopped walking—or limping—grabbed it, and lurched open the back door.

He slammed on the brakes. "Whoa, warn a guy, will ya?"

"You can drop me off at the bus station and lend me some money for the fare. Then I'll give you your phone back."

"Yes, ma'am."

She slid across the seat to the exact middle so she could get an eyeful of his hands. Big. Probably could strangle an elephant.

He turned on his blinker. "So, do I finally get your name?" His voice sounded distant as he turned the ostentatious boat onto Monument Street. People with money really did waste it on a lot of stupid things.

"Aspen."

"Real name or stage name?"

"Does it matter?" She ran her hands over the leather seat, new and expensive. It smelled like her old office, and a pang in her chest took her off guard. "And I told you, I'm not stripping."

"That why one of Jones's boys was after you? Cooked the books for them?"

"I have never done anything illegal in my life." She ground her teeth together. No matter her confiscated computer showed $11,000 had been transferred from her old company's books to her personal checking account, which then promptly disappeared again to God knows where.

"Well, good for you. First night on the job, and Jones get handsy? Yeah, he's got that reputation."

"You ask a lot of questions." She dropped her head against the headrest and slipped off her sandals. "You got any water back here?" Though she really could use something stronger. The adrenaline rush was fading, but she would not disappear into feeling sorry for herself again. She'd allowed herself one day for that—and that day was over.

Max spun his hand on the wheel. "In the fridge. So, you fought back?"

"I stapled his dick." The little mini fridge opened with a sucking pop. *Oh, score.* The limo's liquor stash included Grey Goose vodka.

Max shot a look over his shoulder. "You did what?"

The bottle was chilled and, even better, unopened, which meant *full*.

"Stapler," she said. "It was the only thing handy when he asked for that second audition, if you get my drift." She undid the foil and pulled out the corked top.

He laughed heartily. "Declan would *love* you. Hey, I'll introduce you. He's always hiring."

"Thanks, but I'm through with strip clubs." She'd just have to figure out another way to drum up eleven thousand dollars in twenty-five days. She'd begged for more time, but her jerk-off ex-boss said thirty days was generous enough for her crime. If not, he'd have her arrested.

She lifted a crystal cut tumbler from the little rack, filled it halfway, and took a huge slug. It did little to tamp down a curious lump rising in her throat, probably from having to admit she'd actually lowered herself to peeling off a dress the size of a napkin to Britney Spears crooning "Breathe on Me." Shit. *What* was she thinking? Stripping?

Her second thought was worse. Who fails at *that*? Clearly, she had.

"Shakedown's not a strip club," Max peered at her in the rearview mirror. "Burlesque. Classy joint."

"Sure it is. With a *code*." She took another gulp of vodka heaven. Instead of being swallowed down, that stupid lump remained, threatening to make her emotional. As if that would help anything.

"Mr. Phillips tells all his employees that if someone's in trouble, we should never hesitate to follow our gut and help," he continued.

"Real altruistic guy."

"You have no idea." His eyes stared at her in the rearview mirror. "Declan rescued one of Jones's other girls once. Name's Phoenix. You should tell her what you did. She could tell you things can get better, even after what happened to her."

He didn't need to elaborate on what the bastard had done.

The lump morphed, and her heartbeat ratcheted up. She took another large swallow of vodka, but it did nothing to stop a sob from escaping her throat. She took furious sips, but her teeth chattered against the tumbler.

"Hey." The limo lurched a little when Max hit the brakes, and vodka splashed all over her and the seat. The bottle she'd set between her feet slipped and tipped over, and the glug-glug of vodka escaping onto the floor mats gave her an odd rise of panic. She grabbed it, but her hand shook so badly she couldn't get the little stopper back into the neck.

Doors opened. Dings sounded. There was a dip next to her, and then the bottle was taken from her hands. A strong masculine arm went around her shoulder, and that was when her ridiculous crying really let loose.

"It's okay. You made it out." Max's voice was sincere, which only made her feel worse because she wasn't *out*—not by a long shot.

"I didn't make shit. I—I had $631, and now, it's gone." She swiped at her face, angry she was melting down.

"Hey." Through the tears flooding her eyes, a Grey Goose bottle tipped in her direction. "You need this."

She took a big swallow of vodka and sniffed. The limo smelled like a distillery, masking the expensive leather smell, reminding her of the strip club once more. Whoever said vodka didn't smell hadn't dumped half a bottle onto a car floor.

Max handed her an honest-to-God cloth napkin pulled from

another rack. As she wiped under her eyes, smears of make-up and mascara colored the white cloth.

She swiveled her head to take him in. He gazed at her with pity, which made her feel worse.

The warmth from his body felt good, however. October wasn't exactly tee-shirt and jeans weather, and that was all she had on. Oh, yeah, she'd had a coat, too, but it was back at the club with her bag, cell phone, bus pass, and money. Her breath hitched, and her stupid sobs just would not stop.

"I have got to get a grip." She banged her head against the headrest. "I'm normally not this emotional."

"Take it tonight's not been normal for you," he offered. "More?"

"No, I shouldn't." She held out her glass so he could refill it. "I have a lot to do tomorrow, including finding a new job." She took a sip of the vodka. "Why are you helping me? I mean, you don't even know me. What was your name again?"

He offered a handshake. "Max Torsney. Driver. Club Security. Like I said."

Wow, his hands really were huge. "Aspen Snow. Former accountant. Failed stripper. Unemployed." She left out *accused felon*.

"You need some water." He reached over to the little refrigerator.

She held out her glass. "I'll have more Goose." Who cared if she was hung over tomorrow? She didn't have anywhere to be.

Without releasing her hand, he refilled her glass with the magical, make-everything-alright elixir.

She studied his profile as he put the stopper back in the near-empty bottle. He was the dead opposite of Sol, Jones, Mr. Dollar Bills, and all the other anonymous men she'd feigned interest in tonight. Max was handsome in a rugged lumberjack meets a yacht captain sense.

See? Her brain was definitely not working. Mixed metaphors, anyone?

"Now, beautiful," he said. "Where can I drop you?" His hand had not left hers. All that warmth and masculinity touched her with such care she almost cried again. She pulled her hand free.

She crossed her arms over her chest, splashing a little vodka on the seat. "Do you do this often? Pick up strange women?"

"Never. But you're not strange. You're smart and pretty, and you ended up in a place you shouldn't have."

"How do you know? You just met me."

"You're wearing 7 For All Mankind jeans at two hundred a pop. Your nails were done professionally. And those earrings are real diamonds."

Oh, thank God. He's gay. Or married. Because he also was gorgeous and protective—and vodka always did turn on her hormones like a mermaid sent to lure sailors.

She must have said that aloud because he laughed. "I'm not gay. I'm around dancers—a lot of them nothing like who you've been hanging out with tonight at Maxim's."

Shit. Now he's straight—and gorgeous and protective. Of course, everyone was gorgeous when a third of a bottle of Grey Goose had been consumed.

"And Jones has enough victims on the street—"

"I'm not a victim. I put myself there." Sort of.

"Of course not. But I felt called to help." He scratched his chin, even the sound of stubble sounding masculine if such a thing were possible. Yeah, he was good looking, alright, all that dark tousled hair and a tiny scar across one cheek. And he had that knight in shining armor thing *down.*

"Are you single?" No one like him could be.

His eyebrows shot up. "Asking me out?"

"Maybe." She set her glass down on the floorboard. "But we're already out."

She leaned toward him and kissed his cheek. His five o'clock shadow felt as good as it looked. "So, thank you for being called to help."

He smiled back, confident but not smug. His eyes were a warm brown if that was possible. Kind eyes, her mother would have said. The mother who'd stopped talking to her since she got fired from her job.

"Now, Aspen-not-a-stripper, where do you live? I'll take you." For one brief second, she couldn't remember because he had really nice lips. Who could think when she was less than six inches from those?

She wasn't sure who started the kiss. All she knew was their lips met, his a little hesitant at the contact, hers decisive as if her mouth had a mind of its own. She was just about to dip her tongue between his lips when they opened and he took over. Holy hell, did he take over.

But then, as soon as the kiss began, it ended.

He pulled back. "What are you doing, doll?"

"It's Aspen to you." She dipped her chin and let her eyelashes flutter—trying to look innocent over the devil that clawed at her insides, desperate to get out.

He didn't do anything but stare at her lips. So she licked them. She'd had a craptastic day, and she would never see him again. She wanted to forget all about her situation. She wanted to feel good for ten minutes. Was that asking too much?

She put her hand on his thigh—just a little test to see how he'd respond. "So, how far does this code extend? I mean, if a girl needed help in other ways …" Up close, his eyes were more hazel than brown, confident and kind. But his smile was more of a wicked tilt that egged her on.

He smiled, lifted her hand from his thigh, and placed it back on hers. "The girl drinking straight vodka gets the help she needs by being taken home."

"Why?" God, was that a whine?

Oh, screw that. She didn't wait for an answer. She went for his mouth. Once more, he didn't kiss her back right away, so she pressed forward, dipping her tongue between his lips. Mmm, he was delicious. She might have moaned a little aloud at his taste, which was clearly the right thing to do because that was when he took over. His hands were on her back, his chest pressing against her aching nipples and his lips moving over her mouth like he owned them.

She swung her leg over his lap and positioned herself over his crotch, and, sweet Jesus, he had a package inside those expensive trousers.

He grasped both sides of her face and pulled her from her blitz on his lips.

"Aspen ..." he mumbled. He leaned his head back and took a good long look at her face. Hesitation grew in his eyes, and for a quick second, she panicked that he might consider stopping.

"You promised." That was most *definitely* a whine.

His eyebrow arched up. "What?"

"To help me. I had the worst day of my life today." Well, not exactly. Being escorted out of the building four days ago after being accused of embezzlement was pretty damned bad. Having your mother hang up on you when she learned of your alleged criminal activities was horrible. Being asked to give a blow job to a rotting heap of flesh ...

"Aspen. Look at me." He swiped his thumbs under her eyes. "Don't cry."

Fuck, her eyes leaked more emotion she couldn't control.

"I'm taking you home," he said.

"Not yet. Please." She put a little begging into her tone, and his nostrils flared.

"You need to know there are some good men in the world."

So she'd been told. But was he for real? Turning down no-strings sex? Shit. He was going for sainthood.

The limo door dinged as he folded himself into the driver's

seat again. He slammed the door and adjusted the mirror so she caught those beautiful eyes.

She crossed her arms and huffed. "Now you're going to make me wish you remembered me and called me in the morning, and … I hate that."

"Okay." He lurched the car into drive and spun his hand on the wheel. "I'll call in the afternoon."

CHAPTER 2

*V*odka was the devil's blood. Its retreat from her body left pure fire that now coursed through her head, her limbs, and her stomach.

She rolled to her back.

Oh, God, her stomach had woken up, and it was *not* happy. It roiled. She ran to the bathroom and promptly upchucked. Then she fell back onto the bathroom rug and shivered.

Did last night really happen?

Yep. But it was over.

Time for a self-pep talk.

For one, things could be worse. She could have given in to Jones. She could be out on the street. She could have had to walk home. Instead, she threw herself at a perfect stranger—someone with a *code*. See? More than one thing was good. She would recover from it—all of it.

There was a loud pounding on her front door, and she sat up. Blood pulsed in her head—and her heart. Someone was at her front door, and whoever it was didn't sound patient.

Crap. She'd put a fake address on Maxim's employment document, but her address would be easy enough to find.

Maybe they'd come for her, and if so, something told her it wasn't to return her $631, coat, and cell phone.

Shit, she didn't even have the ability to call 9-1-1.

The knocking sounded again. She crept into the hallway, her tee shirt with the giant kangaroo on the front barely covering her ass. She grabbed the first thing she could get her hands on. A brass bowl where she usually put her keys—which she also didn't have. How did she get into bed anyway?

Oh, that guy with the limo … Where was he now?

"I'm calling the police," she screamed, making lightning bolts go straight through her head.

"You never say that," a male voice said through the door. It sounded familiar.

She crept over to the peephole. Max. Limo guy. His hair was darker than she recalled. She slid the deadbolt over and opened the door.

She held the door open only halfway. "Oh, and what was I supposed to say?"

"You yell out a guy's name like you're calling your six-foot-two Marine Corps husband from the back room."

"They'd get all that from a name?"

"If he's named Max." He held up a plastic grocery bag. "Rescue package. Motrin, an Emer-gen-C, and—" he grinned and lifted a grease-stained bag with his other hand, "—Charger's French fries."

She grabbed the greasy bag, the aroma of roasted potatoes instantly calming her stomach. "You are a god." French fries should never be turned away. Her gut told her if he brought her French fries, he wasn't the assaulting type. Plus, there was that *code* thing, which so far proved real.

She stepped inside, and he followed.

Plunking down onto her couch, she tore the bag open and reached in. Her fingers met the hot, oily, delicious fries, and she stuffed three of them into her mouth. As the salt hit her tongue, she murmured. "God's fooooo." Her mouth was too full, but the magic of grease and potatoes were doing the trick, instantly settling her belly.

Max shook the water bottle, now fizzing and growing orange with the Emer-Gen-C. "You're looking less green."

She swallowed. "Not my best color."

"Oh, I don't know. I imagine you look good in anything." He winked.

Uh-oh. Flirt alert. The fact that she'd straddled his lap last night and practically begged him to nail her in the backseat of a stretch limo she'd defiled with half a bottle of vodka was probably a clue she was open for business.

He must have gotten her home last night. Oh, shit, had they done the deed? Who could tell, given her body was in full revolt? She had a vague recollection of him pulling covers over her shoulder. "We didn't—"

"Relax, Aspen-Anna Davis. Once you showed me where you had a spare key on the ledge—you put up quite a fight there, which was good on you—you passed out."

"I don't usually drink." *That much.* "Wait a minute. How do you know my real name?"

He held out his hand, her cell phone nestled in his large palm.

She grabbed it and squealed. "You found it!" She stared at her phone. He could have handed her a velvet bag full of diamonds, and it wouldn't have compared. Her gaze shot up to him. "How?"

"Told you I'd call you in the afternoon. Only Jones answered, so I stopped by to get it for you."

She harrumphed, checking the time. Two in the afternoon already? "And he just handed it over?"

He lifted his other hand, her purse dangling from it. "He was … accommodating. I took the liberty of looking at your driver's license. Sue me."

She snatched it and hugged it to her chest. So what if the leather got a little French fry grease on it? "Oh, thank you, thank you." She opened it up and rummaged around. Shocking, but her wallet was inside. She broke it open and found bills—lots and lots of them.

Her lips fell open.

Max shrugged. "He gave you a bonus."

A week ago, she'd have waited until Max was gone to count the money. But a week ago, she wasn't an accused felon. She found two thousand dollars inside.

Max settled into the chair near the couch and put his elbows on his knees. "Feeling better?"

He assessed her with his beautiful brown eyes. But he was studying her a little too hard.

"Listen." She moved her purse and greasy paper bag to the side, the edges scratching her bare legs. Oops. Brain not yet on. She pulled the blanket from the back of the couch and draped it over her thighs. "I appreciate all this, but I'm never working for a club again." He clearly was there to recruit her. Strips clubs were always looking for new girls.

"Not even to do accounting work? Yeah, I talked with Declan," he scrubbed his hair and stared down at the floor, "and I usually don't go this far, but let's just say Shakedown is a place of second chances, and it seems like you could use one."

She took a swig of the Emer-Gen-C, which for the record, didn't go with French fries. "This part of the code? Find an almost-convicted felon a job?" Why not go all the way with the truth? By the look on his face, he wasn't expecting that.

"Almost convicted?"

"Sort of. I have until the thirtieth to return $11,000 that I didn't take from my firm but somehow magically appeared in my account and then even more mysteriously disappeared within three hours. Ya know, a typical Monday at the office."

"Declan will loan it to you."

She harumphed. Another stapler was in her future with this guy, wasn't it? "Why would he do that?"

Max shrugged. "He's always doing shit like that."

She cocked her head, not buying this whole scenario.

"Okay," he sighed. "I'll tell you."

Here it came. That Declan guy was mafia, and Max was there to break her legs if she refused.

He reached over and grabbed the paper bag, pulling out a fry from the bag and sticking it in his mouth. "Declan went to jail a long time ago on bogus charges. Not my story to tell. But he tends to believe people when they're telling the truth."

"How do you know I'm not just making it all up? To worm my way into your good graces only to … *cook* the books, as you said last night."

"Like *I* said last night, I can tell you're someone who at least once had money. Besides, you'd have inflated the number. Rounded it to something like twenty grand. Or you'd have charged me for the pleasure of your crotch on mine."

She swallowed hard. She'd connected with him on that level, hadn't she? But prostitution? "No, even I have limits."

"Of course you do. Finish breakfast." His gaze fell to the French fry bag. "Then, take a shower. I'm taking you to meet Declan."

Bossy. "I'm not sure—"

"You got somewhere else to be?"

Truly, she hadn't.

* * *

MAX FILLED her in on the way over about how Declan had met a stripper who really was a very talented dancer, and she'd rescued him, and he'd paid her back … and honestly, it sounded like a Hallmark movie. Only with sex.

Then it got better. Max wasn't kidding about Shakedown being a high-end burlesque club.

The club's outside looked like a warehouse except for the red awning leading up to an etched glass front door. And inside? Pure

1920s glamour. Green tufted booths, a long wood bar with a gleaming brass foot rail, and a large stage framed by heavy red velvet curtains.

But it was the sign above the bar that proved the adage that some things are too good to be true.

Touching any of our performers will result in the offender's permanent removal. Removal in one piece not guaranteed.

She'd most definitely walked into a mob lair. She spun on him. "If you kill me, I will haunt you forever."

A grin broke out on his face. "Too late. You're already doing that."

Her brows pinched together. "Charming me before the axe falls?" Because dying by axe was not on her agenda. Even if she was joking, she still shuddered at the thought.

"You think I storm into a strip club for a woman's cell phone and purse just to try something? I've seen your defensive skills. Jones is walking with a limp, by the way, and not from me. Thought you'd like to know."

"Good." She returned to studying the room as her eyes had adjusted from the bright sunshine outside to dimmer surroundings. "How does this place not have an accountant already?"

"Declan handles all of it by himself, but he recently got hooked up, so—"

"So, he needs to have time for me," a woman's voice rang from the other side of the room. She stepped out from a long line of shadows. Flame red hair framed a drop-dead gorgeous face.

Blue eyes sparkled at her. "I'm Phee, short for Phoenix. And you must be Anna. Or do you prefer Aspen?"

Oh, she was the woman Max had told her about, the one who'd had a similar experience with Jones. Amazing how Anna recalled that tidbit. Word had gotten around fast about her failed employment at Maxim's. Or rather, her humiliating attempt at raising money by gyrating nearly naked before men with folded dollar bills. "Anna. I'm burying Aspen."

"Oh, you don't need to do that. Just bring her back out when you feel like driving some man wild, even in private." Phee winked and looped her arm in Anna's. "Want a tour?"

Max stepped in front of them. "Phee, I've got this."

Anna must have startled and jumped back a bit when he took her other arm. They both quickly dropped their hold on her, their faces dropping into concern.

"Want a stapler?" Max asked, a grin spreading across his face. Making fun of her?

"Max." Phoenix crossed her arms and pursed her lips. She inched closer to Anna. "I guess he didn't tell you much about us. Here's what you need to know. If you want to dance, you have to audition—next year, and there's a waiting list. You're not allowed to take your clothes off. Believe me, my sister Starr has tried to break that rule. Also, Jerk-off Jones is an ass. Declan is the best man I've ever encountered. And," she leaned closer, "Max is a close second."

A puff of air left his lips. "I wouldn't say that."

"Okay," she smiled. "You're fourth or fifth." Phee squeezed Anna's elbow. "Come see me if you want to talk. No one here has to use office supplies to survive." She pointed at the sign over the bar that threatened bodily harm if the dancers were threatened. "They mean it. It's been tested, and they're barred for life." Phoenix waved a hand and then glided away through a set of black curtains.

Anna turned to Max. "You brought her out here to put me at ease, didn't you?"

He chuckled. "Phoenix has never put anyone at ease. She just wants that accountant position filled." He gestured to the black curtains. "The office is that way."

She sighed heavily and was probably about to make yet another bad decision, though stripping still topped the list. Really, how could following him be any worse? She walked through the black curtains.

The mysterious code master, Declan, turned out to be a hell of a silver fox in an antiques-laden office. He asked normal interview questions with only two about the "false accusations," as he called them. Did she take the money? And had she ever thought she could before?

The answers were easy. No, and she wasn't stupid. "Risking my entire life for eleven thousand?"

He'd chuckled and agreed. "I appreciate a woman with a grand vision." He pushed himself off the edge of the desk where he'd been perched. "Fair warning. Our books are quite behind. It's a big job to catch us up. Blame it on a distraction named Phoenix."

"Oh, she's your—"

"Love of my life? Yes." He glanced up at Max and cocked his head.

She'd almost forgotten Max was there in the background. She turned to look at him. He was staring at her intently and turned as red as a firetruck when she caught his gaze. He cleared his throat and shifted in his seat. When she swung her gaze back to Declan, he was smiling broadly. What was going on?

Declan rounded his desk. "Max doesn't normally make such a vehement case for someone. When can you start?"

Oh. "I'm hired?"

"I trust Max with my life." He raised a hand. "Which means he keeps me from dying in Baltimore traffic, which is the same as taking one's life in your hands. Need time to think about the job?"

Time was one thing she did not have on her side. "No. I mean, yes, I'd like the job. But there's a little matter of salary."

Declan smiled at her. "You can start at seventy-five K. I'll loan you the $11,000 and take a little out of your paycheck each month. In the meantime, we'll see what we can do to chase down who might have set you up. Unfortunately, this isn't our first encounter with such circumstances."

Was he kidding? First, his offer was double what she'd made before. And to pay off her wholly-unfair debt? Then to help her figure out how she got into this predicament to begin with? When one encounters something that seemed too good to be true, it generally was, her mother had told her. Then again, that was the woman who'd hung up on her when she'd asked for a loan.

"But you don't even know me. It's just so ... generous of you."

"I don't want you worried about money while you're taking care of mine. So take the night to think about it. Go out and enjoy the show. Have dinner. Phee's favorite is the salmon."

She stood. Everyone in that room knew she'd take the job. After all, what choice did she have? "Thanks for taking a chance on me."

"What's life if we don't give each other chances?"

The "show" turned out to be spectacular. Men, women, all adorned in sparkles and feathers, and not a single strip move in sight. Rather, their acts were storytelling in motion. A Valkyrie taking another woman to Valhalla—or at least she thought that was what was going on. A huntress meeting up with two hunters and besting them. It was downright feminist if she thought about it. But also, their acts were elegant. Sensual.

One performer stood out, however. When the curtains split and the spotlight lit up Phoenix's pale skin and sunset hair, she understood what Declan saw in her. She rode a giant stuffed bull in a matador costume. Smoke billowed from the beast's mechanical, bobbing head. With one arm lifted, she rode the bull into the center stage, and the crowd jumped to their feet. She was pure sexual power, presenting herself without apology or the need to explain herself. It was mesmerizing.

"Wow." Anna couldn't say anything else.

Max bought his head closer to her. "Phoenix doesn't perform much anymore. She owns the dance school next door. Declan set her up." He was so close she could smell his masculine scent mixing with the lavender and vanilla of the club. That was another thing about the place. A few men smoked cigars, but for the life of her, she couldn't smell them.

"Guess love makes you do all kinds of things." She didn't understand why she said that. When had she ever been in love?

Max's eyes glittered from the stage lights in the dark as he looked into her eyes. "Yes, it does." He flushed.

It was so wild that he had blushed a couple of times in her presence. He didn't seem the type to be undone by much. He looked like the type of man who made others shake in their boots. Thick biceps straining his jacket. Hands that were nimble and strong. Then, there were the tattoos she just now noticed. Of course, she was now sober, not hungover or running for her life.

Max's arm was warm against her back. He'd placed it along the back of her chair.

She didn't hate it. "You said you work here as a bodyguard."

"Yep. Driving Declan when he goes to less desirable neighborhoods. General security."

She could believe it. He looked like someone who could handle anything that came his way. And not just because he was sporting multicolor tattoos that climbed up his neck and trailed beyond his shirt cuffs.

He tugged at a sleeve.

"They're nice." She hoped that sounded right. She wasn't used to being around people who supported more than the usual female tramp stamp so popular in the 1990s.

He fiddled with his water glass. He didn't seem to drink at all, sipping ice water all night with his prime rib. She joined him with that choice, given her *poor* choice last night with all the vodka. Her stomach lurched at the memory.

He cleared his throat. "If I could get rid of some, I would. But…"

"Sounds like you have a past, too." She might as well go there with him. He'd heard the worst about her.

"Yes." He took a swig of water and averted his eyes.

"Have I thanked you yet for setting me up with Declan?"

"No."

She chuckled. "Honest."

"Always."

"Thank you, Max. I appreciate you."

His gaze sliced her way. "Does that mean you'll go out with me sometime?" His words were stilted, like he was almost afraid to ask.

She looked at him. Really looked into his eyes. Yes, kindness lived there. He'd said something about good guys last night. She could tell he was. "Tonight sort of counts like a date. I've never been taken to a club like this before."

He nodded slowly. "Okay. A date." Lines in his forehead smoothed.

"You haven't asked out many women, have you?"

"I'm more of a pick them up off the streets in the limo guy." He half-laughed.

"You do seem to have a knack for it. I mean, the limo was …"

One corner of his mouth tilted up. "Want to see it sober?"

The subtext of his question was as clear as the water in his glass. He wanted to pick up where they'd left off.

Did she?

She did.

She'd known this guy for twenty-four hours, and every bit of her said "play the good girl" game. But look where that had landed her. An easy target to defraud and then get accused of embezzlement. Demeaned to stripping, the only way she knew how to raise that much money that fast. Good girls didn't get very far, she decided. And what was the good of feminism if she couldn't do what spoke to her?

She placed her hand on his forearm. "Lead the way."

His nostrils flared, and he scraped his chair backward. "I'll tell you my story there. Then you decide if the limo is for you."

* * *

270

THE LIMO'S window behind Max's head had begun to fog up.

He'd massaged her feet for the last ten minutes as she'd laid against one side of the long bench in the back of the huge vehicle.

"Mmm," she purred. His foot rub was hands down the most sensual thing anyone had ever done to her. His hand covered her whole foot, thick fingers pulling on her toes.

"This is very Kate and Leo," she breathed.

He grunted a little. "Yeah, but I'm not dying at the end. I get on the door."

"Ah, so you know there was room for them both."

"Of course there was." He grinned at her. "But in some people's worlds, dying is the romantic ending."

Her heart hitched. "Not in mine. Remember my haunting warning."

"You're safe with me because it's not romantic in my life either. That's why I got out."

She swallowed. "Out?" She'd learned a lot about Max, even more than the fact that he worked magic on feet. Like how he was a breakfast sausage purist. "None of that tofu turkey crap." And how he loved movies; the older, the better. It was kind of fun, like a conversation you had on a real date.

But as he told her what Shakedown was like, his work there, and how Declan had hired him as fast as the man had hired her, he kept dancing around something. It was as if he didn't really want to let her in on this past he'd alluded to before.

"Yeah. Out." His gaze leveled on hers, and his hands stilled. "From the Flaming Tides. Gang."

She gasped. "Oh, sorry." Was that the right thing to say? In every movie she'd ever seen, if she expressed shock at such an admission, it was usually followed by someone then saying, "Now, you die." She bit her bottom lip and tried not to tremble. "Never heard of them."

"Good. Getting out was … difficult."

"I'll bet."

"Don't take that bet. It involved a lot of … fighting."

She swallowed—hard. "Is this your way of saying you killed someone to escape?" she asked flippantly.

"Yes."

A little gasp escaped her throat. Trouble was the last thing she needed. She needed to rebuild, not get swept into a world of illegal activity. "Oh. That's …" What? She swallowed—hard. "Max, I can't get caught up in anything."

His nostrils flared. "Yeah, I get it." He let go of her feet and slid away.

"W-what?"

"I recognize the look on your face."

She crossed her arms. "What look?"

"Let's go inside."

"No. What look?"

When he didn't answer, she cracked open the door. "Fine. But next time you don't want a woman to be shocked, don't drop 'I killed someone once' on the first date."

"You needed to know," he gritted out. "And if you aren't going to listen to me, then I was wrong about you."

"Oh, really?" *Bastard.* She didn't want to have that conversation right then. Maybe never.

Time to go. Job or not, there was being stupid, and then there was *stupid.* Hanging out with a bunch of ex-cons? Yeah, that wasn't exactly going to get her reputation back on track.

She cracked open the door and scrambled out.

CHAPTER 3

$\mathcal{A}$nna took one long breath and pushed open the front door of Shakedown. It'd been two days since meeting Max, ex-gang member and foot massager extraordinaire, and Declan, who, with any luck, was still her new boss.

She was still miffed. At who, she wasn't exactly sure. Maybe herself, for starters. Almost having sexy times in the back of a limo—twice now—with a guy she hardly knew? Her life had sunk to a new low.

Still, a job was a job, so there she was.

At least Max wisely didn't call her or show up at her front door after she'd hightailed it out of Shakedown's garage last night.

She glanced around at the darkened club. Still elegant. Still scented with vanilla and lavender. Still her only hope of raising enough money to move on with her life.

Once her debt was paid, she could always quit.

"Ah, there she is." She spun toward the black curtain separating the business offices from the club floor. "Right on time, I see." Declan leaned against an ornately carved cane. Max stood behind him, his face schooled to pure granite.

The fact he looked so cold only pissed her off more. Did he

really think he could fill her in on his past and that she'd just act like it was nothing?

"Mr. Phillips, thought I'd get started right away. If I still have a job, that is." She stared directly into Max's eyes. Dared him to say anything.

He chuffed.

Oh, he was angry at her?

"Of course," Declan says. "Why don't you and Max have a moment and then come back to my office when you're ready." He chuckled and limped away behind the curtain.

She charged up to Max. "What did you tell him?"

"Excuse me, Miss High and Almighty, but I don't run to my boss when women run away from me."

"I didn't run." More like acted on a moment of clarity. She'd been too rash of late, and it was time to stop. "You need to give a girl a minute."

"Take all the minutes you want."

Laughter filled the air as two women swept through the curtain. She blinked. She was seeing double—two of Phoenix.

"Oh, hi, Anna. This is my sister, Starr."

"Nice to meet you," the woman said.

Oh, they were twins. Had to be. "Uh, hi."

"Ladies." Max grinned at them. Now, he smiled?

Starr winked at him. "Hey there, Maximillian." It came out like a purr. The kind you heard in movies during seduction scenes.

Max's neck reddened.

He was the club's man whore, was he? Okay, dodged a bullet. Nice guy or not, he clearly had a thing going on with Phoenix's equally gorgeous sister.

The two women sashayed to the front door and were gone.

"They're triplets," Max said.

She faced him. "What?"

"Phoenix, Starr, and Luna. You haven't met L yet. She's the one you shouldn't underestimate."

"I take it you know a lot about those three. Starr especially."
She even had a special name. Unlike Anna. Everywhere she went,
she ran into another Anna.

"She's like that with everyone." He crossed his arms, which was
something given the size of his biceps. "Jealous?"

"You wish. In fact, life-saving door privileges revoked. Climb
on Starr's." She stomped through the curtain. Where was Declan's
office again? She opened the first door she saw and stared into the
parking garage. The limo was parked nearest to the door. She
couldn't get away from it, could she?

"Looking for something?"

She spun at hearing Max's voice and ran right into his chest.
She might as well as run into a brick wall. "I'm *fine*."

"You don't seem fine. Look." He scrubbed his hair. "I'm sorry
my past upset you, but it is what it is. Just like yours is."

Oh, low blow. "Is that what you tell everyone when you have
them in the back of your limo?"

"It's not mine. And we were there to have some privacy. Lots
of ears here."

"They don't know your past?"

"Of course they do. They don't care. Unlike a certain woman
I'm staring at right now." He pushed her forward and let the door
close behind them. "We don't need the whole club listening in."

"I wasn't judging you." She wasn't, not really. "You automati-
cally assumed that I'd run. So, guess what? Expectation fulfilled.
Happy?"

"Not in the least. Though I'm rather glad we're getting our first
fight over with."

"We're not fighting." Her voice echoed against the concrete
walls.

"Yes. We are." His tone matched hers. She turned to go back
inside when he grasped her arm—gently. "Hey." His touch was so
gentle that her eyes pricked. "I expected you to run because most
women do."

His kind eyes stared down at her, and her heart panged. What was it about him? She should be running. Her feet wouldn't move her.

He dropped his hold and scrubbed his chin. "You've had a shitty week? I had years of hell."

She could see it if he had to kill to have a normal life. "I'm sorry. I wasn't judging you." Okay, maybe she had been judgmental.

He rose to his full height. "I'm not in that world anymore. Never going back."

All her irritation drained like a damn breaking.

She grabbed his hand, and he intertwined his fingers with hers and held on. Warmth spread everywhere in her body, and an odd intimacy crossed between them.

"I wasn't running. Seems like I only run *into* you." Twice now if she counted in the hallway.

Finally, she earned a half smile from him. "Didn't hurt."

"Good." She pulled him into the garage and toward the limo. For the life of her, she'd not ever know what caused her to be so bold—for the second time with him in forty-eight hours. But they had unfinished business, and she couldn't go to work with him believing she'd rejected him.

As soon as they were inside, she scrambled up and straddled him. His chin jutted back as if also surprised by her move.

She giggled a little. "Oh, sorry, but to balance on that door in the middle of the ocean, someone would have had to be on top."

"So, my door privileges are back?"

She nodded. "I'm sorry. I understand that sometimes you have to do what it takes to save yourself." After all, look at what she'd attempted to do to manage the embezzlement charges being laid against her.

"Be forewarned, Aspen-Anna." He brushed the hair off her face. "I had to do a lot."

His bald admission sent blood rushing through her ears, but

oddly, she wasn't afraid. More like she was in the presence of someone who'd lived a very different life from hers, one she'd hoped never to encounter. Yet he was able to walk away with his humanity. That was a special human.

Two weeks ago, she'd been living in a utopia, completely unaware of what some people went through. Who would she be if she hadn't lived such a sheltered life? What if she'd stayed at that strip club? Worse, what if Sol had caught her? Stapling a guy's dick was one thing, but to actually have to fight?

"Okay, tell me what you think I need to know."

He cleared his throat. "Got scars."

She folded forward and traced the scar on his cheek with her finger. "This one?"

His face broke into a grin. "Nah. That was from Judy clocking me with a swing when I was five."

She laughed. She couldn't picture Max being five years old. Or anyone, let alone a little girl, getting the upper hand. "Rude."

He shrugged one shoulder. "Eh. I tried to kiss her."

"I wouldn't clock you." (But good on Judy. Consent isn't just a word.) "I mean, if you tried …"

"What?"

"I don't know, really. I mean. Are you good at it? Because I was pretty drunk the other night, and women judge a lot by—"

His lips were on hers so fast she nearly fell backward. His large hands caught her and cradled her back.

As for kissing? Oh, he was good, alright, just as she knew he'd be. The way he slid his lips over hers, almost too much over her smaller mouth, was nearly feral. It was exactly the kind of kiss that got her naked in under five seconds.

He broke his lip lock but barely pulled back. "Scale?" Even that close, she could tell he wore a smug smile.

What a dichotomy. One minute he seemed hesitant and shy, and the other, he was a Casanova.

"Seven." No need for him to get cocky.

"I'll have to try harder." He arched his crotch up. A baseball bat had grown inside his pants in the last two minutes. She'd always loved that game.

Her breath came faster. "I think you're pretty good at hard." She only hoped Declan was serious about them having "a moment" because if he didn't move things forward immediately, she'd die.

The fact she was now employed at Shakedown and he worked there, which meant she'd see him a lot, never arose in her mind. Or perhaps her brain had already gone through mental gymnastics realizing if the boss and the lead dancer were a *thing*, then a little nude baseball action in the boss's limo wouldn't be fireworthy.

Or the fact that he was just so honest about his past and wanted her to hear it before they went any further.

Or perhaps it was because he had a code—and had proceeded to follow it even if she didn't know all the clauses and amendments of said code. For one, they both still had all their clothes on, which was man speak for I-was-waiting-for-you-to-make-a-move. It showed he had some modicum of respect for her, right? He was letting her call the shots.

All those split-second reasons why it was perfectly okay for her to *get some* in a garage, of all places, paled to the truth, however. He just felt right.

Her fingers played up and down his captured hardness. He didn't move to undress her, and she began to worry her he might actually think they were only going to talk.

She leaned down to him. "You're definitely door worthy."

"Now you're just trying to get me naked."

She squeezed his length, and at last, his breath hitched. "What gave you that idea?"

"Never tease where the door is concerned."

Speaking of which. "Will anyone see us?"

2023 RARE AUSTRALIA ANTHOLOGY

"Tinted windows, plus no one comes to the garage this early. But ..."

"What's wrong?"

His eyes narrowed a little. "Am I with Aspen right now or Anna?"

She cocked her head. Should she be offended he thought she might be playing him? "How about Aspenanna? Rhymes with banana. A little bit of each? Phoenix said—"

"I want Anna."

Oh. "Okay. To be honest, I kind of sucked at being anyone else."

One side of his mouth inched up. "You don't need to be anyone else here."

He slid his hands up her thighs and pushed her knit dress up her body until she had no choice but to raise her hands and let him divest her of it—thank God. Her dress—the one she reserved for interviews—got tossed to the limo floor.

And that was how she ended up nude in the back of a limo. At least that was what she'd tell *someone* if she ever got any friends back. How he stripped her of her bra and panties with equal speed. How he kissed her until she could barely breathe. How he wanted her—not some made-up persona.

Still, he was fully clothed.

She fluttered her eyelashes. "Don't I get to see more of you?"

"In time. For now, my most favorite part is all yours." He undid his belt buckle, then unzipped his pants, never taking his eyes off her face. "Be gentle with me." He winked.

"Do I have to be?"

He slowly shook his head.

Her fingers found their way inside his pants, and she nearly choked on her own tongue. She'd grown wet before, but now Niagara Falls threatened. The need to touch him, kiss him, do filthy things with him until they couldn't see through the limo windows from the steam. God, let her not be able to sit down for a week after tonight.

He cupped her face, his fingers threading through her hair. He massaged her scalp. His gaze ran over her body, and his voice grew hoarse. "Very few would be worthy of having my view right now."

"Not many have." In fact, she'd been living in a sexual drought. Now an arousal fog had settled over her, her sex throbbing and demanding to impale herself on him. Her fingers squeezed his cock once more, and his eyes narrowed ever so slightly.

"Good." He dropped one hand, his other still possessively threaded through her hair. Her scalp pulled a little as he began to unbutton his shirt. She couldn't help but drop her gaze to his chest.

He revealed his chest, dusted with dark hair over skin inked everywhere. Black and red images she couldn't quite understand. Circles and fire and … a long red wave seemed to be the backdrop. There was no question he'd told her the truth about the scars, either, as several long gashed marred his skin. But instead of presenting a victim, he presented a warrior.

Her hands moved to his pecs, needing to touch and feel him. His muscles twitched. He was one hundred percent male and pure power. That reality unhinged any last speed limiter she had on slowing things down.

He reached into his pocket with one hand and drew out a condom. He got it on himself, which was a minor buzzkill, even if it was necessary.

But then her lips found his again, and her body got right back on board. The feel of his strength under her hands, the way his deft fingers dug into her ass, she could tell this man knew what he was doing.

He grasped her hips and positioned her over him. The silky head of his cock was right at her entrance when he spoke into her mouth. "Fuck me."

Thank God, because she'd grown desperate.

Her entire identity had flipped in the course of one week. Hesitation, protests, or any other things that "good girls" did or said to feel better when they were being bad weren't even possible with her anymore.

She sank down on him and didn't try to tamp down the long moan that rose in her throat. Nothing had ever felt that good. And by the way he bit down on her bottom lip when she took him all inside, so he might agree.

They rocked together for long minutes until her head spun and her legs ached. Her breath came in gulps, and her sex was clenching. He grasped her face and held her gaze like he wanted to see her come. "From the second I saw you in this backseat, I wanted you riding me."

"But you didn't."

"I did in my mind," he ground out. "And many. Times. Today," he said, pitching his hips hard, thrusting even deeper into her.

"Thank God you're impatient," she whispered. Max's head fell back against the seat, and he hissed as she began to grind herself down on him, and he met her in equal measure.

Her lids drifted half closed, pleasure spiraling through her whole body. She couldn't imagine being anywhere else, doing anything else better for herself than that.

It didn't take long for her orgasm to rise like the cheap date it was—ready and willing to go there as soon as it wanted to. It'd been so long since she'd had sex, let alone *good* sex with someone so clearly in his element fucking.

She let go, and he matched her. And it felt so damned good.

She lay against him for a while, feeling his chest rise and fall under hers. The window closest to her was so fogged beads of moisture clung to the glass. She drew a smiley face in it.

"Anna was here," she whispered.

"She came. She saw. She conquered," he chuckled, sending a rumble through her chest. She eased up to look at him, and his hand returned to the side of her face, those thick fingers once more woven into her hair. "Conquered me."

They stared at one another, something intimate passing between them. It wouldn't to be a one-off. A promise of more hovered between them.

She rolled her lips between her teeth. "So."

"All I'm going to be thinking about from now on is you."

Her breath hitched. She didn't want him to feel obligated to promise her anything. After all, she was the one who'd practically jumped him twice.

Both of his hands held her face. "Anna Davis, only you are allowed in the back of my limo."

"It's the first time I've ever been in one."

"Second. And not the last. I'll drive you home after work. Then we'll talk about how we can get some more practice in."

"*Practice?*" She slapped his pec.

He reached for his shirt. "Well, I have to up my game because my new girlfriend here is a sex fiend."

"What can I say? My new boyfriend's got a *code* and will make room on his door for me. Turns me on."

His smile broadened. "You haven't seen anything yet." He pushed her off his lap and reached for her dress.

"Oh?" She took her crumpled dress from him.

"We're just getting started. Declan's got two limos and an RV. Way better than a carriage in the hull of a ship." He zipped up his pants and buckled his belt. "Though I think you'll look best in my California king."

And she thought she moved fast? Still, what started as her worst night ever just might have become one of the best nights of her life.

"New girlfriend, huh? Does that mean I have to cancel my date with Leonardo DiCaprio?" She pulled her dress over her head.

A low growl came from him. "I don't share—no celebrity clause, either. When I said girlfriend, I meant it. Just you and me and this beautiful ass of yours." He reached over and spanked her butt—the move sending renewed interest straight between her thighs.

How could it only have been two days since she met him? It felt like they'd known each other for months already. Was that what it felt like when you met The One? You just knew?

She sighed dramatically. "Leo's going to be really disappointed."

"Don't worry. We'll invite him to the wedding."

Strange thing, she could picture it. A 1920s Titanic theme, where she'd walk down a spiral staircase, and they'd give life preservers as take-home gifts. She shook her head, amused by her own imaginings.

"What?"

"Nothing." Maybe someday she'd tell him about it.

One thing was for sure. If they were lucky and it really did work out between them, she'd tell their daughter how she could meet a good guy even in her darkest hour.

As for now, she knew one thing. She wasn't going to drown. Not today.

Max smiled over at her, and her insides got all gooey.

Maybe she'd never find herself drowning again.

* * *

THANKS FOR READING! Learn more about my books at www.ElizabethSaFleur.com where you can also join my email newsletter for new release updates and free bonus stories.

Elizabeth SaFleur writes award-winning, luscious romance from sexy romcom to steamy billionaire stories. When not in her writing cave she can be found hiking, drinking good Virginia wine with friends or traveling the world in search of new hero and heroine inspiration. She loves to connect with readers so check out ElizabethSaFleur.com and drop her a line.

MITCH AND HOLLIE: A SHORT ROMANTIC SUSPENSE READ BY NYSSA KATHRYN

This story can be read as a prequel to Declan 's book in my Mercy Ring series. Every book in that series can be read as a standalone.

CHAPTER 1

Thick, corded muscles over bronzed biceps. Well-defined six-pack. Chiseled jaw and piercing blue eyes.

Yep. It was official. Her next-door neighbor was the sexiest man alive. Of course, he seemed grumpy as hell. The few times she'd actually run into the man since moving into this house, she'd given him huge-ass, want-to-get-to-know-me smiles, and all she'd received back was a nod.

Sigh. At least she had eye candy.

Hollie Gibbs watched him through her second-level bedroom window as he stopped by his door. Every day at exactly five p.m., the man went for a run. And no matter how damn cold it was, he always returned an hour later, bare chested with his shirt tucked into his shorts, and man-oh-man did the guy have a body to make a woman stare.

They both lived on large acreage surrounded by woods. She did have a guy who lived on her other side, a flirty middle-aged man by the name of Brad, who thought he was God's gift to women. But she couldn't see his house. Fine with her. From what her nanna had told her, the guy was a drinker and often had not-so-great people show up at his house, so the less she saw of him, the better.

She sighed as Mr. Hottie next door disappeared inside his house. All right, fantasy time was over, and laundry time had begun. Oh, what a glamorous life she led.

With a shake of her head, she moved out of the bedroom and down the stairs. The house was old, but cozy, something her nanna had always made sure of. Oh, Nanna. Her heart still hurt that she was gone. If it had been old age or sickness, maybe it wouldn't have been so heartbreaking. But nope. It was a car accident. That was something no one could have seen coming.

She passed the large living area, her gaze catching on the blazing fire in the grate. She stopped. Joey wasn't in the bed she'd made him.

"Joey?"

She scanned the couches, then the corners of the room. With quick steps, she moved into the kitchen. She was just checking she hadn't left any cupboard doors open when a brush of cold air hit her skin.

Her gaze shot to the dog door that led outside.

No…No, no, no!

She ran over to the door and dropped to her knees. Then she tugged at the flimsy piece of wood she'd used to cover the door, which was currently hanging down.

Oh, God. This couldn't be happening. This had to be a nightmare, right? Some wake-me-up-I-need-to-get-back-to-reality nightmare?

But it wasn't. The evidence was right in front of her eyes.

Shit.

Quickly, she tugged on her jacket, grabbed Joey's pouch bag from his bed and ran outside. The door slammed closed behind her. The cold Heart Valley wind slapped her right in the face. God, it could get cold in Montana. And that cold made dread sliver in her belly. The cold was not good for Joey. In fact, other than making sure he got his medication, keeping him warm had been her main damn job.

Stupid. She was so stupid. She should have done a better job of boarding the door. Hired a professional even.

This was her first day with him. Her first week working at the sanctuary. And what had she done? Let a poor animal escape into the cold evening. He was already sick. She hadn't even given him his antibiotics. What if she didn't find him and he didn't survive the night?

No. She couldn't think about that. She would find him. She had to find him.

Her feet sank into the wet dirt as she headed for the trees, scanning every inch of the property as she went. She wasn't too familiar with these woods. Sure, she'd played in them as a kid, but that was a long dang time ago.

Her nanna had known these woods like the back of her hand. *Nanna, if you're watching, help me find Joey.*

She wasn't an overly spiritual person, but right now she'd take all the help she could get.

She spent endless minutes searching. Behind trees. Beneath bushes. When she heard a shuffle of leaves behind her, she stopped and turned.

"Joey?"

With a gentle voice and quiet movement, she headed back a few steps. She did not want to scare the animal off.

More crunching. But this time, she stopped for a different reason. The crunches didn't sound like Joey. They were too loud to be a small animal.

A frown flickered on her brows. "Hello?"

Silence followed. But it was an eerie silence. The kind that caused the back of her neck to prickle and the fine hairs on her arms to stand on end.

She remained exactly as she was for long seconds before

giving herself a quick shake. She was freaking herself out. New town. New home. And her first emergency.

With deep, calming breaths, she turned and moved through the trees once again. She needed to find Joey and get the heck home. She broke into a jog, scanning the ground as she went. Even though she was moving quickly, the cold began to creep into her bones.

And when the rain started, her teeth began to chatter.

God, the world really did hate her right now, didn't it? She quickened her pace, calling out to Joey in even intervals.

She'd just rounded a tree when she ran smack bang into a big black wall.

A screech slipped from her lips, and she fell backwards. She closed her eyes, expecting the cold, damp ground to meet her backside. Instead, large fingers wrapped around her wrist and tugged her up.

Her eyes sprang open to see the bluest eyes she'd ever seen looking back at her.

Her lips separated.

He was tall up close. So tall he towered over her five foot eight. He wore a large black jacket and jeans that did nothing to hide his powerful thighs. But it was his face she couldn't look away from. Those eyes. That chiseled chin.

"Are you okay?"

God, even his voice was sexy. Deep and smooth and oh-so-masculine. For a moment she struggled to piece together a coherent sentence for her neighbor. Hell, she struggled with basic English.

When the man frowned, she swallowed. *Words, Hollie, he needs words.*

"Yes." Okay, it wasn't a lot, but it was something. Could she blame her sudden loss of words on the fact she hadn't been touched by any man—neighbor or otherwise—in two years? *Yeah, let's blame it on that.*

His gaze shot over her head before returning to her. "Are you lost?"

Lost? Probably. But she had bigger problems than that. "I'm looking for Joey."

She didn't miss how his hand remained on her arm. Firm and warm, even through her jacket. Maybe he was scared she'd fall. Probably wasn't far from the truth. Her knees felt wobbly as hell in his presence.

"Joey?" he asked.

"He's a joey, but his name is also Joey."

The man's eyes narrowed. Okay, now he was just looking at her like she was crazy. Another thing that probably wasn't far from the truth. "A joey as in a..."

"Baby kangaroo," she finished.

His throat bobbed. "Lady, this is Montana, not some country outback, Australian state."

A fat blob of rain hit her nose. "I know. I've been to Australia. I just got back from spending five years there." Exactly why she'd been tasked with caring for Joey. Because she was familiar with kangaroos. Damn that dog door. "I'm working at the animal sanctuary here in town and took Joey home for the night because he's sick."

Another twitch of his brows. "There's really a joey on my land?"

Wait, what? "Your land?"

"The border's about five feet behind you."

No, that couldn't be right. "There's no fence."

"Anna and I never erected one."

She nodded, a slow, I'm-barely-paying-attention-to-your-words nod. How could she pay attention when she was too busy tracing those lips with her eyes? They were full lips. Kissable lips.

A shot of heat spiraled from where he touched her arm to her lower abdomen. Oh God, she needed to get away from this too-good-looking man and find Joey.

"I've got to go." She tugged her arm out of his hold so hard and fast, she fell backward. She threw her arm back to catch herself, and her palm hit the sharp edge of a rock.

A deep curse sounded from above, and a second later, the man was crouched in front of her. She looked up to find his face mere inches from hers, his fingers curving around her hand, his breath grazing her skin.

CHAPTER 2

⌘

*M*itch Baydon watched the flurry of emotions pass over his new neighbor's face. Her dark brown eyes were huge and there was a splatter of freckles over her nose.

Cute. That was the word to describe her. But had the damn woman really lost a kangaroo on his property?

When her gaze lowered to his lips, his fingers tightened around her arm, and heat flared in his chest.

Where the hell did that come from?

A second later, she tugged her arm from his hold, hard, and fell straight back onto her ass.

He cursed as she tugged her hand up and crimson blood ran down her palm. He dropped in front of her and lifted her hand. He inspected the damage, wanting to ask the woman what the hell she was thinking. Instead, he tugged off his jacket then his shirt. "We need to wrap this up."

She gasped, but he didn't look at her as he tugged his jacket back on and zipped it up, before wrapping the shirt around her hand. When she remained silent, he looked up to see her watching him closely, lips separated and chest moving up and down in deep succession. They were close. So close that if he moved his head forward a fraction—

Fuck. He needed to get this woman inside her house and get home.

He tugged her to her feet, and she lifted the blanket that had fallen from her grasp. Her head just reached his shoulder, and she had this scent that toyed with him. A sweet lilac scent.

Shoving down the emotions he didn't know what to do with, he led her back to her place.

"I need to find Joey," she said quietly.

"You really have a joey out here?"

"Yes. And if I don't get him inside where it's warm soon, his pneumonia will get worse."

A baby kangaroo with pneumonia. On his land. As well as his cute, confusing neighbor. Well, his night just got a bit more confusing.

"I'll get you inside then look for him." It was the best option. Not only did it mean she'd be warm, she'd also be away from him. Space seemed like the safer option right now.

They'd almost cleared the trees when her gasp whipped through the air.

"Joey," she whispered.

He followed her gaze to see a small joey peeking from behind a tree.

Slowly, she unfolded the blanket. No, not a blanket, a bag. He watched as she crept toward the small animal and when she was close, she crouched beside him and opened the bag. For a moment, the animal didn't move—then the joey jumped inside.

Well, this was a first for him.

The woman stood, and when she turned to face him, she wore a huge-ass smile on her face.

His heart gave a little kick. Christ, this could be an issue. She was far different from the elderly Anna Parkins who'd been living in the house.

When she was back with him, worry filled her features. "He's so cold. I need to get him back quickly."

He trailed behind her as she took the joey back to the house. Once they were inside, the woman flew into action, setting the small animal in front of the fire, covering him, then making some sort of milk.

His gaze shifted to the broken wood over the dog door. "Is that where he escaped?" he asked.

She sighed from where she fed Joey. "Yeah. I tried to board it over but I did a terrible job."

He studied the nails. They were too small for what she was trying to do. "Have you got tools?"

"In the hall cupboard."

He went searching through the hall and found her toolbox quickly. It was sparse. Almost empty. But it had what he needed.

While the woman continued to feed the joey, he nailed the wood to the door. It wasn't perfect, but Joey wouldn't be getting out today. When he was done, he searched through her cabinets for a first-aid kit. Unlike the toolbox, her first-aid kit was fully stocked.

When she finally finished feeding the animal, her chest seemed to deflate with relief, and her eyes closed. "He's okay." She almost sounded like she was talking to herself. Her gaze swung to the dog door. "And you fixed his escape route. Thank you."

"You're welcome." He pushed off the kitchen counter. "Your turn." He lifted her to the kitchen island.

The woman's inhale was loud. He stepped between her thighs and unwrapped her hand.

* * *

FOR THE LOVE of all that was holy. The man had just lifted her onto the kitchen island like she weighed nothing. And now he was holding her palm in his hand. Grazing her skin. *Caring* for her.

Her heart trilled in her chest.

She remained so still while he cleaned her hand that she was pretty sure she was barely breathing. How much oxygen did a person need to remain alive?

"I'm Mitch, by the way."

Oh, yeah. They hadn't even exchanged names. He was still Hot Neighbor, in her head.

Mitch. She liked that name. It suited him. "Hollie."

His gaze rose and collided with hers. There was a flutter in her belly before he looked back down.

She wet her lips. "How long have you been living next door to Anna?"

Anna had never mentioned this sexy man to her. She'd come back to the States a couple of times over the last five years and had never seen him. And he didn't exactly have a face she'd forget.

"I've owned the house for a few years but was away for missions a lot."

Her brows rose. "You're in the military?" So that was where he got the rock-hard twelve-pack.

"Was," he said quietly. "I was special forces. Got out twelve months ago. I work in construction now."

Special forces? So the guy was badass. Her throat bobbed as she watched him wrap her hand. Desire spidered through her limbs at the sight of his powerful fingers. Yes. Powerful fingers. It was a thing with this guy. He was all power and strength.

"Next time you need to go out in the cold at night, come get me instead and I'll find whatever animal you're looking for." He said it with quiet authority.

Again, his gaze clashed with hers, and all she could do was nod. Because those eyes…it was like they saw right inside her. Like they demanded every part of her pay attention to him.

Without her permission, her gaze dropped back down to his lips. And there it was again. The flutter in her lower abdomen. The jump in her pulse.

"You need to stop doing that," he growled.

Her gaze flew back up to his eyes. Eyes that appeared a shade darker and had never stopped looking at her.

"Sorry." Her apology was a near-soundless whisper.

The fingers she hadn't realized were still on her wrist skirted to her waist. Her breath caught. Heat danced in her belly.

For a moment, she wondered if the man would kiss her. He stood so close she could almost feel his breath brush her skin.

But then he stepped back. His hand slid away. And her heart dropped.

He ran a hand through his hair. "I should go."

She nodded, even though what she really wanted to do was ask him to stay. To step back between her thighs. Which was crazy, right? Because she didn't even know him. Still, there was this pull.

"Don't go out in the woods alone again," he said quietly. Then he left, and the breath she hadn't realized she'd been holding whooshed from her chest.

CHAPTER 3

ollie watched the rain fall outside the coffee shop. She had so many memories of this place. Sitting here with her nanna. Sipping hot drinks and eating cake while people-watching.

Good memories. All of them.

God, Nanna, I wish you were still here.

A couple of days had passed since the incident with Joey. Thank God he was okay. She hadn't spoken to her neighbor since. A small flicker of heat tingled in her belly at the memory of the man. At the way he'd stood between her thighs. Grazed her skin.

God, why did he have to be so damn sexy? It was annoying as hell that she couldn't stop thinking about him. That she'd actually watched his house through her bedroom window this morning like a damn stalker, waiting for the slightest glimpse of him.

Sad. She was sad.

She was just taking a sip of coffee when her phone rang from the table. She rolled her eyes when the name popped up on the screen. That damn real estate agent again. What was this? His fifth call in the last week?

"Still not interested, Tony."

"Mrs. Gibbs—"

"It's Ms., just like I told you the last million times. And I am not selling my land to your big fancy developer."

"He's upped his offer to—"

"Don't care." She was sick of the harassment. "The man could offer me ten times the property and land value and I still wouldn't be interested. I *do not* want my nanna's home, the home she grew up in, knocked down and her land developed to make some men in suits lots of money. No."

Her gaze had just risen when her jaw dropped open as she saw who stepped through the café door.

There were *two* of them.

Well, not two Mitch's...but he had a friend who looked just like him. They both wore t-shirts that stuck to their thick biceps and chests like a second skin. They were both a million feet tall, and both sexy as hell.

She swallowed. Oh man. Someone was taunting her, weren't they? They were literally watching her from some place up high and putting these good-looking men in her path.

She was still trying to control her breaths when Mitch turned his head and their gazes clashed. The agent spoke across the line, but she wasn't listening to a word he said.

He gave her a small nod before hitting the counter.

"Ms. Gibbs? Are you there?"

The guy beside Mitch grinned at her, then thumped Mitch on the shoulder. She sank into her seat. "I have to go, Tony. Not interested. Never will be."

She hung up.

All right, she had to get to work. She finished the last of her coffee and stood. She grabbed her mug and took it to the counter, all the while telling herself she was not doing it just to get close to Mitch. Ha. All the while *lying* to herself.

She stopped at the counter, and when she saw Mitch move toward her, her pulse picked up.

2023 RARE AUSTRALIA ANTHOLOGY

"Hey."

She looked up, way up, into those gorgeous blue eyes. "Hey."

"How's the hand?"

Before she could answer, he lifted her arm. She suppressed a shiver at his gentle touch. At the way those fingers ran along her skin. She didn't have a bandage on her hand today, and she felt all of his touch.

"It's fine," she said quietly. He grazed the skin around the cut. Every hair on her arm stood on end.

The sexy grinning man behind him moved forward. "Well, hello, who do we have here?"

Mitch dropped her hand and she swallowed at the loss of contact.

She smiled at the other guy. "I'm Hollie. The neighbor."

His brows lifted. "Hello, Hollie. I'm Declan. The cousin."

He was probably military too. He looked all tall and strong and powerful like Mitch. "It's nice to meet you." Her gaze flicked back to Mitch, who was doing that watching-her-too-closely thing again.

Her heart thumped. "I should go."

She left the shop, feeling his gaze on her the entire way out.

* * *

"Ah, did you forget to tell me you have a new pretty neighbor?"

Mitch dragged his gaze away from Hollie. What the hell was it about her that made him feel like a fucking teenager again? He shouldn't have touched her just now. But he hadn't been able to damn well stop himself.

He turned back to the counter. "Anna Parkins died and passed on her property to her granddaughter. I met her the other day."

His cousin watched him closely. Too fucking closely. "Interesting. And what happened during this meeting?"

Coffees were set in front of them. He took a sip, ignoring the burn on his tongue. "She cut her hand while looking for her joey. I helped her clean and bandage it."

That was the very short and condensed version of the story.

Declan's brows rose. "Joey?"

"She works at the animal sanctuary."

Since that night, he hadn't been able to get the woman out of his head. The way he'd stood between her warm thighs. The heat of her skin.

Fuck. He needed to stop.

"Maybe you should bake her a welcome-to-the-street cake or something?"

He shoved his cousin's shoulder. "Have you baked *your* new neighbors a cake?"

His cousin had just moved to Lindeman, Idaho, with his former Delta buddies. Unlike Mitch, Declan had adjusted well to life after the military. Probably because his entire team was with him. They'd opened a boxing ring together, called Mercy Ring.

Whereas Mitch's team was still out there, serving without him.

He took another sip of coffee.

"Nah," Declan finally said. "But I have been texting a very pretty lady."

Mitch frowned. "Really? Guessing she's your normal outgoing, loud-personality type."

"Nope. She's quiet. A bit shy. Loves to read. Her name's Michele." A darkness skimmed over his cousin's face. "She has a bad ex though. I think he's harassing her, although she hasn't been too good at asking for help."

Mitch straightened. He fucking hated assholes who couldn't take no for an answer. "Is she okay?"

Declan looked at his phone like he was expecting a message from her. "I text to check on her as often as I can. I just have to convince her to let me in."

"With that big-ass grin of yours, how could she not?"

Declan's smile widened. "That's what I'm counting on."

Mitch turned his head to see Hollie through the window as she slipped into her car across the street. He frowned when he noticed a guy outside the coffee shop.

Was he watching her?

He had his back to Mitch, so he couldn't see the guy's face. When her car left, so did he, walking in the other direction down the street.

"So about that cake for your neighbor…"

He turned back to Declan. "Not happening."

"Come on. I leave this afternoon. At least tell me you're gonna make a move. I saw the way you looked at each other."

If Declan had seen the way she'd looked at his lips the other day… His dick twitched and his fingers tightened around the mug. "Nothing's gonna happen."

But even as he said the words, something inside him rebelled against them. Something that made him want to take them back. Go after her and prove they were a lie.

CHAPTER 4

*ollie tilted her head as she watched Mitch work the pipes in her kitchen. The pipes had started leaking about an hour ago, and she *had* thought about calling a plumber. Briefly. Very briefly. Then she'd popped on over next door and been met with a shirtless Mitch. Yes, shirtless, because apparently that was how he dressed in his house.

Maybe tomorrow she'd run out of milk and have to pop on over again.

"So why were you in Australia?"

His question tugged her out of her thoughts. "I became a shelter veterinarian about eight years ago. Three years into the career and I wanted a change of scenery. So I applied for a working visa and got it. Next thing I know, I'm on a plane to Adelaide."

The muscles in his arms flexed as he tightened a bolt. So. Damn. Sexy. "Anything you miss about the country?"

"The coffee's pretty awesome. And they have these cookies called Tim Tams, which I kind of became addicted to. I never got on the Vegemite train though. I think it's one of those things you have to be raised on."

"I tried the stuff once. It was terrible. Never again." Another flick of his wrist. Another flex of his muscles. Lord help her. "Happy to be back?"

Right now? Heck yes. "It's been nice. And living in Nanna's home has brought back lots of great childhood memories. I used to come here every school break." She swallowed as his muscles flexed. "What about you? Sad to be out of the military?"

"It's been an...adjustment."

When he didn't expand on that, she frowned. Had he not left on good terms?

"I busted my knee on a mission," he continued quietly. "So the decision to leave my team wasn't mine, and adjusting to civilian life has been more...challenging than I anticipated."

Her frown deepened, but before she could ask more questions, her doorbell rang. Strange. She wasn't expecting anyone, and she was too far out to get unexpected visitors.

"I'll be back," she said quietly, moving to the door.

She looked through the peephole and just held in a groan. Brad. Her other neighbor. The one she avoided like the plague. And as usual, he had a sleazy grin on his face.

With a click of her jaw, she tugged open the wooden then the screen door. "Hello, Brad."

"Hey, Hol's. How are you doing today?"

Hol's? "I'm okay. What can I do for you?"

"I was thinking. I haven't given you a very good welcome."

He stepped forward into her house. She stepped back.

"Maybe I could change that? Take you on a date tonight?"

Oh, God. She couldn't think of anything worse. "I'm busy. But thanks."

He tilted his head to the side, taking another step toward her. Crowding her. "Come on. I'll take you to Chilli's, the nicest restaurant in town. Wine and dine you for a bit before taking you home."

He slid a finger up her arm, and her skin crawled.

303

Argh. "I said no."

But instead of stepping back, he pressed his other hand to the door, leaning into her. "Maybe I could change your mind."

She was a step away from kneeing him in the balls when loud footsteps sounded down the hall. Her head whipped up to find a very angry-looking Mitch entering the room.

*   *   *

THE SECOND MITCH saw the hand on Hollie's arm, the way Brad leaned into her, he saw red. He was across the room in a second, pulling the guy off her before standing in between them.

"You don't understand the word 'no'?" There was no hiding the threat of violence in his voice.

Brad's eyes widened. "Mitch. I didn't know you were here."

Mitch lowered his head. "If I ever see you touch her again, I will break your hand. Do you understand me?"

The guy was in his forties and fit enough. But he wasn't a match for Mitch, and they both knew it. He usually kept to himself, but maybe that was because he hadn't had a neighbor who looked like Hollie before.

He lifted his hands in defense. "Look, I wasn't trying to create trouble. Just welcome the woman into town and offer her a date. I'm sorry if I was too forward. I'll go."

Damn straight he would.

The second he left, Mitch took a moment to calm himself. It was only the touch of Hollie's hand on his back that finally had him turning.

His gaze dropped to the place on her arm the asshole had touched. "Are you okay?"

"I'm okay." Her voice was quieter than usual.

Gently, he grazed the skin. When he heard the small hitch in her breath, his gaze rose to hers.

His gut tightened at the look on her face. She got it whenever he touched her. A mixture of desire and heat. Like she wanted more touches. More *him*.

He took a step back and cleared his throat. "The leak's all fixed."

She gave a small nod. Another thing she did after he touched her. She got quiet. Because she felt what he felt? An attraction so intense it took all of his self-control to not act on it?

Fuck, he needed to leave.

He moved into the kitchen and cleaned up his stuff. He was just lifting his bag of tools when he turned and she was right in front of him. That damn sweet smell of lilacs hit him square in the gut. She touched his chest, and his breathing stopped.

"Thank you," she said quietly. "For the pipes and for...the Brad stuff."

She wet her lips, and his gaze lowered. Fuck, she had nice lips. His muscles tightened and his hand twitched to touch her. Pull her into him. Taste her.

Like she heard his thoughts, her hand slid up his chest, then his neck, before resting behind his head. Slowly, so slowly he could stop her at any moment, she tugged his head down.

It would be safer to stop her. He'd been a damn mess this last year. But in the moment, he just couldn't. And the second her lips touched his, there was an explosion of fire inside him.

His hands went to her hips and he tugged her closer, so that her soft pressed to his hard.

When her lips separated, he didn't hesitate, he plunged his tongue inside her mouth. And she tasted as good as he'd known she would. Sweet like fruit.

Her breasts pressed into his chest as their tongues danced. He slipped a hand under the material of her shirt and grazed the soft skin of her hip.

He itched to turn her. Lean her against the wall. He wanted to claim this woman. To explore every inch of her.

Then her soft hum pricked the bubble that was their desire and brought him back to reality.

He was kissing his neighbor. A neighbor he could easily fall for. But he wasn't in a position to fall for anyone.

He lifted his head and broke the connection. A disappointed moan slipped from her lips, and damn if that didn't make him want to pull her right back.

"I should go, honey." The endearment slipped from his mouth before he could stop it.

Her breathing was labored, but she gave another of those quick nods.

It took all of his willpower to step back. To release the woman in his arms.

He did. Just.

Then he got the hell out of there, before he did another stupid thing.

CHAPTER 5

*S*he'd kissed him. On the lips. And man, oh man, the kiss had been perfect. Abso-freaking-lutely perfect.

She grinned as she stripped off her clothes after work and stepped into the shower. A big, can't-get-the-man-or-the-kiss-out-of-my-head grin. Even colleagues at the sanctuary today had been asking why she was so happy.

Okay, yes, the man had pulled away before she'd been ready. *Way* before. He had a tough exterior. Was it because of what he'd said about leaving the military? Did that plague him?

If she was honest with herself, she was maybe a little, teeny-tiny bit disappointed he hadn't called or texted today. But it was only five-thirty. There was time.

She washed quickly, then stepped out of the shower and grabbing her big fluffy towel. It was a kangaroo towel her Australian work colleagues had given her. She also had a mug and about a dozen other things, all with kangaroos and koalas on them. Man, she missed them.

Once she was in the bedroom, she slipped on a black bra and panties. She was just opening her drawer to find her yoga pants when something sounded from downstairs.

She stilled. There weren't any animals from the sanctuary in the house tonight, and she was certain she hadn't left anything open, not with the cold outside.

A frown danced over her brow as she tugged on her silk dressing gown and stepped out of the room.

"Hello?"

Silence. The heavy, eerie type.

Slowly, she crept out of the room and to the top of the stairs. Nothing. No sounds. No movement.

God, she was being silly. New house. New *big* house. She was terrifying herself.

With a shake of her head, she moved back into her bedroom.

Pushing the sound to the back of her mind, her gaze shifted to her phone and thoughts of Mitch once again plagued her. Before she could talk herself out of it, she lifted it and sent him a message.

Hey, how was your day?

There. She'd made the first contact. Casual, no-pressure contact.

She was just about to set the phone back down when it beeped with a message. Her heart thudded. Had he responded already?

She opened the message and a smile tugged at the corners of her lips.

Hey, Hollie. My day was good. Got called out to a couple of mainte-nance jobs, but not too busy. Yours?

She nibbled her lip while writing, then deleting and re-writing a response. God, she was a nervous wreck.

Mine was good too. Joey's doing a lot better. There's an older kangaroo at the sanctuary who's taken him under her wing. I did have a sick horse to care for. Beauty. Yes, her name's Beauty.

She grinned as she set her phone back on the dresser again. Talking to her sexy neighbor about the job she loved. Did it get any better?

She'd just opened her drawer again when a dark figure burst

into her bedroom. She didn't have time to scream before an arm wrapped around her throat.

For a second, shock and fear rendered her still.

Then the arm tightened. Her air cut off.

She burst into action, grabbing and kicking the figure behind her. She pulled at the arm around her throat. Swung her foot back at his legs. The arm didn't loosen. In fact, it tightened.

Black dots danced in her vision and wild panic swirled in her gut.

No. She had to fight. She had to get this asshole off her. Through the blur, she caught sight of the candle she'd lit before her shower. With desperate hands, she wrapped her fingers around it and flung her hand back.

The guy cried out. When his arm fell, she raced out of the room and down the stairs. She'd just reached the bottom when she heard the loud thumping of footsteps above.

Oh God, he was coming after her!

It took her trembling fingers three goes to unlock the front door, then she all but fell out of the house and ran. She ran as fast as her legs would take her. Too soon, a hand grabbed at her from behind, but it only snagged the dressing gown, wrenching it from her body.

Cold blasted over her skin, but she ignored it.

Get to Mitch! It was all she could think about. All she could aim for.

She was halfway there when a heavy weight fell on her from behind, pushing her to the ground. Her face hit the grass hard and her breath was knocked from her chest.

She opened her mouth and screamed. She screamed as loud as she could for as long as she could before strong hands came around her throat.

Tears filled her eyes as she clawed at the man. She wasn't getting enough air. She was going to lose consciousness.

She was almost out, had almost lost that last bit of fight, when the weight suddenly lifted from her body and she could breathe. She gulped down desperate gulps of air.

Two bodies clashed beside her. They were blurry, but she knew one was Mitch, and could just see the black balaclava the other guy wore. She touched her fingers to her aching throat, her heart pounding hard in her chest.

She tried to push up, but her arms trembled so violently she fell back down. She swallowed, and it was painful.

Grunts sounded from beside her. The sound of fists hitting flesh. Then running. Mitch followed for a bit, but she heard his loud curse before he returned to her.

* * *

FUCK. He got away. Mitch wanted to chase him down. Hell, he wanted to get close enough to tear the asshole apart with his bare fingers. He'd had his hands around Hollie's neck. Choking her. But if he ran after the guy, he'd leave Hollie alone. Unprotected. And that was too big of a risk when he didn't know if there were others.

With the click of his jaw, he turned and lowered in front of Hollie. Fury was like a tidal wave in his chest when he saw the bruises on her neck. Her shivering, almost bare body.

Without hesitation, he tugged his shirt over his head and gently fit it over hers, helping her move her arms through the holes. Then he touched her cheek. "Are you okay?"

Her eyes were wide and her face pale. She was in shock. "I-I don't know."

Another click of his jaw. He pushed it down. The anger. The fucking shout in his head to go find the asshole and end him.

Carefully, he slipped his arms around her and lifted her. Her tremors vibrated into his chest. He fucking hated it.

Instead of heading to her place, he went to his. He waited until they were inside, Hollie on his couch, before crouching in front of her. He set a hand on either side of her hips. He needed to touch her right now. Reassure himself she was okay and safe.

"I'm going to call the police. Do you need a paramedic?"

She shook her head, but her movements were wooden, and she was too damn pale.

Gently, he cupped her cheek. "I'm going to stay with you, okay? You're safe here with me."

He wanted to bring her comfort. See some color return to her cheeks.

She opened her mouth like she was going to say something, but instead, she leaned against his chest and pressed her cheek to his heart.

"Thank you," she finally breathed.

CHAPTER 6

*H*ollie stepped out of the shower. Her second shower of the evening, but she still didn't feel clean. Not after having that man's fingers around her neck.

A shudder spidered its way down her spine.

The police had left almost an hour ago. Mitch had stayed by her side the entire time. He'd been her pillar of strength. Always with a reassuring hand on her leg. Answering the officers when she couldn't.

And now, here she was, in the man's guest bathroom, getting ready to sleep in his spare bedroom.

Once the towel was wrapped around her, she stood in front of the mirror and wiped away the fog. Her gaze zoned in on the red and blue bruising on her neck. It looked so much worse than it felt.

Carefully, she touched the skin, flinching at the sting. Okay, maybe not.

Someone had broken into her house tonight. Chased her. Choked her. God, it didn't feel real. How could it? She'd never been in a fight in her life, let alone been attacked by a man who broke into her house. He'd broken the lock on her front door. Would she ever feel safe again?

The question was why? Why had he targeted her? Attacked her? She'd just moved in. She had nothing of value.

She closed her eyes and took a moment to calm herself. She hated that he was still out there. That the police had almost nothing to go on.

With a quick inhale, she moved out of the bathroom and finally slid on some yoga pants and t-shirt. Mitch had gone with her to grab some clothes, thank God. She needed to be in something comfortable and familiar.

She was just lowering to the bed when a knock came at the door.

"Come in," she called.

A second later, Mitch walked into the room. He wore a t-shirt and sweatpants. He still had the same expression on his face. A mix of worry and anger and alertness. Danger. The man radiated danger.

He set two glasses on the side table. "I know you said you weren't hungry, so I just brought a glass of orange juice and some water." He pulled out some pills from his pocket. "And some aspirin in case you're in any pain. Are you sure you don't need a doctor? I could drive you to the hospital—"

"I'm sure." She couldn't think of anything worse than sitting in emergency right now.

He crouched in front of her. Even crouched, he was huge. Her big protector.

There was a flash of fury when his gaze skimmed her neck, but then his eyes rose to hers and gentled. The man had been nothing *but* gentle with her since he'd saved her. "You still doing okay?"

No. She could still feel those hands around her neck. "I just wish I had more answers."

Who was he? Why had he attacked? Would he be back?

The last one made her insides tremble.

His fingers wrapped around her thigh and gently squeezed. "We'll get your answers."

We. Not her. He was not leaving her to deal with this alone.

"Are you going to be okay tonight?" he asked quietly.

Physically, of course. Because Mitch was here, and she knew he wouldn't let harm come to her. Mentally and emotionally? Ha. Yeah, right. Those black eyes and that balaclava would riddle her dreams.

But she forced a smile to her lips. "Of course."

He looked at her like he didn't believe her. For a moment, she wanted to ask him to stay. In this room. In this bed. He stood, and her heart thumped. Her fingers twitched to grab him. Pull him back to her.

But she clenched her hands and forced her lips closed. She couldn't ask this almost-stranger to share her bed.

"Call out if you need anything. I'm in the room next to yours."

She gave another of those small nods she always gave to this man. Then watched as he left. The second the door closed behind him, she snuggled under the blankets. And yep, as soon as she switched off the light and closed her eyes, those black eyes of the intruder were all she saw.

* * *

MITCH SCRUBBED a hand over his face as he turned off the light in the kitchen. He couldn't get the image of that asshole choking Hollie out of his damn head. He was kicking his own ass for not being able to secure the guy.

He moved through the house, checking that each door and window was locked, before turning on the alarm. He didn't always use the alarm. Heart Valley had always been safe. Tonight, it wasn't.

He'd sat there and listened as Hollie told the officers about the asshole attacking her in her bedroom. Thank God she was strong enough to fight him off and run. If she hadn't been...

No. He couldn't think about that. He couldn't accept the reality that might have been. Of the woman being fucking murdered in the house right beside his while he'd had no idea.

Every muscle in his body tightened at the thought.

He moved up the stairs but paused outside her bedroom door. He hadn't wanted to leave her. Hell, he'd wanted to pull Hollie against his chest and not let go.

He listened for sounds. Movement. There was nothing. She must be asleep already.

With a shake of his head, he moved into his room.

His need for Hollie to be safe went beyond his protective nature, and he knew it. He liked the woman. More than he should, based on how long they'd known each other. He'd done nothing but think about her and that damn kiss they'd shared. The way she'd made him feel things he'd never felt before.

The problem was his head was a damn mess since leaving the military. After a knee injury, he'd been forced out. He'd had to leave his team. His job. If he was honest with himself, he'd felt a bit lost. But when Hollie touched him, kissed him, he'd felt like he was exactly where he was meant to be for the first time since serving.

He had a quick shower before pulling on briefs. He was about to climb into bed when he heard the soft whimper. He froze and listened. The next sound was more of a cry.

He was out of his room and in the hall before he could stop himself. He rushed into Hollie's room—and stopped.

There were no intruders. No broken windows or anything out of place. Hollie lay in bed, a scared, almost pained look on her face as she thrashed around, caught in a nightmare.

He crossed the room and sat on the edge of her bed. Then, gently, he cupped her cheek. "Hollie."

Another whimper. Another thrashing of her head to the side.

He raised his voice a notch and gripped her arm with his other hand. "Hollie, wake up."

Her eyes scrunched, but she didn't wake. So he leaned his head down and placed his mouth near her ear. Then he whispered, "You're safe."

Her body stilled. Her quick breathing shifted to long, deep breaths. Then, as he lifted his head, her eyes fluttered open. It took a moment for her to focus on his face. "Mitch?"

"Yeah, honey. I'm here."

Her brows pulled together, then her eyes closed. She remained like that for two breaths, then she sat up and fell against his chest.

"It was so real," she whimpered. "I was out there again. But this time, you weren't there to save me."

His arms went around her, and he held her close. "It *wasn't* real. I was there."

He wished he could offer more comfort. Some sort of promise that he'd always save her. But the truth was, if she hadn't gotten away, if she hadn't screamed, he wouldn't have.

His arms tightened.

They remained like that for long minutes. Her latched onto him, him holding her.

Eventually, he pulled away and studied her face. "Are you okay?"

Her eyes flickered between his. "Could you…"

When she didn't finish her sentence, he cupped her cheek again. "Could I what, honey?" He knew what he was hoping she'd say. But he needed to hear the words.

"Will you stay with me? Hold me?"

He swept some hair from her face. Then, without a word, he switched off the light, moved around the bed, slid beneath the sheets and pulled her into his embrace. The second she was there, he felt it. The calming of the storm in his chest. The peace that had been absent since he'd heard her scream.

Home. This woman felt like home.

She gripped him tightly. Her body was tense. He could almost feel her fear.

"You're safe," he whispered into her ear.

The second the words were out, her body relaxed and finally, a few minutes later, her breaths evened out.

He didn't fall asleep so quickly. He remained awake for a long time, just holding her. Wondering why the hell this felt so right.

CHAPTER 7

*H*ollie scrunched her eyes closed as she rolled from her stomach onto her back. Flecks of sun hit the back of her eyelids, and the sound of an animal chirping pricked at her ears. Slowly, she opened her eyes.

The first thing she noticed was the charcoal sheets. Very different to her pale pink ones. She lifted her head and swung her gaze around the sparse, masculine room. The wooden set of drawers. The glass of water on the bedside table.

The previous night crashed back to her. The attack. Mitch saving her. Him climbing into bed and holding her while she slept.

Her gaze swung to the other side of the bed. Empty. When had he left? The middle of the night? This morning?

Slowly, she climbed out of bed. She quickly used the bathroom and brushed her teeth before padding out of the room and down the stairs. Movement sounded from the kitchen. His house was similar to hers. With a living room and kitchen to one side of the stairs, and all bedrooms on the second floor. But where she kept colors light and neutral, he had a lot of dark wood and barely any photos.

She stepped into the kitchen to see a shirtless Mitch sliding a pancake onto a huge pile. She scanned the kitchen island to see scrambled eggs and juice already waiting.

He turned, and when his mouth stretched into a smile, desire was like lightning down her spine. A shirtless Mitch, smiling at her while making pancakes? God, that's what every woman's fantasies were made of.

"Hey." His voice was deep and husky. "How are you feeling this morning?"

"Better." Particularly after being cocooned in his arms all night.

He lowered the spatula to the counter and stepped toward her. When he gripped her hips, her breath caught. Just like last night, his gaze brushed over her neck and hardened. She realized there was a dangerous edge to this man that she hadn't known existed before yesterday.

"It looks worse than it feels," she said softly. Sure, it stung a little bit, but that was it. It could have been worse. A lot worse.

Gently, he lifted his hand and caressed her skin. "I wish I'd gotten to you quicker."

"You got there as soon as you heard me." He couldn't have done any better than that.

He didn't look like he agreed, but he didn't argue. "You didn't recognize the guy's eyes?"

A shudder coursed down her spine at the memory of those black eyes. "No."

His grip on her tightened. "There's no one you can think of who might want to hurt you? No one you might have pissed off?"

She'd only been here a couple of months. She couldn't think of anyone who—

No. Something came to her. "There *is* this company that's been trying to buy the land. Their real estate agent has called a few times since he found out Nanna's property was left to me. I think they want to develop the area into housing."

Mitch scowled. "Elite Housing?"

"Yes!"

"They approached me too. I was pretty firm when I told them to fuck off and haven't heard from them since."

Her brow creased. "I did a quick search of them online and saw they're a big company. But they'd need to knock down a lot of trees and I just don't think my nanna would have liked it, so I keep saying no. Plus, this was where she lived for most of her life. I can't just sell it." She shook her head. "Still, I don't think they'd go so far as to send a guy to kill me."

Her brows flickered. Would they?

"We'll mention it to the police and they can look into it." His hands lightly grazed her sides. "If you're ever in the position of someone holding your throat again, grab their index and middle finger with one hand, and the ring and pinkie with the other, and pull as hard as you can in opposite directions. It's painful, and the asshole should release you."

She swallowed. The idea of it happening again sent her into a cold sweat, but she nodded anyway.

"I'm glad you're okay," he said a moment later, his voice softening. "But I want you to stay here until they catch the guy."

Her heart gave a big thump. "You barely know me."

"I want you safe."

His deep, rumbly voice rolled over her skin, causing her belly to do a little flip.

Slowly, she skirted her hands up his chest, feeling every hard ridge as she went. They settled on his shoulders. "Thank you."

"You don't need to thank me."

She felt like she did. When her gaze flickered between his eyes, she saw something other than concern. Desire.

Her heart gave a little squeeze, and she grazed his bare skin. The heat in his eyes deepened, then, slowly, so slowly she barely saw him move, his head lowered.

When his lips touched hers, her breath caught. The kiss was

slow and gentle, but it also made every little part of her spark to life.

She leaned into him, a soft moan slipping from her chest. When her lips separated, his tongue slipped inside her mouth and swiped against hers.

God, she wanted to pause this moment and stay right where she was for endless minutes. She wanted to explore this man. To keep him close and devour him.

His hand tightened around her, tugging her closer. The air became thick, her breaths short.

Too soon, his head lifted, and she wanted to groan in despair.

"I don't know if I'm the best person for you to get into a relationship with," he whispered.

"Then why do you feel so right?"

There was a flash of heat at her words. But there was also something else. A flurry of emotions. Uncertainty. Fear. Anger, even.

"I want you," she whispered. "And if you've got stuff to work through, then I want to help you work through it."

She'd never spoken truer words.

The man watched her for another beat, then his head dropped, and he kissed her again. She melted into him.

* * *

MITCH BARELY TOOK his eyes off Hollie the entire breakfast. Even the way the woman spoke kept him captivated. She had this quiet grace about her. This calm that pulled him in and made his own issues feel insignificant. She even made him laugh, which, after last night, he'd have thought would be impossible. And that kiss… it was different to the last, but just as intense. Just as hit-to-the-chest powerful.

"Do you have work today?" he asked.

She shook her head. "Even if I did though, I would have let

them know I couldn't make it. I don't think my head would be in it today."

Some of the calm left him. He still wanted to find and kill that asshole from last night.

"They'll find him," he ground out. "When Jimmy sets his sights on someone, he doesn't stop until he has them."

Jimmy was the chief of police here in Heart Valley. He was good at his job, and they were damn lucky to have him.

"Is your cousin still in town? Declan?"

Mitch shook his head as he stood and lifted the empty plates. "Nah. He lives in Lindeman, Washington, with three of his former Delta buddies. He visits every so often, but I got the feeling he was keen to get back for a woman he's worried about."

He hoped his cousin could sort out that mess. There was nothing he hated more than a woman being harassed by a dangerous ex.

Something behind her in the window suddenly caught his attention. He had a view of not only his land, but Hollie's too.

And there was movement in her woods.

His voice lowered. "Stay here."

Before she could respond, he moved into the living room, opened the hidden safe behind a picture on the wall, and pulled out his gun.

Hollie gasped. "Mitch—"

"Lock the door after me."

With the Glock cocked, he ran across his yard. He kept it aimed as he weaved through the trees toward the men. He stopped a few yards away.

"Turn around slowly and keep your hands where I can see them."

The three men froze, then slowly, they all turned.

Two strangers and Brad.

"What the hell are you doing on Hollie's land, Brad?"

He looked at the gun, then back at him. "Now, Mitch, calm

down. I thought I saw a grizzly bear, so we're just checking over the area."

"A grizzly bear? Where's your weapon?"

Slowly, he lifted his jacket, and Mitch saw the holster holding a gun. Still, he didn't trust the guy.

"Get off her land—and stay off."

There was a flicker of anger on the guy's face. It came and went so quickly, most would have missed it. Mitch didn't.

"We're going," he said quietly.

Mitch didn't lower the gun until they reached the border of Hollie's land. Even then, there was something about the guy that made Mitch stay on alert whenever he was in sight.

CHAPTER 8

*H*ollie rinsed a dish before setting it in the dishwasher. A week had passed since her attack, and everything had been silent. Nothing had happened. Zilch.

What the heck did that mean? That someone wanted to hurt her, but Mitch had scared them off, so they'd moved onto someone else? Or they were just biding their time until she moved back into her place?

She turned her head and surreptitiously watched Mitch putting away everything on the table. She'd stayed here all week. But not in separate rooms. Nope, since that first night, they'd slept in his bed. She'd gone to sleep with the man snuggled around her like a pretzel and woken with her cheek against his chest. Every. Single. Night.

It was bliss. But it was also frustrating as hell, because other than a few more kisses, they'd done nothing. And man, oh man, the sexual tension was through the roof.

When the last dish was in the washer, she turned and studied him. She'd seen little changes in him over the last week. He'd opened up to her a bit more. About his time in the military. About his team over there. And the heated kisses, in combination with the intense looks, told Hollie that he wanted her as much as she wanted him.

So tonight, she was taking a risk.

"Want to watch a movie?" he asked, without looking her way.

"We could." She stepped up to him. Immediately, his arms went around her waist. She was becoming as familiar to him as he was to her. "Or…we could do something else."

She pressed a light kiss to his chest. She felt and heard his sharp inhale. She kissed him again, this time a fraction higher. When he didn't pull away, she peppered light kisses up his chest until she reached his neck.

"Hollie." He whispered her name like a warning.

"Mitch," she breathed.

She reached his jaw and trailed those kisses right across until she reached the corner of his mouth. Then she pulled back and looked at him. A million different emotions flickered over his face.

When several seconds passed, and he didn't make a move, she sighed quietly and started to step away.

Immediately, he tugged her back into him, and his mouth crashed onto hers.

She groaned deep in her throat as his tongue swept into her mouth, colliding with hers.

This kiss was different from others. It was hard and raw, and felt so damn heavy with emotion she could almost drown in it.

She swept her fingers back up his chest and slid them through his hair. Always so soft. In complete contrast to the rest of him.

His hands moved beneath her ass, and he lifted her up his body. Then he spun, pressing her against the wall.

Oh God, the heat. It was like nothing else. The man lit her on fire. He made her feel more alive than she'd ever felt, insanely aware of every inch of him.

His hand skirted beneath her top, grazed over her bare skin, then cupped her breast.

She whimpered when he found her pebbled nipple through the material of her bra and rolled it between his thumb and forefinger.

Yes. So much yes. To this man and what he made her feel.

He continued to roll her nipple while she pulled and tugged at his hair, desperate for more of him.

When his hand slipped out of her top, she wanted to cry out in disappointment. Then the air moved around them as he carried her through the house and up the stairs. A second later, she was sitting on his mattress. He stood at the end of the bed, eyes only for her. He tugged his shirt over his head. She watched as every muscle in his body rippled.

Her breath caught in her throat as he worked the button and zipper of his jeans. Then he tugged them down to reveal his muscular legs. Everything about this man was powerful. He exuded strength like it flowed through his veins.

He leaned over her and his fingers went to the waistband of her yoga pants before tugging them down. His eyes heated, then his head lowered to her foot, where he pressed a kiss to the inside of her ankle. Her breath stuttered. His next kiss was a notch higher.

He continued to kiss up her leg, and every time his lips touched her bare skin, her belly quivered in desire. When he reached the hem of her shirt, he tugged it over her head, then the kisses on her belly began.

Holy Christ. This man destroyed her. He completely undid every part of her in the best possible way.

When he reached around her back, she arched as he undid her bra and slipped it off. The second her breasts were free, he cupped them before taking one hard peak between his lips.

The world around her slipped into a deep gray as the heat in her belly coiled.

She cried out at the feel of his tongue on her hard peak. At the way he flicked her bud while thumbing her other nipple with his hand.

It was like torture and ecstasy mixed into one. It took her right to that edge while craving more.

He released her bud and trailed his lips back up to her mouth. He simultaneously sealed his lips to hers while running his hand down her body. When his finger slipped inside her panties, her breath stopped. Then he ran a finger down her slit.

Her body jolted violently, and she attempted to cry out, but he swallowed the sound.

Her thighs parted to give him better access, and he took full advantage, running his finger along her clit, while she writhed and groaned. He was unrelenting.

Then she felt his finger at her entrance. Her breath stopped in her throat. Slowly, he pushed inside her. She ripped her mouth from his and threw her head back with a cry.

"You're so damn beautiful, Hollie," he growled between kisses to her chin, her neck. All the while pushing inside her and pulling out.

Her breaths were uneven and her limbs in overdrive, but she had to touch him. She reached down, slipping her hand inside his briefs, and wrapped her fingers around him.

His powerful body tensed above her. She stroked his length, long, firm strokes, loving that she could bring him to such stillness. That he thickened in her grasp.

She pressed a gentle kiss to his neck, then another to his shoulder, never stopping. All the while, his finger remained firmly inside her.

She felt like she'd barely had a chance to touch him when he pulled out of her and grasped her wrist.

"I need you," he whispered, his breath brushing her face.

She cupped his cheek. "Take me."

The words had no sooner left her lips than his mouth crashed against hers again. Hands went to the waistband of her panties and pushed down. She did the same to him. Then he left her for a second and grabbed a foil packet from his drawer. The moment he'd donned it, he was back with her, between her thighs, his length at her entrance.

Her heart thrashed against her ribs.

Then, with a slowness that made her body ache, he slid inside.

Oh Lord, that stretch was like nothing else.

He didn't move straight away, instead his eyes remained on hers, holding her captive. That's when she felt it. The flicker deep inside her. Like a place in her heart she'd never known existed had just been filled. With this man, and what he did to her.

His mouth eased to hers, and she knew right then, there was no escaping her feelings for Mitch.

* * *

HIS BODY WAS ON FIRE. With heat, desire, and something else. A deep need for this woman that went further than anything physical.

Mitch lowered his head and kissed her. It was a slow, gentle kiss. So different from everything that had come before it. Then, slowly, he lifted his hips before easing back down. The small moan from her lips made him grow thicker inside her and sent lava burning through his veins. He thrust again and again, alternating between watching the beautiful emotions play over her face and kissing her heated skin.

He reached down and cupped her breast, thrumming the peak. Another moan. Fuck, he loved those sounds. Hell, there was nothing this woman could do or say he wouldn't love. He thrummed her nipple again. Another moan.

He increased his pace. He ached for this woman, to the point it felt like no touch would ever be enough.

His hand left her breast, and he reached down between their bodies and slid a finger across her clit. That's when her body finally arched, and she shattered around him. He watched it all, fucking drowning in her emotions like they were his own.

He thrust twice more, then his body tensed, and he broke.

For a moment, there was a thick stillness, no sounds but their labored breathing. Finally, he slid out of her and pulled her onto his chest as he lay on the mattress. Neither of them spoke. But neither of them had to. He was almost certain they'd both felt it. This woman was his. All of her. And even though he didn't quite feel like his old self after leaving the military, he wanted to fix that. For her.

CHAPTER 9

*H*ollie stretched her sore muscles, a smile playing at her lips at the memory of what had created the tenderness. She'd slept with Mitch, and God, it had been everything she knew it would be.

She reached across the bed but frowned when she touched cold sheets. Her eyes popped open. He wasn't there.

She listened for the sound of running water. Movement downstairs. There was nothing. Then her gaze caught on the piece of paper beside the bed.

Leaning over, her gaze skimmed the note.

I had to pop out to an emergency job in town. I shouldn't be long. Stay inside, everything's locked up. M x

Her smile widened. Man, she was screwed. Royally screwed. What she felt for him went so much deeper than it should after their short time together.

With a sigh, she climbed out of bed. She took her time getting ready. She was due to go into the sanctuary today, but not until later. Maybe she'd surprise Mitch with some pancakes when he got home. She smiled. She was a pretty lousy cook but pancakes she could do.

Once dressed in jeans and a long-sleeved shirt, she slipped her phone into her back pocket and moved downstairs. She grabbed a new bag of flour, and had just grabbed some scissors from the drawer when the doorbell rang.

She stilled. Mitch hadn't mentioned he was expecting visitors.

After setting the scissors on the island, she headed to the door. She almost rolled her eyes when she saw who it was. Brad freaking Baker. Why was he here? To hit on her some more?

She tugged the door open, but kept the screen closed and locked. Then she tried for a smile she didn't feel. "Hi, Brad, did you need something?"

"Hollie! Hi. I have a petition for city council requesting they do something about the grizzly bears in the area. They're dangerous and they're multiplying. I'm trying to get as many locals to sign it as possible."

Her brows flickered. Well, that wasn't what she'd been expecting. She agreed, the grizzly bears were a problem, and they killed a lot of the native wildlife. It was a huge reason they had so many baby animals at the sanctuary, because their mothers had been mauled.

"Come back later today and I'll sign it."

He cringed. "I would but it's a tad time sensitive. I need to get it to the council this afternoon." He lifted a bag in his arm she hadn't realized he'd been holding. "Oh, and I made you some banana bread. I know, a man who bakes, crazy."

Argh, now she just felt bad. "Okay, fine. But we need to make it quick."

She coded in the house alarm to turn it off then unlocked and opened the screen door before closing and locking it straight after him. He walked straight into the kitchen and set the contract and banana bread on the kitchen island. She had to admit, the bread smelled good.

Her stomach growled. Oh, jeez.

She moved into the kitchen and took the pen from his fingers.

She scanned the page. There were a dozen signatures already there.

"Are you getting more signatures before the meeting?" she asked. "Twelve hardly seems enough to get people doing anything."

"Yeah, I'm going around today."

So, more people in town would get a visit from this ray of sunshine? She bit back a chuckle as she pressed the pen to paper and signed her name. She was just lifting the pen when she noticed the paper felt strange under her touch. A slick, smoother kind of texture than usual.

Frowning, she ran her fingers over the page, and when she hit the edge…a thin layer separated from another layer beneath it. What the heck?

Without thinking about what she was doing, she peeled the pages apart.

Her lips separated.

Transfer paper. And a different contract lay underneath. A sale of land contract—which now had her signature on it.

Oh, shit… She'd signed carbon paper that transferred her signature.

The flick of a pistol slide being racked sounded from behind her. Every muscle in her body tightened.

"Turn around, Hollie."

With slow, controlled breaths, she turned. Brad stood in front of her, gun in hand, aimed right at her head.

"What are you doing, Brad?"

"I need the money from the sale of my property," he said quickly, his hand steady on the weapon. "I approached the company a year ago with the idea of development. They liked it but said they needed more land than mine. They were hoping for mine, yours and Mitch's…but said they'd go ahead with just the two of us."

She shook her head. "So you're going to kill me for money?"

"Yes. They're willing to pay a lot. Enough for me to get some people off my back. A lot more than anyone else will pay. But fucking Anna wouldn't sell! So I got rid of her."

Her throat closed, and it took her three tries to get words out. "You killed my nanna?"

"Yes. I cut her brake line. It wasn't hard. I thought her family would sell the property, the developers would buy it, and everything would be okay."

Anger was like steel up her spine. This asshole had *killed* her grandmother!

"You're a murderer," she growled.

"I'm desperate."

And that made it okay?

He kept the gun aimed as he reached around her for the contract. "At first I thought I could fuck some sense into you. Seduce you into selling to me."

Argh. Wait… "Did you send that man to my house?"

"Yes. He was only supposed to scare you into selling."

"But you didn't count on Mitch."

The man sneered. "No. That's man's fucked a lot up for me." He took a small step back. "You've made me do this, Hollie. With your damn stubbornness."

Now the asshole was blaming her? Did he tell himself her grandmother's death was the older woman's fault too?

Her hand crept back on the island behind her, touching the edge of what she was looking for.

"Any last words?" he asked.

Nope. Because she wasn't dying today. She wrapped her fingers around the scissors, then lunged and stabbed them into his leg.

The man howled and dropped the gun, reaching for the scissors as the sharp blade sliced into his skin. She stretched for the gun and took a quick step away when strong fingers wrapped around her calf and pulled her to the floor. The gun slipped from her hand.

Brad crawled over her, his body weighing her down. His fingers wrapped around her throat. Immediately, her air cut off. Seconds later, a fuzzy cloud began to blur her vision.

She tugged and pulled at his arms. Then Mitch's words rushed back to her.

With desperate fingers, she grabbed Brad's index and middle finger with one hand, and his ring and pinkie with the other. Then, using all her strength, she pulled in opposite directions.

Brad howled, and the second her throat was free, she kicked him away.

The gun was too far and on the other side of him, so instead of trying to get it, she ran. She raced straight outside and beelined for the trees.

Her phone vibrated from her back pocket, but she ignored it. All she could focus on was putting space between her and Brad. On surviving.

She'd made it deep into the woods before loud footsteps pounded the ground somewhere behind her. He was close. Too close. He was going to catch her.

The thought had terror crawling up her throat. But she swallowed her fear and dodged behind a tree to hide. Then she forced her breaths to silence.

CHAPTER 10

Something was wrong. Mitch pressed his foot harder to the accelerator. Not only had the house alarm been switched off, but she hadn't answered his call.

He pressed the button on his steering wheel and called again. Again, no answer. *Fuck.* What the hell was going on? Had that asshole gotten inside? Found a way to disable the alarm and attacked her?

Everything in Mitch vibrated with the need to protect her. Save her.

The idea of losing Hollie...God, it tore him apart. It made him regret everything about his hesitancy. He needed the woman, and he needed her to be okay.

The police had looked into the developers. There were no red flags and no connections to any criminal activity. Didn't mean it wasn't them, but if not, then who the hell could this person be?

Like he'd conjured them with his thoughts, his phone rang, but it wasn't Hollie. It was Jimmy.

"You got something for me, J?"

"We found the guy who attacked Hollie. A neighbor spotted his

plates the day he drove away and we matched them to the guy."
His engine was loud in the background.

His gut tightened as he turned a hard corner. "Who is he?"

"A hired contractor by the name of Eli Scott."

"A contractor? Who hired him?"

There was a heavy pause, and Mitch knew he wasn't going to
like this. "Her neighbor. Brad Baker."

Shit.

"I've sent units to his house—"

"He has her," Mitch interrupted.

Jimmy cursed. "I'm heading there now."

Mitch hung up and pulled into his driveway before slamming
his foot on the brake. His heart crashed in his chest when he saw
the open door. He raced inside, then stopped and listened. Silence.

"Hollie?"

No answer. He moved through the living room and into the
kitchen. His gaze zoned in on the blood on the floor. Dread
twisted in his gut. A breeze suddenly hit him. His gaze shot to the
open back door.

He took off. Once outside, he saw the prints in the ground.
They went into the woods. He ran, gun cocked and ready to
shoot. He'd kill any asshole who threatened Hollie. Without
pause. Without hesitation.

* * *

"Get the hell out here, Hollie!" Brad shouted, his voice angry.
"You're gonna die one way or another, whether you like it or not.
Why drag it out?"

God, this guy was an asshole!

Fear flowed through her, but so did something else. Anger. An
anger so raw and real that she wanted to run out there and attack.
She wanted the guy to pay for what he'd done to her nanna.

"If you'd just sold your damn land, you wouldn't be in this position right now!"

No, if her neighbor wasn't such a psychopath, *then* she wouldn't be in this position.

His steps had slowed, and he sounded like he was searching the area.

Oh Jesus.

"I actually liked Anna." Her chest constricted at the sound of her nanna's name out of his mouth. More steps. "But when it became a choice between her and me, I chose *me.*"

Of course, the selfish asshole.

When she heard him pause right on the other side of the tree she was hiding behind, she quietly lowered to a crouch and readied herself. He was going to find her. She couldn't do anything about that. But what she *could* do was fight.

Her muscles twitched.

He rounded her tree.

And she lunged for his middle.

He hit the ground and she landed on top of him. Immediately her hands went to his wrists, pushing the gun up, while she kneed him between the legs.

The guy growled in pain, and the gun went off.

Without removing his hand from the weapon, he threw his elbow forward and hit her in the face, then shoved her off. She cursed loudly and rolled to her back beside him.

He swung the gun around. She stopped him with both hands on his wrist, keeping the gun aimed above her head. Her muscles strained. Inch by inch, the gun grew closer to her face.

No... He was too strong!

She tried to get her knee up, but there was no space between them. Her heart pounded in her chest and sweat beaded her forehead. The gun was almost aimed right at her head when Brad suddenly flew off her.

Her gaze shot around to find Mitch on top of Brad. He threw a punch, and Brad's head snapped back.

She breathed heavily as she shoved up into a sitting position. Her face ached from where that elbow had collided with her cheek. More punches sounded. She looked up to see Brad still on the ground and Mitch hovering, pounding the guy over and over with his fist.

"Mitch!" she gasped.

It was like her voice pulled him out of his fog of rage—and he finally stopped. Brad lay still in the dirt.

Mitch's chest heaved as he staggered toward her. When he cupped her cheek, his touch was gentle. "Are you okay?"

She swallowed. "I think so." Her gaze swung to Brad then back. "He tricked me into signing over my land and was going to kill me." A shudder rocked her body.

The rustle of footsteps sounded from somewhere in the woods.

Another flash of fury and pain overtook Mitch's face. "I should have killed him."

She leaned into his chest, resting her cheek against his heart and letting the beats calm her. "Thank you. *Again.*"

She felt a kiss pressed to her head. Her eyes shuttered and the feel of his body against hers, holding her, eased her fear.

"He killed Anna," she sobbed against him.

His arms tightened. "He'll go away for his crimes. He won't see the light of day as a free man ever again."

When a groan sounded from the ground, they both swung around to look at Brad. Mitch was just pulling her behind him when three uniformed officers broke through the trees.

"Hands where we can see them!"

The next couple of hours were a whirlwind of police reports and medics. Brad was taken away in cuffs, and eventually everyone cleared out of Mitch's home. When it was just her and Mitch left, it couldn't have been too soon.

2023 RARE AUSTRALIA ANTHOLOGY

He closed the door then took her in his arms. "Are you sure you're okay?"

She nodded slowly, touching her hands to his chest. "Thanks to you."

His temple touched hers. "You scared me today, Hollie."

She swept her hands up his neck and tangled them through her hair. She'd been terrified too. Terrified that today was her last day. That she wouldn't have a chance to tell the man what she should have told him already.

She opened her mouth to say those very words, but before she could, he spoke first.

"I love you, Hollie. I know it hasn't been long, but I can't imagine a future without you in it."

Her heart thumped, and the place inside her that ached for her nanna eased a tiny bit. Her gaze flicked between his eyes. "I love you too, Mitch." She grazed his neck with her fingertips. "And the heart doesn't care about time. It knows love. And this is it."

He pulled her into his arms once again...and brought her the peace she so desperately needed with a single kiss.

* * *

THANKS FOR READING! You can read Declan's story here: https://www.amazon.com.au/dp/BoB63WSR45

Nyssa Kathryn is a romantic suspense author who writes about ex-Special Forces heroes and heroines who need saving. Protector romance and HEA's are her jam.

NO MARK: A RUSTED HERITAGE PREQUEL BY M.F. ADELE

The Rusted Heritage is a dark contemporary reverse harem romance rated M for a mature audience. It includes violence, murder, graphic sexual scenes, alcohol and tobacco use, drug use, and explicit profanity.

Reader discretion is advised.

Like most other content rating systems, this should be used as a guide.

Please refer to the author disclaimers in the front of each book if you have triggers, as there are dark themes in these stories that some readers may find unsettling.

CHAPTER 1

❦

$\mathcal{J}$asper

ELEVEN YEARS AGO...

The dark circle tunnels my vision as I adjust my rifle's scope. This was supposed to be a quick job, but my mark has company.

I observe the two men arguing from three-hundred meters away, wishing I could hear the heated debate.

Gavin "Gator" Mendez stands under the streetlamp, toe-to-toe with a tall blonde. The named man faces me, though he doesn't know I'm lurking in the shadows. His brow furrows deep over his eyes, a look I interpret as his attempt to be menacing. But the way he puckers his lips and frowns has the opposite effect.

The blonde man tips his head back, his shoulder rising and falling as he laughs. From the change in Gator's expression, I'm guessing that wasn't the reaction he was hoping for.

My finger rests against the trigger, but I keep it relaxed. Each time I've readied myself to take the shot, they've subtly shifted until the blonde man blocks me.

This is taking too long.

I should have finished twenty minutes ago. Lorenzo is waiting for me, and I still have to trek a mile through Rose Bay with a large rifle case strapped to my back in order to get to him. The one upside to this situation is flat, open land doesn't surround the Asphalt Zombies' clubhouse.

No.

Just several gigantic thickets of overgrown, thorny shrubs littering a slight downhill slope...

Beyond that, I'll hit the barbed fence around the docks. Then shipping containers stacked too high and cameras searching for thieves in the night.

Fuck.

Kiss and makeup, or hurry and leave.

The job itself is simple enough. I'm meant to kill Gavin "Gator" Mendez. The only stipulation is I can't let it look like another biker gang caused his death, hence the rifle. It's just a guess, but I'm assuming whoever the Asphalt Zombies made enemies with wouldn't park out here and wait this long.

Gator would already be dead if I could just march my ass down this dirt and brush-covered slope and shoot him with my 9m.

Or slit his throat...

I'd gladly walk away bloody to end this waiting game.

I don't know who the blonde man is... otherwise, I would kill him too. But I'm only being paid to take out Gator.

Why waste a bullet when Blondy clearly isn't a fan of him either?

My phone vibrates dully against my right butt cheek, and I know without looking that Lorenzo is sick of waiting for me. Or perhaps he's concerned with how much time has passed.

I won't chance him showing up, blowing my cover, or getting us caught.

I'm too far away to shoot Blondy with my pistol, but if I shoot him with my rifle, I'll do more damage than necessary. If I could accurately graze him without blowing a chunk of his leg away, that would be great.

I don't know if I trust myself that much, though.

This is a conundrum I don't enjoy being in... But there aren't any better options.

Leaving Blondy alive is a surefire way to have a witness for the Asphalt Zombies to... consult. Then, they'll turn to Wheeler, their leader, and blah, blah, whatever. I don't care as long as they stay away from me.

It's not something I typically worry about.

Finding out I've killed a member of their precious club would require someone to know who I am.

No one knows exactly who the Ghost is.

And no one knows the Ghost is Jasper Maldonado.

They definitely don't know that I am Jasper.

They all think I'm Gemma Smith, the quiet teenager in the back of her classes at Saint Carmen Preparatory Academy, who gets picked up from school by thugs because my dad deals drugs.

And they all think Jasper is a guy who disappeared out of fear when his older brother was killed three years ago.

Having the money and power to fake birth certificates and government documents is one tiny perk of being a Maldonado. While my grandfather has a minor level of trust with the Lennox family from Silva Meadows, I do not. Peter is scum, but until the leadership of our cartel switches, I can't touch the banking fraud who knows too much about me.

But that doesn't matter here and now. The men before me don't go to school with me or know my secrets. They won't see me... And I'll be gone before Blondy can work his way through the pain to look for threats.

Fuck it. I'm going to shoot them both.

I continue observing them through my scope and witness the moment their argument reaches its crescendo. Blondy shoves Gator, causing the shorter man to shuffle backward.

My finger tightens on the trigger, knuckle bending at a snail's pace until I blow out my breath.

I don't care what the movies try to sell us... There is no being quiet with a rifle.

It's easier to muffle the sound in the city, where there's hustle and bustle and an abundance of noise.

Out here, though?

Not a chance.

If anyone is outside the Asphalt Zombies' clubhouse, they'll hear my shot.

Shots...

Fucking Blondy.

I squeeze the trigger, and my ears ring from the assault.

Gavin "Gator" Mendez jerks from the impact of my bullet sailing through his forehead. Bone fragments and brain matter explode from the back of his skull as his body slams onto the ground, landing atop of the mess we made. It all happens within a split second, but a headshot always looks the same from this distance.

I turn my attention to the next man.

Blondy stumbles backward, shaking his head as if he's confused. But I give him no time to understand what has just transpired.

He steps to the left, and I ready another round. One more foot to the left, and I can accurately aim for Gator's unmentionables and hopefully knick the unlucky fellow in the forearm or something...

As Blondy continues shaking his head in dismay, I squeeze the trigger a second time. He drops to the ground, clutching the ripped left thigh of his jeans while he screams. As my hearing returns, I'm shocked to note his shrieks of pain are more of a growling, angry sound that carries through the night air, and less of a wailing screech that pierces my eardrums like needles.

I don't take my eyes off Blondy as I dismantle my rifle in a hurry and put it in the black case on my right. Every movement I make is from memory, is from doing this one too many times. I check my surroundings before I toss the strap over my head and climb to my feet.

The bush beside me conceals me as long as no one is searching. And sadly, I don't have time to witness a raging group of bikers come to aid their fallen without knowing their leader hired me to kill his second in command.

Club politics aren't my business.

I tuck my hand into the pocket of my hoodie and remove a tiny plastic baggy.

It holds one thing.

One very important thing that will probably go unnoticed if the wind blows before anyone finds where I was lying on the ground.

A Tithonia petal floats to the ground as I turn the baggy upside down.

The Mexican sunflower is my signature. And those spicy pops of reds, oranges, and yellows have littered most of my crime scenes for the last year.

I make my way toward the thorny thicket on my left, keeping my eye trained on Blondy. He turns his head, and I stop in my tracks until I'm sure his eyes are closed as he works through the pain.

But something about him has become oddly familiar now that I can see his face.

I think through all the blonde men I know, only coming up with a handful that fit his description.

The thicket fully hides me as I watch him, trying to figure out where I've seen him from. I pull my phone from my pocket, and it begins vibrating in my hand. Lorenzo's name lights up the screen.

I answer his call, turning the volume down as I wait for someone to show up… Anyone.

Preferably an Asphalt Zombie… But yeah. Anyone.

"What the fuck is taking you so long?" Lory asks, his teeth grinding in his ire.

"Someone confronted Gator while I was waiting, so I had to wait longer."

"Who?"

I sigh as I study Blondy's face. The streetlamp casts shadows against his features, but I can still make out that straight nose and those high cheekbones. His dirty blonde hair is long on top and was artfully messy before I shot him.

"I don't know," I whisper, though as soon as I say the words, I know who he is. "Leave without me, Lory. I'll call a cab."

"In Rose Bay in the middle of a Friday night? Fuck no."

"It's fine. I've got some cash, and I know my way around."

"Gem," Lory growls, but I hang up.

He calls me again, though I simply press the screen to my hoodie so no one sees the light.

The man I shot—the one I didn't kill—is no man at all. He's a sixteen-year-old boy that I go to school with.

Blondy is Riley Barker.

An SUV speeds down the road from the clubhouse, slamming on its brakes when they see the two guys lying on the pavement. The driver fishtails before coming to a complete stop, and two men rush to Riley's side.

Another man checks on Gator, though he doesn't so much as bend down when he sees the blood.

William "Wheeler" Davies, president of the Asphalt Zombies, surveys the scene, his brow raised as he speaks to his guys.

Riley leans his head back, face scrunched in pain as he shrugs.

Wheeler tips his head toward the SUV, but when no one jumps to his silent command, he yells, "Hospital. Now."

Two of the men hastily scoop up Riley, grimacing when he muffles a shout from the unsteady movement. Another man quickly circles the driver's side and opens the hatch so they can shove him inside.

Wheeler and the three men climb into the still-idling vehicle and speed away.

CHAPTER 2

*J*asper

I STARE at the empty road—the near empty road—as I untangle my thoughts. I'm not surprised they took Blondy, but I am surprised they're taking him to a hospital. That tells me more than it should, while somehow telling me nothing at all.

Why is Riley Barker hanging out with bikers? And the Asphalt Zombies at that...

They aren't the type of people a spoiled rich kid should associate with.

I've never shot a kid before, though I wonder if sixteen is close enough to an adult to ease my guilt. The Maldonado family has few morals, but the ones we do have are strong.

My grandfather would kill a kid to prove a point...

I'm not him.

And I'll never be him.

Had I known the man arguing with Gator was a teenager, let

alone one I went to school with, I would have shot my mark and ran... But maybe that would have made this situation worse.

I have no way of going back, so I need to move on, smother my guilt and—

Fuck.

Check on him.

I hang my head as I push through the thicket toward the fence around the docks. The barbed wire at the top juts out, making it damn near impossible to climb without slicing myself open. But I knew this and came prepared.

I swing my rifle case around my chest and unsnap the buckle to dig into the pocket. The bolt cutters are bulky in my grasp, but I use them to cut the chain-link fence away from the nearest post.

The opening is just big enough for me to squeeze through and drag my case behind me, but I don't want it to be too obvious that someone came through here.

I kneel at the fence and pull my phone from my pocket to call a cab, though Lory has beaten me to it.

Lory: A cab will be waiting at 12:36.

Get your shit done and call me.

I don't text him back. Instead, I begin my trek through the docks, between the mountains of shipping containers.

Rose Bay's imports and exports aren't as prevalent as Crimson Bay or Silva Meadows, but there are still plenty of workers milling about.

And cameras.

I stick to the shadows, keeping my face angled to the darkest areas. Everything I'm wearing is black, and my dark hair curtains on the right side of my face... But that isn't always enough, and I need unobstructed vision to weave through the paths unseen.

The shipping containers are three and four units high, creating an ominous atmosphere in the middle of the night. There are too many corners to peer around, too many corners for people to sneak up on me.

My comfort isn't an issue, though.

I lost that freedom several years ago.

Beeps and squeals from forklifts and tires ring through the air. The scent of saltwater clings to my skin as the wind blows my hair away from my face. I take a quick left, slinking further into the stacks to avoid the workers, and head east toward the main gate.

My travel time is a hasty twenty-two minutes... And I worry the cabbie might leave me when I realize I'm ten minutes past the meeting time. But as I get closer to the guards' booth, I see the white sedan idling at the curb of the main road. My phone buzzes in my hand.

Lory: Did you make it?

Me: Yes. I'll call you soon.

I tuck my phone in my pocket and slide around the backside of the guards' booth before heading toward the cab. My stomach churns unsteadily as my guilt surfaces once more.

I shouldn't care...

But I do.

* * *

THE CAB RIDE IS QUIET, though I don't mind. I'm actually pretty fucking ecstatic that the driver doesn't try carrying on a conversation with me.

The M tattooed on his right middle finger is all I need to see to relax a fraction in the backseat. I still keep my rifle case close to the door, out of his reach.

Relaxing and trusting are two totally different things.

I take a good fifteen minutes of him driving in circles before I decide on my first destination.

And it's not the hospital.

I don't know how I would explain my black case if anyone asked... and there's definitely no way to hide the dismantled rifle inside.

"Go to The Flaming Cherry," I direct the driver.

He tips his head and whips us around at the red light, taking us to the center of Rose Bay. We're not far away, so I don't bother texting Rosario to let her know I'm popping in.

I should... But I don't.

A gentleman's club is no place for a sixteen-year-old girl at one in the morning. That never stops me from visiting the cheeky broad that owns the business.

I would say Rosario is a family friend, but that's not really the case. She's a friend of my mother's, not my father or the Maldonado's, though that doesn't stop her from doing some sketchy deals with me.

I might be young, but I'm not dumb. I need to make a name for myself or the cartel will swallow the rest of my freedoms whole and spit out an eighteen-year-old troubled housewife who's waiting for her thug husband to come home and knock her up again.

No fucking thanks.

I'm grateful that Lorenzo agrees with me, and he's *not* a lowlife thug. We're arranged to be married, though the recent influx of attacks from the Estrada Cartel has kept my grandfather busy enough to forget about us.

For now.

We consider ourselves lucky for the break. But we count the days until I'm eighteen, because he won't let us go after that. Eduardo Maldonado Senior won't have to travel to Mexico with two young teens and force them to get married if he can force us in the comfort of his own home.

My grandfather is disgusting, but that thought never leaves my mind unless I know it's just me and Lory.

The Flaming Cherry is quite the hot spot for near naked entertainment. The parking lot is jam-packed, cars lining bumper-to-bumper along the side of the building, blocking the painted flames and neon cherry signs.

"Take me around back."

Again, the driver doesn't speak. He simply nods his head and does as he's asked. Maybe because Lory called him to pick me up, or maybe because he hates his fucking job... None of it matters as long as I get where I need to be.

As he pulls to a stop, I toss a wad of twenties over the seat and hop out of the cab. The black metal door on the back side of The Flaming Cherry reads *employees only*, and I'll get stopped when I walk in, but telling them Rosario is my aunt usually does the trick.

They all know she has a niece, though none of them know we chose each other and aren't blood related. It's not their business.

"Who are you?" a towering Spanish man asks, his accent light after years in the states. "You can't come in this door."

"I'm Rosario's niece," I remind him. "She's expecting me. We go through this every time, Jose."

He looks me up and down. "She didn't tell me."

I shrug. "Are you going to call her out? Or can I go? You can walk me to her office if you still don't believe me."

"What's in the bag?" he inquires, narrowing his eyes.

"What bag?"

"The one on your back."

I roll my eyes. "A rifle."

"Sure." He scoffs. "You walk around with a .50 cal in Rose Bay, and I shit rainbows."

I struggle to keep the smirk off my face. Rosario didn't hire him for his intelligence. I'm convinced she brought him on as an employee so she could drool over his muscles in the tight t-shirts he wears.

If Jose only knew that I wasn't lying...

"It's just a duffle bag with clothes in it," I explain, giving him an answer he can comprehend. "I'm staying the weekend with my aunt. And I like this bag because it's a conversation starter."

"Rose is in her office," he grumbles. "Don't wander."

I mock-salute him as I head down the dark hall toward Rosario's closed door. One knock tells me she's doing paperwork of some sort.

"What?" she shouts.

"It's me."

"Me who?" she demands, aggravation bleeding into her tone.

I turn the knob, leaning my head around the edge of the door. "Me, me... Were you expecting someone?"

Rosario huffs as she drops her pen and rubs her cheek. "Gem, what are you doing here?"

"I need to drop something off," I reply with a grin, lifting my shoulder to bring my case into view. "I'll pick it up in two or three hours, but I can't take it with me right now."

"What is it?"

"My rifle."

She arches a perfectly drawn on brow. "Jose let you in with that?"

"He said if I had a rifle, then he shit rainbows."

"He's fun to look at, but he's such a moron," she mumbles. "I'm going to fire him when Darren leaves, even though I'll get that whole '*I told you so*' speech."

I hold my hands up. "I told him what it was."

"I know you did. It tickles the shit out of you when they don't believe you." She tips her head toward the back wall. "Just put it in the closet, but make sure you pick it up tonight. I don't want someone finding it when they snoop around my office."

"Someone was snooping in *your* office?"

"It's nothing," she assures me as she flips through some papers. "Caught a girl in here looking for something. She said she was just curious. I don't remember stupid being tattooed on my forehead, but it could be the Botox wearing off."

I snort when she rolls her eyes. The wrinkles on her forehead are deep, and I don't think Botox will help them much anymore. I know better than to voice my opinions, though.

Rosario is the most low-key thug I know. She's polished and proper-ish for an ancient dancer, but I've seen her bust a wine bottle over a man's head for calling her an aged-out whore. And I once watched her beat a man to near death with a baseball bat for assaulting one of her girls.

It wouldn't surprise me if she had a gun or two stashed in her desk drawers. Or between her tits. They're big enough to conceal a small pistol.

I close the closet door and wipe the amusement from my expression before I face her. The last thing I want to do tonight is explain why I was thinking about Rosie's melon-sized breast.

"Thank you," I say as I start to leave.

"Where are you going at half-past one with dirt all over you?"

I glance down, frowning when I see how filthy my hoodie is. "To the hospital."

"Are you hurt?"

"No," I answer, taking off the dirty jacket. "I'm going to check on the guy I shot earlier."

"Why?" she asks, clipped as she grimaces in distaste.

I sigh as I turn my hoodie inside out and pull it back over my head. "Because he wasn't my mark, and I didn't realize until after I shot him that I go to school with him."

"That's going to be fun," Rosario murmurs, picking her pen up to finish her work.

"I'm hoping he's unconscious when I get there," I admit. "I just want to make sure I didn't blow his leg off. Pretty sure I grazed him, but—"

"With a rifle?" She snorts as she shakes her head. "That's some aim, Gem."

"We'll see when I get there."

Rosario waves me away. "Should be a cab out front. I'll see you in a few hours."

* * *

355

As MY SECOND cab of the night pulls into the Bayview Hospital parking lot, I ready myself for a silver screen worthy performance. I toss the driver some money and frown at the last of my cash as I stiffly walk toward the automatic doors.

I'll have to call Lory to come get me from The Flaming Cherry, because I don't have enough money to take another cab back to Crimson Bay. I'd have to use my debit card for that, and the answer is no.

The closer I get to the emergency department, the quicker my steps become, until I'm practically running as I rush inside. I slide across the floor, shoving my hip against the check-in counter as I force tears to pool in my eyes and roll down my cheeks.

"My boyfriend," I tell the nurse, gasping a little. "They brought him in about an hour ago. I need to see him."

"Settle down, honey," she placates, reaching up to pat my arm. "I'm not supposed to let you back there. Only family."

A sob spills from my lips that sounds so real I almost believe it. And I lay into the act, stretching my arms across the counter and letting my tears drip onto the sign-in paper. I pant for breaths, working myself into a choked-up frenzy.

The man sitting closest to us shifts uncomfortably in his chair as he watches me fall apart. I endeavor to make a bigger scene, turning the volume up as I bawl my eyes out.

Rules and regulation or not, I'm getting the information I need.

The question is... How many people must witness my theatrics before I get what I want?

It's manipulative, I know. But when you grow up on the battlefield between two cartels, you learn to work the system.

"Don't do it, Kirsty," a second nurse mumbles as she flits by.

"Look at her, Belle," Kirsty the Nurse admonishes. "She's just rushed to the hospital because she thinks her boyfriend might be hurt. Her jacket is on inside out, and her pants are dirty... She's clearly had a night, and now she's devastated."

"You're projecting," the second nurse, Belle, calls as she walks through the triage hall.

I turn my body and sink to the floor, leaning my back against the counter as I loudly whimper, "Please, just tell me he's not dead. Don't let him be dead."

"Aww, honey," Kirsty the Nurse sadly sings. "What's his name?"

"Ri—Riley Barker," I stutter, sucking in heavy breaths.

Her short nails click across the keyboard of the laptop in front of her. And I visually pick the waiting room apart, observing as another nurse waves her hand over the motion detector to open the door into the main portion of the hospital. She pushes a gurney through the entrance, bumping the end into the corner of the wall.

I almost dash in after her.

"He's not in the ER anymore," Kirsty the Nurse informs me, whispering as she glances over the counter. "He's in room 378. Third floor."

I jump up, using my sleeves to wipe my eyes. "Thank you. Thank you so much."

"You're welcome. Now, go before the she-beast comes back to stop you."

CHAPTER 3

J asper

THE SCENT of coffee permeates the third floor, not quite covering the sterile smell, but it's better than nothing. I glide past the nurses' station without acknowledging them. They're too caught up in their hooting laughter to pay me any attention.

Room 378 looms ahead of me, and I almost pause, self-conscious of my actions. I'm already here, though this suddenly seems like a stupid idea.

I don't know Riley Barker. We go to school together, share a few classes... We were lab partners last year, but we could hardly agree on anything. I wouldn't even call us acquaintances.

"It's after visiting hours," a nurse informs me as she rolls a vertical blood pressure machine out of Riley's room. "But since he just got here, I'll give you a few minutes."

She steps to the side, letting me pass her as she closes the door behind me. I stand frozen for a second, hoping like hell he's asleep. I just need to know that I didn't do crazy-serious damage.

A little is fine, but I wasn't trying to take off his leg.

"Camille?" Riley calls out when I don't move.

He can see my shoes.

Fuck.

I should leave.

"Not your sister," I correct as I pull the curtain open, despite my better judgment.

His brow squishes over his eyes, confusion causing him to shake his head. "What are you doing here?"

That's the million dollar question, isn't it?

What the fuck am I doing here?

"I saw you with some bikers when you came in," I say, carefully choosing my words as I walk further into the room. "I thought I'd be nosy and find out why a Barker is hanging out with—"

"So, you're going to tell everyone at school I'm biker trash?" He scoffs. "It shouldn't surprise me. Everyone wants shit on the Barkers."

"Why would I tell anyone anything?" I ask, offended that he assumes I'm here to bask in his injury or some kind of downfall.

"I don't know," he snaps. "Why the fuck are you here?"

I lean against the foot of the bed as I glower at him. "I wanted to make sure you were okay, which is stupid. We're not friends. But I felt bad—"

"For what?" Riley interrupts, crossing his arms over his chest. "Seeing me with helpful citizens who just happen to be bikers? After I was injured. And then jumping to conclusions about why I was with them like it's any of your business?"

"Wow," I drawl, quietly admitting, "Now I regret just grazing you."

He tilts his head. "What did you say?"

"Nothing," I reply, turning for the door. "Forget I was here."

"No. You don't get to just barge into my hospital room under the pretense of being nosy." He chuckles, his anger palpable and contagious. "That might be the case, but I won't have you going back to Saint Carmen and telling them I'm part of a biker gang when you run around with thugs and drug dealers."

"Fuck you. I'm not telling anyone shit," I snarl, stepping closer, ignoring my better judgment again. "The people I run around with aren't a part of whatever this conversation is. I don't care if you associate with bikers or not. You're right. What you do isn't my business. I was just checking on you because—It doesn't matter."

I flail my arms around as I grow agitated, more with myself than with him. "I prefer to stay in my own lane. Clearly, I'm not doing that right now. This whole fucking night has been one mistake after the next. I should have just walked away, saved the job for another day. But no—"

"What job?" he asks, studying me as I bite my lips. "What does that have to do with anything?"

"Now, who's being nosy?" I pop back, admittedly a bit too childish.

The questions make us frown at each other. He wants an answer, though he knows I won't give it to him.

"Tell me why you're here," he demands, more friendly than before, but it's a fucking ruse. "Or at least be a decent person and tell me if you're going to spread rumors about—"

"I'm sorry," I cut in, a sarcastic grin lifting my lips. "Did I miss some memo about how I run my mouth to anyone, ever? I barely even speak to the people at Saint Carmen, much less gossip. Why would I tell them you were with bikers or shot, for that matter?"

I catch my words as soon as they leave my mouth, but it's too late.

"How do you know I was shot?" Riley inquires, livid blue eyes piercing straight through me.

"I read your file."

"They're digital."

I shrug. "The nurse at the ER desk told me."

"That's confidential."

"Then how did I know where to find you?"

Riley narrows his eyes, watching me as if we're animals. Only I can't decide who's the lion and who's the antelope in this instance. It makes me like him a little more than I should after the attitude he's given me.

"You already said you were being nosy," he points out. "Did you come in here to—"

"Jesus." I groan, hating that I'm starting to enjoy the banter. "Clearly you're fine. I don't know what I was thinking. I was never here. Forget you saw me."

I turn for the door, and he sighs heavily. The weight in that sound is one I recognize and feel all too frequently.

"Wait," he calls to me, his glare heating my back. "So, you're not here to find out my secrets and tell everyone?"

"What? No." I spin on my heel to return his ire, but it's not there, so I lower my voice. "Listen. I have no room to speak about hidden identities. I don't care what you do or when you do it. Honestly, I just came to check on you because, for once, the guilt was riding me."

"Guilt?" he parrots. "Guilt over what? What did you—"

"I just shot you," I confess, then slap my hand over my mouth and talk through my parted fingers. "Do you really think I want to explain to anyone why I saw you or where I saw you?"

Riley blinks in slow motion, though a grin creeps over his face as he glances from me to his leg. "You shot me?"

"Yes." I huff as I move closer to him and prop against the right-side edge of his bed. "I'd apologize… But you shouldn't have been there. Getting Gator to wait at that spot was like two weeks worth of work."

"Why didn't you kill me?"

"You weren't my target."

He nods like that's acceptable, and I look around to make sure I haven't entered the twilight zone.

What to fuck is happening?

"Someone paid you to shoot Gator?" he inquires.

"That answer depends..." I lean my back against the footboard and cross my arms over my chest, careful to not jostle him. "How high on pain meds are you?"

He snorts. "Not high enough to forget this conversation."

"Then, no," I tell him, plastering a sardonic smile on my face. "I did it for fun... Just a casual Friday night activity."

Riley watches me too keenly, like a cat stalking the mouse. "They say you run with major thugs, well-known guys in the crime rings."

"Is that another question?" I ask.

"No." He shakes his head. "It's just a statement I've heard floating around the halls of Saint Carmen."

"I don't run with thugs," I respond, though he doesn't need me to.

"But someone in your family is a member of the cartel?" he guesses.

I wobble my head. "No comment."

"What's your name, Gemma Smith?" he queries, making me bristle.

"I have no other name."

"It's not Gemma," he states matter-of-factly, as if he's got me all figured out.

I prop my feet in the chair on the right side of his bed and gaze at beyond him. Saline drips into the IV taped to his left arm and a heart monitor beeps, quietly fading into background sound the longer I'm in here.

Finally, I turn my amber eyes to him, ready to change the subject.

"What about you, Riley Barker?"

"They call me Riot."

"Your biker buddies?" I inquire, though humor lightens my words.

He shrugs. "My dad's club."

"Your dad is the president of the Asphalt Zombies?"

I could kick myself in the ass right now. If Wheeler comes at me for shooting his son, I'll have hell to pay for taking outside jobs. My father may know, but we work diligently to keep my grandfather from noticing. It's why I don't leave the Tithonia petals with marks he's sent me after.

"One and the same..." Riley grumbles.

"Wheeler is your dad?" I ask, needing the clarification.

How is Riley a Barker if his dad is William "Wheeler" Davies?

"His name is William," he tells me.

"I know what his name is."

"How?"

I grin as someone knocks on the door. "No comment."

A nurse comes in, pushing a large white cart in front of her. An open laptop perches at chest level, and she pays us no attention as she types in Riley's vitals.

It's when she's done that she turns her deep brown, disapproving eyes on me. I can say with absolute certainty that she's not a fan of me lying on the hospital bed with him. But she doesn't say anything about our yin-yang position.

"How are you feeling, Mr. Barker?"

"If I say dandy, do I get released early?"

She smiles at him as she opens a drawer on her cart and pulls out a syringe. "The doctor ordered morphine for you since the topical numbing will wear off soon. You should consider yourself lucky. A few more inches and you could have lost your leg."

I brush the invisible lint off the shoulder of my hoodie as I smirk at the only living victim to ever meet my rifle. He rolls his eyes at me before grimacing as the nurse injects the medication into his IV.

"You should wrap up your visit," she advises. "He needs to rest."

"I'll be leaving in a moment. Thank you."

She hums, though she doesn't reply. We stay silent as we watch her leave. As soon as the door shuts behind her, Riley stares at me, his head cocked like he's trying to understand the internal workings of my mind.

"Who are you, Gemma Smith?"

I raise a brow. "Why is my name so important to you?"

"Well, for starters, you shot me," he points out.

"My name is Gemma."

"Second." He glances around the hospital room. "You're here, so I'm guessing you didn't want to shoot me, otherwise you would have killed me."

I shrug my left shoulder. "I missed. Don't flatter yourself."

"No." Riley smirks, his blue eyes glimmering under the dim bedside lighting. "I think you hit me exactly where you wanted."

"Why do you say that?" I inquire, trying to figure out where I went wrong...

I mean, other than showing up and talking to him.

This is a huge fuck up on my part.

"Because you hit Gator directly between his eyes before you knocked me down. I know what you were doing..." He shakes his head, fighting the morphine. "Cleaning up and leaving a witness for the Zombies to question."

"I could have killed you," I reiterate, standing firm on my answer. "I didn't know who you were."

Riley relaxes, squinting at the ceiling as the medicine takes effect. "But you didn't."

"I won't miss next time," I inform him, exasperated with myself.

He chuckles as his eyes fall shut. I sit up, moving to slide off the bed, and he grabs my hand.

"Who are you, Gemma Smith?"

As his grip relaxes, I force myself to leave his side. But before I step away from the bed, I brush his blonde hair off his forehead.

"You know who I am," I whisper in his ear, the confession tightening my chest. "There are three faces to this coin. Gemma and the Ghost are only two of them."

He says nothing, though his eyelids flutter in response.

I kiss his cheek, daring myself to get just a little too close. "And my name is Jasper Maldonado."

"I'll see you tomorrow, Gem," Riley drawls, prying one groggy eye open as he gives me a dopey grin. "Bring ice cream."

"You can't manipulate me. I'm not coming back," I tell him, peeved that he wasn't asleep.

He nods, somehow still the cocky guy from school, despite the gunshot wound on his leg and the drugs. "You will."

"If you blackmail me—"

"You will," he repeats, though his voice is growing distant. "We have nothing to hide here. That's freeing."

I stop at the foot of the bed, observing him for a moment. The steady up and down of his chest is a false comfort now. I'll have to kill him. Eventually. But maybe he's right, and a few days of feeling what it's like to live without secrets will be freeing.

"Gemma?"

I clear my throat. "Yes?"

"Stop staring."

"Go to fucking sleep."

He tries to smile, though it's more a twitching of his cheeks. "Bring sprinkles."

I snort. "Fine. I'll bring ice cream and sprinkles as an apology."

"You said—"

"Oh, I'm not sorry for shooting you," I correct. "But I am sort of sorry for stealing this hoodie someone brought you. Mine is covered with dirt, and I don't expect you to be using this one anytime soon."

His hand barely moves from the bed as he flicks his fingers. "Chocolate."

"One condition, Riot."

He grunts, losing his fight against the morphine.

"If you repeat my name, I'll kill you," I warn.

I stare at him for two solid minutes, though he doesn't move. He's finally asleep, so I tug my inside-out hoodie over my head and toss it in the trash.

His black hoodie swallows me, hanging to the tops of my thighs. But the fresh scent clinging to the fabric is a welcome reprieve to the sterile smell of the hospital room.

The cartoon kangaroo makes me grin, with his plump red boxing gloves poised for attack. It reads *Jump Motherfucker...*

And that feels eerily accurate the moment Riley's whispered words reach my ears.

"I'm already dead, Jasper," he slurs, causing me to frown. "I want to enjoy my last year."

* * *

BLOCK AND TACKLE BY ELISE FABER

This is a novella that fits into my Gold Hockey and Billionaire's Club worlds. If you want to leave more about *the* Devon Scott and his siblings, check out those series! For now, enjoy how it all began...

CHAPTER 1

*I*f ever a time existed for a curse word, this was it.

Becca was five minutes late. Five entire minutes late, and the little screen on the printer was flashing at her with a paper jam.

"Becca! Those files need to be on my desk *now*."

Devon Scott. CEO of Prestige Media Group and her boss. Her *very* demanding boss.

Hence, curse words. Particularly the four-letter one Becca saved for only very special occasions.

The one that began with *"f"* and ended with a perfectly timed and heartfelt *"uck."*

Yeah. The word pretty much summed up her day. No—her week. Heck, if she was already cursing, it might as well sum up her month.

She yanked the tray from the printer, nearly knocking over her mug of tea. Thankfully, she caught it just in time, glaring at the maniacal kangaroo printed on the front, the words "Just keep hopping" emblazoned beneath it. That mantra might apply to her life to an uncomfortable degree, but right at that moment, she didn't need ridiculous things like encouragement. Or hope. Or maniacal kangaroos. Carefully, she set the mug to the side—well out of knocking-over distance this time—expertly cleared the jam, and shoved the tray back in. The printer whirred to life, spitting out pages in a flurry.

"Becca!"

"Coming," she called before dropping her voice and muttering, "Hurry up. Hurry up."

"*Becca.* So help me—"

The last page dropped into the tray. She snatched it up, fit it into the proper place of the file, and all but sprinted through the doorway of her boss's office.

"The printer—" she began.

Devon's eyes locked with hers, and Becca shivered. Not for the same reason that most people did when they met Mr. Scott. Not because his cool, businesslike expression was attributed to icicles or frozen seawater.

She shivered because of chocolate ice cream.

His eyes conjured thoughts of delicious, rich, melt-on-her-tongue sweetness that made her insides go all squirmy.

And along came that four-letter word again, blaring across her mind.

One winged brow arched, dark brown and perfectly formed. It made a crease on Devon's forehead, a rainbow of little lines leading up, up, up almost to his hairline.

Which was the precise moment Becca realized she'd said that curse word aloud.

She clamped a hand over her mouth, smacking herself in the face with the manila cardstock in the process and dropping every single paper she'd so painstakingly fought the printer over.

This was not happening. Devon didn't allow mistakes and… she sighed. She really needed this job.

The phone rang, and Becca lowered the folder, reaching out a hand to grab the receiver.

Devon beat her to it, snatching the phone up and snapping a

terse "Hello" into it. But his eyes didn't leave hers as the conversation went on. They sharpened, holding her in place as effectively as handcuffs—

And *oh God*. Now her cheeks were burning.

Trust her mind to take her straight on a journey to *Fifty Shades*.

She bent, hurriedly collecting and ordering the papers before gingerly setting the file on his desk and beginning to back from the room.

Warm fingers on her wrist stopped her.

Becca's eyes flashed down, and she shivered again. Tanned skin against porcelain. Thick, strong fingers dwarfing hers.

Devon Scott was a former hockey player, and it was easy to see why. He was every inch an athlete.

Every. *Inch.*

Oh good Lord.

She bit her lip and looked away.

"I need to go," Devon said into the phone and hung up, hardly waiting a beat before allowing the receiver to drop.

It clattered and fell to the floor, but Becca barely noticed.

Because Devon was walking around the desk, his grip on her wrist tightening when she tried to slip free.

She always forgot how tall he was. Most of the time Devon was sitting behind his desk when they interacted. But like this— he towered over her, her head having to tilt back so she could look at his face—Becca felt very petite indeed.

And for a woman who was nearly six feet, that was unusual.

"What's wrong?" he asked, calloused fingertips running along the sensitive skin on the inside of her wrist.

"Nothing." She tugged her arm, silently telling him to release her.

He didn't.

In fact, he leaned closer, bringing his face near hers, trailing the scent of pine and spice and *man* alongside.

"I *said* what's wrong?"

The question made every part of her body go all tingly. Head to toes—and in between—each part heated and perked to attention. Those parts told Becca to grab two fistfuls of Devon's white button-down and rip. To pop the row of buttons and bury her face in the broad expanse of his chest.

But she had *some* pride. And a backbone, for that matter.

So she lifted her chin and said again, "Nothing."

His hand wove into her hair, scattering the messy ponytail she'd thrown her brown locks into that morning as she'd run out the door behind schedule.

First the coffee shop for Devon's large latte—she couldn't abide the stuff. Then the bagel shop for his breakfast. *Then* rushing across town to open the office by five-thirty.

Her life was about making his easier.

And that was totally fine. She was the disposable half of their working relationship. She knew the score.

Until she didn't.

One strong arm snaked around her waist and tugged her flush to his chest. The chest she'd admired for so long, the chest that made her want to lick… and squeeze… and stroke…

She didn't have a chance.

He kissed her.

His mouth was firm and insistent, his tongue parting her lips to sneak inside, teasing hers until she broke free of her shock and kissed him back.

His hand slid lower and gripped her butt, pulling her somehow closer as he backed her up against his desk and proceeded to kiss the smart right out of her.

Buttons on her blouse came unfastened, his belt unbuckled, her skirt hitched higher, and—

"Becca!"

CHAPTER 2

*B*ecca jumped up and blinked, struggling to comprehend the chaos that was her workstation. Stacks of paper, a rainbow of Post-its, pens, paperclips, and files were strewn across the surface.

Her gut twisted.

She was in the office. She'd...fallen asleep at her desk.

Which meant...it had been a dream.

Acute disappointment swelled within her, even as she chastised herself. *Of course* it had been a dream.

Devon Scott would never look at her twice. She was a lowly assistant and not even his normal one, since she was just filling in for Clarice, who would be returning from maternity leave in less than a month.

"Becca."

Another snap of sound.

Similar to the one that had snapped her out of her almost wet dream.

Son of a monkey wrench.

She forced herself to meet the chocolate-brown eyes boring into hers. They were liquid and hot, but that was probably just her imagination, considering she'd just been fantasizing about him taking her on his desk.

"I-I'm sor—"

One corner of his mouth quirked up. "You've got..."

She reached up and—Why was this her life?!—removed the paper from her cheek.

The paper that had a lovely drool spot on it.

Devon rested one hip against her desk, folded his arms across his broad chest. "You don't have to be here so early, you know."

"I'm okay. I'm not tired—" She yawned then sighed in defeat, shrugging as she murmured, "I just had a late night."

He studied her for a long moment. "You look exhausted." His hand rose, and she swallowed hard, watching those tanned fingers come close to her face. Goose bumps prickled on her arms. After her dream, she could almost *feel* his roughened skin brushing against hers.

Then his hand dropped back to his side, and the spell broke, the anticipation that had been tightening every nerve of her body gone in an instant.

That buildup and the subsequent letdown were like a balloon popping.

And she was just as disappointed as a kid whose brand new, helium-filled sphere of latex happiness was suddenly gone.

She cleared her throat, her eyes drifting to the side then back to his pretty face. "I'll sleep better tonight."

Devon studied her then nodded. "I'll have Pascal patrol your house tonight."

Pascal was a bodyguard, Devon's security detail since he was so recognizable amongst the mainstream public. Shattering records on the ice and dating famous actresses off it would do that to a fella.

And great. Fella? Now she sounded like her grandmother.

"Mick hasn't called again," she said. "I'm fine."

Mick was an ex-boyfriend, and the reason—scratch that,

reasons—he was an ex were vast. In addition to the whole leaving-the-seat-up situation, playing video games at all hours of the night, not having a job, and moving into her apartment without paying a cent of rent, Mick had been controlling as hell.

She didn't do controlling. Not anymore.

So she'd changed the locks, neatly packed Mick's things, and put them in a storage locker before texting him the combination.

Which had gone over as well as she had expected.

But Becca had it covered. She wasn't a woman who was easily bullied…at least, not any longer.

It was just unfortunate that Devon had overheard Mick threatening her on the phone.

Because now he thought it was his right to stick his nose in her business.

His face had gone hard, his expression recalcitrant. "Pascal will be nearby."

Aw. Heck. She opened her mouth to protest, but he was gone, sweeping into his office and closing the door with a decisive *click*, leaving her protest on her tongue and his nose still firmly in her business.

Becca rested her head on her desk, tapped it against the wooden surface.

Then again.

And perhaps one more time—just for good measure.

Heaven save her from stubborn men and impossible bosses.

The intercom beeped, and she reached a hand up to press the answer button. "Yes?" The word may or may not have been slightly muffled given that her face was still resting against her desk.

"I need those files." A pause. "Preferably minus the drool stains."

CHAPTER 3

*D*evon's morning flew by. There were never enough hours in the day to catch up on emails, to return phone calls, to massage athletes' egos.

But it wasn't the ever-growing to-do list that was hijacking his thoughts.

No, that distraction came in the form of the five-foot-eleven goddess who'd taken to running his life...with better results than when he did.

She was blonde, statuesque, had legs for days, and a steel trap of a mind that never seemed to forget anything, appointment, name, conference call, food preference, or otherwise.

But he couldn't wait for Clarice to come back.

Because he was having a really hard time focusing on anything except attempting to get those gorgeous legs wrapped around his waist, especially when he'd heard the breathy way she'd moaned his name earlier.

Cheeks flushed, hair mussed, Becca had been a tantalizing mix of cute and sexy as hell. He'd been tempted to let her sleep, the circles beneath her eyes blatantly obvious.

Then she'd said his name, and he'd gone hard as a rock. The

simmering attraction he'd always struggled to ignore in her presence had boiled to the surface.

Take her.

Fuck her.

Right on her desk.

Not going to happen. He was her boss...but *damn* he wouldn't mind playing secretary with Becca.

And speak of the devil—

"Devon," her voice chirped through the intercom, "Sam Roberts is here."

He got to his feet and was through the door in an instant, guilty conscience in full effect.

Boss. He was her *boss*.

That was a line he couldn't cross.

"Hey, Sam. It's good to see—" he began, his chest going tight when he saw his old friend perched on the corner of Becca's desk, trademark smile in place. And she was smiling back. Sam could charm the pantyhose off a little old lady and still get her to make him cookies. "Roberts," he said, ice all up in his tone and not giving a damn.

Sam raised a brow but didn't move from Becca's desk.

"As I was saying"—his friend did that smoldering thing that reduced women to puddles of goo—"I know the best little Italian place, and I'll pay."

Becca's eyes flicked to his, a flash of brilliant blue, the worry in their depths easily visible. "Well, as much as I hate to pass up a free meal," she said quietly—quietly, but firmly. "I've got a ton of work to catch up on."

Sam flashed him a knowing look before turning up the smolder on Becca a notch. "Yes, Devon here is a workaholic, but that doesn't mean you have to be."

"I don't mind," she said and made a shooing motion with her hands. "Now go. Devon's got a conference call in twenty-three minutes."

Wearing a bemused smile—probably because the fucker wasn't used to being turned down—his friend rose from the desk and extended his hand as though to shake Becca's. But when her palm met his, the bastard lifted it to his mouth and kissed the back.

"It was a pleasure to meet you, Becca," he murmured.

Fucking hell.

The blush on her cheeks was as bright as a fire engine and… Devon wanted to be the one to put it there.

Idiot.

Him.

Sam.

Both of them. *Fuck*.

Whirling around, he strode into his office, collapsing into his chair and waiting for Sam to shut the door before he dropped his head into his hands.

"What the fuck was that?" Sam asked.

Dev sat back, thrust a hand through his hair. "*That* was my new and terrifyingly efficient assistant."

"Which is not what I was asking, and you know it." Sam took the seat across from him, crossing his arms and waiting with an expectant expression on his face.

"Dude, it's nothing," Devon said and pulled out a file. "Now about this project—"

"Cluck."

Devon sighed, barely resisted the urge to tilt his head back and sigh. Here they went. "You're so freaking—"

"Cluck."

"—im—"

"*Cluck.*"

"—mature."

"Cluck!"

"*Fine*," Devon snapped. "Becca is hot as hell, and I'd rather have her anywhere than sitting out front of my office, distracting me and the entirety of the male populace at PMG. But I can't fire her,

and Clarice will be back in a month, so I've just got to endure it."
His heart pounded, the sexual frustration that had been eating him up for the last five months roiling below the surface of his skin.

He needed to get laid.

Just not with his secretary.

Sam opened his mouth to reply, but the knock at the door cut him off.

Before Devon could call out in answer, the door opened, and Becca walked in.

She didn't say a word, didn't have to. Her body language said it all: raised chin, averted eyes, stiff and slightly slumped shoulders.

She reached across the desk, still not looking at him, and pressed a button on his phone.

The intercom button.

And *fuuuuck* him.

She turned and walked out of the office, quietly shutting the plank of wood. God, it would have been so much easier if she'd been the type of woman who slammed doors. Who pitched fits and was high drama.

But she wasn't.

And that was a big part of Devon's problem.

Because she was so *freaking* likeable.

He lurched to his feet and started after her when Sam's voice stopped him. "Slippery slope, bud. Watch out for it."

CHAPTER 4

*ecca grabbed her purse, a stack of files, and hightailed it out of the office. It was too early for lunch, but she was beyond caring.

Devon wanted her gone.

So she'd disappear.

Three flights of stairs down and she was in the lobby. Twenty-seven strides and she was through the front door. Her car was parked six spots down.

Except her car wasn't the only thing in the sixth stall.

Mick was alongside her Toyota Corolla, a can of black spray paint in one hand as he wrote something...

Not *something*, but an obscenity, and it wasn't the special four-lettered "f" one she used sparingly, but the one that rhymed with a punt, as in football—not that she was opposed to *punting* the jerk through the goalposts of life.

Becca saw red.

She'd always thought it just an expression, but in this moment, after Devon's *confession* and with Mick painting a freaking curse word on her car, she'd had enough.

She took a step forward.

A hand on her shoulder stalled her. "What the fuck are you doing?" Devon snapped.

"Don't curse at me." She struggled, trying to free herself, but only managed to knock her purse down her arm and nearly drop the files. "Let me go. I'm—"

"Going to stay right here while I take care of it."

He released her and crossed to her car, moving like lightning while somehow managing to look casual and unhurried at the same time.

Becca stared stupidly after Devon for a few seconds before managing to pull her head out of her you-know-what. She stormed over, heels clicking on the pavement. Mick had hated her wearing them, hated the way they made her tower over him.

And so she'd given in.

She'd worn flats, because like a little pansy, she hadn't wanted to fight with him over something *"stupid."*

But Becca loved heels.

The rapid *click-click* had always made her smile, a secret internal grin that made her feel powerful, her personal I'm-a-woman-hear-me-roar moment. Today, however, her heels had the opposite effect.

They whipped two sets of male eyes in her direction, one petrified and one furious as all get out.

Devon leaned toward Mick and said something she couldn't hear. It made her ex's face pale before he dropped the paint can and sprinted away.

"What is wrong with you?" she asked—okay, *yelled*—when Mick had gone, jabbing a finger into Devon's hard chest.

"*Me?*" Devon asked—okay, yelled—back, capturing her finger. "You're the one who thought it might be a good idea to confront the man who's been harassing you. Don't you have a restraining order? Why would you think that's a good idea?"

She yanked her hand free, muttered, "I don't have a restraining order because the judge didn't grant it." Turned out, Mick's father was a golf buddy of the one who'd presided over her case.

"What?" Dev snapped. "That's total bullshit." He snatched his phone from his pocket.

"Stop cursing at me," she told him again.

"I'm not cursing at *you*. I'm cursing at the bastard who thinks it's okay to tag your car, send you threatening notes, and come to your apartment in the middle of the night."

"How do you know he sent me notes?" she asked. She hadn't mentioned that to anyone. Nor for that matter, "And showed up at my apartment?"

If she'd ever wanted to witness a man having an oh rhymes-with-*hit* moment, this was it. His eyes widened, a slight rosy tint appeared at the tops of his cheeks, and he actually ground the toe of one shoe into the pavement. "I—uh—"

His phone rang, and the relief on his face was so obvious that even furious, Becca was somehow tempted to laugh.

Despite her car being defaced and her boss telling her she was a nuisance before interjecting himself into her life in a very *nuisance*-like way himself, she was amused. How?

Because Devon.

Because Devon like *this*—chivalrous, concerned, contrite—was almost cute.

And that was a completely different side of him than the powerful, take-no-prisoners executive she normally saw.

"Pascal, good. I need you in the parking lot immediately," he said and hung up. Avoiding her eyes, he moved around the car taking pictures, bending to study the undercarriage, the tailpipe.

"Devon," she said.

He ignored her.

"*Devon.*"

His sigh was audible even though she stood on the other side of her car. "Let me do this first, okay?" He took one more picture, walked around the hood of her Toyota, then got right into her face.

In her three-inch heels, he was still taller, but not by much, and he didn't have to crouch to meet her eyes.

"How did you know about the notes and the apartment?" she asked again.

"It doesn't matter."

Except, it did. Especially if what she was seeing was real.

Concern. Actual genuine concern. And beneath that?

Heat.

She sucked in a breath, and his eyes flicked to her mouth. They tingled, ached, *needed.* Kiss her. She *needed* him to kiss her.

For real this time, not in the fantasy-dream-world of her mind.

One hand came up, cupped her cheek. He leaned in.

Their mouths were so close she could feel his breath on her lips, could smell the cinnamon on his tongue.

Devon moved a hairsbreadth closer and—

"Sir."

CHAPTER 5

Becca gasped and straightened, tugging her purse up to her shoulder. Devon held on to her cheek for a long moment, calloused fingers brushing the skin behind her ear before he dropped his hand and stepped away to greet Pascal.

Stupid.

As in *she* was for falling for Devon's magical man-scent and his hard body and—her heart gave a little tumble—his sweet side.

The man made her stupid…which was exactly why she needed to keep her distance, magical man-scent or not.

She unlocked her car, tucked her keys back into her purse, then reached into the glovebox. After grabbing a handful of napkins, she went to work at wiping off the paint.

Or attempting to anyway.

The black letters smeared and blurred but didn't come off. Though at least it looked less like the c-word and more like a giant ebony blob engulfing one entire side of her car.

"Ms. Stealing?"

She smiled and turned to Pascal. The bodyguard was standing behind her, shifting slightly from foot to foot. Even in her few months at the firm, she'd come to like him. He was a strange combination of awkward and capable, endearing and tough. She'd seen him take down an overzealous fan before he'd reached Devon's side and just as easily comfort a child who'd fallen and hurt her knee.

"Hi, Pascal."

"Your keys, please."

Becca blinked. "For what?"

"He's going to take your car to the shop, get that paint off," Devon said from right behind her.

She hadn't heard him move, but she'd certainly felt him—or her body had.

Raised hairs on her nape, heat between her thighs, a tilt-a-whirl for a heart. She was falling apart...or just falling for Devon. Stupid. So freaking stupid.

"I can take care—"

Dev came close and snatched her purse from her arm. He'd reached inside and plucked her keys free before she'd done more than utter a sound of protest.

"Come on," he said, tossing them to Pascal and picking up the files from where she'd set them on the driver's seat. "We're going to lunch."

He'd rattled her, totally discombobulated her senses.

That was the reason she didn't protest.

Not because he'd snagged her hand after he'd slung her purse over his shoulder—which, for God-knew-why, didn't look ridiculous.

Definitely not because his warm fingers stroking along hers felt incredible.

No. *Definitely* not.

Definitely—

Sigh.

It wasn't until she was in the passenger seat of his BMW and really digging the butt warmer that she found her voice.

"What are you playing at, Devon?"

He'd been shrugging out of his suit jacket and froze at her question.

Chocolate irises flashed to hers, held. His jaw clenched. His nostrils flared as he released a long slow breath.

"I'm not *playing* at anything." He tossed the jacket on the back seat.

She toyed with the seatbelt strap, running her fingers over the nylon, up and down, up and down.

Devon's gaze went hot.

Becca froze, then pressed on. "You want me gone."

He pushed the button to start the car, and it rumbled to life. "Yes."

Her gut twisted.

"But not for the reason you think."

Something like hope bubbled up in her belly, only it couldn't be. Even putting the matter of Devon being her boss aside, he was still way out of her league in everything else.

"Why then?"

Silence.

Dead silence as Devon drove them down the street. Silence as they got on the freeway, silence as they pulled into the parking lot of an Italian restaurant—her favorite, which she was starting to think wasn't a coincidence.

Silence until Devon turned off the car.

"You're fired."

She gasped, opened her mouth—

He kissed her.

CHAPTER 6

*T*his was so fucking stupid. Like beyond stupid. Like making-a-pass-up-the-middle-and-getting-it-picked-off stupid.

But damn did it feel good.

Becca had the most incredible mouth, perfect and pink with a pouty bottom lip and a precise cupid's bow at the top.

Devon knew it was called a cupid's bow because he'd fanta-sized about her enough to Google it.

Pathetic.

But there was nothing pathetic about finally being able to kiss Becca. Her mouth had been stiff in surprise, but the moment he gentled his lips, she softened and let him kiss the hell out of that pout.

She let him in.

Just like he knew she would.

Becca was all softness, sweet kind eyes, and empathy to her core.

But she was also heat. And temper.

Which was a side of her he hadn't seen before.

A side that threatened to ruin everything.

Which is why he needed to stop this. He was going to ruin everything for *her*.

Becca needed this job, and he needed to keep it in his pants.

Devon pulled back. It took every bit of his tenacity to drop his hands to her shoulders and set her away from him, every bit of strength to not kiss her again when he saw the flush on her cheeks, her reddened lips, and the glaze of pleasure in her eyes…

He wanted her so fucking bad.

And he was her boss.

No. Glutton for fucking punishment, *that* was what he was.

He got out of the car, let the cool air soak into his overheated body, and thought about stats and contracts and granny panties until his erection subsided.

Only then did he grab his coat from the back seat then walk around the car to open Becca's door.

She was staring straight ahead, trembling fingers pressed to her mouth.

"You're hired."

Her stare flashed up to his, that hint of her temper sparking to life all over again. He was rock hard in an instant because…this woman killed him.

"You can't just—"

He had no resistance, not when it came to Becca.

"Fired." He slanted his mouth to hers. "Hired," he said when he managed to break away, heart pounding, body aching.

"What the—"

"Also"—he reached across her and unbuckled her seat belt, barely resisting the urge to nuzzle against her breasts, which just so happened to be a hairsbreadth away from his nose—"I can and I will."

And God, the shirts she wore, buttons from top to bottom, always made him want to tear the two halves apart then bury his face into the exposed skin beneath…or better yet, to unbutton it, one by one, kissing, licking, worshiping every inch below.

Which was so *not* helping his problem.

"Let's eat," he said. "I promise I won't kiss you again."

It was a promise he didn't want to make—*fuck no*—but one he felt he had to. Becca was his employee, and their relationship held an inherent uneven distribution of power.

Not only would the media have a heyday with the whole forbidden love, secretary-boss scenario, his HR lead would have his head.

Devon followed the rules. It was one of the reasons his business was so successful. He didn't compromise, didn't flake out on commitments, and he certainly didn't screw over his clients or employees.

Which, of course, meant that he would be screwed in this case...and not in the way he was desperate for.

"What if I want you to?"

The air froze in his lungs, locking him down tight, making *everything* hard. He studied Becca, saw the heat in her expression, the flush on her cheeks.

She was in as bad a way as he was.

Curse words blared through his mind but not his mouth because...because he knew she didn't like it. Instead, Devon snagged her hand and helped her from the car, closing her door behind her.

"Wait," she told him when he started tugging her in the direction of the restaurant.

She pulled her hand free, went back to the car, and bent over —*sweet Christ*—to retrieve her files from the back seat.

A strangled noise escaped his throat. He couldn't help it.

Becca turned, held up the stack of manila, and smiled. "Didn't want to risk leaving these in the car."

He nodded, his voice gone somewhere in the direction of his sanity.

What he really wanted to do was shove her back into the car, drive them back to his house, and park in the garage.

Then show her just how much he appreciated the way her ass looked in that tight skirt.

"Devon?"

He blinked, realized she was staring at him with concern. Which tended to happen when people zoned out in the middle of parking lots while mentally acting out their fantasies about curvy, blonde bombshells who seemed intent on torturing them.

"Food. Inside," he said, pushing the other stuff away and focusing on Becca. Pascal would have dropped her car off at the repair shop by now. Then his bodyguard was supposed to get her apartment fitted up with the best security system Devon's money could buy.

And Devon's money could buy a lot.

"Okay, caveman," she said and strode in front of him, shaking her head and muttering something about men and idiots.

No argument there, he thought, especially when he caught his eyes drifting down again.

He forced them heavenward and prayed he'd have the strength to resist.

And then he trailed after her, not holding his breath that his prayers would make one lick of difference.

CHAPTER 7

*A*wkward. Things were straight-up-vodka-without-a-twist awkward.

Devon stared at her over their respective ice waters. He. Just. Stared.

Finally, Becca couldn't take it any longer. "For God's sake, *what?*" she exclaimed.

He blinked, melted chocolate shuttered for an extended moment before he sighed. "I shouldn't have kissed you."

Oh geez.

"Well, you did." And really freaking well, if she could say so. But since she *couldn't* without exacerbating the buyer's remorse Devon clearly had going on—

"What's done is done," she said, waving her hand in a casual way that was absolutely a falsity. "So let's just move on and forget about it."

"Forget about it?" His brows were sky high, his jaw agape.

The man was actually surprised that a woman might want to forget his kisses.

Well, that was what happened when one went through life as a walking, talking example of sex-on-a-stick.

And it wasn't so much that she wanted to pretend the kisses hadn't happened—hands down the two he'd given her were the best ones of her life—as it was that she needed the money from the job.

Her mom was on the waiting list for an expensive program at her rehabilitation center, and they collected their fee upfront. Which was why she'd been scrimping and saving forever to get her in and couldn't afford to lose a month's salary, even from a mediocre temp job.

"Yes," she said, more firmly this time. "We're going to forget about it. We can eat pasta. I work on these files, and you'll answer the six hundred or so emails floating about your inbox. Then we'll drive back to the office, and you'll forget all about The Kiss as you order me around until six. After which I'll sneak out and drive to McKay's."

He'd been with her until she'd blown it and mentioned McKay's. His frown had smoothed out, one side of his mouth had curled up. Then she'd gone and ruined it all.

"What's at McKay's?"

The waiter came by before she was forced to answer. She ordered the puttanesca—if her words didn't put him off then hopefully the anchovies and garlic would—and Devon asked for a salad.

Seriously. A salad.

But she didn't get to go on the offensive about the salad, not when he was fixing her in place with The Stare. The one that made the most difficult and stubborn of clients sit quiescently and do exactly as Devon wanted.

She didn't have a chance in hell of resisting him, not when he looked at her like that.

"I work there," she blurted.

He frowned, two slashes of black brows pulling down and in. "You work for me."

She rolled her eyes. "Temporarily."

"You've worked for me for five months."

Becca had been lucky enough to get a six-month contract when the norm for maternity leave was only three, but apparently, Clarice had experienced some pretty serious complications. Becca had actually been hired right after Clarice's doctor had ordered bedrest for the final three months of her pregnancy.

"I've only got one more before I'm off contract."

Devon stilled.

She smiled. "Yeah, exactly. I have a life outside of Prestige." A shrug. "I have to, because in a few more weeks I'm gone. Maybe I would get an offer for another temp position, but there's no guarantee."

"And so you work at a bar."

She traced her finger through the condensation on the outside of her water glass. "It's got a restaurant too."

"Which isn't open at night," he pointed out.

She frowned. "And how do you know that?"

"How do I know about one of the rowdiest bars in this whole town?" He went on, probably because her brows had nearly climbed to her hairline. "Because I was a professional athlete. We have the ability to discover the single place in every city where it's the easiest to get into trouble. And trust me, Bex, McKay's is it."

Since she *had,* in fact, seen her fair share of trouble at the restaurant—okay, bar—Becca didn't argue. She also didn't point out the fact that he'd called her Bex.

It seemed both too familiar and comfortably intimate all at once.

And she liked it.

"I need the money," she said.

His brows dragged together. "For what? Drugs?"

Becca was so startled she knocked her water glass over. "You're being ridiculous," she muttered.

Devon calmly swiped the files out of danger and mopped up the mess with his napkin. "So no drugs."

A sigh, her head shaking in disbelief. "How could you honestly—?"

One half of his mouth turned up. "I didn't."

Now it was her brows dragging together. "So why did you *ask?*"

The other half of his mouth quirked up, curving his lips into a sexy smile. "Because I like you a little scrambled."

She scoffed. "You're insane."

"Probably." A shrug as he glanced over her shoulder, and she felt the server come up behind her before setting their plates in front of them.

She decided to scramble him a little in return. "I can't believe you're eating a salad."

He frowned. "Me neither. Hate this shit. Thought I was done with it when I retired."

Becca twined a noodle around her fork and brought it her mouth, sighing in pleasure before chewing and swallowing. "No cursing." Her lips twitched when his expression went contrite. "So why order it?"

Devon's cheeks went slightly pink. "I've gained weight."

Her eyes flicked to Devon's middle—flat, even while sitting—then to his arms and chest. He did *not* look like a man who needed to cut back. "Ummm," she said, "and where'd you put it?"

"Hell—*er, heck*—if I know." He sighed. "I could barely button my pants this morning."

Oh. *Oh!*

An episode from the week before flashed across her mind. Their CFO was Devon's old teammate, and his assistant had offered to pick up Devon's dry-cleaning for her. Becca, feeling swamped as always, had agreed.

"What?" he said grumpily, shoving a bite of lettuce into his mouth.

"I'm sure it's nothing," she prevaricated.

"I'm *sure* it's not."

She took another bite of carb-loaded deliciousness. "Well, Caleb's secretary grabbed your clothes from the cleaner's last week—" His curse halted her flow of words.

"Sorry," he said when she gave him her version of The Stare. "I meant mother*pucker.*"

"Of course you did." A roll of her eyes. "Do you think she gave me the wrong set of pants? They all kind of look the same."

"Except mine have my name sewn in them."

"You have your name *sewn* into your pants?"

Devon waved the question away. "Not the point." A pause. "Caleb did something to them, shrunk them, had the waistband taken in."

"That seems insane."

"Former athletes, remember? Pranking each other is how we pass the time." His expression went from irritated to pleased. "Oh, I *so* know how I'm going to get him back for this one."

"Athletes seem to be a lot like children."

He grinned, flagged down the waiter, and placed a double-order of spaghetti. "Can't argue with you there."

CHAPTER 8

Devon was expecting a fight.

He hadn't driven Becca back to the office after lunch, instead taking her directly to her apartment...where Pascal was supervising the installation of her security system.

She hadn't fought with him, just sighed and shook her head at the sight before walking into her kitchen.

"How much longer?" he asked Pascal.

"Twenty minutes. Then I'll show her how to work the system."

He nodded and followed Becca into the kitchen.

She leaned against the sink, head hanging and the files almost overflowing her arms. Her body language was so forlorn, so sad that he wanted to pull her close and just hold her tight.

Blue eyes flicked up, and Devon's breath caught. If he'd thought her body language was bad, those eyes...

Damn. Or rather, *dang.*

He gave an internal smile. Becca was even censoring his thoughts. But his amusement vanished nearly as quickly as it had come on.

Because she was crying.

It wasn't even a thought, just instinct, to take the files from her arms and set them on the counter, to gather her against him, to brush the drops of moisture from the corners of her eyes, to ask, "What is it?"

She sniffed and shook her head. "Nothing. I'm fine."

"Bullsh—" Her stare met his. "Poop."

The tiniest smile curved her lips, and she released a shuddering breath. "Thank you."

"For what?" he asked. "Cursing is a terrible habit anyway."

"That's not—" She tried to pull free but, for some reason, his arms wouldn't release her. After a moment, her shoulders slumped, and stopped fighting him. "I can't afford it."

"I think I can spot you one meal," he said with a laugh. He wanted to see Becca smile again, hear her laugh, not worry about forty dollars when he had millions to spare.

"It's not that." She struggled, shoved his chest, but they seemed to be finally getting to the crux of things.

"Why do you work two jobs, Becca?"

Her spine went ramrod straight. "I told you," she said. "We all know that the position at Prestige is just temporary. I can't sit around and wait for it to end."

"I know how much rent is in this area. I know how much I'm paying you." He paused. "What else is going on, Becca?"

"Nothing."

A thought occurred to him, and Devon was surprised that he didn't find it nearly as scary as he probably should. "Do you have a kid?"

"Oh my God, we are so not having this conversation."

He pictured a little girl with blue eyes like Becca's, with blonde curls. "How old is she?" he asked, looking around for signs of the little girl.

"How—no! Just *no*." She finally succeeded in freeing herself and leaned back against the sink, arms crossed. "I don't have a kid. I'm not on drugs. I don't have a gambling problem."

He frowned. "Then what?"

Silence.

Then a heavy sigh. "My mom is sick." She shook her head. "No. Not sick exactly. She was in an accident almost a year ago."

Shit. "I'm sorry." An apology, even though it was useless, even though it didn't change anything.

Becca's gaze slid to the side. "She had a spinal cord injury."

Devon closed his eyes briefly. In his line of work, he'd seen too many injuries of that type, knew how devastating they could be.

Knew how expensive.

"So that's why you work two jobs."

"Yes." She shrugged. "Insurance doesn't cover everything, and her rehab facility is expensive and—I just…she needs it right now."

"What about your dad?"

Becca's eyes shuttered. "He's not around."

And now Devon felt like an asshole—okay, in Becca-terms, a jerk.

"I'm sorry," he said again, feeling even more certain that the apology was pointless, not when the words didn't actually *do* anything.

"Yeah," she whispered. "Me too."

And cue the awkward pause.

Pascal, who Devon was starting to think had a super-human ability to solve every problem, saved the day.

"Ms. Stealing?" he asked, coming into the kitchen. "Would you like me to show you the system? The company is finished."

Bex blew out a breath, averted her gaze from Devon's. "Sure. Let me just find my wallet."

"No need," Devon interjected. "It's been taken care of."

If it were possible for human eyes to fill with fire, hers would have. She leveled a glare at him. "Lunch is one thing, an entire security system—"

"I need you safe." Bald words. True words. Even if they didn't completely make sense.

Her jaw fell open. "But why?"

Yes, genius, why? Why did he care so much about a woman he barely knew?

Because that was a giant lie.

He'd come to know Becca well enough over the last months to understand that she was different from most of the women he knew. She was independent, fiercely so, and wasn't looking for a handout.

And he liked her...a whole hel—*heck*—of a lot.

Not that he could tell her that because, boss-secretary thing aside, she looked a heartbeat away from freaking out.

"You're my other half until Clarice gets back," he said, seeing panic swell in her expression then fade at the mention of his normal assistant. "Prestige would fall apart without you. I need... my files in order and my schedule kept straight with your freakish organization."

The rest of the tension faded from her hers. "Yeah?" she asked.

He nodded, had the feeling that he might fall apart too if she wasn't there at his desk every day. Not that he was going to tell her that. "Yeah," he agreed before nudging her toward the hall. "Now go let Pascal show you the system so we can get out of your hair."

CHAPTER 9

cKay's was hopping. A playoff baseball game was on television, and the local favorite was losing— which meant most of the patrons were buzzed and angry.

Not a pleasant combination for a waitress.

Especially one forced to wear Daisy Dukes and a tight, mid-drift-baring T-shirt.

Crappy tips and cranky customers.

Add that to her car being vandalized, and Devon going over her head to have the security system installed at her apartment... well, the last was sweet, except for the fact that it made him even more dangerous to her and her heart.

Good-looking. Powerful. Wealthy. And sweet.

It was a devastating combination.

Rough fingers grabbed her arm, jerked her to a halt. "I *said* I want a beer." A man wearing the losing team's hat and a surly expression glared at her.

Becca forced a smile and tried to free herself, only to have the man's fingers tighten. She winced, knew she was going to have bruises tomorrow. "I'm going to put this order in. Your beer is next."

"I want it now."

"I *could* be getting it now, if you hadn't slowed things down by grabbing me." She yanked, but the guy didn't release her. *"Let go."*

"I—"

The man didn't finish the thought because he was suddenly on the floor halfway across the bar. The skin on Becca's arm felt like it had been scoured, but she wasn't being held captive and knew why even before she turned around.

Devon.

In air thick with the bitter tang of beer, with the not-so-pleasant burn of sweat and man-funk, she could still smell him.

The cinnamon hit her first, a rush of the spicy scent straight into her nostrils. It jolted her system, made her heart race and her nerves fire.

Or maybe that was just Devon.

He came close, near enough that she could smell his deodorant, something indecipherable and utterly masculine. Definitely not floral like hers. And maybe that was an inane thing to think, but with him right there—towering over her, inundating her senses—it was the only thing that came to mind.

"You okay?" he asked. His eyes were wild, the words gritted out through a jaw so tight she was surprised they were clear enough to decipher.

Becca felt shaken but nodded anyway, absently rubbing the sore part of her arm.

Devon's gaze latched onto the spot and flared hot. "I'm going to kill the bastard."

Her own stare trailed down, and she grimaced. Her skin was red, angry-looking, an imprint of four fat fingers on her upper arm. She lifted it and glanced to the back side. Yup. A sausage-sized thumb-shaped bruise was already forming there too.

Cute.

Devon took a step away from her, presumably to kick some ass—

And, oh great, now she was as bad as he was. Cursing. Good Lord.

Which was *so* not the point.

Jumping forward when he took another step, she snagged his hand, held tight, and hoped he wouldn't drag her with him.

But something amazing happened the moment she laced her fingers with his.

He stopped.

She almost stopped breathing. His jaw was no longer tight. Instead, it hung open.

He felt it too?

The spark, the zing, the…Goldilocks' sensation of *just right*.

"Don't," she said.

Dev nodded.

"Come with me." She tugged, and he followed, six-feet-four-inches of suddenly cooperative male.

It was like holding a tiger by the tail. Sooner or later, he'd snap.

Becca made eye contact with Laurie, the other waitress on duty in the bar, silently asking her to cover the section.

The brunette inclined her head, already moving toward the bar to gather the next round. One of the bartenders, Steve, was hustling the drunk and angry patron out the front door of the restaurant. The other, Ben, was quickly filling glasses.

They all knew how close of a call they'd had.

Bar fights meant damage being taken out of paychecks, meant losing tips and dealing with the police.

Bar fights meant getting fired.

And, though they might all have their own reasons, each of them working at McKay's needed their job.

So Becca decided to take Devon out the back.

Tension filled her limbs, making her steps halting and stiff, especially in three-inch heels.

The employee hall leading out of the bar was just exactly as someone might expect: terra-cotta tile that had seen better days, a fixture with a scant two bulbs working, dust in the corners, and cleaning equipment propped against the walls.

She pushed out the door at the end and immediately shivered against the bracing cold. Or what felt bracing, considering she was only wearing one-half of the recommended clothing for normal adults.

Her tremor seemed to snap Devon into motion. He unzipped his jacket and wrapped her in it then tugged her close to his chest and began rubbing her back.

"I'm sorry," he said.

"F-for what?" Her teeth chattered, and Becca realized it wasn't just the cold making her tremble, but the aftereffects of adrenaline.

"Scaring you," he murmured.

She shook her head. "You d-didn't."

"Then why are you freaking out now?"

She stiffened. His words may as well have had a rod of steel inserted straight into her spine. "I'm not freaking out," she snapped. "I'm cold." She reached for the lapels of his jacket, started to pull it off. "Now just go and—"

He brushed her hands away, put a finger under her chin and tilted her head up, studying her eyes. "Ah. There you are."

She hadn't *gone* anywhere.

"You—" She tried to lean back, to pull free.

Devon didn't let her and—*for God's sake*—she'd had more than freaking enough of men manhandling her for the day.

"I thought you were cold," he said, holding her tight, one finger tracing her jaw, sliding across to outline her lips.

Her thighs quivered, her knees threatened to buckle. His touch...was electric.

"I *am* cold."

A half-smile curved his mouth. "I'd think you'd want to stay close then."

She did. But she couldn't tell him *that*. Not when he was staring down at her, looking all smug. "You'd think wrong, then."

"I don't think so."

He bent, closing the distance between them. And hell (curse words, come on!) she wanted him to kiss her. *Needed* it more than air.

Her lips parted, her breath hitched. Ready. She was *so* ready for him.

He bypassed her mouth.

A hiss of disappointment slid from her...at least until he touched the tip of his tongue to the rapidly pounding pulse at the base of her neck.

His words were warm puffs of air, sending a shiver down her spine for a whole other reason than before.

"You're not scared." His mouth moved up, pressed a kiss to her jaw, behind her ear. "And definitely not cold."

No. She wasn't either one of those things. She was turned on as fuc—

He pressed his lips to hers.

CHAPTER 10

*evon was on fire.

Becca's mouth against his was everything, every sensation, every feeling, every need.

He pulled her closer, loving the feel of her breasts against his chest. She was soft and so damned—*darned*—sweet.

Her tongue darted forward, tapped gently against the seam of his lips, and that gesture, the sign that she wanted this as much as he did, threatened to send him to his knees.

He opened his mouth, let his tongue dance with hers, let his hands do some dancing of their own.

Silky skin, a waist with sinful curves, hips he wanted to grab on to…

Becca pulled back, gasping for air. "This is a really bad idea."

"Yes." He threaded his fingers through her ponytail, tugged her close.

She came willingly, even though her mouth kept working. "You're my boss. My life is a mess."

"Mmm-hmm." Devon bit down on the side of her neck, felt himself grow hard at her moan. Then harder still when she grabbed his hair and threatened to pull it from his scalp.

Ah. So that was her spot.

He sucked, probably marking her and not giving a damn.

"Devon," she groaned, "that's—"

The world fell away, and he was aware of nothing more than the sweet floral scent of her skin, the rapid exhales of her breaths, the soft moans as he kissed her throat.

Which was probably the reason he didn't sense the man coming up behind them.

"You whore!"

White-hot pain exploded along the back of his skull, burned down his spine. He staggered to one knee, barely managing to unclench his hands so that he didn't drag Becca down with him.

It was worse than taking a punch from Teddy Burke, the enforcer from his former NHL team, the San Francisco Gold. That had happened exactly once and mostly because Devon had taken a joke too damn far.

He heard Becca scream and got his shit together, straightening and blinking to clear his vision, shoving the past back where it belonged.

Some asshole had grabbed her arm and was dragging her down the alley.

She was fighting the man who held her, kicking, thrashing, shouting.

Devon chased after her, punched the man right in the jaw. "Let her go, you fucking asshole."

Which basically both ruined his anti-cursing trend and hurt like a mother. But was. So. Worth. It. Especially when the man went down like a sack of bricks.

Becca yanked herself free, and Devon shoved between her and the man—Mick, he realized—then put some distance between them.

And just in time.

Something flashed in Mick's hand. A knife.

"Stay back," he ordered Becca.

"Mick," she said, coming to stand beside him. "Just don't. Please."

"You left me!" he screamed from the ground. "*Left me!*"

"Yes. I did," Becca said softly. "But I had to. Don't you see?"

Mick's eyes were crazed. Any sane person could see that. Except, Becca wasn't being rational. She actually took a step forward.

"We weren't good together," she pressed. "You have to see that."

Devon snaked a hand around her waist and tugged her back to his side. She shot him a glare.

"You. *Left*," Mick said, standing and taking a lurching step toward them.

"Stop," Devon ordered, reaching into his pocket for his phone and inputting a code.

Behind, he thought, trying to gather his thoughts. They were spreading out, getting harder and harder to hold on to. But he knew she was better off behind him. Safer. So he shoved her back, was surprised when she didn't fight the action.

Hopefully, she was finally starting to realize how bad of a situation this was.

"Just go, Mick," she said. "This isn't worth it."

"Quiet," Devon hissed when his thoughts scattered again.

His head was pounding, his hand hurt like hell from the punch, and his vision was going suspiciously black around the edges.

Becca stiffened, snapped out, "Devon, I'm just trying to—"

"Shh." He put a hand to his temple, trying to rub the bleariness away. Where the *fuck* was Pascal?

"Don't shush me—"

God, he would have loved the fire in her tone, the spunk in her words…if only he weren't about to pass out.

"Shh." He shoved his phone into her hand. "9-1-1."

"Devon?"

"Fine."

Except he wasn't fine. He couldn't form full sentences, let alone protect her.

"Dev, wait…"

He turned slightly, curled her fingers around the phone. "Call…9-1-1."

A flicker of movement out of the corner of his eye told him that Mick was moving. Unfortunately, he wasn't running away.

He was charging toward them.

Devon turned, but he was too slow.

Mick tackled him to the ground. Devon felt the hot burn of pain, a liquid lightning spurt of hurt in his side before he managed to flip them and pin Mick to the ground.

Black stuck like treacle to the edges of his vision, drawing him in, pulling him under.

He scrabbled for Mick's shoulders, trying to stop the other man's flailing, to just get him to *stop*, but his movements were clumsy and ineffective.

Another sting. Another gush of hot liquid down his side.

Then hands were on his back, pulling him away. Voices yelling to get down, to stay down, the sound of a struggle and the unique *thunking* sound that only came from fist meeting flesh.

"No," he said, struggling to sit up. "Becca. Safe."

"Here," came her voice, tight with fear and worry. "I-I'm fine. But Devon you're—"

Devon managed to meet her eyes, to see she was unhurt for himself.

"Good," he muttered and let the blackness take him under.

CHAPTER 11

◈

*W*aiting room chairs. Stiff. Uncomfortable. Riddled with germs.

Becca hated them with a passion.

And not because of the creepy-crawlies or that it felt like she was sitting on a pile of bricks.

But because she was always out *here*.

And the people she cared about were always in *there*.

Taken behind heavy wooden doors, pushed through stark corridors, cared for by men and women with gloves and masks— who worked tirelessly to save the body and worried about the person inside second.

Which was how it should be.

Trouble was, *she* was out here.

Trouble was, she was helpless.

With a groan, she pulled her knees up, crossed her arms over them, and buried her head in the little makeshift shelter.

Poor Devon. This was all her fault.

Why had she taken him into the alley? Why had she kissed him? Why had she dated a freaking psychopath who pulled knives on people?

A tear leaked from the corner of her eye, and she didn't bother to brush it away.

Misery.

It filled every cell, made her wish for a different day, a different life. When money hadn't been so important. When she hadn't needed two jobs, and she could have shielded a good man from the mess that was her life.

She should have never brought her personal life to work. No. She should have never *taken* the job at Prestige.

But she had. And because of her, Devon was hurt.

It was all her fault.

More tears escaped, dripping down her temples and pooling on the fabric of her jacket.

No, not her jacket. *Devon's* jacket. And great, now she was crying harder because Devon was sweet and kind and had given her his jacket when she'd been cold, and now she'd ruined everything and...and—

"Hey."

Devon's voice.

She opened her eyes, peered through the gap between her legs. Booted feet stood directly in front of her chair.

He sounded exhausted, but she was afraid to look, afraid of what else she might see in his face.

"Becca," he said. "Honey, give me your eyes."

Wordlessly, she shook her head. Or really, rubbed her face against the cotton jacket since she was still ostrich-ing it and wouldn't glance up.

A grunt, and then he was on his knees in front of her.

Gasping, she lifted her head. "Devon, you shouldn't—"

"There you are," he murmured, his tone beyond gentle. "Why are you crying, sweetheart?"

The endearment and soft words didn't help her get it together. More tears pooled in the corners of her eyes and dripped down her cheeks. He was okay. Somehow, he was okay.

And concerned for her.

It defied logic.

Calloused fingers brushed the drops away. "I'm fine, honey."

She nodded. "Right." He'd been stabbed and knocked unconscious. How in the hell was he fine?

"Are you okay?"

Okay?

She was so far from that, she couldn't even begin to quantify it. But…this also wasn't all about her—or it shouldn't be, anyway.

"I'm okay," she whispered.

Fingers on her jaw. "Good."

They stared at each other for a long moment, gazes locked, emotions swirling between them. What Becca most felt was relief, followed a close second by guilt, but underneath both of those was the sense of rightness she always felt when Devon was near. His feelings were harder to deduce. His eyes definitely held relief and discomfort and even warmth, but there was also something deeper underneath it all—a thread of something *more* that made her want to wrap her arms around him and never let go.

Then Devon winced, and she was a flurry of motion.

She burst to her feet, grabbing for his arm. "You shouldn't— You're *hurt*…the floor."

Levering her shoulder beneath his, she lifted, struggled, mentally uttered a really bad curse word, and managed to get him to his feet.

Mostly because Devon helped her.

"I should call Pascal," she said once he was steady. "He'll need—"

"He's pulling the car around," Devon said. "We ditched the wheels." He nodded to the empty blue wheelchair in the corner. "How long have you been here?"

"Not long," she lied.

After the ambulance left, she'd talked to the police and

promised to come down to the station in the morning, if they'd only let her go to the hospital.

They'd been understanding, had suggested that she get checked out herself.

But bruises didn't need an ER doc's attention. Neither did an overdose of guilt.

One of the officers had driven her to the hospital, and she'd parked her butt in the chair.

That had been hours ago.

"Come on," she said, spotting Pascal coming back through the automatic doors. "Let's get you home."

She opened the passenger door and watched miserably as Devon painfully maneuvered himself inside.

Becca didn't speak, and neither did Pascal, but once the door was closed and she had stepped back onto the curb, he touched her arm.

"Not your fault."

She swallowed hard. "Of course not." A pause. "How bad?"

"Three wounds. Thirty-seven stitches. A huge lump on his head but no concussion."

Oh, look at that. The moon was bright and…blurry. At least until she blinked rapidly for several seconds.

"Okay." She nodded, pulled out her phone, opened the Uber app. "I'll see you Monday."

"No, Ms. Stealing." Pascal shook his head at the same moment the window *whirred* down.

"Get in the car, Becca," Devon snapped. "And for once in your life, don't give me attitude."

Her eyes were wide. She could feel it. Devon *never* talked to her like that.

But all things considered—stab wounds, head lumps, crazy exes—she guessed she could give him a pass.

She got in the car.

Pascal came around and slid into the driver's seat. A moment later, they were off.

Becca opened her mouth when they bypassed her exit and headed toward the more-expensive part of town but quickly closed it. She could catch a cab home later. The sooner Devon was resting in his own bed the better.

They stopped briefly at a gate. Pascal pressed a button on a remote to open it before driving up a winding road. Near the top they stopped, and Becca's breath hitched.

It was beautiful.

The huge craftsman-style house was painted in dark gray, the trim a bright white. Flowers spilled from ceramic pots and crawled over the planter beds in cheerful disarray. Stone-covered columns enclosed a tidy porch, completed with wicker furniture and a two-seater swing.

Her eyes were just tracing the lovely woodwork of the front door when the car moved forward again, and they pushed into the garage.

She blinked at the sudden transition, from charming and warm to bland and wholly male. Sports equipment lined the walls —Pascal might as well have been parking in the middle of Dick's. The other side held cabinets and a workbench, drills and hammers and other strange-looking tools all hanging above it in perfect precision.

The car door slammed, and Becca jumped before getting her butt in motion.

She popped the handle, pushed out, and...promptly ran into Pascal.

"Sorry," she muttered, shuffling out of the way as he moved to help Devon, who for some reason decided he was going to try and get out of the car by himself.

"Fuc—" He glanced at Becca. "Frack." He sank back down, his jaw clenched tight, his skin almost gray.

And cue more guilt.

Pascal grabbed Devon's arm and waist, tugging him free of the leather seat. Muttered curses—or rather, aborted ones—rained out of his mouth as they moved and Becca slid by them to open the door.

"Wait—" Pascal began.

Harsh beeping erupted around her. She froze, listening to the alarm before spiraling into motion. Lights. She needed lights. A bank of switches was on the wall near the door, and she scrabbled to turn them on. Except, no matter which one she hit, the inside of the house didn't get any brighter.

A hand reached over her shoulder and calmly pressed a switch. The same one she was sure she'd hit ten times over.

The lights flicked on.

"7-8-4-1 and enter," Devon said, pointing to a panel on the wall that looked frighteningly technological.

Swallowing, Becca pressed the buttons and hit enter. The horrible beeping sound stopped. She blew out a breath.

"The police will be here in—"

"What?" she all but shrieked.

Devon gave her a goofy half smile and chuckled before breaking off with a wince. "Kidding."

"Come on," Pascal said, tugging Devon forward. He nodded at a row of kitchen stools. "Wait here. I'll drive you home."

"I don't need—" Two exasperated sets of male eyes swiveled toward her and, hands raised in surrender, she sank down onto a stool. "Fine," she muttered.

Devon inclined his head at her then let Pascal lead him from the room.

Becca sat…for all of a minute. Which was the point when she began getting antsy and feeling like she should be doing *something*.

She stood and paced the kitchen for a few minutes then remembered Devon's bag of medicine was in the car. She retrieved it and read his discharge instructions so she knew what he would need next and the dosage.

Since one of the meds required food, she bustled around the kitchen until she found the fridge—no easy feat considering the space was sleekly modern with built-in panels on every appliance except the double oven.

Good Lord, she'd love to bake in that.

Which *so* wasn't the point, she reminded herself and extracted a loaf of bread from the fridge before searching out the toaster and popping a slice inside.

While she waited for it to finish, she scrounged out a cup and filled it with water before laying out the pills on a napkin.

By the time Pascal came back into the kitchen, the toast was ready on a plate, and Becca was cleaning the already spotless countertop.

Pascal stopped short at the sight, the corner of his mouth twitching suspiciously. "I'll take you home now, Ms. Stealing."

"It's time for Devon's medication." She picked up the instructions. "They say he's supposed to have a pain pill before he goes to bed."

"Mr. Scott won't take it."

"But the doctor—"

Pascal sighed, shook his head. "He won't. He doesn't believe in taking anything stronger than over-the-counter medication."

She scowled. "This is a stupid male thing."

"This is growing up with a father who was addicted to Oxycontin and making a promise to yourself to never be in the same position."

Becca froze at the sound of Devon's voice then felt her jaw drop at the matter-of-fact statement.

"Oh," she said.

"Yeah." Devon limped into the room, and her jaw dropped again, albeit for a different reason.

He was deliciously rumpled, and, even hurt and pale and clearly exhausted, Devon was still sexy as all get-out. His T-shirt skimmed the muscles of his chest, made her want to trace her hands over the fabric, to feel the muscles beneath. His hair was disheveled, as though some woman—Becca couldn't deny she wished it had been her—had run her fingers through it.

Even the flannel pajama pants he had on were hot, riding low and exposing a strip of skin she very much wanted to taste.

Devon tilted his head, lips twitching. "Something on my face?" Except the way he'd said *face* made it seem dirtier, like he'd caught her eyes drifting south and liked that she'd been looking.

Heat flooded her cheeks, and Pascal coughed—or maybe chuckled, the jerk—before turning away.

"No," Becca said and snatched up the pill before grabbing the bottle of painkillers and taking it over to the sink.

She dropped it down the drain before remembering her ecology class from college and how it was bad for the environment to dispose of medication that way. Poop. Her eyes locked on to the rubber covering of the garbage disposal, and she sighed heavily.

"Becca?" Devon sounded confused.

Her shoulders slumped as she set the bottle on the counter. She couldn't even do a simple thing like throw something away correctly.

Eyes burning, she blinked and forced her voice to be steady. "I'm ready to go home now."

"Hey." He touched her arm. "What's the matter?"

And that was it. All of her calm faded, and the emotions that had been roiling under the surface of her skin for the last hours burst forth.

"What's the matter?" she screeched. *"What's the matter?* You're kidding me, right?" She slammed her hands onto the counter. "You're not seriously asking that, are you? Because in the last twenty-four hours, my car's been vandalized, my boss has kissed me, then was hit on the head and stabbed by my ex-boyfriend, and n-now I've probably *murdered* some poor d-defenseless sea l-lion—"

She burst into tears.

Too far gone to care that Pascal and Devon were probably exchanging the-girl-is-nuts looks, Becca slumped against the counter and buried her face in her hands.

The arm around her shoulders surprised her.

"Hey. It's okay," Devon said.

Which—of *freaking* course—made her cry all that much harder. Because Devon was comforting her. After everything that had happened over the last few hours, he was being nice.

When, for all intents and purposes, he should be fucking pissed.

Oh God. There her mind went again, saying naughty words when six months before, such a thing would have never crossed her tongue, mental or otherwise.

And good grief.

She was an adult. She should be allowed to say the f-bomb. It was just...*not* cursing was burned into her brain.

Fuck.

Fuck!

Fu—

Nope. She couldn't do it.

Straightening, she looked Devon right in his chocolaty eyes and said, "I blame you."

His jaw dropped open in surprise. He glanced down toward his torso, no doubt cataloging the list of injuries that were *definitely* not his fault. "Uhh."

"Oh!" Good grief, her emotions were cycling. Crying one second, cursing the next, and confusing the heck out of everyone else in the process. "I meant the—*shit*." She gasped, clapped a hand over her mouth.

"Becca."

She shook her head. "I need to go." Except, it sounded like *"Shmf a pog."*

Devon peeled her fingers from her lips. "Come again?"

"I need to go." She took a slinking step to the side. "I didn't mean that"—she pointed to Devon's yummy and rather abused torso—"was your fault. Of course not. Just the cursing. I don't curse and it's your fault because you have a dirty mouth."

Yes. That was good. She nodded, wiped her cheeks. Now to make her escape.

"The cursing?"

A breath. Another nod. "Yes."

He raised a brow, and her cheeks went hot. "Dirty mouth?"

Another step toward the garage, her hand was on her purse. She cleared her throat, ignored the implications of that. "You curse too much. And now you're corrupting me."

Devon's eyes danced with amusement. "I do curse too much." He tilted his head. "What kind of curse words are crossing that innocent mind of yours? Dang? Heck?"

Oh really? *Now* he was going to tease her?

"I just said *sh*—" She cut herself off, ignored the mischief in his eyes, and glared. "I'll have you know—"

He smiled. "What's this about a sea lion?"

"I—"

"Where's—?" A frown pulled his brows together, and he swung his head around. "I'm sorry, baby. I didn't mean to interrupt you. It's just...where's Pascal?"

Becca glanced around, saw they were alone in the kitchen. She crossed to the door to the garage, opened it...and sighed.

The space they'd parked in was empty, Devon's car gone, the gears from the garage door's motor still clinking as the panel settled back into place.

Dev came up behind her.

She knew that despite not hearing his footsteps, knew he was mere inches behind her because her spine tingled, gooseflesh spread on her nape, and, of course, the heat. The heat that spread through her limbs, soaked into her skin, burned through her nerves.

417

The spark that always existed between her and him flashed to life, threatened to incinerate the room.

She couldn't risk it, couldn't risk reducing her heart to ashes.

"Pascal. Always with the matchmaking," Dev muttered, and panic gripped her. It was already hard enough to resist him without someone throwing them together, playing matchmaking fairy manfather.

"I can't—"

He shook his head. "Don't worry about it. You can take the Jeep." He nodded toward the old, ragtag vehicle taking up the other half of the garage.

"Okay." At the offer of a car, Becca relaxed.

Unfortunately, his next words made that disappear as easily as chocolate around the office. "You do know how to drive a stick, don't you?"

That very naughty four-letter word—the special-occasion one —spilled from her lips.

CHAPTER 12

evon winced as he stretched. Playing in the NHL, he'd had his fair share of broken bones, stitches, and bruises. This was right up there with the worst of his injuries.

Midday sun streamed through the windows, blinding him, forcing his mind awake even when his body wanted to hunker down into the mattress and not come out for days.

He sat up with a curse. An almost one. A broken-off one.

Then he blinked and stared at his nightstand. A sticky note, bright yellow as Becca seemed to favor, was propped up against his lamp. A little paper cup sat next to a glass of water.

Antibiotics, it read, and he looked into the container to see two huge yellow and red pills. His eyes trailed down, took in the rest of the note. *Take them with the crackers. Not good on an empty stomach.*

Devon stared at the script-like swirls of Becca's handwriting. It had always amused him how gracefully she'd been able to give him written orders.

Today's Post-it note was no exception.

Flowery squiggles did not hide the outright command.

It also didn't mean that Becca was wrong. After swallowing the pills, he choked down a couple of crackers and drank the glass of water.

Using the facilities, brushing his teeth, and painfully changing his clothes went a long way toward making him feel human again.

He opened the door to his bedroom and was immediately assaulted with scents. Cinnamon, chocolate, something savory. They danced around the hall and collided with his senses.

Shaking his head, he walked down the stairs and into the kitchen.

He'd left Becca in a spare room the night before, after they'd waited for Pascal.

After his five phone calls and texts had gone unanswered.

Devon didn't know whether to thank or strangle his head of security.

"I take it that Pascal is still MIA?" he asked.

Becca jumped. "Don't do that!" she said, hand over her heart. "I was just—"

His mouth dropped open as he glanced past her and caught sight of the destruction she'd made of the kitchen. Every square inch of countertop was covered with pots or cookie sheets or ingredients. He flicked his gaze back to hers, watched her cheeks turn a lovely shade of pink.

Devon found he liked the mix of scents, the sight of the cheerfully messy disorder. His chef, on the other hand, was going to lose her shi—*stuff.*

He raised a brow. "Just what?"

"I—uh—thought that you might need some food while you're recovering and…"

He remained quiet as she trailed off, having learned long ago that sometimes silence was the best weapon to gain the truth.

Becca was no exception. She sighed, and her shoulders slumped slightly. "I stress-cook."

"You're stressed?"

It was her turn to raise her brows. "Um, yes. That tends to happen when a girl's ex tries to kill her boss."

She had tried to keep her tone light, but he'd seen it in her expression before she turned away. Guilt. The way her blue eyes had glittered with tears.

"It's not your fault."

A shrug of her shoulders. "Of course not. It was Mick's." But she didn't look at him, and her tone wasn't right.

Devon didn't spend time second-guessing his actions. Not after last night, not after realizing how easily he could have lost her. He might have only known Becca for six months, but he'd never felt so connected to a woman.

When he was with her, the world shined a little brighter. When he *kissed* her, nothing else mattered.

Which, he thought ruefully, was probably why he was sporting more stitches than Frankenstein.

But Devon didn't care. About any of it. He'd find a way to make it work at the office, make sure her psycho-ex was locked up permanently.

Because he'd realized that this was his chance.

His opportunity for something permanent. And he wanted Becca in his life.

So while she was trying to slyly wipe her tears away, Devon snagged a brownie and crossed to her.

"I hear chocolate makes everything better," he said, carefully leaning over her shoulder and offering her the treat.

It wasn't the smoothest line he'd ever made, but it did make her smile. And really, if all she gave him for the rest of his life was that smile, then his heart would be full.

"I baked those for you," she said softly.

He started to shrug, forced back a grimace, and touched her cheek instead. "I can share."

She gave him a crooked grin. "Good," she said and stuffed the square in her mouth.

Her moan of pleasure hit him hard in the gut. And elsewhere. It shouldn't be like this. She shouldn't affect him so strongly. But he was realizing that Becca made all the shouldn'ts and can'ts become possible.

"Hey," he said after she'd swallowed. The skin on her neck was delicate, pale honey, and his mouth watered with the urge to trail his lips there.

Not yet. She was primed to bolt, and Devon knew he would need patience if he wanted to catch her.

Resisting the urge to kiss her was tough, but he understood how to play the long game. So instead, he laced his hand with hers, got close enough to feel the heat of her body, to smell the aroma that was wholly Becca—floral with a touch of spice.

"It's not your fault."

She stiffened, tried to pull free.

Devon held on and continued, "You don't believe that right now. I get it. But that doesn't mean I'm going to stop telling you." He bent and put his face right in front of hers. "I'll keep telling you that until you realize it's true. I'll keep telling you because it *is* true. This guilt will eat you up inside."

Becca was silent for a long time. "It was my fault—"

"I told—"

She closed the inch between their bodies and rested her forehead against his shoulder. "Not that. My mom's accident."

"You said she was in a car wreck. That kind of thing just happens sometimes." He stroked a hand through her hair, feeling the strands slide like silk through his fingers.

"Not this one." She leaned back, misery in her eyes evident. "We were talking on the phone. No"—a bitter laugh—"arguing is more like it. My mom wanted to talk later, said traffic was bad, but I couldn't let it go. I couldn't hang up, a-*and* she got into an accident."

"Shit."

He didn't even bother to stifle the curse. Because, well, shit.

Becca didn't seem to hear him, or maybe the adjective didn't bother her because she was so distraught.

That's why she was working so hard, why she was so intent on paying her mother's rehab bills. That was why she thought last night—

"I'm sure your mom doesn't blame you."

And that was precisely the wrong thing to say.

"She should," Becca said fiercely and pulled back.

Devon let her go, not able to find the right words.

Then—*screw that*—he closed the distance between them and gathered Becca in his arms. "It's not your fault."

A snort. But she didn't fight his hold.

"*Not* your fault," he murmured into her ear.

Her breath caught, but she shook her head.

"Not." A kiss behind her ear. "Your." To her jaw. "Fault." The corner of her mouth.

"Dev—"

He pressed his lips to hers. The kiss was gentle and sweet, penance and persuasion wrapped in one. And yet the underlying heat threatened to singe his very soul.

Becca just meant so much more than he could have ever expected.

He pulled back way sooner than he wanted to, resting his forehead against hers, breaths coming fast, heart pounding.

"It's not your fault."

Her eyes welled with tears, and she gave a small nod.

"More chocolate?"

She smiled. "God yes."

CHAPTER 13

The next ten days were a blur.

Pascal did eventually come back that morning, the car filled with files and two laptops synced to the office's server in hand. He drove Becca to the police station to give her statement before returning her to Devon's house and disappearing to who-knew-where.

She and Devon worked in his home office while he recovered, Becca organizing the client files and returning emails while Devon took calls and made deals, talking all the while as though he hadn't been hurt the previous day.

The media had picked up on the story and called for a statement, but Devon knew how to underplay incidents with the best of them, and within a day or two, the next celebrity scandal swallowed up interest.

And so it went.

Every morning Pascal would show up in her parking lot then drive her to Devon's. They'd work all day together, stopping for breaks only when she forced Devon to—or bribed him by cooking up something extra delicious.

At the end of the day, Becca would make dinner, and she and Devon would eat together.

It was decidedly domestic.

It *felt* decidedly right.

She was also learning more about him. He'd always seemed so big, so fierce and untouchable, but getting to know him, working side-by-side so intimately without all of the other stressors of Prestige's work environment somehow blurred the edges of him.

He was softer, more approachable, and wore casual clothes. Or maybe she was just more comfortable with him.

Or maybe it was the kisses.

Devon was the *best* kisser.

At first it had scared her, how powerful his hold was over her, how much the spark between them threatened to incinerate her.

Then she realized he was in the same boat.

And so work got...fun.

A stolen kiss here, a brush of fingers there. She found that touching him made the day a lot better.

Snorting to herself, she flipped through the file in her hands to make sure it was all in order before moving to the next.

She was on the couch in Devon's office, curled up near the gas fireplace and enjoying the warmth radiating over her skin. Nice to be able to get that with only the flip of a switch.

It was Friday evening and past time that she should wrap up things and head home.

Except...she didn't want to leave.

Behind her, Devon talked quietly on the phone, and his voice never failed to make her inner teenager sigh. It was slightly rough, had just enough texture to feel like a physical caress down her nape.

It was even better when he held her tight against his chest, the words rumbling through his body and into hers, vibrating her nerves pleasantly.

She set the file back on the stack and laid her head on the arm of the sofa, closing her eyes, listening, wanting to find the courage to take the next step with Devon.

The stitches had been removed that morning. He would be returning to the office on Monday, and this intimacy would be gone, tempered by HR policies and prying eyes.

And *she* would be leaving soon.

In a little over a week, Clarice was coming back. Her time at Prestige would be done.

Why did that make her so sad?

Fingers combing her hair back from her face made her eyes fly open.

Devon. Of course Devon. And he was so close, his mouth just inches away, his delectable body *right* there, calling to her to touch.

And so *finally* she did.

This was their swan song. Their last bit of time together before the real world intruded, and she was so damn—yes, *damn*—tired of resisting, of ignoring, of downplaying the pull between them.

For once, she wanted to give in.

And so she did.

Becca reached up, wrapped two hands in his T-shirt, and yanked hard.

Nothing happened.

"Bex?" he asked, glancing down at her clenched fists.

"This is so much easier in the movies," she muttered, tugging the two halves again.

With a lopsided grin, Devon shrugged off his shirt. "Better?"

Her mouth watered, her head wobbled like one of those bobbleheads. Somehow, she had ended up still gripping the cotton T-shirt, probably because she hadn't wanted to release him.

Now she dropped the slip of fabric like a stick of dynamite and touched...skin. Hot. Smooth. Skin. And muscles. A light dusting of hair covered his chest—except for three bare patches that were bisected by angry lines.

She swallowed hard at the sight, flicked her eyes away.

A finger under her chin. "Not your fault," Devon murmured.

Blinking, she nodded, indicating the bald spots. "The guys are going to give you hell."

He chuckled. "Yup. Except I get to play the hero card."

"Yes, you do." She leaned forward and gently kissed the red marks. The space between her thighs warmed at his rough inhale of breath. "You'll have scars."

He shrugged. "What's another couple?"

God, she liked this man. Maybe even—

No. She pushed that aside and gave into the urge to kiss him. It was...coming home.

Their lips met, melded together. Heat zipped down her spine, lifted the hairs on her neck, her arms. She didn't hesitate when his tongue touched the seam of her mouth, just parted and let him in.

The same as she'd let him invade the rest of her life. Her heart.

She gripped his shoulders and pulled him toward her, cognizant that he still might be sore, but needing him tight against her all the same.

He stretched out atop her, pressing her body into the cushions, parting her legs and resting his hips between her thighs.

He was hard. *Everywhere.*

Those were the last two thoughts she had before Devon ramped up the kiss. He plundered her mouth, delving deep inside and basically transforming her into a puddle of goo.

But just as things were starting to get really good, he softened the kiss and began to sit back.

Becca let him go. "Hurt?"

His mouth curled as he rested against the cushions. "Not in the way you mean."

"Good." She straddled his hips, wrapped her arms around his shoulders, and licked his neck. "Because I don't want to stop."

"Bex—"

She kissed him, and since it felt so freaking good, rocked her pelvis against his.

He groaned and grabbed her waist, but instead of urging her on, his hands stayed her motion.

"We shouldn't."

They should. They *definitely* should. Especially since everything was going back to normal in two days.

And because she wanted. So dang—no, *damn*—much.

For once, she wanted to put her heart on the line.

Her hand slid down his bare chest, toyed with the waistband of his sweats.

He sucked in a breath.

"I'm saying yes. Please don't say no."

CHAPTER 14

*D*evon stared down at Becca's face, trying to judge her sincerity. Did she really want this? Had he somehow manipulated her? Shouldn't he just wait one more week until Clarice was back—

Her finger brushed the tip of his erection, and things went hazy, really hazy.

"Please, baby?" She leaned forward and bit his neck, flicked her tongue against the tiny hurt.

And how in the hell was he supposed to resist *that*?

He tucked his hands under her ass—not minding the grip in the least—and stood. She gasped, held on tight to his neck.

"Your side," she said, worry in her tone.

Yeah no. Worry was not what he was going for. If they were finally taking the plunge in this, then he wanted her boneless and limp, satiated and flushed. He walked to the fireplace and set her down on the rug.

But he had to be certain.

His mouth hovered an inch above hers. "You sure?"

A nod made him grin. "Kind of need the actual words, sweetheart."

"I'm sure, Devon." She touched his cheek. "I'm clean, I'm on the pill, and I've got a condom in my pocket. Can you get inside me already?"

Not a naughty word in sight, and yet that was the single sexiest thing a woman had ever said to him.

"Yes. I can do that." Slipping his fingers under the hem of her sassy little button-down, he reveled in the silk-like texture of his skin. For the life of him, he couldn't remember ever having touched something so soft. He lifted the material, pressed a kiss to her stomach, loving the way her breath hitched.

"Devon?" she asked when all he did was stroke the exposed skin.

"You're overdressed," he murmured and slipped the bottom button free. He touched his lips to the space just above her navel.

Another button. Another kiss. Another. Another. *Another.*

Until all that creamy skin was visible. Her breasts were swathed in pink lace. Pink *see-through* lace.

"I really want to curse right now," he said, running a finger under the flimsy material, "in a good way."

Becca's cheeks were flushed, and she arched up, reaching behind her and unhooking the strap of her bra. "Me too..." A pause as she shrugged out of the lace. "...in the absolute *best* way."

Then her breasts were in his hands, and Devon was spinning, curse words forgotten, nothing filling his mind except the drive to please Becca.

He flicked the button on her slacks and slid them down as she kicked off her shoes. The lace below wasn't the same pink, but he couldn't care less. He swept it off, stroking and caressing, kissing and licking every inch of her. Only when she was writhing and begging—and uttering his favorite curse word—did he pull off his pants and roll on the condom.

"Last chance," he said, sweat beading his brow, his body aching...and not because of his healing wounds.

Becca was everything. If she said stop—

She grabbed his hips and pulled down, and *fuck yeah,* he was there.

The world went blank, nothing existed except the two of them and their race to the peak. He tried to go slow, wanted to draw their first time out, but it was impossible to fight his rising desire. Not when Becca was so sweetly sensual below him, meeting him thrust for thrust, holding on tight and making the hottest little moans in the back of her throat.

And when she cried his name, convulsing around him, that was it for his self-control.

He exploded.

* * *

AWHILE LATER, they forced themselves to move upstairs, and Devon coaxed Becca into a repeat performance in the shower.

He had set her on the marble countertop and was patting her dry with a towel when he noticed the red abrasions on her skin. His brows pulled together. *Damn.* He touched his face, felt the sandpaper-like texture of his unshaved face.

He'd done that.

She glanced down at where his hand rested against the abused spot and smiled. "Don't worry. It doesn't hurt."

"I'm going to shave." He tucked the towel around her then bent and pulled his razor from the cabinet. But just as his fingers wrapped around the handle, his stomach growled loud enough to shake the foundation of the house.

"It doesn't matter." She touched his chest. "You're hungry. Let's go eat first."

"No," he said and flicked the switch, filling the space with buzzing.

"Dev—"

"Are we going to play a game of *Who's More Stubborn?*" he

asked, running the electric razor along his neck. "Because I'd put your bet on me."

She stared at him before sighing. "I'd bet that too." A kiss to his chest. "How about I heat up something to eat?"

He used his free hand to tug her ponytail. "I could get on board with that."

"And a salad? Since you're getting so fat?" Her eyes danced in amusement.

His lips twitched. "Touché." He set the razor aside and helped her down before giving her a little tap on her butt. "You can wear my robe if you want. It's on the back of the door."

"Thanks."

She dropped the towel, and he almost sliced his carotid.

"Hurry down," she said as she slipped into the robe and then walked through the door, hips swaying as she went.

He said that word again, and meant it again, in the *best* way.

CHAPTER 15

$\mathcal{B}$ecca walked down the stairs, knowing she was grinning like an idiot and totally unable to stop.

Unfortunately, the sight in the kitchen had her skittering to a halt, the smile fading.

Clarice stood in front of the sink, arms crossed, prim suit in proper form, deadly stilettos on foot. She was thin and beautiful and perfect, the kind of woman who made other women insecure, especially since she'd just had a freaking baby three months before.

But she'd always been a friend and sweet, a kind look in her hazel eyes.

That definitely was absent today.

"H-hi," Becca said, cursing the way her voice shook. She set her shoulders and indicated Clarice's outfit. "You look amazing. How's the baby?"

"Fine." Her foot tapped angrily, and Becca sucked in a steadying breath, knowing that the fury in Clarice's eyes was seconds away from being unleashed.

Why hadn't she gotten dressed?

And to make matters worse, she couldn't stop the idiotic

words from slipping out. "We're moving back into the office on Monday. All the files are up-to-date. Client meetings booked. Contracts signed and mailed out. We'll be good to go for your return in a week."

"I thought better of you."

The icy words slid down her spine, but, *dang it*, the situation with Devon wasn't like that. What they had was *different*.

Except…was it?

She was there, easily available, and she'd seen plenty of news stories of Devon's conquests. What made her any different? *He* certainly hadn't said anything.

No. That wasn't it. He wasn't a predator; he'd tried to resist her. This was on her. Her fault. Her—

"I took the liberty of preparing your final check." Clarice set an envelope on the counter. "We won't need you back on Monday."

The statement was a punch to the gut. "But I—"

"Okay, what's for dinner—" Devon's voice came around the corner before he did, fully dressed, of course. "Clarice!" He swept right past Becca and pulled the other woman in for a hug. "I've missed you. How's the baby?"

Clarice softened in Devon's arms. You could see her actually melt against him, and when they stepped back, her expression was loving. "He's the best baby. Sleeping and"—she pulled out her phone—"look! He's getting ready to roll over."

Devon watched the video dutifully then looked up at Clarice with genuine happiness. "Yeah, he is. What a champ. Good job." He bumped her shoulder, laughed when she bumped his in return.

"I'm coming to back to the office on Monday."

"Awesome." His eyes didn't stray from Clarice, not even for a second. "The crew has missed you."

Devon's words were worse than a punch to the gut. He'd just casually taken a knife to Becca's heart.

And all the while, she stood on the outside. In a freaking robe.

"About the Carlson contract..." Devon began, and they were off.

Becca was frozen there for a minute, waiting for them to include her in the conversation. When they didn't, she swallowed hard, turned away, and left the check, left the kitchen, left her shattered heart right there on the travertine floor.

She'd been an idiot, an idiot to rival all idiots. Devon was—

He laughed at something Clarice said, and she felt her eyes well.

No. Not here. Not yet.

She stumbled into the study and snatched up her clothes. Numb fingers buttoned cotton, shaking hands pulled on slacks and pumps.

Pascal was at the curb when she walked out of the house, and she'd never been more thankful to see him.

"Can you take me home?" she asked, opening the car door and sliding inside. Her hair was a mess, her clothes rumpled.

His eyes swept down then up before flashing back behind her shoulder.

She knew what he was seeing. Clarice drove a bright blue SUV. It was quite distinctive, and everyone in the office knew it by sight.

That same SUV was parked smack dab in the center of Devon's driveway, as overtly as Clarice had situated herself in Devon's kitchen.

Pascal was quiet for a beat then nodded, put the car in gear, and drove away.

About halfway through the drive home, he turned on the radio.

Becca didn't mind.

She was just thankful he didn't mention the tears streaming down her cheeks.

CHAPTER 16

*D*evon came up for air around an hour after he'd walked into his kitchen.

Clarice tucked the folder she'd brought to go over with him—full of contracts he'd needed to sign, travel documents for an upcoming conference, a proposal for an endorsement deal that had just come into the office that morning—under her arm, bussed him on the cheek, and headed for the front door. "See you Monday," she called.

He waved and turned for his study. Quite frankly, he was relieved that Clarice was back and that Becca wouldn't be his secretary any longer.

No conflict of interest. No HR disaster. Just him and her and that explosive chemistry.

Of course, it was more than just heat between them.

Becca was spunky and sweet, wholly capable and enduring. He admired her work ethic, loved how comfortable he felt in just being with her.

Spending time with her was—

Damn.

Devon stopped right there in the hall, his hand coming up to touch his chest. Below his fingers, beneath the muscle and bone and sinew, his heart pounded.

Because he loved her.

Suddenly he needed to be right next to her, to hold her close and tell her exactly what she meant to him.

He hustled down the hall, bursting into the study in a flurry of limbs and—

She wasn't there.

Frowning, he turned and hightailed it up the stairs.

But his bedroom was empty. The bathroom too. And aside from the containers of food crowding his fridge and dotting his countertops, so was his kitchen.

Not a sign of Becca anywhere.

And the more he searched, the deeper his heart sank.

Finally, he pulled out his phone and called Pascal. "Did you take Becca home?" Maybe she'd left something at her house and hadn't wanted to interrupt.

A beat of silence.

"Pascal?" he demanded.

"What the hell are you doing to that girl?" Pascal said, his tone as sharp as Devon had ever heard it. Usually, his bodyguard was about as emotional as a piece of plywood. "First you lead her on, then you sleep with her, and *then* you fire her at the first opportunity. She's a nice woman and cares—cared…"

Cared?

The past tense was the only reason that Devon stopped and tried to process what Pascal was saying before laying into him.

He was the boss. His people weren't supposed to question his actions.

Except—guilt sliced through him—those actions *were* kind of questionable.

And then there was the whole past-tense thing.

Pascal was still talking, but Devon didn't have time for that. Not when panic was bubbling up in his gut, burning a fiery trail up his throat.

"Did you take her home?"

Pascal stopped ranting, but his reluctance to answer the question was clear in the weighted silence.

"Did you drive her back to her apartment?" Devon pressed.

"Yes." A grudging response.

His panic calmed slightly. Devon would go over there, explain what had happened. Clarice coming back was a good thing because he and Becca could be together without worry.

"Good. I'm giving you the weekend off. See you bright and early Monday morning."

"Sir—"

Devon hung up, hit ignore when Pascal called him back. He didn't have time for phone calls. He had to go make things right with his girl.

A minute later, he'd thrust his feet into shoes and was driving down the street, his recently healed side protesting slightly as he maneuvered the Jeep. But the pain was negligible, and he couldn't ignore the niggling in his mind.

The voice in his brain telling him that he needed to get to Becca.

That he needed to let her know how he felt.

That—

When he knocked on her door, she didn't answer.

He let himself in via the code he'd had the security company make for him and found...her apartment empty. Or at least empty of Becca. All her stuff was there. Her car was even in the lot.

But *she* wasn't.

He called her phone. No answer.

He drove to the office. Not a single light on.

When he finally went full circle and drove home, he found she wasn't there either.

The panic, the same he'd managed to squelch earlier, reared its ugly head.

She was gone.

And it was his fault.

CHAPTER 17

The call from the rehabilitation center couldn't have come at a better time for Becca. Space had finally opened up for her mother in the rehab program they'd been waiting for, but all the paperwork and transfer documents needed to be taken care of ASAP.

It was an inconvenience, but one of the best kind.

Her mom would be getting better care, and she was getting an escape from Prestige, from Devon, from the bleak reality that was her life.

Five minutes after her cell had rung—and no, she hadn't been hoping it was Devon…really, she *hadn't*—she'd requested a Lyft, packed a bag, and headed for the airport.

The center was in Arizona, so the flight from northern California had been short.

But not short enough to keep Becca from her thoughts.

With a sigh, she'd disembarked the plane and rented a car for the drive to the center. It was closed to visitors, of course, but she'd grabbed a motel room and met with the facility director early the next morning.

Her mom had protested about the cost involved during the

entire transfer process—proverbially dragging her feet since she couldn't physically drag them yet—and fought Becca tooth and nail over any upgrade.

She had finally lied and told her mom she'd gotten a permanent position with Prestige just to cease the worst of the battling.

It felt like days later before she was walking out of the center, when in reality it had been only a couple of hours.

But since she'd worked the full day before then played hanky-panky with her boss, which had been followed by buckets of tears, a plane ride, and a sleepless night, she was done in.

So she wasn't happy when her cell rang as she'd barely cleared the door of her motel room.

"What?" she asked with a sigh. It was probably her mother, getting ready to argue with her about buying a cheaper set of sheets or some other nonsense.

"Uh, Ms. Stealing?"

Crap. So not her mother. Rather, it was Stephanie, the director of the rehab center.

She cleared her throat and resisted the urge to bang her head on the doorframe. "Hi, Stephanie. Sorry. I just—"

"No problem, Ms. Stealing. I know. I-I, um..."

Oh good God, what had her mother done now?

"I'll talk to her. I promise," Becca said. "She wants to get better. She's just worried about the cost. But I've got it covered—"

"I know. I just—" Stephanie sighed. "Well, I don't really know how to say this..."

What the hell—*heck?* Becca bumped her head against the motel door anyway. It hurt...but kind of in a good way. "Say what exactly?" she asked.

"Your mother's account has been permanently covered."

Her eyes flashed open, and she winced as she had an extreme close-up with the bright pink trim of the motel's paint job. "Wh-what?"

"I know." Stephanie sounded excited now. "I couldn't believe it when the man came in, but the paperwork is all in order, and he's set up a trust for your mother. There's enough money in that account to make sure she'll have the best treatments, the best teams. Your mother is going to get better..."

Becca's breath caught; her throat tightened. Luckily, Stephanie kept talking about plans and doctors and medicines, and she didn't have to say a word.

Because Devon.

Somehow, she knew in her heart that Devon had done this.

"What was the man's name?" she asked when Stephanie finally took a breath.

"He wouldn't give one, but"—Stephanie gave a little giggle—"I've never seen a member of the male population as hot as this one. Tall, dark, built like a god, eyes like chocolate—"

Clearly, Stephanie didn't watch sports. Or pay attention to Hollywood starlets.

"Devon."

"You know him?"

Becca sniffed at the same time her neck prickled and her skin heated from the inside out. Turning, she saw the man himself. He stood there in all glorious *hunky*-ness, ready to crush her battered heart for the second time, just for fun.

"I know him."

Stephanie blew a breath out, and it rattled through the speakers. "Good. I just wanted to make sure you knew, and that you were okay with it."

Okay? Not really. But it was the best thing for her mother, and that meant the majority of her was thrilled, touched even. The small piece of her that still ached from Devon's dismissal was what smarted.

A parting gift, payment for services rendered.

"I'm o-okay with it." A sob caught in her throat. "Thank you," she choked out and hung up.

Devon took a step toward her.

She backed up and promptly smacked her head against the frame, except this time a lot harder than her little love-tap from before. "Stop," she said, putting her hand up.

The word sounded broken and desperate even to her own ears.

But did the man ever listen to her? He'd said he could out-stubborn her, and he was right. He closed the distance between them, pushed her hand aside, and swept her into his arms.

And, dammit—yes, a *real* dammit—she liked it. Reveled in it, hugged it to the depths of her soul.

He'd ruined her, she realized as she sank into his embrace. She had no resistance or armor when it came to Devon.

He guided her to the bed, closing the door behind them with a soft click, and sat down on the edge with her in his lap.

And just held her.

And it felt really freaking good...and—she hiccupped, coughed, sniffed, tried every trick to keep the tears at bay.

None of which worked.

She cried. Devon held her, stroking her back, cradling her close, until she finally stopped, feeling as wrung-out as a dish-towel on a laundry line.

He didn't say a word until her breathing slowed and even then, his words were a riddle. "I think we're laboring under a misapprehension."

Her head throbbed, and she struggled to make sense of his words. "Wh-what?"

"I'm happy Clarice is back."

Her lungs hitched, the slice of pain deep.

But Devon continued on, seemingly oblivious that he was hurting her. How could she have been so wrong about him?

He tucked a strand of hair behind her ear. "I can't have you working for me."

Becca stiffened and tried to wriggle out of his arms. "Yeah. Reading that loud and clear."

"Because I love you."

"I can't believe—" She froze. "What did you say?"

Devon smiled down at her, warm brown eyes threatening to suck her into the depths of Willy Wonka's chocolate river. And she'd happily take a dip in *that*.

"I." A pause. "Love." Another pause. "You." He tapped her nose.

"You." Becca shook her head. "It's not— I— *You*—"

"The reason I'm happy Clarice is back is because I want us to have a chance at something special without all the barriers of work."

Becca blinked at him. "But you just—" She broke off. "And Clarice said—" *Oh jeez*. What did it matter anyway?

Devon frowned. "I fuc—*screwed*—up at the house. I didn't handle the situation well. I was so relieved to see Clarice because I thought she was the solution to our problem. I forgot that she can be overprotective."

Ha. Yeah. Now *that* was an understatement.

Except Becca couldn't be too mad. Insinuations aside, Devon deserved to have someone looking out for him.

But who was going to look after her? asked the little voice in her head.

"Clarice and I had a chat," Devon said. "She understands that what's going on between us is none of her business."

Becca snorted.

"Sweetheart…" He touched her cheek. "…I love you. I need you to know that. You've been different from the beginning. Clarice is going to have to understand that, or she's going to have to go."

"I—" Becca shook her head. "No. I don't want to be the cause of anything. Clarice is excellent at her job. I shouldn't—"

"Which is exactly why I love you so much." He ran a thumb along her bottom lip. "You care about other people. You work hard. You're smart as hell. Anyone would be lucky enough to have you as their assistant, let alone to have you gracing their life."

The knots in her stomach loosened; the wounds in her heart closed up. "You think so?"

One-half of his mouth did that sexy, slight curve that never failed to make her insides all gooey. "I *know* so." His lips brushed across hers. "Forgive me for being such an idiot."

"Maybe." She smiled, kissed him back. "Thank you for my mom. I shouldn't accept it, but…"

It was for her mom, and it was a gift she didn't have the strength to return.

"You will," he ordered, brows pulling into a fierce frown.

"Maybe," she countered, giggling when he started to mutter a curse then cut the word off.

"You're a bad influence." He glared.

"I think you mean a *good* one."

His fingers laced with hers. "Yes, I do," he said and raised their hands to his mouth before kissing the back of hers. "Give me, give *us* a chance?"

As if he had to ask. Devon was… well, he was pretty much everything.

"Okay."

Brown brows came up. "Okay? Just like that?"

Becca leaned forward and hesitated with her mouth a half inch from his. "Just like that." A pause. "Because I fucking love you too."

The look of surprise on his face was why she saved that word for very special occasions.

EPILOGUE

Three months later

"I can't believe he stole you from me," Devon grumbled as Becca slid out of bed and started for the bathroom.

It was obscenely early, but she had a flight to catch.

"I should have gutted him when he offered you the job."

She flicked on the lights in the bathroom and paused in the doorway. She was naked of course—clothes, pajamas, and sexy lingerie alike all seemed to melt away in Devon's presence.

"You like Sam," she reminded him.

"I *used* to like Roberts," he muttered, throwing the covers back and advancing on her. "Until he took advantage of you."

"By offering me a great job that is both fun and pays really well? That took me away from the HR mess that was PMG?"

Devon just grunted and an edge of annoyance gilded her tone. "I'm a good executive assistant, and you know it." She bent, pulled her toiletry bag from beneath the cupboard of Devon's sink.

446

She was still paying rent on her old apartment, not that there was any point. Not when she spent every free minute with Devon.

Except for the next forty-eight hours. Those would be with Sam Roberts, closing the deal he and Devon had been putting together.

While Devon stayed home. Which was why he was so grumpy.

At her tone, his grouchy expression faded. "I do know it. You're the best executive assistant around." His face screwed up. "I just—"

"Am going to miss me." Silly man. She was going to miss him desperately too.

His face softened. "You're darned right I am."

Her lips turned up. "I love it when you don't curse for me."

He put his hands on her waist and tugged her close. "I love you. Period." He gave a kiss that would have singed her socks, had she been wearing any, then reached behind her to turn on the shower. "Now get ready. I'll make you breakfast. You'll need something in your stomach for all the proverbial names you're going to take and butts you're going to kick."

Her heart swelled so big it threatened to burst right out of her chest. "Devon," she said and ran over to him when he paused in the doorway.

He didn't miss a beat when she threw herself against him, just caught and slanted his mouth across hers.

"I love you," she said.

A wicked grin. "I know."

After another kiss, he released her and tapped her bottom. "Go on now. I'll be waiting downstairs. With chocolate."

"You're my hero."

He touched her cheek, smiled down at her. "And you're mine, Bex. Always."

* * *

THANK YOU FOR READING! You can find information about all of my books—including those featuring the troublesome Scotts—on my website, www.elisefaber.com.

USA Today bestselling author, Elise Faber, loves chocolate, Star Wars, Harry Potter, and hockey (the order depending on the day and how well her team—the Sharks!—are playing). She and her husband also play as much hockey as they can squeeze into their schedules, so much so that their typical date night is spent on the ice. Elise changes her hair color more often than some people change their socks, loves sparkly things, and is the mom to two exuberant boys.

She lives in Northern California. Connect with her in her Facebook group, the Fabinators or email her at elisefaberauthor@gmail.com

Manufactured by Amazon.com.au
Sydney, New South Wales, Australia